THE RULES of DATING
My Best Friend's Sister

VI KEELAND
PENELOPE WARD

THE RULES OF DATING MY BEST FRIEND'S SISTER
Cover Designer: Sommer Stein, Perfect Pear Creative
Editing: Jessica Royer Ocken
Formatting and Proofreading: Elaine York, Allusion Publishing
www.allusionpublishing.com
Proofreading: Julia Griffis
Cover Photographer: Ashraf El Bahrawi, @byashrafb
Cover Model: Giorgos Mavrogiannis, @gio_mavrogiannis

HAPTER 1

Holden

What the heck is this?

I picked up the envelope my parents had mailed me and looked again at the smaller envelope I'd found inside. The bigger one had definitely been addressed by my mother. But the handwriting on the other one looked a hell of a lot like mine, only messier. I hadn't mailed myself anything, though, and definitely not to my parents' house in Philly. And why would someone send me mail at my parents' place and then also put my name as the return address?

Then it hit me.

Holy shit!

No freaking way!

I *had* addressed the envelope, a long-ass time ago!

Back in tenth grade, my creative writing teacher, Mr. Wolf, had made all of his students write a letter to our thirty-year-old selves about what was important to us at the time. We'd handed them in, sealed and stamped, and he'd promised to mail them all the year we turned thirty. Of course, I'd lived at my parents' house then, so that's where I'd addressed my envelope.

Holy shit. I had zero recollection of what the hell I'd written, but I was definitely curious to find out. Fifteen-year-old me hadn't been so well behaved. So I tore the letter open and unfolded a ratty piece of loose leaf.

Dude,

In case you've forgotten—because by the time you receive this letter, you're going to be ancient—Mr. Wolf made us write letters to ourselves. We're supposed to write about what's important to us, because he thinks our priorities will be different when we're thirty. This might be the one homework assignment I actually liked this year, mostly because it's about me, and I'm damn awesome. So here goes…

What is important to Holden Catalano today? Well, this is a very easy question to answer. HEAD. It's fucking amazing. Laurie Rexler introduced me to it last month, and it's pretty much all I've been able to think about since. She's in eleventh grade, and she said it was her first time giving it. But I think she's full of shit since she didn't gag or anything. Anyway, HEAD is glorious. It's probably why there are so many names for it—blowjob, blowie, slurping the gherkin, fellatio, oral, deep throating, knob gobbling, hummer gummer, jingle bob, sucked off, dome polish, playing the skin flute… Notice, there is only ONE word for homework. Why? Because homework sucks and HEAD is THE SHIT.

Side note—Mr. Wolf, you said you weren't going to open these. But in case you do, I hope you're getting lots of HEAD. Especially from Ms. Damarco, across the hall. Because she's smoking hot and looks like she'd give a good BJ. I bet she even swallows. Laurie Rexler doesn't…yet. But I'm working on that. If we write ourselves another letter, I'll let you know how that turns out.

Anyway…back to me and what's important these days… The drums are right up there with HEAD. I couldn't live without music. And of course, my bros—Colby, Ryan, Owen, and Brayden. They're pretty high on the list, too. Though let's not tell them that, because I'd get my balls busted for a month for saying they were important to me. Other things…

Freedom

My hair (which I better still have when I'm thirty)

My parents

Lastly, drums. (I know I said that already, but everything begins and ends with drums. Note to self—playing the drums while getting HEAD just went to the top of my to-do list. How has it taken me this long to think of it?)

What else is important? I'm almost afraid to write this in case I drop this letter and Ryan somehow gets ahold of it. But Mr. Wolf said if we couldn't be honest with ourselves in a letter, we'd never be. So I have to mention Lala. AKA Laney Ellison, my best friend Ryan's little sister. She's the only girl I can really talk to about life. I've had a thing for her as long as I can remember. But she's eighteen months younger, and Ryan would KICK MY ASS if I tried to go there. I can't say I'd blame him, either. Because Lala Ellison can do a fuck of a lot better than me. She's a brainiac, a real genius. She'll probably wind up curing cancer or something someday. But even though she's off limits, she still makes the list of things that are important to me. In fact, I like her so much, if I were putting these things in order, Lala Ellison would come before HEAD. Now that's saying something, isn't it?

3

I guess that's about it. Not much else I give two shits about. Plus, I'm getting bored. This is more writing than I've done in the last two years.

Later,

Holden

P.S. If you haven't been on the cover of Rolling Stone by now, please kick your own ass.

P.P.S. If Lala is single when you get this, and you still haven't taken your shot, you're a giant pussy.

"It's about damn time." Colby shook his head. "We were about to start our meeting without you. You know the old ball and chain only lets me out once a month, and I need to take advantage and get my post-meeting drinking started."

I shook my head. This guy was so full of shit. *Old ball and chain my ass…* He was the happiest married man I knew, married to one of the coolest women I'd ever met. But since I was late, I didn't call him on his shit, and instead shook hands with Owen and Brayden before taking a seat at the table. My three best friends and I owned an apartment building together. Once a month, we met at the local bar to discuss building business. Our meetings generally only lasted about a half hour. Then we'd move on to a night of drinking.

"Sorry I'm late," I said. "The band's van broke down again."

One of the regular waitresses walked by and brought me a beer, without my even having to ask.

I winked at her. "Thanks, gorgeous." Leaning forward, I held out the bottle and the four of us clinked—our version of a gavel calling the meeting to order.

"Before we start," Owen said. "Did you guys get the letters Mr. Wolf made us write to ourselves in tenth grade?"

Colby nodded and laughed. "You guys got yours? I got mine last year since I'm a year older than you babies. But I wrote *a lot* about my hair and the importance of a clean bong."

We chuckled. "I shouldn't tell you guys this, because it's an open invitation for ball busting," Owen said. "But I wrote that my SAT score was important to me. Then I dedicated a half page to Mrs. Wagner's tits. I forgot I had a big crush on her."

My face wrinkled. "Mrs. Wagner? The math teacher? She was like fifty, dude."

Owen crumpled up the napkin under his beer and chucked it at me. "She wasn't fifty, you idiot. She was like thirty, and she had a great rack."

"Sorry," I said with a shrug. "Guess I was too busy noticing girls closer to our age. You know, because I could actually *get girls our age*, unlike you."

"Bite me." Owen chugged half his beer and lifted his chin to me. "What did yours say? Your dream was to have a car that worked." He elbowed Brayden, who sat next to him. "Some things never change."

No way was I going to mention that I'd written about our buddy Ryan's little sister, Lala. I'd either get punched or lectured, probably both. And I was definitely not going to share that I'd had a little too much to drink last night and called her. *Thank God she didn't answer.* What the hell would I have even said, calling her like that out of the blue?

"Mine was about the truly important things in life, gentlemen," I told them. "Apparently I was mature for my age, because my priorities haven't changed."

Brayden nodded and grinned. "You wrote about jerking off, huh?"

"No, dumbass. I wrote about playing the drums and getting head."

The guys all laughed. "Sounds about right," Owen said.

I pointed to Brayden. "What'd yours say?"

He grinned. "I wrote two sentences: *It's important to me to do less homework. Therefore, this is the end of my letter.*"

I shook my head. "Figures."

We ordered another round of beers and got down to business. Colby talked about replacing some of the old air conditioners in the building with new, energy-efficient ones. He thought we could make the cost back in electric-bill savings in only two years. Owen told us about a building a few doors down that had sold for way more than we thought it was worth, and I passed around the estimates I'd gotten for the new roof we desperately needed.

We'd just moved on to talking about the tenant leases up for renewal and how much we were going to raise rents, when my cell buzzed in my pocket. I pulled it out, and my heart leapt into my throat. Lala's name flashed on the screen. My first instinct was to let it go to voicemail, but then I'd be up all night tonight wondering if everything was okay with her. It was bad enough that I'd had to get myself wasted last night to stop thinking about her long enough to crash. So I excused myself from the table and walked outside the bar to take the call.

"Hello?"

"Holden?"

"Yeah?"

"It's Laney…Lala."

I tried to play it off cool. "Oh, hey, Lala. Long time no talk. What's up?"

"I just saw your name in my missed calls from late last night. I wanted to make sure everything was okay."

Shit. "Uhh…sorry. I must've butt-dialed you or something." I lied straight through my teeth. "I didn't even know I'd called."

"Oh, that's funny. Because I was actually going to call you this weekend."

"You were?"

"Yeah, I'm coming into town for a night next week. I have an interview in the City for a research grant I'm trying to get. I thought maybe I'd stop by the apartment building you guys bought and check it out and say hi to everyone while I'm there. You all live in the building, right?"

"We do. Which night are you coming?"

"Wednesday. My interview is early Thursday morning."

"Where are you staying?"

"I didn't book a hotel yet. I just got the call about the interview yesterday afternoon."

"Stay with me." I shook my head. "I mean, you can stay with us. We use one of the units in the building for short-term rentals. We're testing out renting it as an Airbnb. The rates are higher, and so far the demand seems to be there."

"Oh, wow. Do you think it's open next Wednesday for the night?"

If it isn't, I'll be canceling a reservation. "I'm pretty sure it is."

"Alright. That would be great. Then I can see you guys and won't have to rush to find my hotel. I get so lost in Manhattan."

"Are you driving or taking the train?"

"I think I'm going to drive."

"I'll text you a good place to park near the building that isn't too expensive."

"Perfect. Thanks so much, Holden. I'm looking forward to seeing you guys."

After I hung up, I stared at my phone for a while. Growing up, my mom's favorite saying was, *There's no such thing as a coincidence.* I never paid it much attention, but right now, I was kind of hoping she was right…

I hadn't gone on Facebook in probably two years. But that's exactly where I found myself after getting home from the bar with a buzz at midnight and re-reading the letter I'd written to myself three times. One sentence in particular I read over and over:

> *If Lala is single when you get this, and you still haven't taken your shot, you're a giant pussy.*

I typed *Laney Ellison* into the search bar and frowned at the profile picture that popped up. It was of her and Dr. Douchebag, so I grabbed another beer. The photo must've been taken the day she'd gotten engaged, because the cardigan-wearing scientist had one arm wrapped around her shoulder, and she was holding her hand out to the camera, showing off a ring. I zoomed in on her finger as I guzzled back half my beer. *That's a fucking pebble. Lala deserves a rock.*

It made me dislike Dr. Douchebag even more that he hadn't bought her a decent ring. "Cheap bastard," I muttered and clicked over to the rest of her photos.

The next picture was of her graduating Brown with her PhD. Her mom and dad stood proudly by her side. I zoomed in and noticed the small cross around her neck. It had been Ryan's, a gift from his parents when he'd made his first communion—the same day as me. He used to wear it all the time. After he died, Lala put it on, but I hadn't realized she was still wearing it. I wasn't surprised. Those two weren't like most siblings. Ryan and Lala had actually gotten along, even when they were younger, before his diagnosis. He'd been super protective of her. Hence the reason that on one of his final days, he'd asked me to keep an eye on his little sister… but not "*too good of an eye.*" My buddy was probably looking down right now, cursing me just for stalking.

I clicked over to the next picture, and my eyes grew wide. *Holy shit.* Bully is still alive! Ryan had adopted that fat bulldog when we were in high school, so it had to be at least fifteen by now. I couldn't believe he was still kicking. The picture showed Lala kneeling in front of the Christmas tree with one arm around Bully, and the dog was wearing a Christmas sweater. If Ryan wasn't already pissed off that I was stalking his baby sister, this photo of his dog wearing a *sweater* was certainly gonna do it. I raised my beer can to the sky. "Sorry, buddy. I didn't know."

I spent the next fifteen minutes going through the rest of Lala's photos, though I may have stalled on one in particular for most of that time. There was a shot of Lala in a bikini. She'd always been beautiful, with a nice figure, but the years that had passed since I'd stolen glances of her in a bathing suit in Ryan's backyard had turned the skinny girl into a woman with dangerous curves. Curves that would *definitely* get me into trouble if I went too close.

When I clicked onto the very last picture, it felt like the breath had been knocked out of my lungs. It was of Ryan and Lala sitting on a piece of driftwood on the beach, and I was the one who'd taken it. Ryan had no hair from his third round of treatments. I remember he wasn't supposed to be released from the hospital for a few more days, but he'd convinced everyone to let him go early so he could spend his twenty-second birthday with his crew. Me, Owen, Brayden, Colby, Ryan, and Lala had driven to Ocean City—the place we'd all gone to after prom that had so many good memories. We'd spent the entire day on the beach and then made a bonfire, which didn't go out until after the sun came up. It was a day I'd never forget, especially because it was the last good day we'd all have for a while since Ryan passed away the very next night.

On that note, I closed my laptop. I guess the upside of seeing that picture was that it stopped me from stalking Lala. If the photo of her in a bikini had gotten me hot and bothered, that last one had poured a cold bucket of water over me. Which was exactly what I

9

needed. Lala Ellison was off limits, the one woman in the world I wasn't allowed to go near with a ten-foot pole. Well, at least until she arrived next week…and stayed the night in the apartment that happened to be right next door to mine.

Knock. Knock. Knock.

Jesus Christ, my palms actually started to sweat. What was I, twelve?

Lala had texted a few hours ago to say she'd probably arrive around five o'clock, and the time on the microwave read 5:01. The last time I felt this nervous was when my band played at a festival in front of ten-thousand people. I had to wipe my palms on my jeans.

"Hey." I smiled as I opened the door. But my smile wilted when I realized Lala wasn't alone. There was someone standing next to her.

Lala looked over at the buxom redhead and motioned between the two of them with a hesitant smile. "We took the elevator up together and got off on the same floor. Turns out, we were going to the same place."

Fiona—the woman I'd met at a bar last weekend—shrugged. "Sorry to stop over without calling, but I was in the neighborhood and thought I'd see if you were home. I forgot something at your apartment when I was here."

"You did?"

She winked and pointed inside. "I believe they might still be attached to your headboard." Fiona looked over at Lala and back to me. "Can I just go grab them, and I'll be out of your hair?"

Not knowing what else to do, I stepped aside for Fiona to enter. Meanwhile, Lala remained outside my door with her suitcase. I shook my head and reached for the handle. "Sorry about that. Come on in."

Before I could wheel in Lala's luggage and shut the door behind us, Fiona came strutting back out from my bedroom. She held up a set of handcuffs. "Found 'em."

I shut my eyes. *Great. Just fucking great.*

❤CHAPTER 2

Lala

The door shut behind the redhead. When I looked back over at Holden, you could've heard a pin drop.

"I can explain…" he finally said.

I held my palms out and laughed. "I'm sure you could, but I don't think I want to hear about it."

Holden ran a hand through his thick mane of shaggy hair. "Fair point."

Then his face turned red. Holden seemed embarrassed. It wasn't like his history with women was a secret to any of us, so that surprised me.

"Well, that was a fucking awkward way to greet you." He held his arms out. "Anyway, welcome to the building, Lala."

"Thanks." I fell into his warm embrace. "I'm so excited to be here." My body buzzed at the contact of his chest against mine.

I could feel his heart beating fast, which was interesting. He had that delicious fresh-out-of-the-shower scent—soap and cologne—mixed with an intoxicating smell that was all his own; I remembered it from the last time we were this close—when we'd danced at Colby and Billie's wedding.

I looked around. "Your place is exactly how I might have imagined it, Catalano."

He cocked a brow. "Why's that?"

"Drum set in the corner. Black furniture…"

"Please don't say handcuffs on the bed post."

I sighed. "That, too."

He shut his eyes again, in apparent embarrassment, and then flashed the most beautiful smile.

I'd always had a crush on Holden. But believe it or not, it wasn't purely physical. When we were younger, we used to talk a lot. Ryan never knew about all those private conversations. I suppose I'd had mini crushes on all of Ryan's friends at one point or another, but nothing touched the one I had on Holden, and it had never gone away. That said, of all of my brother's friends, Holden was the last one Ryan would have approved of for me. Holden wasn't boyfriend material, even if women—myself included—couldn't take our eyes off of him. Actually, Ryan had picked up on my admiration for Holden once. He'd caught me staring as Holden climbed out of our backyard pool and dried off his half-naked body one summer when we were all teenagers. My brother had warned me "*not to even think about it.*" Ryan loved Holden, but the idea of me and Holden together would have probably killed him—if he weren't already dead.

"So…" Holden clapped his hands together. "Should we go next door?"

"Yeah. I'm excited to see it. Thank you again for letting me stay here."

"Of course. Anything for Ryan's little sister."

"Thanks, although I'm not exactly *little* anymore."

"I've noticed." He smiled.

A chill ran down my spine as I followed Holden out to the hallway and watched as he opened the apartment next door for me.

I took a look around. *Wow.* The place was stunning.

The living room featured cream-colored leather furniture that looked brand new. A couple of chunky knit throws on the sofa and loveseat gave the space a cozy yet trendy feel. Everything smelled new. It was an open floorplan with the kitchen adjacent to the living area, and the light-colored granite countertop complemented the earth tones of the rest of the apartment.

"You guys did a great job setting this up. It's beautiful."

"Yeah, thanks. Like I said, we're experimenting with renting it out as an Airbnb. You got lucky that it was available."

"I should say!" I wandered over to the kitchen. "Oh, thank God. There's a coffee maker and pods. I was wondering if I'd have time to get coffee in the morning."

"If there's anything you need, I'm right next door," he reminded me.

How could I forget? "Thank you."

The fact that this apartment happened to be *right next door* to Holden's made me nervous as much as it was comforting.

"So tell me about the geek adventures that brought you here."

I crossed my arms. "You mean the research-project interview."

"I'm teasing. But you *are* too damn smart for your own good. Always made the rest of us look like bigger idiots than we are." He sighed. "Anyway, seriously, tell me about it."

"It's an interview for a research grant on the effects of dopamine in relation to Alzheimer's disease."

"Interesting." He scratched his chin scruff. "Dopamine is like a sex hormone, right?"

Of course, his mind would go straight to that. "It's a type of neurotransmitter that the body makes. It impacts how we feel pleasure. Too much or too little can affect us negatively. But yes, it is produced in response to sexual stimulation, among other things."

"So, wait, too much dopamine can be a bad thing? It can make someone lose their mind?"

"Well, anything in excess is bad, right? But this particular study is focusing more on *low* levels of dopamine and the increased risk of Alzheimer's."

He nodded. "Ah. So the more sex someone has…the less likely they'll get Alzheimer's?"

I cleared my throat. "The research seems to point in that direction, yes."

"Damn. I'm all set then. My brain will be sharp as a whistle." Holden winked.

I rolled my eyes. "Sex does have many benefits. And very few downsides—as long as you're careful."

"I'm always careful," he said, his expression sincere.

"Good."

"Especially with Colby as an example," he added.

Colby had impregnated his daughter's mother during a one-night stand about five years before he met his wife, Billie. Saylor was a gift, but certainly that had been a hard lesson for all of the guys: one lapse in judgment could change your entire life.

He tilted his head. "So, tell me more about the benefits of sex."

"Are you serious?"

"Sort of. I'm mainly enjoying watching your face turn red right now."

I felt my cheek. "Am I?"

"A little. But really, I'm intrigued. I never think about hormones and shit and how all of that can impact someone for the long term. But good to know that sex has health benefits."

"The increase of both oxytocin and dopamine during orgasm wipes out cortisol, which is the stress hormone."

He nodded. "That's why people feel so relaxed after."

"Right."

"But I never knew those hormones could, like, protect your brain. That's huge."

"Almost every decision we make—what we put in our bodies, food or *otherwise*—has an impact on our overall health." I smiled. "You know what else increases dopamine levels?"

"What?"

"Music."

"Ah. Nice. Another win for me."

"The chills I bet you get in the middle of a great set? A lot of that is dopamine."

"But like you said, too much can also be bad, right?"

"There are *some* negative side effects of too much dopamine, like anxiety, insomnia, too high of a sex drive."

"So my memory will be perfect, but I'll continue to go through life as a horn dog with occasional anxiety." He nodded once. "Got it. Sounds about right."

I laughed.

"Thanks for the education, Lala. You're so smart." Holden smiled. "It's good to see you. It's felt like forever."

Dare I bring it up? "Yeah, I think the last time was Colby's wedding, huh?"

"Yup." He nodded slowly. "A year. Too damn long."

His eyes locked with mine, and I immediately thought back to the dance he and I had shared at the wedding. Warren had disappeared to the bathroom. I'd looked up, and suddenly Holden was standing there in his place. I remember hoping to God Warren didn't come back to find me dancing with Holden. It had been a slower song, and I didn't want him to think anything inappropriate was happening. But maybe that's because *I* was the one thinking inappropriate things. Like clockwork, the song had ended, and Holden left the dance floor right before Warren reemerged. My fiancé, therefore, had no idea that I'd just shared a dance with my childhood crush.

It was like it never happened—except for the fact that I had continued to think about it all night. I'd steal glances over at Holden and feel guilty because I couldn't put my finger on it, but there'd been something special about that dance. Did I think Holden liked me *like that*? No. But his cutting in when Warren left did seem quite intentional. Maybe the sentimental feel of the wedding had gotten to him. Weddings are a huge milestone. They have a way of making you realize life is passing us all by. And I wondered if the song made him emotional about missing Ryan. Since I was the closest thing to Ryan there, maybe that was why he'd latched onto *me* in that moment.

"Anyway…" Holden interrupted my thoughts. "I know there are a lot of people eager to see you tonight. Colby and Billie are making dinner. They wanted me to bring you over to their place when you're done settling in. I think we're already late, actually."

I rubbed my belly. "Oh my gosh. That sounds great. I'm starving. Give me just a second."

I went to use the bathroom, then met Holden back out in the living room, and we headed over to Colby's apartment.

Colby's daughter, Saylor, answered the door and jumped up and down. "Lala!"

"Hi, honey! I'm so happy you remembered me." I bent to hug her. "You're getting so tall. I can't stand it."

She and I had only met a couple of times, but we'd spent some quality time together at the wedding. Saylor's mother had never been in her life. When Colby got married, his wife, Billie, had taken on the role of her mother. It seemed to be working out great.

Saylor reached up to touch my hair. "Your hair is so curly!"

I fluffed my blond mane. "I know! It's a crazy mess."

"It's wild. I love it," Holden said from behind me.

"Thanks." I felt a little flushed.

Billie came over to hug me. "We thought you'd never show, Lala! What took you so damn long?"

Billie was a super-cool person I was eager to get to know better. She owned the tattoo parlor in the building; that's how she and Colby had met.

"I'm sorry!" I said. "There was tons of traffic. And then Holden was showing me the apartment."

"I had her tied up for a while. It's my fault."

Wait, what? The fleeting image that conjured was quite vivid. I cleared my throat. "The apartment is beautiful. I can't thank you guys enough for letting me stay here."

Still dressed in a three-piece suit, Owen came over to hug me. "Are you kidding? This is Ryan's building. There will always be a place for you here. Even if we have to kick Holden out to make room."

"I'll volunteer to kick his ass out myself," Brayden said as he opened his arms to hug me next.

I'd really missed being around these guys. They reminded me so much of my brother, and I could feel Ryan here, too.

Colby was the last to appear. He'd been in the kitchen and came out holding a plate of something, which he placed on the dining room table.

"Hey, Lala!" He wiped his hands and came over to embrace me.

Shortly after that, we all sat down to a dinner of pasta, meatballs, salad, and garlic bread. Saylor proudly proclaimed that she'd arranged the salad all by herself.

During our meal, Colby grilled me a little.

"So, Lala…" he said. "Being that Ryan isn't here, I hope you'll understand that we have to play the role of the protective older brothers. Unfortunately, you get four for the price of one."

"Four brothers, huh? That sounds like…a lot." I chuckled.

"I have four uncles!" Saylor chimed in. "Three here and one in heaven."

I smiled. "That's true."

"So, I have a few questions," Colby continued. "For one, I don't really know much about Warren. He seemed like a great guy when I met him at the wedding, but I don't really *know* him. Tell me more. Why is *he* the one, out of all of the men in the world?"

"Oh, leave her alone." Billie smacked his arm. "She doesn't have to explain her feelings to anyone. You can't always articulate what it is about someone that makes you love them. When you know, you just know." She smiled at me.

"Sorry." Colby shrugged. "I think it's a fair question."

I looked over at Holden, who stared back at me. He, like everyone else, seemed to be waiting for an answer.

I wiped my mouth, looking over at Billie. "It's okay. He's right. Ryan would've asked me that question a while ago. He would've insisted on spending time with Warren and vetting him."

Brayden crossed his arms. "Okay, so why should we approve of him?"

"Well…" I paused. "He's super smart. Funny. He truly cares about me. He makes me feel safe. He's honest, which is *very* important to me…" I looked around the table.

"That's it?" Colby chuckled.

Billie smacked his arm again. "What more do you want?"

"He's curing cancer or some shit, right?" Owen asked.

"He's a cancer researcher, yeah."

Holden played with his pasta. "I don't mean to sound stupid, but what *exactly* does a cancer researcher do? Like he goes into work and does…what?"

I straightened in my seat. "Well, a typical day for Warren might be putting cancer cells under a microscope and seeing how they interact with a particular organism. It takes many hours of work, trial and error, to make small gains in discovering what works and what doesn't in terms of diminishing cell growth and therefore reducing disease burden."

"That's a very honorable job," Billie said.

"He's an honorable nerd, yeah," Holden added.

I raised a brow. "Well, I guess we're perfect for each other then, since that's what you used to call me—a nerd."

"Yeah, but you know I mean it lovingly." Holden winked.

Colby looked between us. I hoped he didn't sense my weird feelings for Holden. I remembered Colby watching Holden and me dance at the wedding. He'd seemed to be the only one who took notice.

After dessert, I stood from the table. "Well, I'm sure you guys have to get Saylor to bed, and I have to get ready for the interview tomorrow, so I should get out of your hair."

Billie stood. "We need to do this all the time, if you end up getting the position. Maybe make it a weekly thing."

I nodded. "I'd love that."

Holden stood and accompanied me to the door.

When he opened it and went out, I looked up at him. "You're leaving, too?"

"Yeah. Dinner's over, right?"

I said a quick goodbye to everyone and followed Holden down the hall. We walked together back to the adjacent apartments.

Holden stopped at my door and handed me the key. Our fingers brushed together as I took them.

He stood in place for a moment, then suddenly asked, "Would you want to come in and have a drink with me?"

My stomach fluttered. Why did a simple question make me react that way? It was just a drink. But somehow anything having to do with Holden felt...dangerous. It wasn't that I didn't trust him—or myself. I just didn't think it was a good idea to fan the flames of whatever had been going on in my head since the second I'd arrived.

"I'd better not," I told him. "I have a lot to unpack. And I need to be in tip-top shape tomorrow morning."

"Right. Of course." He looked down at his shoes. "Another time then." He sighed. "*When* you get the job. You will. Because you're Lala."

"I wish I felt that confident."

"You'll do great." He smiled, his eyes lingering on mine for a moment.

Yeah. There was undoubtedly an odd tension between us. It was the same tension I'd felt at Colby's wedding and intermittently over the years. I just couldn't be sure he sensed it the same way I did. I held up my hand. "Well…goodnight."

"'Night, Lala."

Holden waited for me to enter the apartment. After the door closed behind me, I took a deep breath in and tried to find my bearings. Relief washed over me. *I'm finally alone.*

I took a hot shower, which was badly needed, before drying my hair. I probably should've gone straight to bed after that, but I was wired. I ventured over to the refrigerator, assuming it would be empty. But I was shocked to find cream for coffee and a box of something inside. My chest tightened when I opened it to find a dozen Boston cream donuts. Ryan's favorite. There was a sticky note on the top of the box.

Ryan says: "You got this, sis. Knock 'em dead tomorrow."

Tears formed in my eyes. I reached for my phone.

Lala: You did that? The donuts?

Holden: Figured you needed breakfast in the morning.

Lala: You made me cry. Thank you. That was the sweetest gesture.

Holden: You're welcome, sweetheart.

That made me tingle all over. I was a crying, tingling fucking mess. *Jesus.* I had a fiancé. I needed to stop reacting to Holden like this. Maybe it was just the excitement of being here. If I got the grant and came to live in the City, my emotions would settle down. And anyway, even if I didn't have a fiancé, Holden Catalano would not be an option for me. He was every headache I didn't need in my life. That moment we'd had at the wedding was apparently still messing with my head.

After devouring one of the donuts, I brushed my teeth and tucked myself into bed, once again impressed with the quality of this place as I felt the comfortable, memory-foam mattress beneath me. I briefly tested the sound of the alarm on my phone to make sure it would go off in the morning.

Just as I laid my head on the pillow, I heard a knock on the bedroom wall. At first I thought it was my imagination, but then it happened again.

I grabbed my phone again.

Lala: Is that you?

The three dots moved as he typed.

Holden: What are you talking about?

Then came another knock.

Lala: The knock on my wall!

Holden: What knock?

It happened again.

Lala: Did you hear that?

Holden: Of course, I did. I'm doing it.

Lala: Holden! LOL

Holden: Did you know our bedrooms are back to back?

Lala: I do now.

Holden: LOL

Lala: Oh God. I'm not going to have to listen to you "entertaining" people, am I?

Holden: I'll try to be extra cognizant of the fact that you're here.

Lala: Well, thank you in advance for agreeing to keep it down.

Holden: The only time it gets too loud is during sex parties. But those only happen once a month.

Lala: Sex parties?

Holden: Whips. Chains. (Handcuffs.) The whole nine. Dopamine OVERLOAD.

Is he serious?

Holden: LOL I'm just joking. No sex parties.

Lala: I never know with you.

Holden: I sort of wasted that one since I couldn't see how red your face turned.

Lala: Sigh. I gotta go to sleep.

Holden: Okay. I won't bother you anymore.

Lala: 'Night, Holden.

Holden: 'Night, Lala.

I forced myself to shut my eyes. I should have been practicing my interview answers as I drifted off. Instead, I imagined myself chained to Holden's bed at a sex party.

CHAPTER 3

Holden

Sniff. *Sniff.*

How the hell does a sheet still smell like a person when they've been gone for four days?

Whatever. I needed to ignore it because I had to get this apartment ready for the Airbnb renter checking in tomorrow. I walked around the bed, yanked the last corner of the fitted sheet off, and bunched it into a ball.

But as I lifted it into my arms, that smell wafted through the air again.

I looked around the empty apartment, as if someone other than me might be inside, and then brought the sheet to my nose.

Deep inhale in. Big exhale out. Damn it. Did she have to smell as good as she looked these days? *Lala freaking Ellison.*

The woman was making me nuts. She was all I'd been able to think about since that letter from myself arrived, and I hadn't had a good night's sleep since the one she'd spent here. As if on cue, I yawned.

I really could use a little nap. I looked at the sheet in my hand. *No. Don't do it.*

But why the fuck not? a different part of my conscience asked. It's just a bed. And this one is so new and comfy—unlike my own, which I'd had to fix twice in the last few months. I just needed to get a few solid hours of decent shut-eye.

Yeah right. Lie to yourself. Go ahead, fuckboy.

But it made sense, didn't it? I was tired, standing in front of a nice, new bed, and I happened to have had a mostly clean sheet right in my hand. I could just pop it back on. I wouldn't even need to put on all four corners—two would be enough. Lord knows I'd slept like that before. No one would even know I'd taken a little nap.

Except you, you low-life sheet sniffer.

"Shut the hell up."

I was now not just thinking to myself, but talking out loud too. *Great, just great.* I *really* needed some sleep. So I tamped down my ridiculous thoughts, put the fitted sheet back on, and climbed into bed.

I took a big, deep inhale…

Because that's what one does when they're exhausted and trying to fall asleep, and not because it smelled just like *Lala freaking Ellison.*

For the record, the smile that stayed on my face for my three-and-a-half-hour nap *also* had nothing to do with *Lala freaking Ellison.*

"What's up, ladies?" I smiled at the guys as I walked into Owen's apartment for our monthly card game. They were already seated in their usual spots. I plunked down a twelve-pack of Coors Light and pulled one out for myself.

Owen had the cards in his hands, itching to deal. "You're freaking late, that's what's up."

"Sorry." I twisted off the cap and tossed it into the center of the pot as my ante. "I just woke up from a glorious nap. Which means I also didn't have time to run out and get cash, so I'm going to have to use beer caps for dollars."

Brayden shook his head. "You got some racket going, dude. You never have any cash on you, and you take afternoon naps."

I grinned and pointed to my face. "Needed my beauty sleep. Otherwise how am I going to get women to buy me drinks when I don't have cash?"

Colby chuckled. "Pass me one of those beers, jackass."

I pulled another bottle out of the case and draped it over one arm like a maître d' showing a bottle of champagne. "I hope the year is to your liking."

Owen went around the table, dealing the cards. "You're in an awfully good mood. I take it you weren't alone in bed this afternoon?"

I sucked down some of my beer and leaned back with a big *ahhh*. "All by myself, my friend. I'm just happy to be here with my dearest mates."

Colby positioned his beer cap between his thumb and middle finger and snapped. It went flying through the air, bounced off my forehead, and landed in the middle of the table.

I grinned. "Guess my ante is two bucks."

Owen finished dealing out five cards each and set down the deck. "Any of you know how far out we have reservations on the Airbnb unit?"

"I think we have one at the end of the month, but that's it. We only opened the reservation calendar for six months."

"Can we cancel that reservation?"

I shrugged. "Person probably won't be happy about it. But yeah, we have the ability to cancel. Why?"

Owen looked around at all the guys. "Because Lala got the grant she applied for."

26

I froze. "How do you know?"

"She called me today. They want her to start Monday. It's a government grant, so if they don't begin spending the money by the end of the month, they lose it from their budget next year. She wanted to know if we'd rent the apartment to her. I told her I'd get back to her after I checked whether it was available, but I wanted to see how you guys feel about offering it to her rent free. Her grant lasts for six months, so we'd be forgoing rent for half a year. But we wouldn't have this building if Ryan hadn't made us the beneficiaries of his life insurance policy. It seems like the right thing to do."

The guys all started nodding. "Absolutely," someone added. But I was still stuck on Owen's first sentence. "Why did she call you and not me?"

He shrugged. "Probably because I'm nicer and better looking. Oh, and I'm an adult *who doesn't take naps*."

I was offended that Lala had chosen to call Owen, but when Colby's eyes slanted to mine with a knowing look, I covered up as best as I could. "Yeah, sure. That's fine."

"So we're all good with giving it to her rent free?" Owen asked. Everyone nodded.

"Alright then," he said. "I'll call her back later and let her know she has a place to stay for as long as she needs it."

"Hey, I'm glad you're home."

I opened my apartment door to find Owen on the other side. "What's up?"

"Lala is supposed to be arriving about two today, and I just got a call from a client who wants me to show them an apartment right now because they're very interested, and I already have an offer coming in on it from another agency. I was supposed to give Lala and Warren a hand moving her stuff in. Any chance you could help them out in my place?"

I felt bad saying no. But Dr. Douchebag should be able to carry the boxes himself. The apartment was fully furnished, so it wasn't like he had to carry anything big. "Sorry." I shrugged. "I have plans."

"Shit. Okay. I'll try Brayden and Colby."

"Alright. Good luck today."

"Thanks, man."

Owen started to walk away, but turned back. "By the way, I caught Frick and Frack, the teenagers from hell in 410, up on the roof again last night. They had buckets of water and were trying to dump them on unsuspecting pedestrians this time."

"Seriously? Mrs. Martin from 408 called me to complain two days ago that they'd been blasting music all night. When I went up to tell them to knock it off, they were home alone. I thought I scared them a little. Guess not. Have you seen the mother lately?"

"Nope. And we didn't get rent this month either."

I shook my head. "They're old enough not to need a babysitter, but they're not old enough to live alone. I'll see if the mom is around later and have a talk with her if she is."

"Thanks."

I shut the door, feeling like a complete piece of shit for saying I couldn't help Lala. But the last thing I needed was to be around her and her fiancé. Since she was moving right next door, I was bound to hear them when they arrived, and that would make me feel like an even bigger scumbag for hiding out in my apartment. I needed to make myself scarce, so I scrolled through my contacts for someone to make plans with. I didn't have to scroll very far.

I'd hooked up with Anna a few times, and just last week I'd run into her on the subway. She'd told me to text her. So I did. I asked her to a daytime movie, though I had no interest in seeing one. She texted back quickly, sounding excited about getting together, which made me feel like shit yet again.

I wanted to be gone by the time Lala arrived. So after I took a shower, I figured I'd take a slow walk uptown to the theatre where I'd told Anna I'd meet her in an hour. But when I got outside in front of the building, there was some sort of commotion. A guy was yelling and flailing his arms, standing beside a car pulled halfway into a parking spot, nose first. Meanwhile, another car was backed halfway in. It wasn't until a woman got out of the other car and slammed the door that I realized it was Lala getting yelled at. *Shit.* I ran over just as the other driver began walking toward her.

"Hey." I stepped in front of her and put my hands up. "Slow your roll, buddy. What's going on here?"

Lala pointed to the guy. "I was trying to back in, and he raced up out of nowhere and is trying to take the spot. He was definitely not behind me when I reversed to parallel park."

I looked at the guy. He was bald, with a big belly and ruddy face. "Listen, dude, the lady is moving into this building right here today."

"I don't give two shits where she's going," he spat. "I saw the spot first."

Lala put her hands on her hips. "You did not!"

"Come on, buddy. Even if you were here first, can't you just be a gentleman and let her take the spot?" I pointed to the backseat of her car, which was filled with boxes. "She's got a lot of stuff that needs to get moved."

He folded his arms across his chest. "Blow me."

"Very nice." I shook my head. "You're a real peach, I can see."

Lala opened the back door to her car. "Fine. If you're not going to move, I'm just going to leave my car parked like this and carry my boxes up. I have a lot of them, so if you're thinking of waiting until I'm done, it's going to be a while."

"Uhh, Lala," I leaned in and whispered. "I'm not sure you should leave your car parked like that."

She pursed her lips, reached into the car, and grabbed a box anyway. "Oh well."

I looked at the guy and shrugged. "You heard the lady." Then I loaded a few boxes into my arms, and Lala and I headed to the front door of the building. The guy screamed something about having her car towed.

Lala stopped at the door and yelled, "Go suck an egg, baldy!"

Inside the elevator, I grinned. "That was pretty badass."

She set her box down and showed me a shaking hand. "I guess it was the adrenaline pumping because I'm shaking now. I'm a big chicken."

I chuckled. "Could've fooled me."

The elevator dinged on our floor, and I motioned with my chin for Lala to step off first. Halfway down the hall, the bottom of the three boxes I had stacked in my arms burst open, and everything inside fell to the floor.

"Shit."

Lala and I put everything down, and I attempted to reseal the box where the tape had come undone. I shook my head. "This isn't going to hold. I need to put this box in the middle of the other two, so there's support on the bottom, then we can toss everything back in just to get the stuff into the apartment."

"Good idea."

We scooped everything back into the box and stacked the third on top. Lala picked up the box she'd been carrying, and we walked another five or six steps...until the box in her hands gave out, and the contents spilled all over the floor.

"Oh no!" Lala bent down. "Does tape go bad?"

"If it's old enough. The stickiness dries up. Why? How old was the tape you used to make these boxes?"

She made a face. "I found it in Ryan's closet. I'm pretty sure it's from when we packed up some of his clothes for Goodwill a few months after he died."

Oh shit. "Did you use it for *all* the boxes?"

She nodded and bit her bottom lip.

I chuckled. "I have packing tape in my apartment. We'll bring it down with us and reinforce the rest of the boxes before we carry them up."

Together, we repacked the second broken box and managed to get all of the first batch into the apartment before anything else busted. I went next door to grab fresh tape and came back a minute later. "I thought Warren was coming to help you move in?"

"He's busy working on a project deadline, and I thought I could handle it myself."

That's strike number three against Dr. Douchebag. Two was that pebble of an engagement ring he bought her, and strike one…well, that was because he existed.

I frowned. "We better head back down."

"Do you mind if I use the bathroom first?"

I gestured toward it. "Help yourself."

While she took care of her business, I went back next door to my apartment and got us two bottles of water. I offered her one when she came out.

"Oh, thank you. I'm actually really thirsty. I didn't drink anything before I left because I didn't want to have to leave all my stuff alone at a rest stop."

"Good idea." I twisted the cap and chugged some water. "You ready to do the next trip? Mr. Happy out there is probably stomping his feet by now."

But when we walked outside, Mr. Happy wasn't pouting. The fucker was all smiles. His sudden good mood was most likely due to the *tow truck* lifting the front of Lala's car into the air. I ran over to the guy running the crank.

"Hey, come on, man. The owner of the car is right here." I pointed to the guy who'd started this. "This dude tried to steal her spot and picked a fight with her. We were only gone for ten minutes, max. She's moving into that building right there, and she has all these boxes to carry up. Can you cut her some slack, please? We'll move the car right after you unhook her, I promise."

The tow truck driver lifted a foot onto the bumper of his truck and spoke to the other driver. "I don't know, Officer Agostino, what do you think? Should I give the lady here a break?"

The dickface flashed an evil smile. "Definitely *not*. Get that piece of shit out of here, Johnny."

Oh fuck. I hung my head. *The asshole is a cop...*

I let out a sigh of defeat and spoke to Johnny. "Can we just pay you for the tow, you can unhook it right here, and we'll move the car? At least save us from having to go down to the impound lot to get it."

The tow truck driver looked to the cop again. The dickwad shook his head with a smile so big it made me think this was the most fun he'd had in a long-ass time.

The tow truck driver finished cranking up Lala's car and handed me a card. "I'm probably going to stop for some lunch, so it might be a while."

"Can we at least take the boxes out before you go? Things are going to rattle around from all the potholes and being towed with the front end in the air."

"Sorry. No can do." He walked toward his truck.

I looked at Lala. "Sorry."

"It's not your fault." She pointed to the cop. "It's his."

The officer flashed one last smug smile and got into his car. "You two have a *great fucking day*."

Things didn't get any better after that. Lala and I took an overpriced Uber to Brooklyn to get her car from the impound lot. But when we arrived, the car wasn't there yet. The damn tow truck driver moseyed in almost an hour later. Then we went to pay and found out they didn't take credit cards, and neither one of us had enough cash on us. So we had to walk six blocks to the nearest cash machine. After, when we returned with the three-hundred-and-fifty bucks they had the balls to charge, the clerk at the lot didn't want to release the car to Lala because she didn't have the registration on her. Once we finally convinced them Lala wasn't a car thief trying to steal her eleven-year-old piece-of-crap car from the tow company, her car wouldn't start.

"They messed up your car. I'm gonna kill that tow truck driver." I started to get out, but Lala reached for me.

"No. I don't think they did anything, Holden." She shook her head. "I had to get my neighbor to come over and give me a jump before I left this morning. He said it was probably the alternator."

"Oh. Alright." I looked around, but the impound yard was empty except for cars. "Let me go back to the office and see if the clerk can get someone to give us a jump. I'll be right back."

But our string of bad luck didn't stop there. The car wouldn't start, even after half an hour of trying to jump it and letting the battery charge.

I finally closed the hood of Lala's car and wiped my hands on my pants before extending a hand to the woman who'd helped us. "I really appreciate you trying. Is there a mechanic nearby who won't gouge her for an alternator if we have you guys tow it there?"

She nodded. "Banner Auto Repair is about a mile down on the right. He's fair."

"Can you tow it there?"

She looked at the time on her phone. "It's almost six on a Sunday. He's closed for the day by now. I can get it towed over first thing in the morning, but I'm going to have to charge you for it."

I blew out two cheeks of hot air and looked over at Lala.

She shrugged. "What choice do we have? But what about all my boxes? I don't even have a toothbrush or clothes to wear to work tomorrow without them."

"I'll call Dylan, my bass player, and see if he can come get us and the boxes. He lives in Brooklyn and stores the band's van in his driveway."

Dylan was able to help, but we didn't get back to the apartment building and finish unloading everything until almost eight thirty.

Lala looked around the living room, littered with boxes. "Could you please call my cell? I have no idea where I put it down. I really hope I didn't drop it in the van since Dylan just left."

I held up my phone. "I would, but mine died hours ago."

Lala covered her mouth and giggled. "Oh my God, Holden. If I don't laugh at the day we've had, I might have to cry."

I smiled. "Today was a real shit show, wasn't it?"

"I told a cop to *go suck an egg* and called him baldy!"

The two of us cracked up, and I nodded toward the door. "Come on. Let's go to my place. I'll grab a charger so we can find your phone, and you'll grab us some cold beers from the fridge."

"That sounds heavenly. Thank you."

But as soon as we stepped out of Lala's apartment and into the hall, I realized *heavenly* was still a speedbump away. A woman stood in front of my door—a woman I'd *completely forgotten* I was supposed to meet at the movies hours ago.

Anna looked at me, then Lala, and her lips twisted.

Crap. This wasn't going to be pretty.

"You are *such an asshole.* I can't believe I came all the way back over here because I was worried something happened to you since you stood me up and haven't answered your phone all day." She looked over at Lala. "Enjoy your fun night because that's all you're gonna get." She stormed off.

"Anna, wait! I'm sorry! Something came up and my phone died and then—"

Her response was to flip me the bird over her shoulder and keep walking.

"I'm so sorry," Lala said. "I didn't realize you had plans."

I shook my head. "It's my fault. I totally forgot I was supposed to meet her at the movies."

"Well, I think you're being kind. Will you please let me buy you dinner? It's the least I can do after the mess I've made out of your day and ruining your date."

"Only if I can supply the beer and wine."

She smiled. "It's a deal."

Lala and I ordered Chinese food, and we ate out of the cartons it came in as she unpacked and I broke down boxes. Despite all the hassle, today had left me feeling close to her the way we'd been years ago.

"Can I ask you something?"

"Sure. If I get to ask you something." She held out her container of chicken with broccoli. "Want the rest? I'm full."

I squinted at her. "Did you spit in it?"

She looked shocked. "What? No!"

I chuckled and swiped the carton from her hand. "I'm kidding."

Lala rolled her eyes but smiled as she used a box cutter to open the last box. "What did you want to ask me?"

"Why did you call Owen to see if the apartment was available, and not me?"

Lala froze. "Ummm... I'm not sure. I guess he was just first in my contacts."

That made no sense, since my first and last name both came before Owen's. But she was suddenly avoiding eye contact, and I didn't want to make things weird between us again, so I dropped the subject.

"Your turn..." I said.

"Hmmm?" Lala's nose wrinkled. "My turn for what?"

"You said I could ask you something, if you got to ask me something. Now it's your turn."

"Oh." She took a bunch of towels out of her box and went to the bathroom. "Okay, there is something I'm curious about," she said when she returned.

"Shoot." I put a piece of chicken in my mouth.

"How many women do you sleep with in a month? I mean, that's the second one I've seen at your apartment already."

I started to choke on the chicken.

Lala's eyes widened. She ran to get my bottle of water and held it up to my face. "Drink. Or do you need me to do the Heimlich maneuver?"

I coughed a few more times but managed to swallow the piece of chicken. My eyes watered. "Wrong pipe," I said, taking the bottle.

Lala watched me drink. "Thank God! I haven't done the Heimlich since eighth-grade gym class. I'm not even sure I remember how."

It took another minute to stop the burn in my throat, but at least I could breathe.

"I'm sorry," she said. "I shouldn't have asked such a personal question."

"No, it's fine. I never want you to feel like you can't ask me something." Though I had no idea what the answer to her question was. How many women *did* I sleep with in a month? It wasn't like I kept count, but whatever number I gave her was going to make her think I was a manwhore. "I guess the number varies. Sometimes it's none and sometimes I go out a few times."

"Do you…bring someone home *every* time you go out?"

Fuck. I was making this worse. "Not always, no." *Because there was that one time four months ago that I wasn't feeling so good and left the bar early alone.*

She shook her head and held her hands up. "I didn't mean to intrude or offend you by asking."

I shrugged. "It's fine."

She stared at me for a few seconds. "I bet you're really good at it then…"

My brows shot up.

Lala covered her mouth. Pink bloomed in her cheeks. "Oh my God. I can't believe I just said that. It's just that…you know, practice makes perfect."

I smiled. "I love that you still turn red when you're embarrassed, like you did when you were a kid. You didn't outgrow that."

"Yeah well, obviously I haven't outgrown saying embarrassing stuff, either. I'm sorry for being so inappropriate. I'm not sure what came over me."

"It's fine."

Lala finished unpacking the last box, and I broke it down. We were done now, but I wasn't ready to call it a night. "You up for a glass of wine? I have white and red next door."

Lala hesitated, but then smiled. "Sure. That would be great."

"Red or white?"

"White."

I nodded. "I'm just going to take these boxes down to the dumpster, and then I'll be back."

"Okay."

After I ran downstairs, I went back to my apartment and grabbed a bottle of pinot grigio and two glasses. But rather than go next door, I opened the window in my kitchen and climbed out onto the fire escape.

"Hey, Lala!" I leaned toward her apartment window a few feet away and yelled. When she didn't come, I cupped my hands around my mouth. "*Hey, Ellison! Open the window!*"

A few seconds later, she lifted the window in her apartment and stuck her head out. "I couldn't figure out where you were yelling from."

I waved to her. "Climb out on your fire escape."

She looked down. "Is it safe?"

"Safer than sitting on the roof of your parents' house when everyone else was sleeping like we did when we were kids."

Lala smiled and climbed out. There was only about a foot between my fire escape and hers. I poured two glasses of wine and slipped her one through the metal balusters.

She took it and looked up at the sky. "God, I used to climb out on that roof all the time to study the stars."

"I know. I used to join you whenever I slept over and Ryan would fall asleep before me. You always had your astronomy textbook and a bunch of colored pens with you."

She sipped her wine. "I liked to write down the stars I could identify and color code them based on the constellations they belonged to."

"Ursa Major, Cassiopeia, Orion, Canis Major, Centaurus Crux, and Carina," I said. "Your favorite was Carina. At one point, you wanted to change your name to Carina."

Lala looked over at me. "I can't believe you still remember that."

"I remember a lot about those nights we used to talk…" I probably should've stopped there, since I'd already taken this conversation further than I should've, but I'd always had boundary issues. "You know, you were the first girl I ever felt like I could be myself with when we were out there on the roof. Like, I would tell you dumb shit I dreamed of doing someday, and you never made me feel stupid. You always listened and made me feel like anything was possible."

Lala nodded. "Do you think Ryan knew we used to sneak out and talk like that?"

"Definitely not," I said. "He would've kicked my ass for it."

"Why? We were just two friends talking."

"First of all, I was letting his little sister sit on the roof, when I should've dragged your ass back inside the house where it was safe. And second of all, Ryan knew me well. My intentions always started good with a pretty girl, but they didn't always end so well."

"You…thought I was pretty?"

"Of course I did. Any guy with one eyeball did."

Lala looked into her wine glass with a shy smile. "I thought you were kinda hot, too."

I grinned. "I know."

Her eyes widened. "What do you mean, you know?"

"I used to notice the way you'd check me out, like when I got out of your pool and stuff. Sometimes you'd do it from your bedroom window when you thought no one could see you."

Lala covered her face with her hands. "Oh my God." She laughed. "And here I thought I was so sly."

I leaned a little closer, against the railing of my fire escape. "I'll tell you a little secret."

"What?"

"You know how Ryan and I used to go to the garage and lift your dad's weights before we went in the pool?"

"Yeah? You went in the pool to cool off after."

I shook my head slowly. "Wrong. I made Ryan pump iron with me before we went in the pool, so I'd look more jacked when I got undressed, just in case you were watching."

"Oh wow." Lala gulped back the rest of her wine. "I definitely didn't know that."

I held up the bottle. "You want more?"

Lala bit her lip. It looked like she was considering it—at least until her phone rang. She looked down, and her beautiful face wilted. "Thank you for the offer, but I should take this. It's Warren, and I have to work early tomorrow morning, anyway."

My heart sank, but I forced a smile. "Yeah, of course."

She climbed to her feet, and I followed suit.

"Thank you again for everything you did for me today," she said. "And for the wine and talk, too." She extended her empty glass over the railing to me. "Goodnight, Holden."

"Goodnight, Lala."

Back inside my apartment, I set the bottle of wine on the kitchen counter and placed my glass in the sink. But when I went to put Lala's down next to it, I noticed lipstick marks on the rim.

Don't do it, you dick.

Why not? You already slept in her sheets, bozo.

I clenched my jaw and tried to walk away—really, I did. But I was going to be pissed at myself tomorrow for saying inappropriate shit to Lala anyway. What's a little more self-loathing? So I picked the bottle of wine back up and filled Lala's glass, lining my mouth up where hers had been to drink.

By the time I was done, I'd already started berating myself.

What the fuck, Holden? What's next—stealing her underwear to sniff?

CHAPTER 4

Lala

At the end of my first week in New York, my new admin, Tia, and I were eating our lunch outside of the Department of Health headquarters where I'd be conducting my research for the next few months. I'd just filled her in on my current rent-free living situation.

"I can't believe they're letting you stay for free. That's so nice of them."

"Yeah. These guys are like brothers to me." *Well, except for one.* Holden was more like a wicked, hot stepbrother, perhaps. But there was nothing brotherly about the way my body reacted to that man.

"So...*like* brothers, but three of them are single?"

I cleared my throat. "Yup."

"You've never hooked up with any of them?"

I narrowed my eyes. "I'm engaged." She knew about Warren, so I wasn't sure why she'd asked me that question.

"I know, but I mean in the past?"

I shook my head. "Nope."

"Are any of them good-looking?"

"They're all great-looking, actually."

"Really…" She wiped some mayo off the side of her mouth. "Well, I should come by and, you know, meet you for a drink there some weekend." She winked.

I smiled back, but as a breeze blew my curls around, I hated where my thoughts had gone. I wouldn't mind introducing Tia to Brayden or Owen, but I wanted to gatekeep Holden. And that was ridiculous. Holden Catalano could not be gatekept. Holden freaking belonged to the world; he was with a different woman every week, for heaven's sake.

The afternoon flew by after lunch. Thank goodness it was Friday because my first week on the new project had been pretty grueling. After some early confusion about which space the Department of Health would be providing me to conduct my work, I was finally able to settle into a corner of the building. And I'd been promised more than one admin, but so far it was just Tia. So things were off to a slow start.

I got home from work that afternoon around 4 PM. I couldn't wait to kick my feet up and pour myself a glass of wine to start the weekend. Or maybe I'd crack open a pint of ice cream and do dessert before dinner. Who was I kidding? Wine *and* ice cream before sushi takeout sounded perfect.

But after I took a shower, my plan to have a relaxing early evening was thwarted by a beeping sound coming from somewhere in the apartment. I walked around until I figured out it was coming from a detector in the ceiling in the hallway. I dragged a chair over to check it out, but there was nothing to press to stop it. The battery probably needed to be changed, but I didn't have a screwdriver to get inside.

I really didn't want to have to bother Holden. Somehow, I'd managed to avoid contacting him for anything all week. It surprised me that I hadn't run into him by chance, since he was right next door, or that he hadn't stopped by. After our conversation out on the fire escape—when we'd both admitted our past attraction to each other—I didn't want to reach out to him for no good reason. And maybe he felt the same. Almost every encounter with him left me feeling guilty, even if nothing ever happened. It was all guilt over my thoughts, which I seemed incapable of controlling.

After almost an hour of putting up with the beeping sound, I caved and picked up the phone.

Holden answered on the third ring. "Lala Ellison...wassup?"

"Hey."

"I've been thinking about you," he said. "How did your first week go?"

I let out a deep breath. "It was rough, actually. Some stuff hasn't gone according to plan. But things will hopefully be better next week."

"Damn. Okay. Well, TGIF then."

"Yeah. Seriously. I was hoping to chill tonight, but there's a beeping sound coming from one of the detectors that's driving me bonkers. I can't open it without a screwdriver, which I don't have. I was hoping you—"

"Ah. So this call wasn't just to say hello," he teased.

That made me feel kind of bad. "Not exactly."

"Handyman Holden to the rescue." He laughed. "I'll be over in five."

It was more like three minutes that passed before he knocked rhythmically on the door.

Goose bumps peppered my skin as I opened. "I'm surprised you didn't use your key."

I knew Holden had a master key to every apartment in this place.

"You want me to come in here without knocking? That could be arranged, but I figured I'd be respectful."

"Yeah. On second thought, knocks are appreciated."

"Figured." He winked. "Except on your bedroom wall at one in the morning, right?"

I shook my head. Holden wore a gray beanie over his shaggy brown hair. I'd always loved that look on him—a little too much, perhaps.

Beep. Beep. Beep.

"There it is!" I looked around. "Isn't that annoying?"

"I didn't hear it," Holden said stone-faced.

"No?"

He shook his head.

Then it happened again. *Beep. Beep. Beep.* The chirps seemed to be coming closer together.

I lifted my pointer finger. "You heard that, right?"

Holden chuckled. "Really? I didn't hear anything."

I scratched my head.

He burst out in laughter. "I'm just screwing with you. The battery needs to be replaced."

I smacked his arm. "Thanks a lot. You had me thinking I was losing my mind."

"You losing that brilliant mind of yours, Lala, would be a massive blow to the world." He turned back toward the door. "I'll be right back. Gonna go grab a battery from the supply closet."

Holden returned soon after with a nine-volt. His abs peeked out as he reached up to the carbon monoxide detector and replaced it. I caught a glimpse of a tat that was particularly low on his abdomen, but I couldn't make it out. Something told me many women had gotten an up-close-and-personal look at that one when they were down on their knees. I cringed.

The detector beeped loudly as he tested it. "Working great now. You won't be getting that warning sound anymore."

"Thank you."

Our eyes locked for a moment. "So, you said your week was crazy. What happened?"

"Well…" I sighed. "I was supposed to be assigned more than one admin. And for now, it's just one. This girl named Tia."

"What's wrong with her?" He leaned against the counter.

"Nothing, aside from the fact that she doesn't have a clone. Things are just moving more slowly than I'd hoped. I need help setting up a database, going over the medical files for potential study participants, and setting up interviews and such. Because it's just her and me right now, I've been bogged down with the admin work instead of getting the live study started."

He nodded. "It must be frustrating to not get the ball rolling."

"It is, because I'm very eager."

Holden tilted his head and smiled. "You truly love what you do, don't you?"

I shrugged. "What can I say? There's no greater thrill than discovery—contributing to our growth as humans by tapping into knowledge that hasn't been realized before."

"Damn. I've been tapping the wrong things." He grinned mischievously.

I arched my brow. "Drumsticks and women?"

He laughed. "That's something I've always admired about you, Lala. Your quest for knowledge. It's like you can't get enough." He sighed. "Most days I feel like a cat chasing his tail. Same old shit. Different day. Nothing new."

"Well, we're not all the same. I couldn't put two beats together with your drumsticks. We're meant to have different talents and purposes in life. Maybe mine is to research and yours is to entertain."

"Well, this morning my purpose was to eat Hot Cheetos and patch up what I'm pretty sure was a glory hole in one of the apartments a tenant just vacated."

I laughed. "Someone's gotta do it."

"I guess."

A moment of silence passed. "You must have had a busy week yourself."

"Not too bad. Why do you say that?"

"Well, I didn't see or hear from you. Not that I expected to, but…" *Uh, I shouldn't have said anything.*

"I figured you saw enough of me when you moved in. I was trying to give you some space. I don't want you to feel like I don't think you're a big girl who can handle herself in the City."

"Oh, that's interesting. I never would've thought you were specifically giving me space."

"What *did* you think?"

"Like I said, that you were busy."

"Busy doing what?"

I shrugged. "Busy doing…what Holden does?"

"Busy messing around with random women when I'm not being Mr. Fix It? Is that what you mean to say?" He cocked a brow.

"I didn't say that. You did."

"Well, I'll have you know, there were no hookups this week."

"None *this week*—quite the dry spell," I teased.

"Even though you're mocking me, it actually is." He sniffed.

"I'm sure that will change tonight."

"Why tonight?"

"It's Friday. You must have big plans."

He ran his tongue along his bottom lip. "Actually, I have a gig in Connecticut."

My eyes widened. "Oh wow. Really?"

"Yeah, it's at this club in Danbury. We're opening for another band." His eyes met mine. "You should come."

My stomach did a little flip. The thought of going to see him perform excited me, but it also made me nervous, and I wasn't quite sure why.

"You look like I just asked you to go to a goddamn funeral."

"It's not that I don't want to go." *Translation: I have a fiancé back in Philadelphia and going out with you at night feels dangerous.* "I just don't know if I should. I have to organize all of my stuff that we unpacked." God, that was the lamest excuse imaginable.

"Oh yeah," he mocked. "Cuz all that stuff won't be here to-morrow." Holden's smile faded. "I'm just messing with you. It's not a big deal if you're not in the mood. I just figured I'd ask." Disappointment crossed his face.

Had I insulted him? I hadn't meant to. Gosh, I *really* wanted to go. I just felt…guilty? Nervous? Out of my element? I couldn't put my finger on it. But I *did* want to see him play. *Screw it.* "You know what? Sure. That would be awesome." I exhaled. "But how would I get there?"

"There's a car picking me up at eight before we scoop up one or two of the guys. There should be plenty of room. If there isn't, I'll make room."

My pulse sped up. "Okay…I should start getting ready then. What's the dress code there?"

"The dress code is wear whatever the fuck you want. Ripped jeans, a hat, and a clean, black T-shirt for me."

Holden could wear a paper bag and still look hot. "A lot of help you are," I told him.

"There's no dress code, as far as I know. But feel free to wear something sexy so I can rip some guy's head off later for messing with you. I'm kind of in the mood to fight. It's been a while."

A chill ran through me as I remembered again what Holden had admitted during our talk out on the fire escape. But I was foolish for looking at it as some kind of special compliment unique to me. He likely told a lot of women they were pretty on a regular basis.

Holden went back to his place and left me alone to get ready. I opted for a short, black skirt and a vintage, off-the-shoulder Blondie T-shirt. Debbie Harry's face was deliberately weathered on the front. Leather booties finished the look. I sort of felt like I was channeling the 1980s. Given that it was drizzly out, I didn't bother trying to tame my wild blond curls too much. My hair might start out looking like Carrie Bradshaw's from *Sex and the City,* but I'd end up looking like I'd stuck something in an electrical socket by the end of the night.

Holden knocked on my door at a few minutes before eight. He looked me up and down when I answered. "Damn. Funky look, *Blondie*. I like it."

"Thanks. Not sure my hair will hold up in this weather, though."

"No offense, Lala, but when has it ever held up? It's wild as fuck. Your hair is like a whole vibe."

"It has a personality of its own, and it's pretty good at predicting the weather, too." I laughed.

He smirked. "Remember when you had to cut it, though?"

I gave him a sharp look. How dare he bring that up? "Yeah. How could I forget? You and Ryan had a contest to see who could stuff the most gum into your mouth. I planted my butt down to watch *Jon & Kate Plus 8* in the living room, and when I tried to get up for a snack, my hair was stuck in a wad of gum Ryan had stuck temporarily to the back of my chair." I shook my head. "Five inches gone with my mom's kitchen scissors after we tried to remove it to no avail."

Holden snorted. "You were so fucking pissed. I think that might have been the first time I ever saw you lose it on Ryan."

I looked away, feeling my eyes well up unexpectedly. Grief was weird. I could go six months without shedding a tear over my brother, and then one pesky memory about gum pulls the trigger in a matter of seconds.

Holden's expression fell. "I'm sorry. I didn't mean to—"

"No. Not your fault. It comes in waves, you know?" I sniffled.

"I do, Lala," he murmured. "I do."

"Let's go." I wiped my eyes and hurried to the door.

The mood was quiet as we took the elevator downstairs and walked out to where a black SUV waited.

A man was already in the backseat. Even though it was an SUV, it was a tight squeeze in the rear. And we apparently had to pick up one other band member, too.

Holden introduced me right away. "This is Monroe, our lead singer."

"Nice to meet you," Monroe said as he offered his hand, which was adorned with silver rings and finger tats. He had longish black hair and a neck tattoo.

"Before you say something fucking dumb," Holden interjected. "This is Lala."

"Oh." Monroe smiled. "Your friend's sister. I'm glad you told me."

"Watch your fucking mouth and keep your hands off her," Holden warned.

Monroe looked unfazed. "You're engaged, right?"

"I am."

"Lucky guy."

Holden shot daggers at Monroe but didn't say anything.

As we drove the streets of New York toward the highway, it was a bumpy ride with lots of stop and go. My knee kept bumping into Holden's, and his scent was all I could smell. It frustrated me that I felt so much sitting close to him. Aside from our dance at Colby's wedding and the occasional fleeting and friendly hug, I couldn't say I'd ever been pressed against Holden like this for any length of time. It's one thing to control your thoughts, but how does one control their body's reaction to someone they're attracted to? I guess the answer is…you can't. You just deal with it and pretend like it's not happening.

We must have gotten to the venue in Danbury just in the nick of time because Holden apologized for having to rush off. The guys barely had five minutes to spare before they were on stage. The air was thick, saturated with the smell of alcohol and various colognes and perfumes. I'd just situated myself in a corner when the band, After Friday, started to play.

Nothing compared to seeing Holden in his element. It filled me with adrenaline—the speed at which he maneuvered those sticks, the intensity of his focus, the way he'd toss the sticks in the air occasionally and catch them. Monroe had a really smooth voice, too, but I couldn't take my eyes off of Holden.

When the performance finished, several women went up to them. Their approach seemed very methodical. It gave me the impression that they'd been waiting in the wings, and perhaps they were regular groupies. One in particular, with long, straight brown hair, was hanging all over Holden before he'd even had a chance to exit the stage. I wondered if I'd have to sit next to her on the way home—or if I'd be riding home alone while Holden went back to her place.

Before I could ponder it much more, my phone buzzed.

My heart sank when I saw it was Warren calling, but I pressed the button to answer. "Hey."

"Hey."

"What are you up to?" I said, holding my opposite ear closed to hear better.

"You sound like you're in a bar."

I hesitated. I couldn't lie to him, as much as I didn't want to admit who I was with. "Holden's band had a gig. So I went to see the show at a club in Connecticut."

He hesitated. "Ah. I see. Any good?"

"Yeah." I breathed out. "It was really good, actually. Well, except that I'm by myself at the moment since I don't know anyone here. Holden's still with the band."

"Lala! What are you drinking?" he suddenly yelled from behind me, making me jump.

I held my finger up, asking him to hold on. But instead of shutting up, he said, "A finger of whiskey? Is that what you want?"

"Who's that?" Warren asked.

"That's Holden. He just came over to get my drink order."

"Well, make sure you know where your drinks are coming from, please. Don't leave anything unattended. The last thing I need is for you to be roofied out there."

I knew he'd be concerned, but jeez. "That's sort of an odd thing to say… But of course, I'll be vigilant."

"Just…be careful, okay?"

I felt bad that my being here made him anxious. I couldn't say I blamed him. I wouldn't have been thrilled to find out he was at some bar with a bunch of female musicians. Actually, the thought of Warren in his glasses and cardigan in that scenario made me chuckle. He was such a good guy, but this definitely wasn't his scene—any more than it was mine, actually.

"Okay." He sighed. "Have fun."

"Thanks. I'll call you in the morning."

"Alright. Goodnight." He paused. "I love you."

"I love you, too."

Beads of sweat formed on my forehead after I hung up. I looked around and found Holden beaming as he walked toward me, lifting two drinks.

He spoke into my ear. "I figured you didn't really want a finger of whiskey, so I got you a vodka cranberry. I remember you ordering one at Colby's wedding."

The warm heat of his breath in my ear made me tingle. It was messed up how one small bit of contact could make my body feel like it was on fire.

"Very observant," I said as I took the drink.

"I take it that was Warren on the phone? You looked a little flustered."

"Yeah. I didn't want him to think…" I hesitated.

Holden finished my sentence. "That you were having fun?"

"I guess I just felt guilty…for having fun here without him, yeah."

"Well, I give you credit." He took a sip of his drink. "It can't be easy doing the long-distance thing."

I changed the subject. "Anyway, you guys rocked it out there."

"Thank you. I felt good about it." He grinned proudly. "And it was cool to be able to play for you."

For me. "Ryan used to love to watch you play, too."

He nodded. "I feel his spirit with me a lot when I'm performing."

The same brunette who had rushed over to him after the performance appeared. "Hey! There you are," she said before turning to me. "Who's this?"

"This is Lala, my best friend's little sister."

"Oh…" She stared down at Debbie Harry. "That's cute."

Holden laughed, somehow knowing that the girl's use of *cute* annoyed me. "Lala, this is Carmen."

I nodded. "Nice to meet you."

"You, too."

She turned to Holden. "You wanna come back to my place tonight? It's closer to here than yours."

Yep. Just as I thought.

"I can't, actually," he answered. "I'm going back with Lala to make sure she gets home safely."

Carmen frowned, obviously pissed that Debbie Harry and I were cockblocking her this evening.

She disappeared not long after that, and I celebrated by downing a long gulp of my drink.

Then things got a little hazy. Holden kept going back to the bar to get me vodka cranberries. At one point, the room started to spin.

The next thing I knew, I was back in the car with Holden, Monroe, and the guitar player, Kevin. Once again, my leg was pressed against Holden's. Except this time, my drunken state amplified the arousal. My nipples were hard, the traitorous bitches. And my inebriated mind was going to places it had no right to, imagining what it might be like to be Holden's groupie for one night—what that experience back at his apartment would be like for *her*. The muscles between my legs tightened as I anticipated getting home and relieving myself under the hot shower.

Holden seemed buzzed but not impaired like me. When he reached over and spoke into my ear, my internal alarm bells went off. "You might be getting tired, but I don't think your hair is ready to stop partying."

"That's called frizz."

"Don't ever straighten it."

"I don't have the patience anyway." I hiccupped.

For some reason, the guys decided to start ranking on Holden, making him the butt of their jokes for the latter half of the ride home. Holden explained that they loved throwing "drummer jokes" at him, and this was a regular tradition after a show.

"What do you call a drummer without a girlfriend?" Kevin asked.

"Homeless," Monroe chimed in.

They laughed as Holden rolled his eyes.

"What do you call a drummer with brains?" Kevin paused and smiled over at me. "A guitar player."

"I got another one!" Monroe yelled. "What do a drum solo and a sneeze have in common?"

"What?" Holden rolled his eyes again.

"You know it's coming, but you can't stop it, even if you want to!"

Kevin high-fived him. "Good one."

I decided to give them some of their own medicine. "What do you call a singer and a guitar player who like to make dumb jokes about drummers?"

"What?" they asked in unison.

"Jealous because all the girls seem to want to fuck the drummer." I hiccupped and looked over at Holden. "Must be doing something right."

They fell silent.

I wouldn't have said that if I was sober, but it gave me pleasure to shut Kevin and Monroe up, as did the smug smile on Holden's face.

CHAPTER 5

Holden

Holden: How's the party girl doing this morning?

It was almost noon, and I hadn't heard a peep from next door. I was pretty certain Lala wasn't a big drinker, so I suspected the four vodka crans she'd knocked back last night might be taking their toll on her today. It took about ten minutes, but my phone finally buzzed with a response.

Lala: In case I forget to mention it, I appreciate how clean the bathroom floor is in this apartment. And how cold...

Uh-oh. That didn't sound good.

Holden: Rough morning?

Lala: Rough eight hours. As soon as I closed my eyes and got into bed, the room started spinning. So I came to the bathroom, just in case I got sick. I've been here on the floor ever since.

Oh man. Been there, done that. It sucked.

Holden: I'm heading out to get a smoothie. You want one?

Lala: If it comes with Motrin, sure.

I laughed.

Holden: I'll be there in fifteen minutes with your cure. Hang tight.

Lala: Okay. But can you please let yourself in? I don't think I can lift my head or walk to the door to open it.

Holden: Sure thing.

A little while later, I used my master key to bring Lala what I'd dubbed the *love your liver* smoothie. Her apartment was quiet, so I lightly knocked on the bathroom door.

"Come in."

I creaked open the door to find Lala in exactly the position she'd described: lying on the bathroom floor. She had a towel wrapped around her like a blanket, and last night's eye makeup stained her cheeks.

I sat down next to her, peeled the wrapper off the straw, and popped it into the top of her smoothie.

"Head up, sweetheart. This will help. I promise. It's loaded with vitamin C, wheatgrass, ginger, and echinacea. But you won't taste any of that because the peanut butter and banana hide it all."

She lifted her head with a groan and used both hands to push herself upright.

I smiled. "You're a bit of a lightweight, huh?"

She narrowed her eyes and sucked from the straw. "I was overserved."

"The last two drinks were just cranberry and lime. You only drank two with alcohol in them."

"Apparently that was enough. And please tell me I didn't do anything embarrassing. Last night is kind of fuzzy."

"Nah, your voice isn't *that* bad."

She started to choke on the smoothie. "Wha—what?"

"You don't remember getting up on stage?"

Her eyes widened. She looked pretty horrified, and I felt a pang of guilt for screwing with her while she was in this condition, yet I didn't let her off the hook.

"Oh my God, no. What did I sing?"

"'Call Me', by Blondie. You held your cell phone up to your ear while singing and acting it out. It was really funny."

"*Holden, how could you let me do that?* I'm a terrible singer!"

I nodded. "That's what the brunette said, the one you punched in the ladies' room."

"Oh my God. *Please tell me you're joking!*"

I grinned. "I'm joking."

"Are you really?"

I chuckled. "Of course. I wouldn't let you get up on stage. I've heard you sing. The point of a gig is to bring people *into* the club, not chase them out."

She smacked my arm. "You're a jerk."

"But a hot one you want to see naked—you told me that yourself last night."

Lala turned beet red. "Really?"

"Nah." I laughed and pointed to her face. "But Jesus, you're as red as an apple. It goes really nice with the black streaks down your cheeks."

Lala reached up and touched her face. "I must look like a disaster."

Her curly hair was wild, she had makeup smeared all over her face, and she'd slept in her clothes, yet she was still gorgeous to me. "Maybe. But you're one beautiful disaster, Laney Ellison." I climbed to my feet and extended a hand. "Come on. Let's get you out of this bathroom."

Twenty minutes later, she slurped the last of the smoothie from her cup with her straw.

"Feeling any better?" I asked.

She nodded. "Actually, I am."

"Sounds like you're ready for phase two then."

"What's phase two?"

I plucked the empty smoothie cup from her hand and tapped it to the top of her head. "Coffee. For both of us."

While I made us two cups of joe in the kitchen, Lala went into the bedroom. When she came back, her face was washed, hair tied into a big, messy bun on the top of her head, and she had on new clothes.

"Look at you," I said, passing her a steaming mug. "Good as new."

She tucked her feet under her on the couch and sipped her coffee. "Am I keeping you from doing something? You look like you're all showered and ready to go somewhere."

"I have an appointment with Billie in a half hour. I get pretty sweaty playing the drums, so I figured she'd appreciate it if I washed after last night's gig."

"Colby's wife Billie?"

I nodded. "One and the same. I'm getting a tattoo finished. The outline is done. Today she's going to fill in the color."

"What's it of?"

"An owl."

"Can I see it?"

"Absolutely." I stood and grabbed my zipper. "It's on my ass."

Lala's eyes widened.

I chuckled and sat back down, lifting the hem of my shirt. "I'm kidding. For a smart lady, you're pretty gullible. It's on my ribs, right here."

Lala checked out the owl outline, but then her eyes took a little detour. They dipped down to my abs and lingered for a few seconds before returning to the outline. Three seconds later, the same thing happened, only this time her tongue peeked out and ran along her lower lip.

Fuck me. She's checking me out.

I knew I should do the right thing and lower my shirt, but I couldn't get enough of the way she was looking at me. "You want to see the others?"

She nodded and swallowed.

And because I was a giant dick, I took off my shirt completely.

"This was my first one," I said, pointing to two drumsticks. "I think the meaning is self-explanatory." Next I pointed to the one over my heart, a bunch of numbers in a straight line. "The night before I moved out, my mom got really upset. She cried and told me I'd better not forget where she lives and to come visit a lot. The next day I got the coordinates of my parents' house tattooed here so she would know I could never forget how to get home."

"Aww… That's so sweet."

For the next ten minutes, I gave Lala a tour of the ink on my body. When I got to the cross with the date tattooed below it, I didn't have to say a thing. It was the date Ryan died. Lala reached out and traced her finger over the outline of the cross. Goose bumps prickled all over my skin.

"I've always wanted to get something for him," she said. "But I'm a big chicken. Does it hurt getting one?"

"A little at the beginning, but it goes numb after a while. Then it's more tender than painful."

"Is the skin more sensitive with a tattoo on it?"

"Right after, but not after a few weeks, if that's what you mean."

"So this doesn't hurt any more than it does on regular skin?" She scraped one fingernail down the edge of the cross, and my mind immediately imagined what it would be like to feel her nails do that on my back.

My voice was hoarse. "I'm not sure. Do that again. Harder."

She dug her nail in a little deeper the second time, and my dick twitched to life.

Fuck. What was I doing? I needed to nip this shit in the bud before I embarrassed myself. Abruptly, I grabbed my shirt, yanked it back on, and stood. "I should get going. I don't want to be late to my appointment with Billie. You know, in case she's ready early."

Smooth, Catalano. Really smooth.

"Oh, okay." Lala set down her coffee and walked me to the door.

"If you feel up to it, stop down and you can watch Billie work. Maybe it will help you feel more comfortable about getting the one you want for Ryan."

"Alright. Maybe. Thanks again for the smoothie, Holden."

I winked. "I'm here to serve."

Since it really was almost time for my appointment, I went directly downstairs to Billie's shop. After a five-minute wait, I was lying in her chair.

"What's new with you, pretty boy?" she asked. "Did you stay in last night or something? You look pretty good for this early on a Saturday."

I shook my head. "I actually had a gig."

"Ummm… Last time you were in here the day after a gig, I had to spritz you with cologne because I couldn't take the smell of the alcohol wafting from your pores."

"I only had one drink last night. Thought it was a good idea to keep sober."

"Were you driving?"

"No."

"So why was it a good idea to keep sober?"

"Lala came out with us. She came to see the band play."

"And you can't drink around her for some reason?"

I definitely couldn't drink around her last night, not with how smokin' hot she looked. I was too afraid I'd say something—or worse, *do* something—stupid. But I wasn't about to get into that with Billie. So I shrugged. "I guess I just didn't feel like drinking a lot."

Billie narrowed her eyes. "The apartment she's staying in is right next to yours, right?"

"Yep."

"Do you ever go over there?"

"Sometimes." I shrugged. "If she needs help or something."

"What kind of help does she need?"

Damn, Billie was like a dog following a scent. So I decided to redirect our convo. "I don't know, fixing things around the apartment and whatnot. Which reminds me, how's your dishwasher doing? Colby said the door pops open mid cycle sometimes."

"It does, and it's driving me damn nuts because I can't figure out why. I've taken it apart twice."

"I'll try to stop over later when Colby gets home and take a look."

"That would be great. Thanks."

Just when I'd finally gotten Billie off the subject of Lala, none other than the woman herself walked into the shop. Billie set her needle down and gave her a hug.

"Hey, Lala," she said. "It's so good to see you!"

"You, too, Billie. I hope you don't mind me dropping by. Holden suggested I come since I'd like to get over my fear of getting a tattoo. I've never watched anyone get one."

"Of course not. Pull up a chair. I'll make sure I push the color extra deep, so we can watch pretty boy here wince."

Lala smiled. "Pretty boy?"

Billie shrugged. "It's a fitting name, isn't it?"

Lala's eyes washed over my face. "I suppose it is."

"So you'd like to get a tattoo? Do you have something particular in mind?"

Lala nodded. "I'd like to get one in memory of my brother."

"Do you have any ideas?"

"I think something similar to what Holden has for Ryan—a cross, but a lot smaller and a little more feminine."

Billie's eyes moved to mine. "Matching tattoos, huh?"

"I think Lala meant a cross, not that it had to match mine," I said.

"Uh-huh…" Billie grinned. She picked up the tattoo needle and pressed the pedal on the floor with her foot. "Your real name is Laney, right?"

Lala nodded.

"So how did Lala come about?"

Lala smiled and pointed to me. "Pretty boy made it up. When I was eleven, my brother and all of his friends were thirteen and fourteen. Colby, Owen, Brayden, and Holden practically lived at our house. And they talked about girls nonstop—kissing, feeling them up… They had no shame. They didn't even care if I was in the room. A couple of years makes a big difference at that age, so I still thought it was all gross. A few times when they were bragging about their conquests, I stuck my fingers in my ears. Of course, that only made them talk louder. One afternoon, they were particularly obnoxious with their stories, and I wound up running out of the room with my fingers in my ears, yelling *La La La La La*. Holden called me Lala the next day, and the name just stuck."

Billie snort-laughed. "That's hysterical."

"Ugh, the five of them were horn dogs. That's *all* they talked about."

"And all you talked about was physics and astronomy," I said.

"Well, those subjects are a lot more fascinating than the conversations you had." Lala looked at Billie. "It's no wonder I didn't date much growing up. I had to listen to them talk about accidentally *farting* while getting a blowjob."

"Oh my God. Please tell me it wasn't my husband who did that."

"It wasn't," Lala said. "It was Owen."

For the next hour, Lala and I told stories about when we were kids. We kept Billie laughing the entire time. At one point, Lala's phone buzzed. She didn't answer, and I couldn't see who it was, but her face changed, so I suspected I knew. Right after that, she stood.

"I should really get going into work. I'm hoping to spend a few hours catching up today while it's quiet since I didn't get to everything I needed to accomplish this week."

"Stop down and visit anytime, Lala," Billie said. "I'm always game for collecting new ammunition to rank on the fab four."

Lala laughed. "I have plenty of that." She looked to me. "Thanks again for this morning, Holden."

I winked. "No problem. Have a good afternoon."

After Lala left, Billie pounced. "Spill, pretty boy. What's the deal with you two?"

"What do you mean?"

"There was so much chemistry sparking in here, I could have used it to run my tattoo machine. Did you have a thing together once or something?"

I sighed. "Not like you're thinking."

"Then what?"

"I had a big crush on her growing up."

"And…"

"And that's it. She's Ryan's little sister. Plus, she's super smart and not into guys like me."

"What does that mean, guys like you?"

"Lala's a researcher, and her fiancé is trying to cure cancer. A woman like that doesn't want to date a musician, especially not one whose most stimulating conversation recently has been debating whether I would chop off a finger for a million bucks. Brayden and I don't agree, by the way."

Billie put her needle into its holder. "While I think it's smart for you to keep your distance, because she's engaged and there's clearly a spark between you, you shouldn't put yourself or Lala in boxes like that. Look how different Colby and I are. He designs buildings, and I used to get chased by the police for spray painting them. Just because people are different doesn't mean it can't work.

Why would you want someone similar to you anyway? You'd never learn anything new."

She had a point. But still…

At home later that night, I was still replaying the conversation I'd had with Billie. One way or another, I hadn't thought about much except Lala since she came to the City for her interview. As fucked up as it was, I put my ear against the wall in my bedroom to see if I could hear whether she'd gotten home from work yet. It wasn't like I was going to go over if she had; I just needed to know. But the only thing I heard was silence, so I was glad when my phone buzzed with a distraction.

Sienna: Hey. Are you around to hang out tonight?

I'd hung out with Sienna a few times before. She was really nice, not to mention sexually adventurous and no commitment required. A few weeks ago, I would've jumped on the offer, but I just wasn't into it tonight. So I lied.

Holden: Sorry. Plans with the guys tonight.

Her response was quick.

Sienna: If you change your mind, I'll be at the bar where we met last time, the one around the corner from your place. And just in case you need a little incentive…

A sexy-as-shit cleavage selfie followed. I hung my head, hating myself for still not wanting to go. I had no desire for a hookup because of a certain *engaged* Goldilocks next door.

I wound up lying on the couch and flipping through channels on the TV, but I couldn't stop berating myself for being such a piece of shit and thinking about Lala.

You live in a city with four-million women—why are you obsessing over the one *you can't have?*

She's getting married.

She's Ryan's little sister, for Christ's sake.

After a while, I dragged my ass off the couch and got dressed, forcing myself to head to the bar. My intention had been to go meet Sienna, but one block out, I took a detour and walked into a local old-man's bar instead. I needed a minute to get my head screwed on straight.

There were only three guys sitting at the bar, each one alone, and all looking as miserable as I felt at the moment. The bartender took one look at me and pointed over his shoulder. "Bathroom is in the back right corner."

I walked to a stool and sat down. "I don't need to use the bathroom. Came in for a drink."

"Oh. Sorry. You don't look like my usual crowd." He tossed a cardboard coaster onto the bar. "What can I get you?"

"Jack and Coke, please."

He rapped his knuckles against the top of the bar. "Coming right up."

When he returned with my drink, he extended his hand. "Evan."

"Holden. Good to meet ya."

"You from out of town?"

I shook my head and sipped my drink. "Nope. Live a block away."

"You meeting a woman here on the sly?"

"Nope."

Evan leaned an elbow on the bar. "Okay, I give. Why are you here in this shithole?"

I chuckled. "Do you really want to hear it?"

He pointed to the other patrons. "That's Fred, Ken, and Walt. I've heard their stories five hundred times. So yeah, why not? It's not like I have better options."

"How about a shot first? Yours is on me, too."

"Alright. What would you like?"

"Your choice."

Evan came back with a bottle of tequila and two shot glasses.

He filled them both to the brim. "We don't do salt or lime or any of that fancy shit here."

I picked up the shot and sucked it back. "That's fine with me." It burned going down, but I liked it.

"So what's your story? You look like you belong on one of them Abercrosley ads in Times Square. So it can't be about a woman."

I smiled. "It's Abercrombie, and yeah, it's about a woman. Isn't it always?"

"You got a point. She married or something?"

"Engaged."

"Oh boy." The bartender refilled our shot glasses. "This one's on me." He held it out to clink, and we sucked our second tequilas back.

Then I filled my new friend Evan in on Lala—starting from my school-age crush and ending with her currently living in the apartment next door.

"Oh, and I forgot to mention that I'm currently hiding out here instead of meeting a free-spirited woman at the bar a block away, a woman who wants nothing more than a fuck from me."

Evan shook his head. "You got it bad for this Lala, huh?"

I gulped the rest of my Jack and Coke. "What am I supposed to do about it?"

"There's only one thing you can do, my friend."

"Go meet Sienna and forget anyone else exists for a few hours?"

"Nah. That never works. You'll just hate yourself after."

"Sit here and get loaded then?"

"Nope. You gotta try to break up that engagement, Abercrosley."

I shook my head, not bothering to correct him this time. "I don't think that's gonna happen."

"Trust me, you'll get over the guilt of stealing some other

guy's girl. But you'll never get over letting the woman you love slip through your fingers."

I wasn't in love with Lala, though, was I? Then again, how the hell would I even know if I was? The only person I'd ever been capable of being committed to was me.

"Let me tell you a little story," the bartender said. "When I was twenty, I met a woman. Her name was Elizabeth, and as stupid as it sounds, I knew in the first hour that she was the woman I was supposed to marry. There was just one problem."

"What was that?"

"She was my best friend's girl."

"Oh, man."

Evan nodded. "I had just joined the military. My buddy Phil met Elizabeth while I was at boot camp. They were going to college together. After about a year, I went to visit Phil while I was on leave. He worked and went to class, so I spent a lot of my visit hanging out with his girl. I fell head over heels, and she felt something, too. But she was my buddy's girl, so I wasn't going there. Fast forward four years. I married Catherine, and Phil and Elizabeth got married the following summer. It took me five more years in a miserable marriage to realize I'd married a woman I wasn't in love with. Because when your heart belongs to someone else, it's not available to give to anyone, even when you want to."

"What happened with Phil and Elizabeth?"

"They were having marital trouble, too. But Phil and Liz moved out to Long Island, and we lost touch. I hadn't seen them in a few years. Long story short, they got divorced, and six years later I ran into her. The chemistry had never dulled, even after all that time. We wound up getting together, and I was happier than I'd ever been. So was my Lizzy. Then one day, she goes for a routine exam at the doctor, and they find a lump in her breast. Six months later, she was gone. Metastatic breast cancer. She was only thirty-three."

"Jesus, I'm sorry."

"So am I. But you know what I'm most sorry about?"

"What?"

"Losing the ten years we could've been together but weren't. Life's shorter than you think."

I slammed back two more Jack and Cokes and decided not to go meet Sienna after all. Instead, I walked home with a nice buzz and a lot to think about, courtesy of my new bartender friend. My head was all fucked up from the story he'd told me, but I knew for certain that I needed to keep away from women for a while—*all women*.

But when I got into the elevator and turned around to push the button on the panel for my floor, that vow flew out the window faster than Sienna's clothes would have come off.

Lala.

She'd just walked through the front door. I put my hand on the elevator doors to stop them from closing while my heart sprinted off in a gallop.

"You're not just getting home from work now, are you?"

Lala nodded. "I am. I had so much to do and lost track of time." She stepped into the elevator. "And where are you coming from?"

"I was just at a bar down the block."

"How can that be?" She flashed a cheeky smile and looked around the elevator car. "You're all alone."

"Cute." I pushed the button to our floor. "You know I'm not half the manwhore you think I am." *At least not lately.*

When the elevator doors slid open on three, I held my hand out for her to exit first. Then I tried my best not to look down at her ass, but failed miserably.

"You staying in for the rest of the evening?" she asked as she took out her keys.

"Yeah. You?"

She nodded. "One wild weekend night is enough for me."

I smiled. "You want to come over for a glass of wine?"

Lala chewed on that pouty bottom lip of hers. It looked like she was about to say no, so I threw out an alternative that sounded less suggestive than inviting her over to my place.

"How about a fire escape nightcap? You on yours, me on mine, like the other night?"

She smiled. "Okay. That sounds good. Just let me get changed."

Inside, I opened a bottle of white and grabbed two glasses before climbing out onto the fire escape. Lala joined me a few minutes later, wearing a T-shirt and leggings. I poured us each a glass and passed her one through the balusters.

"So tell me, what's a day at the office like for Dr. Lala Ellison?"

She sipped her wine. "Well, today I went through the rest of the applications for my study and finalized the candidates who are going to participate."

"They all have Alzheimer's?"

She nodded. "It's a controlled study, so I picked people who live in assisted-living facilities within a twenty-five-mile radius. And they all have the same ADAS Cog score—it's a scale that grades the level of cognitive dysfunction."

I smiled. "I always knew you'd do something big."

"Thanks. Though I haven't done anything big quite yet."

A light breeze blew, and Lala rubbed her arms. "It's chillier than I thought," she said.

"The night air gets chilly this early in May. I'll grab you a sweatshirt."

"It's okay."

But I stood and climbed through my window anyway. I came back with a sweatshirt and passed it over the railing to her.

"Thanks." She pulled it over her head. "So I've been thinking about getting a tattoo all day."

"Thinking about getting a tattoo or thinking about all of

mine?"

"Uh…"

I chuckled. "I'm teasing. So you're really gonna get one?"

"I want to. I think I'd like to get a small cross on my wrist. The cross would be in the center, and I'd put the date Ryan died on the side."

"That'll look awesome. You should make an appointment with Billie."

"Yeah…maybe. I'm just not positive yet."

"What's holding you back? The pain?"

"That and, well, I've mentioned it to Warren before, and he was sort of against it."

My jaw clenched. "Does he have a problem with tattoos?"

"He doesn't think it's a good idea for me to get one where anyone can see it. He thinks it looks unprofessional and will hurt my credibility."

"I think his view is pretty outdated, Lala."

She sighed. "Yeah, that's what I said, too."

"Will he give you shit if you get one anyway?"

"I don't know. I don't think so, but…" She trailed off as her cell started to buzz. Just like the last time we sat out here, her face fell.

Dr. Douchebag is a judgmental fuck, but he certainly has good timing.

Only Lala didn't say she had to go this time. Instead, she pushed the button on the side of her phone and stopped it from buzzing.

"Speak of the devil." She smiled. "It's Warren. I'll just call him back later."

As meaningless as it probably was, I took it as a win. Lala had the choice to talk to him or me, and this time, she'd picked me. *Progress.*

We talked for another half hour, and then I made the mistake of asking her if she wanted a refill.

"I should probably get to bed. I can't even believe I drank one glass with how I was feeling earlier today."

I would've stayed out here all night with her, but I nodded. "Yeah, I should get some shut-eye, too."

Lala got up and handed me her empty glass. "Thanks for the wine. Goodnight, Holden."

"'Night, Lala."

She ducked to climb in her window, then stopped and stood straight again. "Hang on a second." She reached for the hem of the sweatshirt she'd been wearing and pulled it over her head. "Thank you for the loaner."

"No problem." *It would really be fine for you to keep it.*

Back inside, I set both wine glasses in the sink. I was pretty damn proud of myself for putting the one with her lip marks down so easily tonight. But then I looked at what I'd thrown over my arm: *the sweatshirt.*

No, you're not.

Definitely not.

No way, Catalano.

Listening to my conscience for a change, I tossed the damn sweatshirt on the couch and rushed out of the room like it had something contagious. But five minutes later, I found myself back in the living room, staring down at the goddamned thing.

This is getting ridiculous.

I really need to get laid.

I scooped the sweatshirt from the couch.

Or jerk off while wearing this…

❤CHAPTER 6

Lala

After another week in my new position—one slightly more productive than the first—I went home to Pennsylvania for the weekend to visit my fiancé. I'd gotten in late last night, but Warren had cooked me a delicious dinner of beef stroganoff this evening, and we were just finishing up when he seemed to notice that I'd been distracted.

"Are you alright?" he asked.

I nodded, willing myself not to turn red or look guilty. "Why do you ask?"

"You just seem a bit out of it."

I moved the last of my noodles around on my plate. "The stress at work is getting to me, I think. And I'm a bit tired from the drive over here last night, I guess."

Or maybe it was my several late nights last week thanks to a certain neighbor.

"Okay." Warren used his index finger to adjust his glasses upward. "Well, I was kind of hoping to have your undivided attention tonight. I need you to be of clear mind because I have something important to talk to you about."

I straightened in my seat. "What's going on?"

He cleared his throat. "I found out about a lead researcher position at UCLA, at the cancer center there. I'd like to put my hat in the ring for it. I think I have a very good chance because my old boss from PENN is now over there. He'd be able to put in a good word for me."

California? "Um…wow. Okay. When will you know?"

"I haven't applied yet. The position opens in six months because the current guy is relocating to Europe to head a large study over there. But they're taking applicants now. I'm not sure when they'll make a decision, but going for it means I need to be prepared to relocate if I get it."

"Which means *I* need to be prepared to relocate." I gulped some water.

He nodded. "How do you feel about that?"

Staring down at my plate, I shook my head. "I don't know, Warren. It's not that I don't want this opportunity for you, but being so far away from my family? That would be really hard. I'm all my parents have now. At least in New York, I can drive home whenever I want."

Maybe that was selfish, but he needed to know how I felt.

"Of course it would be difficult, my love. That's why I would never go for this unless you were okay with it. It would need to be a team decision." He stood up and grabbed a notepad. "Let's go over some of the pros and cons together, shall we?"

I rubbed my temples. "Alright."

Warren loved making lists and drawing diagrams. Any excuse he could find to do that, he took it.

He sat back down. "One major pro, which I haven't told you yet, is that the salary would be almost double what mine is now, Laney." He wrote down a number and underlined it before turning the paper toward me, displaying a ridiculously huge amount of money. *Holy shit.*

My jaw dropped. "Oh my God."

"Yeah. Is that crazy or what? You know I don't do what I do for the money, but *this* kind of money would be life-changing for us."

How could I keep him from this? I blew out a breath. "Well, that's obviously a very big pro."

"And the research facility is twice as big and twice as modern. They have equipment I could only dream about getting where I am now."

"I guess that's an even bigger pro than the money."

"Indeed." He examined my face. "But let's go to the cons. You'd obviously be farther away from your family. And me from mine." He wrote the word *distance* down on the paper. "But with the extra money I'd be making, we could afford plane tickets home whenever we missed them."

He had a point. "Okay…" I stared into space, imagining myself stressed and rushing through airports. It might've been doable, but that didn't mean I wanted to have to get to the airport anytime I felt like seeing my mother. God, this sucked.

"There are many research opportunities for you out west as well," he added. "I've already spoken to a few contacts. Once New York is over, things were going to be up in the air for you anyway, right? You don't have anything lined up. This timing might be perfect. So that's a pro."

Feeling extremely unsettled, I licked my lips. "Maybe."

"If I'm counting correctly, that was three pros and one con. Can you think of any other cons?" he asked.

The only thing that flashed through my mind was Holden. And what did *he* have to do with this? I wouldn't be living in New York once my current project was up anyway. But I'd been enjoying Holden's company in New York. And being back home with Warren made me realize just how guilty I felt about that.

Warren interrupted my thoughts. "Well?"

What choice do I have? "I can't think of any other negatives," I conceded. "I think you should go for it, see what happens, and we'll figure it out if you get it."

He let out a huge sigh. "You have no idea how happy this makes me. I suspected you'd approve once we worked out the pros and cons, but I didn't want to apply until we'd had a chance to talk."

"Thank you for waiting to clear it with me."

He beamed. "The weather in Cali is amazing, Laney. We could have so much fun on the weekends, exploring the Pacific Coast. There are so many geological wonders out there. I know that's your thing." He smiled.

"Yeah," I muttered.

If only geology were my thing lately. My *thing* as of late was far more dangerous.

Since Warren and I had spent Friday night together after I arrived and all day today, I went over to see my parents after having dinner with him this evening. My mom had made a special lemon dessert for me, and since Warren had said he was behind on some work, I planned to spend the night here in my old room, snuggling with Bully, Ryan's old dog. Mom and Dad were thrilled to have me all to themselves.

My mother poured hot water into my mug of Darjeeling tea. "I really miss having you around, Laney. I know you're not that far away, but it's been hard not being able to just pop over to your apartment whenever I want for a quick coffee chat. It'll be nice to have you back in a few months."

Interesting timing for that statement. I sighed. "I know."

Over dessert and tea, I filled them in on the bomb Warren had dropped during dinner.

The creases in my mother's forehead grew prominent as she took it all in. "This is not welcome news. Can I be selfish and admit that I don't want him taking my baby away?"

My dad turned to her. "Jean, if they're getting married, she has to go where he goes. It wouldn't kill us to go out there and visit her, if she has to move. Don't make her feel guilty."

Mom frowned. "That's a very old-fashioned way of thinking, Bill. Laney has an important job, too. She doesn't have to go where he goes. Why can't he stay where her job is?"

"Actually…" I sighed. "My grant only runs for six months to do the initial research. After that, I have to figure out what I'm doing or make a new proposal. So I'm not really tied down. And the timing sort of works because Warren wouldn't start the position for six months."

"Of course it's a decision they should make together," Dad piped in. "That's not what I meant. You're just arguing against anything I say that might support Laney moving because you don't want her to move."

"I'm sorry. Maybe I am, but I can't help how I feel. I know Laney is a strong, independent woman. She has a right to live wherever she wants. But she's my best friend. I love her company and would hate to not have her near us."

I placed my hand on hers. "I know, Mom. There's no part of me that wants to move that far away, but I didn't have the heart to tell him no. Warren works so damn hard and deserves this opportunity."

"Well…" She smiled. "I guess we have to make sacrifices for the ones we love. But is it okay if I secretly pray he doesn't get the job?"

"You're totally allowed. I'll be over here doing the same." I stuffed my mouth with dessert, though there wasn't enough lemon tart in the world to make me feel better tonight.

Melancholy continued to haunt me all through our tea time. Maybe I was jumping the gun, but I felt like Warren was going to get this position. His intelligence and hard work knew no bounds. And with his contacts, he had this job in the bag. I felt sick.

Then my phone chimed, interrupting my thoughts.

I looked down to find a text from Holden. It included a photo of him holding up a drink at a bar.

Holden: Having a vodka cranberry in your honor. Your drunk ass is missing out.

Lala: I take it that's the actual alcoholic version and not one of the Shirley Temples you scammed me with?

Holden: Only your lightweight ass could get drunk off a placebo effect. And it's called protecting, not scamming. But no Shirley Temple for me. This is the real deal.

Lala: Where are you?

Holden: We're about to play in a bit. Just a small bar in the city. Not as big a gig as the one you saw.

Lala: Aw. Well, I wish I could be there. That still sounds like fun.

The three dots moved around as he typed.

Holden: I wish you were here, too.

My heart fluttered. *Stop.*

"What on Earth has you smiling like that?" my mother asked.

My hand jerked, and the phone slipped out of my grip. I picked it up and turned it face down. *Jesus.* I hadn't even realized I was smiling.

"Nothing."

"Was that Warren?"

Damn it. I'd *never* been able to lie to my mother. She could always see through me. This time would be no different.

I swallowed. "No, actually. It's…Holden."

My father's eyes widened. "Holden Catalano?"

"Yes, of course."

"Why is he texting you?" my mother asked.

"He just texted me a funny photo."

"A photo of what?"

"Just a cocktail. He's at one of his band's shows in the City."

"What's so funny about a cocktail?" Dad asked.

"He knows I like vodka cranberries."

My mother's forehead wrinkled. "How does he know that?"

"I went to one of his shows the other night and had one."

Or two or three. I can't remember.

Her stare intensified. "You've been going out with him?"

"No. He just invited me to watch his band play once."

"Does Warren know?" she asked.

"Yes." I gulped.

My mother continued prodding. "He doesn't mind that you've been galivanting around with Holden Catalano?"

I laughed nervously. "Mom, it's not like that. His apartment is next door to mine. And he's a good friend. That's all."

"Try to give Laney some credit," my father intervened. "She's a smart girl. We all know that Holden, as much as we love him and as much as Ryan did, would be nothing but trouble. But I'm sure he's a lot of fun. Laney wouldn't do anything to jeopardize her relationship with Warren."

I nodded, feeling my throat close.

My mother crossed her arms. "Men like Holden can be very captivating, but he's not the best influence. Sometimes in the presence of someone like that—particularly when alcohol is involved—our judgment can be compromised. Especially if you're away from home."

Feeling hot, I said, "I'd appreciate it if we could stop talking about this. It was a friendly text. That's all."

Beads of sweat now formed on my forehead. If only I believed my own words. It seemed my mother knew me better than my father.

A little while later, still feeling extremely unsettled, I retreated upstairs for the night.

But I stopped in front of Ryan's room instead of my own. When my brother was at his sickest, he'd moved back home with my parents. They still kept his room here the same as it always was. Whenever I was feeling sad or conflicted, I'd sneak in and lie in his bed to feel closer to him.

I opened the door, and the first thing staring me in the face was the collage of photos on the bulletin board across from his bed. There were so many photos of the five guys. Memories of all of their fun times together had kept my brother going at the end.

Fishing trips on Owen's father's boat.

Holden and Ryan playing beer pong.

Ryan and Colby at a football game.

Brayden and Ryan dressed up for Halloween.

Because my brother hadn't found love before he died, I was certain those guys were the most important people in his life, besides his family. My heart clenched. Ryan would have made someone the best husband.

There was a photo of my brother and me when we were little, too. I was dressed in a long gown and wearing my mother's oversized heels. I used to beg Ryan to play prom with me because I'd been captivated by our teenage neighbor in her pretty dress taking photos outside before her big night. I'd put on the long princess Halloween costume and make my brother hand me flowers picked from the garden. I'd pretend I was the big girl going to the prom, and my poor brother had to go along with playing my date. That was probably the girliest thing I'd ever done before I stopped being interested in frilly things and transformed into a "science nerd," as Holden would put it.

Speaking of Holden, when I looked down at my phone, I noticed he'd sent another text earlier.

Holden: Wild night.

There was a photo of him, home in bed, eating Hot Cheetos. He was shirtless. Only Holden could make eating Hot Cheetos look sexy.

Lala: Home already?

A few minutes later, he responded.

Holden: Yep. Didn't feel like partying after the show tonight. Came straight home. Showered. And already in bed.

Lala: Who dis?

Holden: I know, right?

Lala: You have a reputation to uphold, Catalano. Going home alone goes against that.

Holden: I didn't say I was alone. I have a girl with me.

My heart sank. *How do I even respond to that?*
My finger hovered over the keys.
And then he sent me another photo. Holden had a guinea pig sitting on his bare chest. He was feeding it greens.
What the?

Lala: Who is that?

Holden: Colby's daughter is getting a surprise tomorrow.

Lala: OMG what?

Holden: Colby pissed me off the other day. So Saylor is getting a gift.

I cracked up.

Lala: Oh you're bad.

Holden: He told her she couldn't have a dog right now. He never specifically mentioned anything about guinea pigs. She's gonna love me. Favorite uncle award is mine.

Lala: Awfully cute.

Holden: Her or me? ;-)

I rolled my eyes and laughed.

Lala: Sigh. Thank you for cheering me up.

Holden: Why? Everything okay over there?

I kept typing and erasing words, unsure if I wanted to get into the California thing with him.

Lala: Something did come up today, but I don't want to rehash it right now, if you don't mind.

Holden: Talk to me.

Lala: I'll fill you in soon. It's nothing bad...just something that might make my life a bit complicated. I'm too exhausted to get into it tonight.

Holden: Got it. Won't push.

I looked back over to another photo of Holden and Ryan.

Lala: I'm looking at you right now, actually.

Holden: Crap. You can see I'm not wearing pants?

Lala: No, on Ryan's bedroom wall.

Holden: Wait...you're in Ryan's room?

Lala: Yeah. I come in here sometimes.

Holden: That's cool to know your parents still keep it the same.

Lala: They do. It was the same when he moved away to college and the same when he came back.

Holden: I'd love to visit sometime.

Lala: You should come by the next time you're home visiting your parents.

Even though my parents might give you the stink eye now.

Holden: I might.

Then Warren popped up on my phone.

Warren: Goodnight, my love. Heading to bed. See you tomorrow before you head back.

Laney: Me too. 'Night, babe. Xo

I was just about to put my phone down when another text came in.

Holden: Damn guinea pig just stole one of my Hot Cheetos. Can they have those?

Holden is nuts.

Lala: I'm thinking...no.

Holden: She better be okay.

Lala: Maybe you should put the Hot Cheetos down.

Holden: She has the hiccups now! What the fuck. I didn't sign up for this.

My shoulders shook with laughter.

Lala: LOL I'm sorry.

About a minute passed before he texted again.

Holden: I just Googled it and some guy says he gave his guinea pig Cheetos and it DIED. Holy shit!

Lala: You can't believe everything you read. It was just one Cheeto she had, though, right?

Holden: HOT Cheeto. But yes.

Lala: I think it'll be okay.

Holden: I should've stayed out tonight. This never would have happened. Fuck! I'm afraid to go to sleep now.

This wasn't supposed to be funny. But I couldn't stop laughing.

Lala: Do you need me to stay up with you?

A couple of minutes passed before he responded.

Holden: No. She seems good.

Lala: Yeah. It was only one Cheeto.

Holden: I think she's gonna live.

Lala: Me too.

Holden: Thank you for your support during this trying time.

I wiped another tear of laughter.

Lala: Of course.

Holden: You're laughing at me, aren't you?

Lala: Yes.

He sent a voice recording. When I hit play, it was the sound of the guinea pig hiccupping. I burst into laughter again. Holden had managed to break me out of my funk from earlier.

Lala: You weren't kidding.

Holden: No. Even I can't make up shit like this.

Lala: Thanks again for the laugh.

Holden: Anytime, Lala.

Lala: I'd better go to sleep.

Holden: Sweet dreams.

Lala: 'Night, Holden.

I fell asleep in my brother's bed that night, with thoughts of Warren, California, Holden, and hiccupping guinea pigs swirling around in my head.

♥CHAPTER 7

Lala

What the heck?

I'd stepped on the gas to speed up before changing lanes, but my car had slowed down, rather than going faster. I pressed the pedal all the way to the floor, yet I kept decelerating. *Ugh. You've got to be kidding me.*

Searching for the hazards button on the dash, I kept driving, but moved over to the right lane, rather than the left that I'd been trying to merge into. Less than a minute later, the car was practically crawling, and I had no choice but to get off at the nearest exit. Luckily, there was a gas station at the first intersection, so I pulled in and parked. But when I got out, I realized there was no mechanic's garage. It only had one of those mini marts attached.

Shoot. What the heck do I do now? My first instinct was to call Holden, but I was only an hour and fifteen minutes into the two-and-a-half-hour drive from Philly. So I went into the mini mart to see if there was anywhere nearby I could take my car.

"Hi. I'm having some car trouble and was wondering if you could tell me where the closest mechanic is located?"

The girl behind the Plexiglas looked like she might not be old enough to drive. She shrugged. "Sorry. I have no idea. My dad fixes all our cars."

"Thanks anyway."

Back outside, I leaned against my piece-of-shit car and dug my phone out of my pocket. I could've called Warren, but he hadn't been able to get a piece of toast out of the toaster the other day when the edge got stuck. I'd had to stop him from sticking a fork in it while it was still plugged in. So I sucked it up and called the only man I knew who could fix anything, besides my dad. My dad was *not* who I wanted to call right now.

"What's up, neighbor?"

I smiled. "Hey, Holden. I'm sorry to bug you, but I'm having a little car trouble. Uh, again."

"Where are you?"

I looked around and sighed. "I actually have no idea. I'm not sure what exit I got off on. But I'm about halfway into the drive back from Philly."

"What's going on with your car?"

"It was driving along just fine, but then it started to slow down, even though I hadn't taken my foot off the gas pedal. Even when I stood on it, it kept decelerating. By the time I got off at the next exit, I was only going about twenty miles per hour."

"Could be a clogged fuel filter. Have you gotten gas anywhere you didn't know lately?"

I cringed. "I actually got gas at some really sketchy place yesterday. I think it was called Joey D's or something like that. The sign on the road was a piece of plywood with the name painted crooked. But I was running on fumes, and it was the only place around."

"Welp, it might very well be a clogged fuel filter from bad gas then. Send me your location, and I'll be there as soon as I can."

"I can't ask you to do that. I'll just call a tow truck. I guess I hoped maybe you would know a trick for getting it to run right again."

"First of all, you didn't ask. I offered. And second of all, you shouldn't waste money on a tow truck that's going to take you to some mechanic we don't know, at least not without me taking a look and seeing if I can get it fixed. A fuel filter is usually only about twenty bucks. A tow alone will be a hundred-and-fifty bucks or more."

"Are you sure you don't mind? I'm probably over an hour away still."

"Not at all, sweetheart. That's what I'm here for. That's what me and all the guys are here for when it comes to you."

For such a wise-ass jokester, Holden really could make my insides turn to mush.

"Thanks, Holden."

"Send me your location. And if you're waiting in the car, keep your doors locked. Roadside gas stations aren't the safest places."

After I hung up, I shot a pin of my location to Holden's cell and decided to go back into the mini mart to treat myself to some junk food. I liked to have something sweet at the end of a stressful day, and this weekend had been full of those. But my fiancé was an ultra-healthy eater, so I always felt bad eating the stuff I liked in front of him.

It was going to take Holden a while to arrive, so I went on a little shopping spree, perusing the aisles and grabbing things with lots of gluten, extra nuts, extra dairy, and loaded with sugar. When I went up to the counter, the cashier wrinkled her nose. "You want all this?"

I narrowed my eyes. "I have six children."

She looked like she didn't believe me, but she rang me up without any other comments, at least. "That'll be twenty-two forty-nine."

I glanced down at the pile of candy. Maybe I *had* gone a little overboard. But what the hell? I swiped my credit card and rushed to the car to feast on my goodies.

Holden pulled up exactly one hour later. He parked next to me in the band's van and, once I unlocked it, opened my passenger door. Unfortunately, I hadn't cleaned up my sugar party, and his eyes snagged on the four—yes, four…don't be so judgy—wrappers.

He picked up the Reese's package. "Are these all from today?"

I grabbed the empty KitKat, SweeTARTS, and Utz Cheese Balls packaging. "I've been dying for some candy, but Warren is gluten free, nut free, dairy free, and sugar free, so I didn't have much of anything this weekend because he was around."

Holden's brows rose. "Gluten, nut, dairy, and sugar free? Sounds like he's *fun free* too. What the hell does the guy eat? Water?"

"Pretty much…"

He lifted his chin with a chuckle. "Pop the hood. I'll tell you when to start it."

"Okay."

A few minutes later, he poked his head around the raised hood. "Okay, start it now."

I turned the key, but nothing happened. The engine didn't even attempt to turn over.

Holden made a key-turning motion with his hand. "Turn the key!"

I opened the door. "I am! It's not starting!"

"Shit."

He shut the hood and smacked dirt from his hands. "I still think it's the fuel filter." He pulled out his phone and looked at the time. "Auto parts stores close by five on a Sunday, so we only have about twenty-five minutes. I think we should go grab a filter before it's too late. We can always return it if it turns out to be something else."

88

"Do you know how to change it if we're able to get one?"

Holden nodded. "I gotta get under the car to reach the fuel line, but I've done it before."

"Okay, let's do it."

After I locked up my car and got into the van, I Googled the closest parts store. "There are two," I said. "One is north of here about ten minutes and one is south about the same distance."

"Pick one and read me the directions."

Unfortunately, the one I picked didn't have the part in stock. So we rushed back to try to get to the other store before it closed, but when we pulled up, the parking lot was empty and all the lights were already off.

"Shoot. What do we do now?"

Holden shook his head. "It's a Sunday, so we're probably not going to find anywhere open now. I guess we can call a tow truck, go home, and come back tomorrow after the shop has it fixed. But if we're going to make the trip back anyway, why not just stop on our way and grab a fuel filter so I can fix it and not waste the money on a tow and a mechanic?"

"I definitely have to be at work tomorrow afternoon. I have an appointment to meet the manager of one of the senior-care facilities where people who are part of my study live. But I can come early tomorrow. Do you have anything in the morning?"

"I'll make it work."

I sighed. "God, Holden. You've done so much for me. I don't know what I would've done without you the last few weeks."

He winked. "You'll never have to find out because I'll always be here for you, babe."

I needed to go back to get my work files from my car. Plus, I thought I should talk to the gas station attendant and let her know I was going to leave my car there overnight. But a few minutes into the drive, there was a loud pop outside, followed by a whooshing sound.

"What the heck was that?"

Holden had been casually driving with one hand, but now he gripped the wheel tightly with two. "That was our tire. We just had a blowout."

Thank God we weren't on the highway because the van started to pull hard to the right. Holden maneuvered us into an empty parking lot, but it was still pretty scary.

I shook my head. "I cannot believe that just happened."

"Me neither."

We got out of the van and walked around to the front passenger side. Sure enough, the tire was completely flat already, though it was still making a loud hissing sound.

"What is it with us and car trouble?" I said.

"I think it has something to do with the fact that we both drive hunks of junk."

"First I got towed for the way I parked, then my starter went, now I have a clogged fuel filter, and you got a flat. I've had more car trouble in the last few weeks than I have had the last ten years."

Holden opened the back van doors. "That's how it happens with old cars. One thing goes after another." He lifted a concealed panel in the floor of the van and hung his head. "You've got to be freaking kidding me."

I walked over to see what he was looking at. "What's wrong?"

"The jack is gone." He looked around the interior of the van. "Shit. So is the spare. I think we took them out to make room for our new amps the other night before a gig. I guess we never put them back. They're still in Dylan's garage."

"Oh boy. What do we do now?"

He put his hands on his hips. "I suppose we could call *two* freaking tow trucks and take a two-hundred-dollar Uber back to the city. Then spend another two hundred to Uber back tomorrow morning to pick up the cars at the repair shop. Or…" He pointed down the block to a building I hadn't noticed. "There's a Holiday

Inn up ahead. We can stay the night, and I'll pick up a new fuel filter first thing in the morning and fix your car, then deal with the van situation. That makes the most sense. Otherwise, between Ubers and tow trucks, it'll be three times the cost of staying the night. Plus, we can get an early start and not have to fight traffic to get back here. Auto parts stores are usually open by eight or nine because mechanics get started early. What do you think?"

I bit my lip. "I don't know."

"Well, it's up to you. I'll do whatever you want."

Of course it made sense to just stay here, both financially and timewise. Yet the thought of spending the night with Holden made me nervous. Then again, I wouldn't be *spending the night* with him. We'd get two rooms. Even if they were right next to each other, it would be no more inappropriate than the apartments we lived in. I was just overthinking things.

I nodded. "Staying the night makes more sense. But I insist on paying for your room and mine. You wouldn't be in this predicament if it weren't for me."

"How about we make sure they even have rooms before we fight over who's paying."

"Fine. But I'm paying."

Holden's lip twitched. "We'll see."

We locked up the van and walked the block or so to the Holiday Inn. The registration desk was empty, and the eyes of the pretty woman behind it lit up when she got a look at Holden.

"Can I help you?" She smiled.

Feeling like she hadn't even noticed me yet, I answered. "Yes, do you have two rooms available for tonight?"

"Just for the one night?"

I nodded. "Yes, please."

She began typing into her computer. "We're pretty booked up because the boat show opens down the road tomorrow, and we're the sponsoring hotel. But let me check." She looked up after a minute. "We do have a room, but only one."

Holden and I glanced at each other. "Does it have two beds?" he asked.

The woman shook her head. "Sorry, just one king."

Holden pointed over his shoulder toward the door. "It's fine. I'll sleep in the van."

"No way. I can't let you do that."

"I've done it before. It'll actually be a treat sleeping in it all by myself. Usually I'm stuck in it with the guys from the band after a show because we can't get a hotel room for one reason or the other."

"I'm not letting you sleep in the van, Holden." I looked at the clerk. "Are there any other hotels nearby?"

"Not really. That's why we're all booked up. There's a Days Inn, but it's about a twenty-minute drive. Though they might be booked up too since they're usually cheaper."

I sighed and looked at Holden. "I'll just sleep on the floor. You can have the bed."

"*I'll* sleep on the floor. *You* can have the bed."

"No, Holden. This is all my fault."

The clerk motioned between us. "I take it you two aren't a couple?"

"We're old friends," I said.

She smiled and spoke to Holden. "I get off at twelve, if you want a place to sleep, and I won't make you sleep on the floor."

Seriously? I felt like punching this ballsy woman. I dug into my purse and pulled out my credit card, giving her a big, fake smile. "We'll take the room and figure it out."

"What's the matter?"

"Nothing," I said, fishing through my overnight bag.

Holden had taken an Uber to my car to get a few things I needed and talk to the clerk at the gas station. Then he'd stopped at Wendy's to grab us some dinner on the way back.

"Is something missing from your bag?" he asked.

"No. I just realized I don't have anything to sleep in." I shrugged. "It's fine. I'll just sleep in what I'm wearing."

"You don't have a T-shirt or something?"

"I do. But it won't even cover my butt."

"Well, I usually sleep naked, but I'll spare you and keep my boxers on." He reached for the hem of his T-shirt and pulled it over his head, tossing it to me. "You can use this. I just put it on before I left the apartment. It'll be a nightgown on you, you're so small."

I swallowed at the full visual of Holden's naked chest. He was tall and lanky, but damn, he still had that great six pack that I'd loved to check out when I was a teenager. When he caught me ogling, I rushed into the bathroom to get changed and put some distance between us. But when I slipped on his T-shirt, it felt like he was all around me. The damn thing smelled so good, *so very, very Holden*, and I couldn't help but lift the fabric to my nose and take a deep whiff. After, I berated myself silently in the mirror for what I'd done.

You're engaged.

You love your fiancé.

Don't be an idiot.

It helped. For about two seconds. Until I walked out and saw Holden making his bed on the floor wearing nothing but tight black boxers. I froze.

God, he's beautiful.

So damn sexy.

I bet he's sooo adventurous in bed, too.

"You okay?" Holden looked at me funny.

I blinked a few times before darting to the bed and burying myself under the blanket to cover up. "Yeah, fine. I just didn't want to interrupt you while you were setting up."

Holden flashed a crooked smile, and his eyes sparkled. "Sure."

He finished with his makeshift bed and pointed to the lamp on the nightstand. "Can you hit that light next to you? I'd do it, but I don't want you to feel guilty for checking me out again…"

My eyes widened. "I was *not* checking you out."

He chuckled. "Whatever. Just turn off the light, Lala."

I did, and we were both quiet for a few minutes.

"You know," Holden said. "It's okay to look at other people. It's natural to appreciate the human body."

"I wasn't checking you out, you egomaniac. I'm not fourteen peeping through my bedroom window anymore."

"Nope, you are definitely *not* fourteen anymore. You're all grown up. Not a chance in hell I missed that."

"What's that supposed to mean?"

"It means you're a beautiful woman, Lala. Any man who tells you he doesn't notice is full of shit. Unlike you, I don't feel guilty about it."

"Maybe that's because you're not *engaged.*"

"Maybe, but I don't think so. I think I'm just okay with looking. I mean, what do you do when you watch porn? Not look at the guy's junk?"

"I don't watch porn."

Holden was quiet for a minute. "Like, ever?"

"Warren thinks it's degrading to women."

"Degrading to women?" His voice was terse now. "Not to men? Maybe you're not aware since you don't watch it, but *men* and women are naked in porn."

Between seeing Holden's half-naked body and talking about porn, I was growing hot and bothered. "Let's change the subject or maybe just try to get some sleep."

"Fine. Let's sleep."

But sleep was impossible. For the next half hour, I tossed and turned, and I heard Holden doing the same on the floor, which I felt bad about. Then there was a bang, followed by Holden groaning.

"Fuck," he grunted. "*Motherfucker.*"

"What happened?"

"Nothing. I just rolled over and whacked the corner of the dresser with my shin."

It didn't occur to me until that moment that I was making one of my oldest friends sleep on the floor. I mean, I knew he was down there, but I hadn't looked at it like that. Holden was like a brother to me, and I was being ridiculous.

"This is stupid, Holden. I'm sleeping in a king-size bed, and you're on the gross hotel-room floor. There's no reason we can't share. We've been friends since we were kids."

"It's fine."

I sat up. "No, it's really not fine. And you know what? I did check you out before. I'm making you sleep on the floor because I think you're attractive and have guilt over that. But you're like my big brother, and that's ridiculous. So get your butt up here."

"You sure?"

"Positive."

I was all bold and righteous until Holden slipped under the covers. Then my body became acutely aware of just how close he was. He rolled onto his side so we were facing each other and tucked his hands under his cheek. I could see his eyes, even though it was dark.

"How was your weekend at home?" Holden spoke softly. "Do anything special?"

"Not really. Just hung out with Warren and my parents."

"Where do you sleep when you go home?"

"I slept at Warren's one night, but I stayed at my parents' the next."

"That's right. You were in Ryan's room when we were texting. But how come you slept at your parents' on your last night?"

I shrugged. "I guess I just wanted to spend some time with my mom. And…Warren sort of sprung something on me last night, and I needed a little space to clear my head."

"What did he spring on you?"

"He's applying for a job in California. He wants us to move there."

"What? Are you going to go?"

I sighed. "I don't know that I have a choice. It's his dream job."

"But what about you, Lala? What have *you* always dreamed of?"

"I'm not sure I've had a lifelong dream like Warren has. He's a cancer researcher because his mom died from cancer when he was only seven. Don't get me wrong, I love my job, but it's not the same. When I was seven, all I wanted to do was marry Beast from *Beauty and the Beast.*"

"Beast? Not the handsome dude he turns into at the end?"

"No, I actually had a big crush on Beast. I thought he was cute." I laughed.

"Not surprising. You also used to dress up in your communion dress and make Ryan officiate your wedding to your stuffed sloth."

I laughed. "I can't believe you remember that."

"Of course. And you stole that shark tooth necklace I used to wear to dress your sloth up for the wedding."

I bit my lip. "You know why I did that?"

"Why?"

"Because I was pretending *you* were the sloth. I had the biggest crush on you back then, and I liked to pretend we were getting married." I laughed, but Holden didn't. His eyes were so damn serious.

"I had the biggest crush on you, too, Lala."

Oh God. I had the craziest urge to lean in and kiss him. My attraction was so intense, stronger than ever. My breath came out in small pants, and I started to fear that if I didn't rein things in, I might do something stupid. So I feigned a giant yawn, stretching my arms over my head and all.

"Man, I'm so tired all of a sudden. I should get some sleep." Without waiting for a response, I flipped over, putting my back to him. "'Night, Holden."

He waited a few heartbeats before responding. "Goodnight, Lala."

I'm not sure how long it took me to fall asleep, but it was definitely a few hours. And when I woke up the next morning, Holden was…*spooning me.*

I could feel his dick against the crack of my ass.

Oh.

My.

God.

His gentle snore told me it wasn't intentional, but that didn't stop my body from reacting. My nipples hardened, and I felt myself swell and grow wet, as if getting ready for action to come.

What if I pushed back? Rubbed myself up and down the length of him, just once. He wouldn't even have to know.

Then again, *I would know.* And I'd probably wind up with a rash every day from stressing over what I'd done. So instead, I forced myself to slip out of the bed. Morning sun was already streaming in through the windows, and a cold shower was in order, for sure.

Inside the bathroom, I turned the water on and undressed. Just as I put one foot into the shower, something buzzed loudly from the other room.

Shit. My phone! That was probably my alarm going off.

Not wanting to wake Holden, I grabbed a towel from the rack, wrapped it around me, and rushed out of the bathroom. But in my haste, I ran smack into Holden standing outside the bathroom door. And he had a massive hard-on bulging from his boxers.

Seeing my eyes grow wide, Holden looked down. "Shit. Sorry. I didn't realize. I was just bringing you your phone." He held my phone out, and Warren's name flashed between us like a lighted billboard in Times Square.

Welp, that worked better than a cold shower...

❤CHAPTER 8

Holden

Lala disappeared into the bathroom to talk to Warren in private, right after she'd ogled my morning wood, which didn't help my predicament one single bit.

Why did it fucking piss me off that she was talking to her fiancé?

Was I pissed, or was I guilty? It was probably both. I didn't feel guilty because of him. I felt guilty because I knew I'd put her in a position where *she* experienced guilt.

I slipped my pants on while listening to the muffled sound of her conversation, struggling to make out what she was saying over the fan she'd turned on in the bathroom.

I walked over to the window and opened the curtain, letting some of the morning sun into our hotel room. As I looked down at our parking lot view, I thought about the way she'd backed into me last night.

Lala had drifted off to sleep before I had. I'd stayed awake for hours, struggling with my thoughts and the fact that my body was on fire despite my best efforts to remain neutral while lying next to her. And then at one point, her ass had shifted back toward me, positioned directly on my dick. I'd wanted to freaking explode. I didn't think she knew what she'd done because I'd heard little snores at almost the same moment. But my dick, which had already been struggling, had risen to full staff.

Aching for more, I'd done the opposite of what felt natural—I'd moved the comforter to act as a barrier for my cock before pushing my hips back. Then I'd reached out and wrapped my arms around her instead, because I couldn't help it. That was a lot more innocent than grinding my cock against her ass, which was what I'd really wanted to do.

It had been physically painful to move back. I'd ended up falling asleep with my arms around her. Not sure what my dick or my body had decided to do while I was sleeping, but I figured I couldn't be responsible for anything if I was unconscious.

Lala's face was red when she emerged from the bathroom. She also had what looked like a rash all over her neck.

My eyes widened. "Is everything okay?"

"Yeah." She sighed. "He was just checking in since he hadn't heard from me."

"What did you tell him?"

She sighed. "I told him you came to help me, but I lied and told him that we were in separate rooms. And I feel terrible for doing that. I know we didn't do anything wrong, but—"

"Fuck no, we didn't, and you shouldn't feel guilty." I stepped toward her. "But I can understand why you couldn't tell him we shared a bed." I looked down at her neck. "You're breaking out from stress. Stop beating yourself up about it."

"I didn't have the heart to tell him we slept in the same bed, even if it was innocent. It wouldn't have made sense to him." She muttered, "It doesn't even really make sense to me."

It *wasn't* exactly innocent. We both knew it, even if we weren't saying it. That was the problem.

"I get it. You're trying to protect him. I can respect that. But we didn't…" I chose my words carefully. "Cross any lines. So you have nothing to feel guilty about."

"Yeah, I know. I know." Her eyes momentarily fell to my chest before she shook her head. "Anyway…let me go change so I can give you back your shirt."

She returned to the bathroom for a few minutes, then emerged and handed me my shirt. As I slipped it over my head, I breathed in deeply. This shirt was going to mess me up for the rest of the day; I wouldn't be able to think straight.

We checked out of the hotel and headed to the auto parts store to get what I needed to fix her car.

Once the job was done, Lala hit the road, since she was already missing the first part of her workday. There was no time to talk about any residual awkwardness left over from last night or this morning.

It took me a little while to get the tire on the van replaced, but then I headed back as well. The drive to New York was crappy, to say the least. Not only could I still smell her all over my damn shirt, but now I was smelling her *with* the memory of what it felt like to hold her, to have her ass pressed against me. I'd actually fallen asleep with a woman in my arms. You know how many times I'd done that in my life? Never. Not intentionally, at least. Sounds crazy, but I'd never had the urge to do that. As many women as I'd slept with, I couldn't remember a single time I'd specifically wrapped my arms around someone. There might have been some tangled bodies here and there, but nothing as intimate as holding someone.

I'd told Lala we didn't do anything wrong. And maybe *she* didn't do anything wrong, but I'd crossed the line the moment I made the decision to get up off that floor and join her in the bed. I knew it was dangerous—especially after she admitted she was nervous because she was attracted to me. I'd made her believe she could trust me.

But she shouldn't.

An evil part of me *wanted* to tempt her. I hated myself for that because I knew a girl like Lala would never forgive herself if she cheated on her fiancé. Why would I put someone I cared about in that position? But my feelings for her were very complicated—and selfish.

The ride went by in a blur because I was so stuck in my head, and it seemed like just a few minutes before I arrived home and parked the van in a lot down the block.

If I thought my day was going to get any better once I got back, I was sorely mistaken. Owen stormed down the hall toward me as I entered the building.

"There you are! Where the fuck have you been all morning, and why aren't you answering your phone?"

"Sorry, dude. Phone is dead." I hadn't brought my charger with me on my unexpected trip.

His ears were red, and a vein looked like it was ready to pop out of his forehead. "I had to miss a fucking important meeting because of a leak you were supposed to be here to fix. The least you can do is charge your damn phone."

My head was killing me. "What happened?" I asked as I opened the door to my apartment.

He followed me inside. "Sink leak in 410 was causing water to come through the ceiling in the apartment below it."

"410? That's where Frick and Frack live. Did you fix it?"

"No! I put a Band-Aid on it, but it's not fixed. And those two little shits greased the pipes under the sink and the faucet to fuck with me. They're out of control."

"I'm sorry, man."

"You were at some chick's house, I assume?"

"Actually, no." I hesitated, dreading having to tell him. "I was helping Lala."

His eyes narrowed. "Helping Lala with what?"

"Her car crapped out on the way home from Philly, and she called me to help her get back."

He arched a brow. "Is that all you helped with?"

I wanted to punch him right now. "What kind of a question is that?"

"Your crush on Lala is the worst-kept secret in the world. You're wondering why I asked you that?"

"She fucking called me!" I spat. "What do you want me to do?"

"How about get one of us to do it because you know you can't be trusted."

"Since when do you know how to fix cars, jackass?"

Owen had no answer for that, so he continued his inquisition. "Where did you spend the night last night?"

I blew out a long breath and gave him the details—without mentioning that we'd slept in the same bed. That would have to remain a secret.

"You slept in the same hotel room, and you don't think you're playing with fire here?" He shook his head. "You know damn well that she's with a good guy who'll take care of her and treat her right. Why would you want to jeopardize that? If she ends up cheating on him with you—because you can't fucking stop coercing her—it would be one of the biggest mistakes of her life."

His words felt like a sucker punch. Mainly because I believed them. Lala falling for me would be a huge mistake. Still, I found myself on the defensive. "Thanks for the confidence, asshole. I thought you were supposed to be one of my best friends."

"Do you seriously think that if she gave in to your goddamn charms she would end up in a better place than if she married him? You need to think about what's best for her, Holden. I know what you're up to."

I raised my voice. "What part of my going out there to fix her fucking car don't you understand?"

"You could've slept in your van like you have before. You didn't have to spend the night in a hotel room with her."

If he only knew. I looked down at my shoes.

"I know you, Holden. I feel like I'm the only one keeping tabs on this situation lately. Colby's so damn busy, and Brayden seems to have his head up his ass per usual. But *I* see the way you look at her. And this whole situation concerns me. She's like the last piece of Ryan we have left. You *cannot* fuck with that girl." He relaxed his tone. "Ryan would kill you, man. He'd *kill* you."

I pulled on my hair. "Look, you don't need to say it. Okay? I know I'm not right for her. I also know that there's *something* between us—it's always been there. Things you don't even know about…from when she and I were younger." I paused. "And I also know I need to do everything in my power to make sure nothing happens. But I *do* care about her. It's fucking complicated. As my friend, I wish you would *listen* to me rather than lecture me." My lip trembled as anger coursed through my veins.

Maybe he finally saw the torment in my eyes because Owen softened. He nodded. "I'm sorry I was so harsh. It's been a rough morning, and I was really pissed that you weren't here. But now that I know you were helping her, I can't stay pissed." He scrubbed his hand over his face. "Look, I gotta get to work. I'm already late enough. You should head back over to 410 to fix the shitty job I did patching up the situation. And maybe tie up the Satan siblings to get them under control."

After he took off, I made a quick stop in my apartment and then went upstairs to get to work on that leak. Owen's words about me being the biggest mistake Lala would ever make continued to plague me all afternoon, though.

I made a mental vow—yet again—to distance myself for a while, as hard as that might be.

A few days had passed, and I'd kept my promise on staying away from Lala. I hadn't heard from her and hadn't made contact.

I had a few hours to kill before leaving for a gig tonight and found myself falling into rumination again. Staying away from her was one thing, but thinking about her was another—that I hadn't been able to stop.

She hadn't texted me or anything since we got back on Monday, which made me think she was still feeling guilty over the other night and had decided to distance herself. It was just as well and made things easier for me, but it bothered me that she might have been upset about it.

I'd done everything I could to try to move on from thoughts of her. I'd even gone back to a girl named Cara's apartment after my show last night. She and I had kissed, but when she tried to go down on me, I stopped her. I'd never stopped a blowjob in my life. Eager head from an attractive woman wasn't something you refused. And it's not that my body wasn't ready for it. I'd been so damn horny lately. I just wasn't in the mood for *her*.

Ever since the other night, all I'd craved was to be back in that warm bed with Lala, which was beyond fucked up. I ended up leaving Cara's pissed at myself, while also patting myself on the back for at least moving on far enough to kiss her. Because I really fucking needed to move on. Kissing random women used to be a nightly occurrence, and now I apparently thought I deserved a gold star.

A knock on the door snapped me out of my thoughts. When I opened, Lala was standing there holding two smoothies.

My heart wanted to burst. Her hair was especially unruly and wind-blown. And her scent, which had unfortunately begun to fade from my shirt, was back in full force as it wafted toward me. Despite everything, I'd missed her so damn much.

"Hey!" I smiled.

"Hi." She lifted one of the cups. "I, uh, know you like that smoothie place. I passed by on the way home from work and figured I'd bring you one."

"Thanks. That was sweet of you." I stepped aside. "Come in."

"Is…everything okay with you?" she asked.

"Yeah." I swallowed. "Why do you ask?"

"I feel like maybe I made you uncomfortable the other night at the hotel. And that's why you've been quiet."

Fuck. "No, Lala. You didn't do anything to make me uncomfortable. Trust me."

"Okay. Well…I can get out of your hair if you're busy."

"Stay," I insisted. "I don't have anything going on. Just a gig later tonight."

"Oh. Is it in the City?"

"Yeah. At a bar. We played there last night, too."

She sat down on my sofa. "What have I missed in Holden's world?"

"Not much." I sat down, took a sip, and kicked my feet up. "The band has been busy, and I fixed not one, but two leaky sinks this week. Other than that, things have been pretty boring. What about you?"

"The research project is going more smoothly. I got a second admin finally."

"Nice."

"Hey…" She grinned. "You never told me what happened with the guinea pig. Did you give it to Saylor?"

"Well, after her triumphant recovery from the Hot Cheeto incident, I took her to Colby's the following morning. Right before you called me about the car, actually." I laughed. "Colby's still pissed at me. But, yeah, Saylor was psyched."

"He's gonna let her keep it, right?"

"Yep. He and Billie basically had no choice. That's why he's pissed."

106

Lala laughed. It was good to see her smile.

I ran my finger along the side of my cup. "Any more news on the California situation?"

She shook her head. "He won't find out anything for a while. It's been weighing on me, though. I've been in kind of a funk about it ever since I got back."

Don't ask her to come out tonight to break out of her funk. "You should come to the show tonight. Let loose."

She didn't immediately answer.

"I don't know." She bit her bottom lip. "It's a work night."

Good girl, Lala. Stay away from me. "No pressure."

Silence filled the room. Then out of nowhere, she seemed to perk up.

"You know what? The days are passing fast. I won't have endless opportunities to see you play. So, yeah. I'll go." She smiled.

Inwardly psyched, I also felt like I'd taken a hundred steps back in my resolve to distance myself. *Nice going.*

There was nothing like looking out into the audience and seeing Lala watching me play. It wasn't always easy to identify faces, depending on the lighting. But I made sure to take note of where she was going to be standing. Tonight at this smaller venue, I found I had a clearer view than normal. My performance was also on point.

As I stepped off of the platform at the end and looked over at Lala's smiling face, all seemed right in the world. Well, except for the fact that Lala was still with Warren, and I still seemed incapable of staying away from her.

Wiping sweat off my forehead, I asked, "What did you think?"

"Was it just me or were you particularly amazing tonight?"

"It wasn't just you. I felt the same. Thank you for noticing." I lowered my mouth to her ear. "How about a vodka cranberry to celebrate?"

"Just one. I have to be alert tomorrow," she yelled through the noise.

"You got it."

I went to the bar and fetched us two vodka cranberries. I only ever drank them when I was with her—or when I was using that particular drink as an excuse to text her.

We chatted and sipped for a while, and then since it was a work night and Lala had to get back at a decent hour, I opted to get us our own car rather than wait to share the SUV with the guys.

As we were exiting the bar, Cara—the girl I'd kissed the night before—stopped me.

"Hey, Holden, you left this at my place last night."

Shit. When she handed me my beanie, my stomach sank. "Thanks."

I resumed walking, placing my hand on the small of Lala's back to guide her forward and away from Cara. I couldn't even look at Lala because I realized the conclusion she must have drawn. But why did it matter? That was the fucked-up part.

Lala's face had turned beet red by the time we faced each other on the sidewalk outside. "I guess you lied when you said not much has been going on, huh? Or maybe sleeping over at some rando's house isn't all that special? Just par for the course?"

I looked her straight in the eyes and told the truth. "I went back to her apartment last night. We kissed. But I left before anything else could happen. I wasn't into her."

Lala stayed silent and shook her head, almost in disbelief. "Jesus. What's wrong with me?" She blinked. "You don't owe me an explanation, Holden. I'm sorry I reacted that way." She blew a breath up into her hair. "This is not a good look on me. I have no right to be jealous right now. I should be minding my own damn business instead of wanting to rip that girl's head off."

Damn. That's kind of hot. "I don't know what to say, Lala."

That was the truth. I almost always had an answer for everything, but I didn't know how to respond. I'd wanted to rip *Warren's* head off for calling his own fiancée the other day, for Christ's sake.

The fact that she'd admitted her jealousy gave me a massive high at first, but I came crashing down pretty fast as we entered our ride and went home in silence.

Because it hit me: It didn't matter that she was jealous; it didn't change anything. She *still* had a fiancé. She *still* chose to be with him. She was *still* leaving New York after this contract was up and possibly moving to California. And I was *still* supposed to be protecting her from me. I was *still* not right for her.

Lala had a crush on me. That was it. She liked me because I was forbidden—her older brother's best friend. The second she felt she could truly have me, she wouldn't want me anymore. Reality would set in fast. She would soon realize I could never be the safety net she needed.

CHAPTER 9

Lala

"**O**h no…"

I frantically turned the bathroom knob back and forth a third time. But it still didn't budge. It was like someone had locked it from the outside.

Feeling a panic attack coming on, I grabbed the doorknob with both hands and yanked as hard as I could.

Still nothing.

Leverage…leverage is what I need.

So I planted one foot on the wall to the left of the door and gripped the knob with both hands again. This time, when I pulled back, I let my weight do the work while I pushed from the wall.

It worked! The knob moved…

Only the door didn't come with it, and I flew backward across the bathroom, landing on my ass with the knob in my hand…

And the door still shut.

Shit.

I didn't even have my phone in here. Not to mention, it was probably around two in the morning. I'd been up all night working on the presentation I had to make tomorrow—or today, that is—to the grant committee, and I still had another hour or two of work before I'd be done. I needed to get the hell out of here.

But playing with the mechanics inside where the knob used to be proved fruitless, and the damn doorknob wouldn't click back into place. After about twenty minutes, I had no choice but to try to wake Holden. I felt terrible doing it at this hour on a Monday, but I couldn't be stuck in here all night. Luckily, our bathroom walls were adjoining, though I wasn't sure if he would hear me. Or if he was even home. But I had to try.

"Holden!"

Bang, bang!

"Holden! It's Lala. I'm stuck in my bathroom and need help!"

Bang, bang, bang!

That went on for a few minutes, and then suddenly I heard a crash inside my apartment.

"*Lala!*"

"I'm in here, Holden! In the bathroom! I'm stuck!"

"What the hell?" He stood on the other side of the door. "Where's the doorknob?"

I leaned down and spoke through the hole where the knob used to be. "It's in here with me. The lock jammed, and the knob came off in my hands when I tried to pull it open."

"Alright. Give me a minute. I need to run next door to get a screwdriver."

"I have one now! I picked it up after the beeping incident, so I wouldn't need to bug you again. It's in the top drawer in the kitchen!"

"Okay, great. Hang on."

Two minutes later, the door popped open. It wasn't until I saw Holden's face that I remembered I was only wearing a tank top and underwear, sans bra.

He gulped and took a long look before turning his head. "Sorry. I didn't realize you weren't dressed."

I wasn't the only one scantily clad. Holden had on only a pair of boxer briefs, his beautiful tanned skin and carved six pack on full display for my eager eyes, *yet again*. I couldn't stop myself from staring. Silence ticked by until Holden turned his head back, probably to see why I'd grown quiet. "You oka—"

My eyes rose to meet his, but not before he'd caught me ogling him.

I shook my head and laughed nervously. "I'm sorry. I didn't mean to stare. I just hadn't expected you to be in your underwear either, I guess. It caught me off guard."

Holden ran a hand through his hair. "Yeah, I'm sorry if I checked you out, too."

I should've just left the bathroom and covered up with a robe, but something about being near this man made me say and do things that were completely out of character. "Would you mind if I…looked a little more?"

Holden's brows shot up to his hairline. "You want to check me out?"

My face heated. I shook my head and looked down. "Oh my gosh. I'm so embarrassed. I think the lack of sleep and stress from being locked in here made me a little bonkers. It's just that maybe we both have some pent-up curiosity about what we look like as adults. I mean, I've only stolen glimpses of you without a shirt on since we were teenagers in my backyard pool. And you certainly haven't seen me in a skimpy bottom and no bra since then. I guess I was thinking if we took a good, long look, once and for all, we might get it out of our systems."

Holden stared at me. I could see the wheels in his head spinning. Eventually, his eyes dropped to my chest. "You have no bra on…"

I shook my head. "No bra."

He swallowed. "Let's do it."

"Really?"

He nodded. "Fuck yeah. I'm going to hell anyway. Might as well enjoy the ride down. But you have to stay in the bathroom, and I'll stay on this side of the doorway."

"Okay." I bit my bottom lip. "You look first."

"Why don't we look at the same time?"

I nodded. "Good idea. How long should we do it for?"

Holden shrugged. "A minute?"

"Do you have your phone?"

"No. I thought someone broke in and you were being attacked. My phone was the last thing on my mind."

"Mine should be on the coffee table. Do you want to grab it so we can use the timer?"

Holden walked away and came back ten seconds later. "What's your code?"

"Zero, seven, one, three."

He started to type and then froze before looking up at the ceiling. "That's the day you're getting married, isn't it?"

I nodded.

Holden cursed as he went back to typing. "I'm *so* fucking going to hell."

He called up the clock app and then turned the phone to show me. The countdown was set for one minute. His finger hovered over the green button. "You ready?"

I nodded.

Holden pressed the button, and we began to openly ogle each other. Without having to steal glances, I noticed things I hadn't before—like how muscular his thighs were and the sexy line of hair that ran from the waistband of his underwear up to his belly button. God, I wanted to trace that with my tongue in the worst way. After about thirty seconds, Holden caught my eye. His voice was low and strained when he spoke. "Turn around."

I swallowed and nodded. Thankfully, I had on a lacy thong and not some ugly old panties. When my back was fully facing him, Holden groaned.

113

"Jesus Christ. Your ass is fucking perfect."

He stayed quiet until the timer went off. Since I'd kept my back to him for the last thirty seconds, I hadn't really gotten to look at him for the full minute. I was about to suggest I should get a little more time, when I turned around and my eyes snagged on Holden's boxers. *Holy freaking bulge!*

Holden was hard, or at least *growing hard*. Or maybe a tallboy beer can was trying to escape from his underwear…

Seeing my eyes grow wide, Holden looked down and used both hands to cover his crotch. "*Shit.* Sorry. Maybe this wasn't a good idea. I'll be back in two minutes."

He disappeared from my apartment for at least fifteen minutes after that. I'd started to think he wasn't coming back when there was a soft knock at my door. I opened to find Holden fully dressed—sweatshirt, socks, sweatpants, even a hat and gloves. It was exactly the moment we both needed, because I had on a matching outfit, only I'd paired my hat and gloves with a scarf, too. We both started to crack up.

"Oh my God, Holden," I snorted. "Have we lost it?"

He bent over in laughter. "I think so."

After we wiped tears from our eyes, Holden held up a roll of duct tape. "I'm just going to put some duct tape on the lock so you won't accidentally get locked in again. Tomorrow I'll get a new doorknob set."

I stepped aside for him to come in. "Thank you."

After he finished taping the door, he looked around the living room. Piles of papers were spread all over the place. "Bomb go off in here?"

I sighed. "I have a presentation to make tomorrow—today—to the grant committee. I still need to finish matching the initial lab results to the participants and then compile information about the test subjects."

"You need help?"

"What I *should've done* is taken the help my two assistants offered, but I was too afraid to not have my first presentation be perfect. But it's okay. You should go back to sleep. I'm sorry I woke you."

Holden smiled. "Trust me, sweetheart. After our little show and tell, I'm not falling back asleep anytime soon."

I knew the feeling. Earlier I'd gone into the bathroom to pee and splash some cold water on my face because I was starting to fall asleep while I was working. But there was no way I could go to bed now. Plus, I could really use the help.

"Are you sure?"

"Positive. Tell me what to do."

For the next hour, Holden and I matched lab results to patient-intake sheets. Since it was a blind study, everyone was identified by number rather than name. It was pretty ridiculous in this day and age that the lab hadn't given me some sort of a spreadsheet that I could sort easily, but they hadn't. So after we paired results to patients, Holden read off the numbers I needed while I typed them into a database.

"How does this study work? I know it's something to do with dopamine levels and Alzheimer's."

"Well, the dopaminergic neuron system has been studied before as it relates to the progression of Alzheimer's. But the results have been pretty inconsistent. It's my theory that more than just dopamine has to be examined. My initial research shows that low levels of three combined hormones: dopamine, oxytocin, and norepinephrine together cause neurodegenerative disease. So my study raises the levels of all three hormones in early Alzheimer's patients so we can study the rate of progression of the disease."

"You said sex increases the levels, right? So do you hand out Viagra and put on some Marvin Gaye?"

I laughed. "Close. We split the test subjects into two groups. One gets a handful of placebos for control purposes, and one gets the actual drugs that raise the levels of the hormones."

Holden got quiet after that. I hoped that my laughing at his Viagra-and-music comment didn't make him feel bad.

"Is everything okay?" I prodded.

"Yeah, sure." He neatened a stack of papers that were already neat. "I was just wondering, have you only ever dated smart guys?"

"Well, I've only ever dated two men, and both happened to be smart. So yeah, I guess so."

"Two men?" Holden's brows pinched together. "You mean you only had two serious relationships? But you must've dated other guys, right?"

I shook my head. "No, I've only dated two men in total."

"Wow." Holden blinked a few times. "So then you've only… you know…with two men?"

"Actually, I only slept with one of them. I went out with the other one for a few months, but I was young, and our relationship never progressed there."

Holden's eyes widened. "So you're going to marry the only guy you've ever fucked?"

When I started to blush, he held his hands up. "I'm sorry. That was crass. I shouldn't have put it that way."

"It's fine." I pointed to my rosy cheeks. "Maybe if I'd had more sexual escapades, I wouldn't turn red every time anyone mentioned the word. I swear if you want me to look like an apple, just say *sex* or make me tell a lie."

"Don't you ever wonder what it would be like? I mean, how do you know if you should pay for the goods if you haven't shopped around?"

"I've actually been wondering that a lot lately." Our eyes met. "In fact, it feels like I *can't stop* wondering about it."

Holden opened his mouth to say something, but then seemed to think better of it and nodded.

I brushed a lock of hair behind my ear. "Can I ask you a personal question?"

"I'll tell you whatever you want to know."

"How often do you…take care of yourself?"

Holden's eyes dipped to my lips before returning to meet mine. "Are you asking me how often I masturbate?"

I nodded.

He shrugged. "It depends. If I'm sexually active, not as often. But if I'm going through a dry spell, maybe every other day or so? I guess it also depends on how frustrated I'm feeling and how active my imagination is." He held my eyes, and his face grew serious. "There have been days when I can't stop imagining what it would be like with a particular person. Those days, I might take three showers."

I swallowed. "Have you ever been in love, Holden?"

He thought about his answer in silence for a moment. "I think so. Once."

"What happened?"

"Nothing." Holden looked down. "She's with someone else."

I nodded again.

"Is it my turn to ask you something now?" he asked.

"Sure."

"If you were in love with someone, and they were with someone else, would you tell them how you felt anyway?"

"I guess that depends. If I thought the person might love me back…" I nodded. "Yeah, maybe I'd tell them. I think you can get over making a fool of yourself, but regret lasts a lifetime."

When I looked up, Holden was staring at me so intensely that it felt like everything else in the room faded away. The two of us were in a narrow hallway where the magnetic pull toward him was extra strong. I had the strongest urge to lean in and take the flesh of his bottom lip between my teeth and tug. Hard.

Catching myself as I actually started to lean forward, I blinked some sense back into my head and sat up straight. "I, um, I really should get my presentation finished. Thank you for the help. I can take it from here."

Holden forced a smile, but I saw sadness lurking in his eyes. "Sure. No problem. I'll head out. Goodnight, Lala."

The next morning, I packed everything I needed for my presentation into three boxes. Hundreds of individual pages had been summarized neatly into a dozen slides, but I liked to bring the source materials in case anyone had questions. When I put the top on the last box, I noticed something sticking out from under the couch, so I pulled it free.

Holden's wallet.

Last night he'd been sitting on the floor with his back against the couch. I definitely needed to return it before I left, but I couldn't help but be nosy and peek inside. Not surprisingly, I found two condoms and a few girls' phone numbers scribbled on napkins, in addition to some credit cards, his license, and a couple of twenties. Just as I was about to close it, a leather crease inside puckered open, and I realized there was a hidden pocket behind one side. Since I'd already been a shitty friend and violated his privacy, I stuck my finger into the slot. The picture I pulled out made my heart hurt.

It was me, Ryan, and Holden on my high school graduation day. I remembered it like yesterday. Ryan had been diagnosed a few weeks before, but no one told me until the week after graduation. They hadn't wanted to ruin my big day since I was class valedictorian.

Pulling the picture closer to examine it, I studied my brother's face, looking for any signs he was sick. But there weren't any visible ones yet. My eyes shifted to Holden. He looked just the way I remembered him back then, which wasn't all that different from now—shaggy hair, crooked smile that made you think he was up to no good, and eyes that made you feel like you were the only woman in the world.

It was odd that Holden had kept that picture. He had to have a million of him and Ryan alone, or better yet, him and all of the guys. I was going to be late to my presentation if I didn't hurry up, so I'd have to mull over that more later. Right now, I needed to drop the wallet off next door and get to work.

Holden answered wearing low-hanging sweats and no shirt.

My eyes immediately found the thin trail of hair that ran up his stomach between his sculpted V muscles. Apparently, that one-minute staring session last night hadn't been nearly enough.

Holden raised a brow with a smirk. "See something you like?"

I rolled my eyes. "Oh my gosh. You're attractive. I looked. Big whoop. I don't have time for this." I grabbed his wallet off the top of the boxes I'd set down on the floor and practically flung it at him. "Here's your wallet. I found it where you were sitting last night. I thought you might need it." I bent and picked up the three boxes and started toward the elevator. "Have a good day," I yelled without turning back. "Gotta run, or I'm going to be late."

"*Whoa*. Hang on." Holden stepped out of his apartment. "How are you getting to work with all that crap? You usually take the train."

"There's no parking near my office. It's actually less walking if I take the train."

"Hang on. I'll drive you. I have the van parked right around the corner."

I was about to argue, but Holden disappeared inside and came back out with keys. He was still pulling a T-shirt over his head when the elevator doors slid open. Once we were inside, he took the boxes from my hands.

"I'm perfectly capable of carrying them," I said.

"I know you are." He shrugged. "But your brother would kick my ass if he saw you like that and me with empty hands. Besides, you might not believe this because you think I'm a manwhore, but I'm a gentleman at heart."

I smiled. "Okay. Thank you."

We made it three quarters of the way to my office with small talk, but then we stopped at a light and Holden looked over. "Thanks for returning my wallet."

"Of course."

"Did you snoop and look inside it?"

"No," I answered curtly. A little *too* curt and *a lot* too quick. Unfortunately, I was a shit liar and felt my face starting to heat under Holden's stare.

Come on, light… Come on, light…change already.

But it didn't happen fast enough. A slow, cocky grin spread across Holden's face and he pointed to mine. "Liar!"

"Oh my God!" I covered my face with both hands. "*Fine, I did.* I snooped, okay? I just couldn't help myself, even though I knew it was wrong."

He shook his head as the light turned green. "Sweet little Lala Ellison, AKA the good one, turns out to be a criminal."

My face was bright red when I took my hands away. "I'm really so sorry, Holden. Can you forgive me?"

He glanced over with a mischievous smile. "Of course I can."

I breathed a sigh of relief. "Thank you. I thought you were going to give me a harder time about it."

Holden put on his blinker as we approached my office. He held up his pointer. "Not so fast. I wasn't finished with my sentence. What I was going to say was, of course I can forgive you, once I get to invade *your* privacy."

"Invade my privacy? What does that entail?"

Holden pulled into a spot in front of my office and shifted the van into park. He held out his right hand. "Let me see your purse. *Tit for tat.* I get to see what you keep in there. Then we'll be even, and I'll forgive you."

"What? No!" No way was I letting him look inside my bag, especially since I hadn't unpacked it from my trip home yet.

But Holden reached over and snatched my purse from my lap. He immediately switched it to his left hand and held it up in the air and out of my reach. I lunged for it, but the damn seatbelt snapped me back into my seat.

"Holden, give it back!"

"Oh? Did you have something private in here? Like the *things in my wallet*?"

In my panic, it took me longer than normal to release the seatbelt. But when I did, I jumped from my seat and grabbed for the purse. Holden was laughing and smiling. I yanked it from his hands, but the strap was still caught around his arm, which caused an unexpected pull back, and my purse flipped upside down, spilling its contents all over…

Including my vibrator.

My.

Vibrator!

I froze.

Holden's eyes flared wide.

And of course, Holden being Holden, he proceeded to reach down and grab it.

"What do we have here, lovely Lala?" He waved it around between us. "Were you using this magic wand while watching porn after I left last night?"

I was pretty sure my face was glowing with fire. Snatching it from his hands, I shoved it back into my purse and opened the van door. "I wasn't watching porn last night! Were *you* watching porn while you jerked off last night? Are you projecting your guilty conscience on me now?"

"No, ma'am. I haven't watched porn lately." Holden's eyes dropped to my lips. "I'm too busy thinking about the one woman I could never have while I jerk off."

There was only one way to respond to that comment. Jumping out, I grabbed my boxes, then the door handle, and…*slam!*

CHAPTER 10

Holden

Thinking about what Lala does with that damn vibrator was the only thing that had been able to get me off lately. Believe me, I *wished* another woman would capture my attention. This forbidden-fruit fixation on Lala wasn't healthy, and it was time I moved on from it; I just didn't know how. The more I tried not to think about her, the more I did.

All this week, I'd once again attempted to put some space between us. But as always, the need to see her eventually wore me down. I'd always convince myself that *this time* it would be innocent. Such as tonight, when I'd decided to knock on her door to see what she was up to and if maybe she wanted to grab a bite to eat.

To my surprise, when she opened the door, she wasn't alone. There was a woman there I'd never met before.

Lala's eyes widened. "Holden."

"Hey." I turned to her friend. "Who's this?"

The dark-haired girl answered before Lala could. "I'm Tia. And Laney *clearly* has been holding out on me."

Lala cleared her throat. "Tia is one of my admins from work and a friend."

"Oh, yeah. Okay." I nodded. "Nice to meet you."

Lala turned to her. "Holden is one of my brother's friends and my next-door neighbor."

"And sometimes I rescue her from broken-down vehicles and locked doors." I winked.

"I might have to fake an accident so you can rescue *me*." Tia laughed.

Well, alright then. This chick was nothing if not forward. She was practically fucking me with her eyes, too.

Meanwhile Lala's face was beet red. Of course, I could've gone easy on her and left right away. But I was sort of getting off on the fact that my being here made her all flustered.

She finally stepped back, allowing me to enter her apartment, and I made myself comfortable, leaning against the arm of the couch. "What are you guys up to this fine Friday evening?"

"Actually," Lala answered, "we're getting ready to go out dancing."

"Oh, nice." I nodded. "You deserve to unwind. You haven't been out with friends—besides me—since you got here, from what I can remember. Right?"

"Well, I don't have too many girlfriends here."

Lala looked really cute, dressed once again in a black leather skirt and her off-the-shoulder Debbie Harry shirt. Her hair was off-the-charts wild too—just the way I liked it. Her friend wore a tight green dress with tall leather boots. They were definitely dressed to go clubbing.

"Where are you guys going?" I asked.

Lala looked over at her friend for guidance. She wasn't the one making the plans.

"Zanzibar," Tia said. "You know it?"

"Yeah. I pretty much know all of the dance clubs."

"You're the drummer, right?" Tia grinned.

"That's correct." I nodded.

"I could tell."

"Because I look homeless or something?"

"No, because you're super hot. Most drummers I know are."

Lala looked ready to crawl out of her skin, so I decided to put her out of her misery.

"Anyway, ladies. I should let you get ready. I hope you have a fun night. Just wanted to check in and say hi, Lala, since it's been a couple of days."

Lala perked up, seeming relieved that I was halfway out the door. "Okeedokee."

But then her friend called after me. "Wait! Why don't you come out with us? The more the merrier!"

I turned. "No, I don't want to interrupt girls' night."

"But it's *not* girls' night." She turned to Lala. "You invited one of the other guys already, didn't you?"

I froze. *Hold up. Say what?* I narrowed my eyes. "Is that right…"

"Uh…" Lala sighed. "Brayden is coming out with us, yeah."

What the fuck? I took a slow breath in to calm myself. Before I got all pissy, it occurred to me that maybe she was trying to set Brayden up with her friend; that was probably the only excuse that wouldn't totally offend me. But still, she could've asked me to hang out, too. She'd specifically chosen not to.

Tia got a phone call and wandered over to the corner of the apartment to talk in private. I took the opportunity to grill Lala.

"So…" I crossed my arms. "Brayden. Since when do you invite him out with you?"

"Okay…" She sighed. "I know it seems weird, especially since I didn't tell you. But Tia had asked me to introduce her to one of my single guy friends. And Brayden was the first person who came to mind."

I decided to mess with her. "That's interesting. Because *I'm* single. Why didn't you want to introduce her to *me*?" I snapped my finger. "Oh, let me guess. You think I'm too much of a manwhore or something? So you chose Brayden?" My eyes seared into hers. "Or…is it something else, Lala?"

What looked like a faint rash started to form on her neck as she lowered her voice. "I don't know why I chose Brayden. And I knew she would want you if she saw you. I just—"

Before we could get into it any further, Tia returned from her phone call. Now that I knew fucking Brayden was going out with them, I decided to take Tia up on her offer.

"You know what?" I flashed an evil grin. "I don't have any plans tonight. If it's not a girls' night, I think I *will* join after all." I turned to Lala. "If you don't mind."

Lala blew out a long breath and shrugged.

A half hour later, it was all aboard the Clusterfuck Express, also known as an Uber SUV Brayden had called to pick us all up. It turned out to be a bigger group than anticipated, since Brayden had also decided to invite Owen, who apparently had a rare night off where he wasn't buried in work. I had to wonder, though, if Owen wanted to come merely to keep an eye on me when it came to Lala. Pretty sure that was it.

Brayden seemed somewhat interested in Tia, asking her some questions about her job and flashing that flirty smile he was known for. But unfortunately, Tia only seemed to have eyes for… me. *Whoops.* Not only had she asked Lala if she could switch seats to be next to me, she kept placing her hand on my knee as she talked. I wasn't one to get uncomfortable from such things, but I felt awkward because I sensed Brayden getting annoyed. He could be competitive sometimes—especially when it came to me stealing his thunder. But you know who was getting even more annoyed? Take one guess. *Yeah.* Lala sat there looking miffed, and her eyes kept landing on Tia's hand whenever she touched me.

Owen was being Owen and seemed disinterested in the entire thing after having forced himself to go out. He certainly wasn't expressing any interest in Tia. He was probably one of the pickiest dudes I knew. He had to be equally as mentally stimulated as he was physically attracted to someone. In the past, I'd been the opposite: it didn't matter to me if a hot girl had marbles. But lately? I could definitely relate to how Owen felt. Brains *and* beauty got me off these days. More specifically, scientists with crazy-curly hair who wore hot-ass thongs and carried vibrators in their purses.

Once we got to the club, the dynamic was weird, to say the least. Tia continued to stick by me, even though I tried my best to seem uninterested. My eyes wandered over the club as she talked my ear off, and I was looking anywhere but at her. This girl just did not take a hint. Clearly, she also couldn't see that she was pissing off her friend. Lala had a permanent look of annoyance on her face.

Tia returned from the bar with a drink—I'd declined her offer to get me one. "Would you want to dance, Holden?"

"No, I'm good," I told her. "Thanks for asking, though."

That was finally the beginning of the end. Tia now started to gravitate away from me—thank fuck—spending more time talking to Lala while scoping out the place for fresh meat. Brayden had already started chatting up some girl he'd met, so he'd given up on Tia a while ago.

When Lala and Tia took off to the bathroom, Owen slipped into the spot next to me.

"I assume someone's getting laid tonight?" he said, raising an eyebrow. "That Tia chick has made no secret of the fact that she wants you."

I tried not to make a face as I responded. "Yeah, well, I'm not interested."

He arched a brow. "Oh yeah? Why *ever* would you not be interested in a hot piece of ass like that?"

"I don't know. You tell me. Why aren't *you* interested in her?"

"Come on, Holden. Cut the shit. You know you don't typically come out and *not* flirt with a zillion women. You haven't so much as looked at anyone because your eyes have been on Lala all night. Once again, you're setting yourself up for trouble."

Brayden suddenly appeared next to us, placing his hand on Owen's shoulder. "Who's in trouble?"

Owen was about to fill Brayden in when Lala and Tia returned from the bathroom, stopping all further conversation on the matter. I wore a scowl on my face for the next several minutes. Owen had once again managed to piss me off, so I decided to take it out on him by asking Lala to dance. That killed two birds with one stone: piss Owen off and get a few minutes to talk to Lala in private, something I hadn't been able to do all night.

"Lala, let's dance." I pulled her gently by the arm to the dance floor. We could barely move to the music amidst the crowd of sweaty people. "I'm sorry," I told her.

"Sorry for what?" she shouted through the noise.

"Sorry for ruining your night. I know my coming out made you uncomfortable. It was a dick move. I got pissed that you invited Brayden and not me. But I should've trusted your judgment on that. You wanted to set him up with your friend and didn't need me around messing that up. I should not have acted like a fucking child about it."

"Pretty sure *I'm* the one acting like the child, because she wants you, and it's pissing me off." She wiped her forehead. "I don't have a right to gatekeep you, Holden, just because you and I have had some awkwardness lately."

"For what it's worth, I wouldn't be interested in her anyway— even if she weren't your friend. She's not my type. And I get why you didn't try to set her up with me. I sure as fuck wouldn't have set *you* up with someone." I clarified, "You know, if you weren't already engaged."

Lala had been carrying her bag with her all night. Right now it acted as a barrier between us as we danced.

I looked down. "Is that a vibrator in your purse, or are you just happy to see me?"

She clutched it tighter. "Very funny."

"I try."

"You *are* funny." She rolled her eyes, swaying her hips a little. "I wish I didn't find you so damn amusing."

I leaned in and spoke into her ear, "I think you find me a little *more* than amusing."

She shook her head slowly. "Admitting my attraction to you was a huge mistake, not to mention completely inappropriate."

"Don't worry. You'll go back to Philly—or worse, California—and all this weird tension between us will be a mere memory. Out of sight, out of mind."

While that was meant to reassure her, the words left a bitter taste in my mouth.

Because they were the truth.

I was just the fuckboy she found tempting, not the guy she'd end up with.

By the end of the night, Tia was sloshed. Owen was even more bored and unimpressed. Brayden had exchanged numbers with that girl he'd been talking to. And me? I was painfully sober. Not sure why, but I felt like if I'd gotten drunk tonight, I might've said or done something *even* more dumb than I already had. So, I'd limited myself to one beer. Lala had one vodka cranberry, followed by a Shirley Temple she had no idea was a Shirley Temple.

We dropped Tia off first to make sure she got home safely. Then the four of us headed back to the building.

Once inside, Brayden went on ahead of the pack to his apartment while Owen seemed to be following me back to mine, and he then decided to linger in front of my place. I knew he was doing it because he wanted to make sure I went to my apartment and not to Lala's, or vice versa. God, he was such a dick sometimes.

But even when Lala had bid us both goodnight and disappeared inside her apartment, Owen still hung around.

"Can I help you?" I asked as he followed me inside my place.

"Just making sure you don't do anything stupid, my friend."

"You don't need to babysit me."

"Not babysitting you. Just looking out for Ryan's little sister."

I opened my fridge to grab a water. "What makes you think I haven't had multiple opportunities to tempt her that I've passed on? You seem to think I can't be trusted when all I've been fucking doing is staying on my best behavior. In fact, being good is nearly killing me."

"I don't believe that you'd pass up an opportunity to go in for the kill if she really weakened to your charms."

He had no freaking clue. I slammed my water bottle on the counter. "Do you have any idea how much restraint I've exhibited, Owen? Let me tell you!" I paused, giving myself one last chance to stop before saying *fuck it*. "I slept in the same goddamn bed as her that night we had to stay in a hotel together. Because *she* insisted I not sleep on the floor. Then sometime after she fell asleep, she unknowingly pushed her ass right against my dick. You know what I did? I fucking moved. Put some space between us. Hardest thing I've ever had to do in my life aside from burying my best friend. So tell me I don't have restraint," I spat. "Tell me!"

I stopped short of telling him about the timed, mutual peep show she and I had done. *Details.* That I *would* take to my grave.

Owen kept blinking, as if trying to process. "You slept in the same bed?"

"That's the part you're stuck on? Did you not hear everything else I just said?"

"Yeah. I heard you, and I still can't believe it. Ultimately, it was your decision to get into that bed, even if it was her suggestion."

"Sue me for wanting to sleep in a warm bed." *With Lala.*

He pointed up at the ceiling. "You do realize Ryan can probably see everything you're doing from wherever he is?"

While that idea made me cringe, I snapped back, "You know what, Owen? If he *could* really see inside my head, he'd know how damn hard I've been trying to do the right thing and control my actions. Feelings? They're not so easy to control. I made a decision not to cross a certain line with her as long as she's engaged. Because of my feelings for her, I've toed the line—I admit it. But I haven't *crossed* it, even though I wanted to a long time ago. You got to give me some credit for that."

Owen just stood there, shaking his head. Then he rubbed his eyes and muttered, "You know what? It's late. I'm going to sleep."

I smirked. "I love shutting you up almost as much as I love proving you wrong. When I get to do both at once? Even better."

"Don't get too confident, jackass." He pointed to his eyes then back at me. "I'm still going to be watching you."

I gave him the finger. "Here's an idea. Why don't you find yourself a woman so you're not constantly up in my business?"

"Find me someone I'm interested in," he said as he opened the door to leave.

"I'll have to go to Mars," I called after him as he headed down the hall. "Because you're the pickiest motherfucker on the face of the Earth."

Feeling restless after he left, I took a shower before going to bed. But I was still wide awake as I sat up against my headboard.

Then Lala sent me a text.

A flash of panic hit as I worried she'd heard our conversation through the wall. But her text was about something else.

Lala: Why do you keep a photo of me, you, and Ryan in your wallet?

Oh. When she'd admitted to going through my wallet, I'd been more concerned with the condoms in there and hadn't even

130

thought about that photo. I could've told her the truth—that I loved her smile in that photo and it made me happy to have two of my favorite people in the same shot. But then I reminded myself of my vow to Owen—that I'd do everything I could not to encourage anything between us while she was engaged. I needed to keep myself in check.

So, I lied.

Holden: I just like the way I look in it, I guess.

The dots moved around as she typed.

Lala: Conceited, aren't we?

Holden: Yup. Sorry. I am who I am. ;-)

After a minute, another text came through.

Lala: Sorry if I made things weird tonight.

Holden: You've always been weird. It's one of the things I love about you.

"Love" about you? *Really, Holden?*

Lala: Speaking of weird... Owen was acting weird tonight.

Great. I was hoping she hadn't picked up on his policing me.

Holden: He's just trying to make sure I don't get you into trouble.

Lala: You've been a Boy Scout, Holden. I'm the problem.

It sucked that she blamed herself when I'd been flirting with her and egging her on this whole time. It'd been a two-way street—with me directing traffic.

Holden: Don't beat yourself up for having a little fun in a new city. You're only young once. And as much as you think you've been "bad," you really haven't.

I couldn't help adding one more thing.

Holden: Believe me, if we ever truly crossed the line, you'd know it.

CHAPTER 11

Lala

"**M**om! Oh my gosh. What are you doing here?"

My mother was the last person I'd expected to find on the other side of my door bright and early on a Saturday morning. Sadly, I felt a twinge of disappointment since I'd thought it might be Holden.

Mom held her arms up. "Surprise! I came to take you shopping."

"Shopping?" My forehead wrinkled. "For what?"

She stepped forward and hugged me. "For wedding dresses!"

Oh.

Ugh. Wedding dresses.

That wasn't exactly what I felt like doing, but I didn't want to make my mom feel bad. Plus, I *should've* been ecstatic to go dress shopping. "Wow. Okay. How…awesome." I waved her inside. "Come in, come in."

My mother clapped her hands. "I got you an appointment at Kleinman's for twelve o'clock today."

"Really?" I blinked a few times. When I'd first gotten engaged, I'd found a few wedding dresses I liked in bridal magazines, and they all seemed to come from Kleinman's in Manhattan. I'd tried to make an appointment, but they were booked solid three months out. "Did you make it a long time ago?"

Mom shook her head. "I signed up to be notified of any last-minute cancelations. Last night I got a text that an appointment had become available today, so here I am."

My mom was the best mother in the world, and I was happy to see her, even if the thought of dress shopping made me a bit queasy right now. I'd probably get over it once I started to try things on. "I can't believe you're here." I smiled. "Thank you so much, Mom."

Two hours later, I was standing on a round modeling pedestal wearing the Vera Wang tulle-bottom dress I'd loved in a magazine. My mother's eyes welled up.

"Oh my God, Laney. You look like a princess."

I stared at my reflection in the mirror. The dress was gorgeous, and it fit me like a glove. Yet something about it didn't feel right.

"It's really beautiful, but I'm not sure it's the one, Mom."

"Really?" She forced a smile. "Well, you need *the one* when you marry *the one*, so we'll just have to keep looking."

I tried on a dozen more dresses after that, with each successive one becoming harder and harder to look at in the mirror. It was causing me so much stress that the rash I often got when I was anxious broke out.

My mother noticed. "Oh honey, your neck is all red."

I covered the skin with my hand. "I think the fabric on that last dress may have irritated it a little. It's fine."

But by the time we left the store, the rash covered my chest, neck, and the upper part of my back. We'd told the saleswoman I was going to think over a few dresses I really liked and would be in touch soon. Then Mom and I went to lunch at a little café down the block. We both ordered chicken Caesar salads and a glass of white wine.

"Is everything okay, sweetheart?" My mom tilted her head. She was so good at reading me. "You seem a little preoccupied today. Sad even."

I shook my head. "I'm sorry. I'm not sad. Maybe a little tired. I went out with my friend Tia last night." I omitted that the guys had joined us. "Also…things have been busy at work. I guess it's weighing on me more than I realized."

Mom was quiet for a long time. "Are you sure you're not having second thoughts about the wedding?"

I stared at my mom, willing myself to tell her she was crazy and *of course* I wasn't having second thoughts. But as I tried to get my jaw to move to speak, tears started trickling down my cheeks.

"Oh no…" My mom scooted her chair closer and took my hand. "Talk to me. What's going on? Are you okay? Did something happen with Warren? Is it the possible move to California?"

I started rambling while fat tears streamed down my face. "I swear, Mom… I didn't want it to happen, but I can't stop thinking about this other guy. I have these fantasies… Warren is the only man I've ever been with. So how can I be sure he's the right one? I mean, I love chicken, and if I had only ever eaten chicken, I'd probably be happy because it's good, you know? But steak is ridiculously delicious, and what if I never tried steak to realize I like it better than chicken? Does that mean the chicken is less good? Or would I spend the rest of my life bored with eating chicken? What if chicken isn't enough for me to eat for the rest of my life?" I felt a little panicked. "Do I need to eat steak, Mom? *Do I?* You'd tell me if I did, right?"

Mom smiled and patted my hand. "I think what you're asking is if it's normal to fantasize about another man. Am I right, sweetheart? Because I like pork better than chicken or beef, so if that's not what you're asking, I think I might be even more confused than you are."

I laughed and swiped at my wet cheeks. "I've been having these dreams about a guy here in New York. Is that normal?"

"Well, I sure hope so, because I've had a thing for George Clooney for years. Your father thinks I like when he wears a tuxedo because it means we're going out somewhere fancy, but really, it's because he reminds me of George." My mom leaned closer and lowered her voice. "This one time, the news covered him going to a White House state dinner of some sort. I recorded the news and watched it a dozen times."

But George Clooney didn't live one thin wall away from my mother…

And George Clooney didn't tell her how perfect her ass is…

And I was pretty certain she hadn't slept in the same bed as him.

"I think some level of fantasy about other men is normal," Mom continued.

Some level? But not twenty-four-seven obsessing, right? "How do you know when it's too much, though?"

"I guess when real feelings become involved. I can stare at Mr. Clooney all day long, but I don't have real feelings for him. There's a difference between playful fantasy in our head and emotional cheating. You can't feel guilty because you have a sexy dream or two about a handsome man. Thoughts are only thoughts, sweetheart. Unless you're considering acting on them, you aren't doing anything wrong."

But I had acted on them, hadn't I? Even if I hadn't technically cheated, I'd run my toe right across the line on more than one occasion—sleeping in a bed with Holden, looking at him practically naked—letting *him* look at *me*. When it came down to it, that was the real reason I'd felt like shit putting on a pure white wedding dress today. It was a stark reminder of the *impure* thoughts I couldn't seem to get out of my head about Holden lately.

"It's normal to have pre-wedding jitters, sweetheart. Really, it is. You shouldn't be so hard on yourself for some innocent fantasies."

The problem was, none of it was innocent. But I didn't want to upset my mom or have her think less of me by telling her the full truth. So I nodded. "Thanks, Mom. I'm sorry if I ruined our shopping trip or put a damper on lunch. You're right. I'm sure it's just pre-wedding jitters."

Luckily, I managed to not cry or break out in additional rashes for the rest of our lunch. But when we got off the elevator, I knew that was about to change.

Holden was pulling his apartment door shut.

My mom knew me so well, and she would be able to read what was going on in my head just from the way I *looked* at Holden. Yet there was no avoiding him. He turned, and Mom's face lit up as she stepped off the elevator.

"Holden Catalano! How are you, honey?" She walked over and engulfed him in a big hug. She held onto his shoulders. "You look wonderful. Then again, you were always a handsome boy. How long has it been?"

Holden's smile was genuine. "It's been too long, Mrs. E. That's how long it's been."

"It must be at least five years now?"

He shook his head. "I'm not sure how that's possible since you look younger than you did last time I saw you."

Mom waved him off, but I could tell she enjoyed the compliment. Holden had that certain je ne sais quoi that charmed women from eight to eighty.

"Where are you running off to?" Mom asked. "I want to hear all about what's going on with you."

Holden pointed his eyes down to the toolbox I hadn't noticed in his hand. "I was just going up to the fourth floor to fix a garbage disposal. There's a set of kids in one of our units who are giving me a taste of what I was probably like at thirteen. Those unruly little brats live to amuse themselves. I wouldn't be surprised if I get up there and a frog jumps out of the disposal."

"Oh my. Well, come in for a glass of wine first. I insist."

Holden's eyes flashed to me for approval. But it didn't matter that I was trying to keep my distance from him if spending a few minutes together made my mom happy. So I smiled and nodded, and the three of us wound up spending the next half hour talking and finishing off a bottle of wine. Holden told Mom about his band and how he spent his days making repairs at the apartment building where he acted as the super, and Mom told him all about a month-long cruise she was planning for when my dad retired next year.

"Oh, that reminds me." Mom pointed toward the bathroom. "Since you're the maintenance man, there's a leak in Laney's shower. It's coming from the faucet. I heard the drip when I was in there earlier, so I took a peek. The tiles underneath are starting to come loose from it, too."

"Mom, we already made Holden late for one repair, and now you want to give him a new job? He's already fixed so much around here, and they're letting me stay for free."

Holden put his hands up. "It's fine. I'd actually rather know when the problem starts, rather than waiting for it to grow into something bigger. A little leaky faucet is easier to fix than retiling an entire shower."

"Well, there's no rush in getting to it," I said.

"I have some time tomorrow. Will you be home?"

I shook my head. "No, I have a lot to do at work, so I probably won't be around much on Sunday."

"Alright. Well, if you don't mind, I'll work on it then. That way I can fix the loose tiles after I fix the leak, and they'll have time to set before you need to get in there again."

"Sure. Whatever works best for you."

Holden nodded and slapped his hands on his thighs. "To-morrow then. But right now, I need to get upstairs before the tenants who *aren't* so easy burn the place down." He stood. "It's really nice to see you, Mrs. E. Tell Mr. E I said hello."

Mom stood. "I will."

I walked Holden to the door, while Mom went into the bathroom.

"It's really good to see her," he said. "I don't remember you mentioning she was coming. Was it a last-minute trip?"

I nodded. "She surprised me this morning. I had no idea until she knocked on the door."

"It's not your birthday, is it? That's in December, right?"

"No, it's not my birthday." I hesitated, but it felt weird not saying more. "She made me an appointment at a bridal-dress store that's hard to get an appointment with. That's where we were coming back from."

Holden's face fell. "Wedding dresses…"

I nodded.

"Did you buy one?"

"No. Nothing felt right."

Holden looked back and forth between my eyes. For a second I thought he was going to say something, but then he looked away. "I gotta run. See you around, Lala."

I shut the door feeling terrible, even though I had no reason to. After trying to collect my thoughts for a moment, I found my mother in the kitchen, opening another bottle of wine.

"More? When did you become a day drinker, Mom? Not that I'm complaining. I never do this."

"I figured you might need another glass while we talk."

My brows dipped together. "Talk about what?"

Mom's back was to me as she pulled the cork out with a loud *pop*! She refilled both our wine glasses before turning and holding one out to me.

She sipped. "While we talk about how long your feelings for Holden have been back, and what you're going to do about the fantasies you've been having about him."

♥

The next morning, I bolted upright in a cold sweat, completely out of breath.

Holy shit. I glanced next to me at the bed. Of course it was empty, but it still took me a couple of seconds to accept that my dream had only been a dream, and I hadn't actually been *riding Holden.*

Oh my. That was the most vivid dream of my life.

The way he'd had my ponytail wrapped around his fist and yanked my head back.

The way he'd topped from the bottom, telling me to ride him harder. Faster. *Take my cock.*

I reached back and touched my ponytail. Goose bumps ran up my arms as I thought about how passionately we'd gone at it. Things were certainly not that intense with Warren—not by a mile. It completely freaked me out that my *fantasy* of being with Holden was better than the real thing with my fiancé, so I got up to splash some cold water on my face. When that didn't work, I decided to take a long shower.

I was still pretty worked up even after drying my hair and getting dressed. But I was determined to get myself in the right headspace. So I made a resolution to focus on the things I *should* be focusing on for the rest of the day, namely my fiancé and my work.

First, I went back to the bridal salon Mom and I had gone to yesterday. I didn't have an appointment, but the salesperson who'd helped us yesterday was there, and she helped me place an order for the dress I'd liked most. After, I needed to go into work for a while, but my head was still not fully where it needed to be, so I went back to the apartment to do something I'd never done before. During the train ride, I'd decided the only way to get Holden out of my head was to *replace him* with Warren. There was absolutely no reason I couldn't get off to my fiancé. In fact, maybe part of the problem was that while I was taking the initiative to spend time with Holden, I hadn't been taking any initiative with Warren. So I walked straight to my bedroom with my cell to my ear, determined to be more creative.

"Hi."

"Hello, my love. This is a nice surprise. I didn't expect to hear from you until tonight."

"Well, I'm sort of…needy…and I thought maybe you could help me take care of that need."

"Oh? What is it that you need?"

I sighed. God, he didn't take a hint too well. "I need…an orgasm, Warren."

"An orgasm?"

"Yes, I was thinking maybe we could…you know, have phone sex."

He was quiet for a few heartbeats too long. "I'm not sure how good at that I'll be. I'm not even very good at Zoom calls for work, Laney. What were you thinking this would entail, because I have a haircut appointment in forty-five minutes."

Oh my God. I was sooo frustrated. "Warren, *fuck your haircut.* I *need* you."

"Okay, okay. You don't have to get so angry about it. Just tell me what you want me to do."

What I want you to do is not *need to be told what to do.* "I don't know…maybe talk dirty to me? I'm going to take off my pants and put my hand in my underwear, and you tell me what you would do to me if we were together."

"Should I remove my trousers as well?"

"*I don't know! Do whatever you think, Warren!*"

"Okay, okay. I'll leave them on."

"Great." I unbuttoned my jeans, pushed them down my legs and stepped out. "I'm going to put you on speaker so I can use both hands."

"Okay."

I hated that he sounded so wary. Nonetheless, I got into bed, hit the speakerphone button and closed my eyes as I slipped my hand into my panties.

"I'm ready. Tell me what you'd do to me if you were here."

"Okay, well, I'd kiss you first."

I ran my fingers up and down my center. "Okay, then what?"

"Then I'd kiss your breasts."

"Okay…"

"Then I guess I'd probably touch you between your legs. Rub you."

Finally. "Go on…"

"Next, I'd insert a digit inside you."

My eyes flashed open. "*A digit*, Warren? Really? Can't you use a sexier word?"

"What would you like me to use?"

"Finger, Warren. *Finger fuck me.*"

"Okay. Well, I'd stick one finger in and move it around a bit. Then I'd add a second one. Before we go any further though, what word would you like me to use for the male genitalia? There are so many choices there."

Grrrr. This was a bad idea. "You know what, Warren. I'm not really in the mood after all. Why don't you get ready for your haircut."

"Are you sure?"

"Yeah. I was just…trying to have a little fun. But I shouldn't have sprung it on you like that."

"Well, if you'd like, I can work on some things I might say to better prepare for next time. Maybe we can schedule a call for one evening this week, so I have time to get ready."

I smiled sadly. "Yeah, sure. Sorry if this was weird."

"I'll call you later?"

"Yep. Have a good day."

After we hung up, I still had pent-up frustration. So rather than get dressed, I slipped my hand back inside my panties, closed my eyes, and began to rub my clit. Sadly, the silence was better than Warren's version of dirty talk. After a few minutes, I found my rhythm, and my mind started to drift back to the hot dream I'd had about Holden last night. Rather than fight it anymore, I pushed my fingers inside myself and let my imagination take over. It felt good. *Really good,* even. *Riding Holden.* Oh yeah. *Harder.* That's it… I was sooo close. Until…

Someone knocked.

And not on my front door.

On my bedroom door!

"Lala? Are you in there?"

Holden.

My eyes flared wide, and I froze.

Oh my freaking God!

Locked in fear, I stayed quiet.

"Lala?" *Knock. Knock.* "Are you in here?"

My heart pounded as I held my breath, waiting for him to walk away.

After thirty seconds of silence, I thought he might've…until the doorknob started to turn.

Oh shit! I jumped up on the bed and dove at the door as it opened. It worked. The door slammed shut. Only Holden's fingers were still inside.

"Fuck!" he screamed.

"Oh my God!" I yanked the door open. "Holden, are you okay?"

His other hand grabbed the fingers that had been stuck in the door. "What the hell, Lala?"

143

"I'm sorry! I wasn't dressed and I…I screwed up."

Holden's fingers were already swelling and turning purple.

"Go put ice on them. I'll be right there."

I frantically dressed and met Holden in the kitchen, where he sat with a bag of frozen broccoli against his hand.

"Do you think they're broken? Should we go to the hospital?"

Holden flexed his fingers with a wince. "They'll be fine. I can move 'em. They're just throbbing."

"I feel awful. I had no idea you were in the apartment."

"I told you I was going to come fix the shower today. You didn't hear my music?"

"I did, but I assumed it was coming through the wall. I hear your music a lot."

My heart continued racing out of control as the last few minutes sank in—though my horror was now less about getting caught and more about what Holden might've heard.

"How long were you here for?" I asked hesitantly.

Holden looked up and our eyes caught. "Are you asking me if I heard your conversation?"

My face heated. "Oh God… This has to be the most embarrassing day of my life."

"I'm sorry I overheard. Once I realized what was going down, I wasn't sure how to handle it. I didn't want to walk out in the middle of it and have you see me and make it even worse. When it got quiet, I tried to sneak out, but then I heard what I thought was crying coming from your room."

I closed my eyes. "I wasn't crying… I was…you know."

Holden nodded. "Yeah, I get that now."

I shook my head and sighed. "You must think I'm such an idiot."

"No, Lala. I don't think you're an idiot at all. I think a woman who's in the mood and tells a man what she wants is one of the sexiest fucking things in the world. Warren, on the other hand, is the biggest idiot I know. For a guy who might be able to cure cancer, he hasn't figured out some basic shit. Like if you don't give your woman what she needs, there's always someone else willing to."

My eyes caught with Holden's again. His were now filled with so much intensity that goose bumps prickled down my arms. It wasn't lost on me that this was the way I'd woken up from my dream, too. It felt like my fantasies and reality were starting to blur. Desire had my lips parting, though thankfully, it also seemed to paralyze me and keep me from jumping into the man's arms.

"Holden…" I whispered.

He swallowed, then stood. "Lock the door behind me. *The top lock*. I can't be trusted."

"Where are you going?"

"To take care of something."

Before I could ask any other questions, Holden stalked toward the door. He slammed it shut behind him and left me sitting with a crush of emotions. I had no idea what to do with myself.

Then my phone rang from the bedroom. Feeling lost, I walked to it and found Holden's name flashing.

"Hello?"

"Did you lock the door?" His voice was deep and throaty.

"Not yet."

"Go do it."

I didn't think it was really necessary, yet I did as he asked anyway. Sliding the chain across the top, I nodded, though he clearly couldn't see me. "It's locked."

"Now put the phone on speaker and go back into your bedroom."

"Why?"

"Just do it, sweetheart."

I walked back to my room on autopilot. "Okay, I'm in here."

"Good. Now take your pants off."

I froze. Was he saying what I thought he was saying? "Holden, I…I'm not sure…"

"Get on the bed, Lala. Get your sexy ass on the damn bed now, or I'm coming over there and we're going to get you off in a very different way."

"But…"

"Quiet. I don't want to hear another word. Unless you're telling me yes or moaning my name, not another word, babe."

Oh, God. Why did I like the way he was talking to me so much?

"Now get your ass on the bed, and tell me you're there by saying yes."

I couldn't believe I was doing this, even as I climbed onto the bed. My voice was barely a whisper. "Yes."

"Now slip your hand into those pretty little panties I know you have on."

I did.

"Put your middle finger over that swollen bud of yours." Holden groaned. "God, you're so fucking sexy. I want to lick your pussy so bad. You're going to rub yourself while I tell you everything I would do to you if I ever had the chance."

I closed my eyes and started to rub my clit.

"I'm going to tie you up and lick you until you're begging for my cock."

A shiver ran through me. *God, I'll beg now if you'll give it to me.*

"I bet your pussy is so hot and tight. I want to lick you until you're trembling and make you come all over my face. I'm going to swallow every last drop of your sweetness."

Oh fuck. I parted my flesh and began to shamelessly finger myself.

"When you're good and wet, I'll still keep you tied up. I'll climb up your body and feed you my cock. I'm going to hold your face between my hands and not give you any choice in the way you take it, fucking your mouth and your throat like I own them. You'll gag a little, but you'll love every minute of it."

My fingers moved in and out faster, and my breath seemed to chase their speed. I didn't say a word, yet Holden seemed to know exactly where I was.

"That's it. *Faster.*" His voice was so gravelly and strained. "Pretend it's my cock, baby. I'm inside you, and you're so tight and wet. You're squeezing me like a vise, and I can barely hold on. I'm going to explode and fill that beautiful pussy with my hot cum."

My orgasm brewed like a storm, everything swirling around and sucking me into the vortex where I had no control over anything.

"Come, sweetheart. Give it all to me."

I climaxed almost violently, my body writhing on the bed as I moaned. It was the single best orgasm I'd ever had, and I panted to catch my breath. For a minute, I almost forgot I wasn't alone.

"Holden…" I whispered.

He took a few seconds to respond. "Yeah, babe?"

"Thank you."

I heard the smile in his voice. "Anytime, beautiful. I'm going to hang up now. Stay in bed and relax for a while, okay?"

"Okay."

After we disconnected, I expected the reality of what I'd just done to seep in. I'd just let another man get me off, so guilt would surely consume my thoughts. Yet the only thing I could think was…

If phone sex was that good with Holden, *holy shit…*what would the real thing be like?

❤CHAPTER 12

Lala

"**W**hen you're good and wet, I'll still keep you tied up. I'll climb up your body and feed you my cock."

Holden's words had haunted me for two days straight. I couldn't even count the amount of times I'd replayed them.

"Come, sweetheart. Give it all to me."

We hadn't spoken since, and I was all sorts of messed up inside, my body in constant arousal.

As I stood at my bathroom mirror, blow-drying my hair, I felt like I was going crazy, once again replaying everything. I'd go from being horrified to smiling uncontrollably about it.

You know who I felt like right now? Diane Lane in that movie *Unfaithful*. Ironically, I'd watched that once with Warren. There was a scene in the film where Diane's character was on a train, heading home to her family in the suburbs after having amazing sex with the French artist she was having an affair with in New York City. She was manically laughing and giddy while somehow also overwrought with guilt and looking like she was about to cry. She deserved an Oscar for that scene. While I was watching, I remember thinking: "How could she do that to her family—no matter how good the sex with the artist was?"

I'd never imagined that there would come a time in my life when I could relate.

You didn't have sex with him, Lala. This is nothing like that movie.

You're okay.

Holden never even touched you.

These were the kinds of neutralizing thoughts I'd use to attempt to feel less guilty, only to be immediately followed by other, less-forgiving thoughts.

Who are you kidding?

You're a horrible person.

I needed to talk to someone rational before I exploded.

Thankfully, I had dinner plans with Billie Lennon tonight, and she was the unlucky person I was going to open up to about all of this. *Poor, unsuspecting Billie.* Colby's tattoo-artist wife was really cool and someone I felt like I could talk to, although I still wasn't sure exactly how much I should divulge.

As I walked to the restaurant to meet her, I started to feel anxious, my palms growing sweaty. I didn't want her to think I was a horrible person—because that's exactly what I thought of myself.

Billie had already gotten a table at the Mexican restaurant a couple of blocks down from our building. She waved to me from a corner of the dimly lit place as faint mariachi music played on the overhead. Billie was stunning with her long black hair and vibrant body art cascading down her arm. It was hard not to stare at her because she was so beautiful.

"Sorry I'm late," I said as I slipped into my seat.

"No worries. I'm enjoying the quiet. It's not every day I get a girls' night."

"Yeah," I breathed. "I really needed this night out, too. You have no idea."

She tilted her head. "Everything okay?"

I licked my lips. "Um…"

"You look a little frazzled."

I shook my head. "No. I'm good."

"Really? Because as dark as it is in here, I can see that your neck is all red."

"I'll fill you in once I've had a drink."

"Okay." She flashed a sympathetic smile.

I opened the menu. "Anyway, I'm so glad we could do this. It was long overdue."

Billie grinned. "So many times people say they're gonna get together for lunch or whatever and never follow through—it's all talk. I hate that bullshit. I appreciate a girl who walks the walk, so I was glad when you texted me."

I hoped she wasn't disappointed when she figured out that I had an ulterior motive and needed to unload on her. I took a long sip of my water as I perused the menu. "What's good here?"

"I love the chicken taquitos. Colby's favorite is the chimichanga."

"Both of those sound great," I said, though my nerves had made me not at all hungry.

A waitress appeared. "Hello, ladies. Can I start you off with something to drink?"

"Do you have vodka cranberries?" I asked.

"Sure, we can make that for you." She turned to Billie. "And you?"

Billie held her palm out. "Oh, just water for me."

The waitress nodded. "Got it."

After she left, I said, "Well, now I feel stupid drinking if you're not having anything."

"Oh, believe me. I would partake if I could."

It took me a few seconds to notice the look on her face, like she was waiting for me to figure it out.

"Oh my God." I covered my mouth. "Are you…pregnant?"

Billie nodded, unleashing a huge smile.

"No way!" I stood up from my seat and pulled her into a hug. "I am so freaking happy for you guys!"

"Thank you!"

I returned to my seat and leaned in. "Tell me everything. When did you find out?"

Billie clasped her hands together. "So, first off, you're the only one from the crew who knows right now. Colby and I are planning a get together to announce it to the guys and Saylor at the same time. I'm just telling you right now because I need to tell someone. I'm going crazy keeping it inside."

Damn, could I relate to that feeling. "Wow. I'm super honored that you're trusting me with this. How far along are you?"

"Two months. So, we're not out of the woods yet. They say three months is a safer time to start announcing it."

"Have you been sick at all?"

"Surprisingly, no. I haven't gotten morning sickness. It would suck if I had to work on clients like that, so I'm grateful. But the one bummer is that coffee now turns me off, so I haven't been drinking it. I used to love my cup in the morning."

"Yeah, I've heard you can get aversions to certain things."

Billie was always gorgeous, but she was absolutely glowing right now.

"I'm so excited, Lala. I never expected it, you know? A biological child wasn't something I had to have because Saylor is truly my daughter. And believe me, she's more than enough. For a while there, I wasn't even sure I *could* get pregnant because we hadn't been using anything in forever and nothing happened. But then one day, I just felt different. Not bad…just different. And I had a feeling. So I took a test, and there it was."

"Are you gonna find out the sex?"

Even the word *sex* coming out of my mouth brought a fleeting wave of guilt.

"Actually, we've been talking about keeping it a surprise."

"Really." I moved some ice around with my straw. "Gosh, I don't know if I could be so patient."

"I think not knowing makes it so much more exciting."

"Well, I'm very happy for you and Colby."

"A baby might not be that far off into the future for you," she said. "Do you want kids?"

My stomach churned. "Oh, yes. I've always wanted kids."

"Is that something you and Warren want to get going on soon after you're married, or do you think you'll wait?"

My drink arrived before I could answer. *Thank God.* I took a long gulp as Billie watched me. Then I started fidgeting in my seat.

"What's going on with you, Lala? You don't seem like yourself today."

That was my cue.

"I'm not myself, Billie. I don't even recognize myself anymore." I took another sip and when my straw made a slurping sound, I realized I'd already finished the damn thing.

She looked down at my empty glass. "Whoa. Okay. Take a deep breath. Then tell me everything."

"I feel horrible bringing this up after the news you just gave me. This dinner should be about you."

"Fuck that, Lala. This baby will be incubating inside me for another seven months. There's plenty of time to talk about me. Whatever is going on is eating away at you. You need to let it out now."

I nodded. "When you mentioned Warren just now, and what I want in the future, the most incredible guilt came over me. I should be thinking about my upcoming marriage and babies. I should be yearning for all of that. And I do—I want that stable kind of life. But my mind has been somewhere else completely lately. I have these…" I paused. "Desires that I can't seem to shake."

She crossed her arms and nodded. "It's Holden, isn't it?"

Shocked by her perceptiveness, I blinked. "How did you know?"

"The last time you guys were at our apartment, I got a vibe. The way he jumped to leave with you, the way you guys danced at our wedding. Don't think I didn't catch that. There's a vibe for sure." She raised her brow. "It's not exactly new, though, is it?"

I looked away. "Holden and I have a connection that goes way back. We used to have these conversations when no one else was around—that Ryan didn't even know about. It was all very innocent then, though. Whatever is happening now…doesn't feel so innocent."

"What are we talking about here, Lala? I need you to be upfront with me. No bullshit." She sighed. "If all this is just flirting, I wouldn't beat yourself up over it. I mean—"

"We had phone sex," I blurted before sucking down the remnants of my basically empty glass.

Slurp. Slurp. Slurp.

Billie's eyes widened, and she lifted her hand to the waitress. "She's gonna need another drink."

I blew out a long, shaky breath. "Not so innocent, huh?"

"Okay. Back up. How did that happen?"

I proceeded to tell Billie everything that'd happened in the month since I'd arrived in New York, from going to Holden's shows, to the hotel-room stay, to the phone sex. She listened intently with a look of complete nonjudgment, which I appreciated more than she could know.

"Okay…" she said. "So while not *innocent* by any means, when you originally said you had phone sex, I assumed it had been a little more interactive. No offense, but I couldn't even picture you doing that, for some reason." She laughed. "Not that the one-sided stuff you participated in was right. But you literally just listened to something and got off. Sort of like porn. So, it's not as bad as it could be."

"It was bad enough."

"Let me ask you something, though. Is this attraction to Holden *more* than just sexual?"

The woman came by to take our order, which gave me a minute to think about Billie's question. I chose the beef tacos while Billie ordered taquitos.

After the waitress left, I returned to Billie's question. "So… like I said before, he and I have always had a connection. I don't think these feelings would be messing me up so much if they were purely sexual. Holden is not what anyone in their right mind would consider boyfriend material, but he does have some really good qualities. He's incredibly down-to-earth, wears his heart on his sleeve, and would do just about anything for anyone. I never feel judged by him. I feel like I could tell him anything."

Billie leaned in. "I'm gonna be straight with you, Lala. I don't know how to feel about this. On one hand, I know Holden's reputation and history would seem to make him a bad partner. On the other hand, I'm a believer that everyone has to grow up sometime. Maybe he does have the capacity to change. I mean, my husband was apparently just as big a playboy as Holden at one time. He's not anymore—otherwise he'd be dead." She chuckled. "I guess what I'm saying is, if you have true feelings for Holden, maybe you need to consider pausing your plans with Warren."

I swallowed. "Cancel the wedding, you mean?"

"I hate to say it, but yeah. I'm not saying break up with him, even. But for fuck's sake, sort this shit out before you end up marrying the man."

"Not sure how I end our engagement and keep the relationship alive, though. It's either break up or don't."

"Do you love him?"

"Who?"

Billie's mouth slowly opened. "Oh my God...you had to think about *who* I was referring to? Think about *that*, Lala." She shook her head. "I was talking about Warren. But in your mind, you were also considering whether you loved Holden."

Jesus. I rubbed my eyes. "I do love Warren. But I don't know what that means anymore. I care about him deeply. Is that really enough? I think the scariest part is that I don't know whether all of this is a phase. My biggest fear is letting go of someone who will truly make a great partner because of a fire inside of me that could eventually burn out. Or worse, it destroys me. What happens then?"

"You might be alone. That's the truth. I'm not gonna sugar-coat it. But life is about taking chances, Lala. The safe route isn't always the best. What if you missed out on something mind-blowing because you weren't willing to risk losing everything? I get that Warren is safe and you love him on some level. But as someone watching from the outside? It's clear to me that you're looking for more."

The room felt like it was swaying. "Yeah," I muttered.

"Whether that *more* comes from Holden or not, I can't be sure. I also don't want to put all of my faith in him because I don't know that I can do that, either. I would *love* to believe he could change, though." She smacked the table. "Do me a favor. Don't waste any more time beating yourself up over what already happened. Just vow to do better. Make wise decisions that won't put you further into a state of guilt. That doesn't mean taking the safe way out, either, Lala." She leaned in and whispered, "If you want to fuck Holden, do it. But handle things with Warren first. Tell him you need space to sort things out. Make a clear decision one way or the other. Because it's this in-between shit that's driving you mad."

"You're right," I murmured, feeling tears form at the thought of hurting Warren.

"I'm not telling you anything you don't already know, babe."

I nodded. "I know you and Colby probably share everything. But if you could not tell him about this conversation, I would appreciate it."

"He doesn't need to know about this. I won't say anything. But don't be surprised if Holden eventually clues him in. Holden has a pretty big mouth."

The thought of Colby finding out what Holden and I had done the other night made my stomach sick. I also didn't want the guys giving Holden hell for anything because it was just as much my fault.

It felt good to bounce all this off of Billie, even if she spoke some harsh truths. I certainly had a lot to think about.

Once our food arrived, we managed to keep the rest of the evening light. After our meal, Billie went ahead of me back to the building because I needed to stop at the pharmacy for a few things on the way home.

During the walk back, my phone lit up with a text from Warren.

Warren: Are you alone?

Laney: I'm walking home from dinner.

Warren: I have no pants on.

Laney: Oh?

Then it hit me what he was trying to do. Before I could respond, he wrote back.

Warren: I was hoping you'd want to duck.

Warren: Duck.

Warren: Duck.

Warren: Damn autocorrect!

Warren: Fuck! You know, do it virtually. Over the phone. Tonight. I felt bad about how the other attempt went.

My sweet boyfriend. Overcome with emotion, I stopped in the middle of the sidewalk and closed my eyes. I couldn't do this anymore. It needed to stop.

My renewed determination to avoid Holden ended the following evening when my smoke alarm started beeping randomly. It reminded me of what had happened with the carbon monoxide detector when I'd first stayed here. The battery probably needed to be replaced, and I didn't have one. I didn't want to have to call him, but this was going to drive me absolutely bonkers and keep me awake if I didn't. So, I finally gave in and texted Holden.

My heart thundered against my chest when the knock on the door came.

I opened. "Hi."

"Hey." He smiled. "I've got the battery. Should only take me a few."

"Great." I moved aside to let him in, instantly buzzed by his musky scent.

The tension in the air was thick as I stood watching him loosen the detector from the ceiling. Neither of us said a word, which was certainly odd.

When he finished, he turned to me. "Anything else you need?"

I cleared my throat. "No. Thank you."

He stared at me for a few moments. "Is this how it's going to go down now? You not saying anything to me while you turn red?"

I let out what felt like all the air in my body. "Even hearing your voice now makes me think about it, Holden."

"I'm not gonna lie, Lala. I haven't been able to stop thinking about it, either."

"We took things too far," I said.

He looked down at his shoes a moment. "I'm sorry."

"Don't apologize. You didn't force me to do anything. I wanted it."

Holden groaned and ran his hand through his thick hair. "No one but us will ever know about it, okay? Choose to give yourself a break. I was helping you get a little relief. That's all it was." He paused. "We're still friends. Right? I don't want to lose you because of some impulsive decision I made." He sighed. "I promise I won't pull anything like that again." He smirked. "I mean, unless *you* happen to call me some night after midnight." He winked. When I didn't laugh, he frowned. "I'm kidding, Lala. Look…my intent was to make you feel good. That was it. You deserve that."

I cocked my head. "What about you?"

"What *about* me?"

"This whole dance we're doing? You act like it's all about me. But it's messing with your mind, too."

"I'm not going to deny that."

"Did you get off too…the other night?" I asked.

His eyes bore into mine. "You're gonna have to be more specific."

"Not sure how to phrase it any better."

"Are you asking if I came *while* I was getting you off?"

I nodded.

"I know you, Lala. You're asking me that so you can feel *more* guilty if I tell you I did it along with you, right?" He exhaled. "I was turned on. You know that. But I was focused on you, not me." He muttered, "I mean, I did jerk off after we hung up. But…" He shook his head. "Again…*you* didn't do anything wrong. We didn't even touch. It is what it is. And I *do* take the fall for it. Even though you say it takes two. This one's on me. And I'm telling you, it *won't* happen again."

"Okay," I whispered, feeling no less unsettled.

Silence filled the air again. "Let's change the subject," he said after a moment. "How was your mom's visit? I mean, besides the part I was there for."

"You want to know the truth?"

"Yeah."

"It was a little weird. Not only did I find out that my mother sometimes day drinks, which is kind of cool, but she was definitely on to the vibe between you and me. That was unsettling."

"Shit," he muttered and looked away. "That whole wedding-dress thing. It made you getting married feel very real."

"Yeah, you're telling me."

"I know it may not always seem like it, but I want the best for you, Lala. I swear, I'm not trying to mess up your life." His eyes were sincere.

"I feel like you have just as much control as I do lately, Holden. And that's really not that much."

"You'd be surprised how much control I have, sweetheart. It's hanging on by a thread sometimes, but I have control. There's a lot I've wanted to say and do that I haven't." He shook his head. "Look, I'm going to back off, okay? This is your life. It's not a game. And I'm not gonna make it complicated for you anymore." We stood in silence again before he simply said, "I'd better go."

Then Holden stormed off.

I lay in bed that night feeling empty, like I was at a crossroads. I could take the safe direction with Warren. In my head, the Warren road was perfectly paved and tree-lined, with classical music playing and the sound of children's laughter in the distance. It was peaceful and safe. Then there was the Holden road: bumpy with cobblestones and flashy lights, rock music—plus lots of sex. That road made my heart race. And there was a big sign at the entrance that read: *Enter at your own risk.*

CHAPTER 13

Lala

Twenty-four long hours passed, and I hadn't seen or heard from Holden. Even though I couldn't seem to stop my mind from visiting him, I'd managed to keep a physical distance. Since my well-behaved streak needed all the help it could get as of late, I decided to stop downstairs and ask Owen for the ride I was going to need later, rather than knocking next door.

He opened with his toothbrush in his mouth. "What's up, Lala? Come on in," he mumbled through foam and stepped aside for me to enter, holding up one finger. "Just give me a second to rinse."

"Sure. Take your time." I walked a few steps into the apartment and froze, finding that Owen wasn't alone. None other than Holden leaned against the kitchen counter. "Uh...what are you doing here?" I asked.

He lifted a coffee mug to his mouth. "Owen has a fancy new cappuccino maker. He needed a ride this morning, so I traded him the ride for *being my bitch*, which included making me this deliciousness and avocado toast."

Owen walked back in the room. "Sorry about that. What's going on, Lala?"

Ugh. This sucked. I knew Holden wasn't going to be happy that I'd come to ask Owen for a ride instead of him. And it also seemed Owen wasn't going to be able to help. "Uh, I was hoping maybe you could pick me up from the PATH train later?"

Through my peripheral vision, I saw Holden frown. "The PATH? You going to Jersey?"

I nodded. "Today is the first day of interviews at one of the nursing homes where the participants in my research study live. The oil light in my car is on, so I don't want to drive that far without getting it checked. I'm also overdue for an oil change. Tia is picking me up so we can drive together, but she's visiting her mom who lives in Jersey after. So I'm going to take the PATH home. But I'll have a bunch of boxes on the way back, so the subway will be kind of difficult to navigate."

"Makes sense you'd ask *Owen* to pick you up," Holden said evenly. "You know, with your arms full of boxes and all."

"Right. Well, I figured the PATH isn't too far from his office…"

"Sorry, Lala," Owen said. "Holden's actually dropping me off at the airport in a little while. I have to go up to Boston on business for the night."

"Oh." I forced a smile. "No biggie. I'm sure I can just grab an Uber or something."

Holden lifted his mug to his mouth. "Or I can pick you up."

"No, it's fine." I waved him off. "I don't want to impose any more than I already have. I was only asking Owen since it was near his office, and I know sometimes he drives because he picks up clients."

"Where in Jersey is the nursing home?"

"Hoboken."

"Well, you're in luck. I've been putting off going to The Heights, which is right next to Hoboken. I have some equipment the band borrowed from a friend that I need to return. I can do that this afternoon and then swing by and pick you up right from the nursing home. That way you don't have to take the PATH or the subway."

"Oh, no. I don't want to put you out."

Holden's jaw flexed. "I insist. Text me the address, and I'll be there."

Damn it. This was exactly the reason I'd come to Owen and not Holden. Now I was already excited for the day to end, just because he'd be picking me up. The man was like kryptonite. I forced a smile. "Thanks, Holden."

Owen put his coffee mug in the sink and thumbed back toward his bedroom. "I gotta finish packing. Sorry I couldn't help out." He narrowed his eyes at Holden. "But I'm sure Holden will be on his best behavior when he picks you up."

Holden glared back at his friend. "Aren't I always?"

Owen sighed. "Have a good day, Lala."

"You, too, Owen."

Left alone with Holden, I motioned toward the door. "I should be running too."

He nodded. "Don't forget to text me that address."

"I won't."

"Oh, and Lala?"

"Yes?"

Holden smiled. "Owen's office is *nowhere near* a PATH stop. So if you're going to pretend you're asking one of the guys because it's more convenient for them and *not* because you're trying to avoid me, you should probably look at a train map first."

"Don't you worry about that." Theodore Mills waved me off as I straightened the covers on his bed after helping him up. "My Clara does that. She hides a piece of chocolate every day while making up the bed and pretends it wasn't her. Been doing it since we were sixteen."

My heart warmed. "Wow, since you were sixteen?" I walked around the bed and offered my arm. "The nurse said it's either me or the walker. You don't want me to get in trouble on my first day here, do you?"

Theo made a face, but took the arm I held out nonetheless. We walked side by side, at a snail's pace, to one of the lounges and sat down on the couch. Today had been about assessing the participants' memories, so I'd sat in on some standard tests the neurologist had given each patient—things like being asked to remember a few random words, answering a series of questions for five minutes, and then having to repeat the initial words at the end. But standardized tests didn't always tell the full story, so I wanted to get to know the subjects a bit more.

"How did you and Clara meet?"

Theo smiled. "We met at a Halloween party. She was dressed as Marilyn Monroe, and I was Joe DiMaggio."

"Wow. Sounds like it was meant to be from the start."

"I was smitten the moment she walked in. I'd had my eye on her all night, but she was talking to a vampire. At one point, she took off her shoes. So when she wasn't looking, I picked one up and held onto it until she was getting ready to leave. I knew she'd have to find it before she went home, and I didn't want to miss a chance at meeting her, even if it was only to give her back her shoe."

I laughed. "Oh my gosh. That's so sweet."

"When she came looking for it, I knelt down and slipped the shoe onto her foot. She said she felt a little like Cinderella, so I suggested that's what we come dressed as the next year—Prince Charming and Cinderella—since they found their happily ever after and Marilyn and Joe got divorced."

"How old were you guys when you got married?"

This was the first time today Theo hadn't had the answer on the tip of his tongue. His face wrinkled as he tried to remember.

Eventually he just shook his head. "When I walked her home that night, I told her my favorite candies were Now and Laters—they made them in a factory in Brooklyn, not too far from where I grew up. The next day when I put on the jacket I'd worn the night before, I found a few in my pocket. My Clara had slipped them in without my knowing. I have a sweet tooth, and she's been hiding candies ever since."

Forget Warren and Holden, Theodore Mills might be the man who won my heart. I'd been spending ten or fifteen minutes with each patient today, but I sat and listened to story after story about Theo's life. There was something so sweet about how he never referred to his wife as Clara—it was always *my* Clara. At one point, we were both laughing when a woman approached. She smiled warmly.

"It's good to see my man can still charm the young ladies."

"He most certainly can." I smiled and stood. "Your husband has shared so many amazing stories. I'm glad I got to meet you today. I'm Laney Ellison. I run the research study your husband is participating in. You must be Clara."

The woman's smile wilted. "Mary, actually."

"Oh. I'm so sorry. I thought you were Mrs. Mills, Theodore's wife."

"I am Theo's wife. He sometimes confuses my name with someone else from his past." She paused. "His first love was Clara."

Oh, Jesus. Where was a giant sinkhole when you needed it? Right about now, I wanted the Earth to open up and swallow me. I felt like a complete jerk.

The nurse who had drawn everyone's blood today walked in. "Theodore, it's time for your meds. You want me to bring them in here?"

Mrs. Mills, whose name was apparently *Mary*, looked down at her husband. "Do you want to rest for a little while before you have dinner?"

He nodded. "Yeah, that sounds good. Okay."

The nurse came over to help Theodore up.

"Thank you for today," I said. "It was a pleasure meeting you. I'll see you again soon."

"You got him, Patti?" Mrs. Mills asked. "I'd like to stay and speak to Ms. Ellison for a few minutes, if that's okay?"

"Sure, take your time," the nurse said.

Once we were alone, I closed my eyes. "I am *so sorry* for calling you the wrong name."

She smiled. "It's fine. No big deal at all. He calls me Clara quite a bit lately." She motioned to the couch. "Why don't we sit for a few minutes? I can fill you in on some of the things that are going on with Theo."

"Sure, that would be great."

Once we were seated, Mary sighed. "Theo and Clara met sixty years ago, when they were just sixteen. She was the love of his life back then, but eighteen months into their courtship, Clara's father lost his job, and they had to move two-thousand miles away. They wrote letters back and forth for several years after that and had planned to run away together when they were both twenty-one. Theo and I met in college and had become good friends. Well, at least he considered me a good friend. I had a giant crush on the man." She smiled reflectively. "He was always a charmer. Anyway, one night we were at a party. We both had a little too much to drink, and one thing led to another. I wound up pregnant. I knew Theodore was in love with Clara, but he insisted that he loved me, too, and we needed to get married. He's a good man. And he's been a good father and husband for the last fifty-five years, but his torch for Clara never really extinguished. My husband's mind is going. Some days he can't remember me, but he never forgets his Clara."

I had no idea what to say, but I hated that I'd dredged all of this up for her. "I'm so sorry."

She squeezed my hand. "There's no need to be sorry. I'm not telling you to make you feel bad. I thought it was important for you to know how his mind works and what state he's in. It's easy to think a lot of these people in here are of sound mind when you talk to them, and sometimes they are. But it's often difficult to ascertain when their mind isn't as sharp as you might think."

I nodded. "I appreciate you letting me know. You're right. I had no idea Theo and I were talking about someone from so long ago in his past. And properly measuring the stage of his disease is key to obtaining the right results in my study."

Mary smiled. "Well, next time you visit, if he talks about Clara again, he might actually mean current times. I've invited Clara to come visit Theo. I want him to be happy while he can still remember how to be happy, so I thought the two of them might like to spend some time reminiscing."

"Wow." I shook my head. "That's...very generous of you."

"It's the least I can do after the many years of generosity Theo has given me." Her eyes welled up. "Sometimes I feel like I robbed him of something irreplaceable. I assumed their connection had been extinguished long ago. But this disease has taught me a lot about love. True love doesn't extinguish when people are separated. True love is when people are separated and your feelings never extinguish." She wiped her cheeks and stood. "I better go make sure Theo isn't giving the nurse a hard time about taking his meds. It was lovely to meet you, Ms. Ellison, and I wish you the best of luck in your research. God knows we need a cure for this terrible disease."

"Thank you, and please call me Laney. It was very nice to meet both you and your husband."

After that, my mood could best be described as melancholy for the rest of the day. I couldn't stop thinking about whether maybe Holden was my Clara. It sounded like Theo and Mary had had a wonderful life together, but there was something tragic about their story, too. I knew I could be happy with Warren. We'd live a very pleasant life together. But was that enough to wipe away the

166

lingering questions about my feelings toward Holden? Or would I still be thinking about *what might've been* when I was Theo's age? It was a lot to consider, and it weighed heavy in my heart for the rest of the afternoon—at least until Holden arrived. He strolled in and smiled, and my pathetic heavy heart took off in a gallop.

"Hey. You didn't have to come in," I said. "I didn't want to make you park."

He shrugged. "You said you were going to have boxes, so I figured I'd help carry them."

"Thank you."

I wound up having eight boxes filled with patient files and notes. So even taking the PATH train would have been difficult, let alone the subway. Holden and I loaded them into the band's van and got situated in the front.

"Thanks again for picking me up."

"No problem." He had his hand on the key in the ignition, but then he stopped and shifted in his seat. "Talk to me before we get on the road. Why did you really go to Owen for a ride instead of me?"

I looked down. "I've just been asking you for a lot. I'm like the pain-in-the-butt little sister you never had."

When I didn't look up, Holden reached over and put two fingers under my chin. He lifted until our eyes met. "Bullshit. Look at me and tell me you aren't avoiding me because of what happened between us the other night on the phone."

When I couldn't, Holden blew out a jagged breath. He hung his head. "Fuck. I royally screwed up."

"We've already talked about this, Holden. It's not all on you. I could have hung up. Besides, you're the one who's single."

He rubbed the back of his neck. "I don't want to lose you, Lala. I care about you. A lot."

"You won't."

He caught my eyes again. "It feels that way. You can't even come to me for a damn ride home."

"I'm sorry. Me not coming to you is more about the stuff going on in my head. It doesn't have to do with our friendship. Things will go back to normal once I'm not so jumbled. I promise."

Holden's shoulders slumped. "Okay."

He started the van, and we headed back to the City, mostly making small talk. Holden was quieter than he'd ever been and seemed lost in thought. I felt bad about the distance between us, but I decided it was probably a good thing at this point.

When we arrived at the apartment building, Holden double parked and helped me carry up the boxes. After, he said a clipped goodbye, mumbling about how he needed to move the van, but I had a feeling it was more than that.

Hours later, I tried to fall asleep, but my mind wasn't having it. So I got out of bed, poured myself a glass of wine, and decided to get some fresh air out on the fire escape. But when I climbed through the window, I realized I wasn't alone.

"Oh!" I froze. "Sorry. I didn't realize you were out here. I couldn't sleep, so I thought I'd get some air and have a glass of wine."

Holden held up a bottle. "Same."

"Are you…just drinking it straight from there?"

He took a big swig and looked out over the City. "Yep."

His tone wasn't exactly welcoming. "I'll leave you alone then?"

"Why would you do that when I haven't left *you* alone since the minute you arrived in town, Lala…*Fa la la la la, la la la la*." He sang that last part to the tune of "Deck the Halls."

My brows pulled together. "How much of that bottle have you had?"

He brought the top of the bottle to his eye and peered inside. "Enough that I don't think I can share."

I laughed. "It's okay. I poured my own glass. But are you sure you want company?"

"I'd love your company, Laney Jane Ellison."

I sat down. "Uh-oh. You're calling me by my full name. I must be in trouble."

Holden shook his head. "I think I'm the one in trouble. I've been a bad boy. A very, very bad boy."

"What are you talking about?"

He wagged a finger at me. "Do you know how long it's been since I've been with a woman?"

Before I could even answer, he pointed to me.

"*Wrong!* Longer than that."

I chuckled. "Dry spell, huh?"

He pointed to his crotch. "He's lost interest in other women."

Other women? Holden was at least a little drunk, but it sounded like he was saying the only woman he had an interest in was *me*.

"How come?"

"How come my dick's lost interest? Because he's stubborn. He always has been." Holden looked up at me. "He wants you more than you can imagine. But don't worry…" He tapped his pointer to his temple. "I've got control of him now. For a while there, things were touch and go about who was steering the ship. But not anymore."

"What do you mean?"

"I made him a date."

I felt panicked. "What?"

"He needs a distraction. Kayla Weathers is one with a capital D." He snort-laughed. "And she likes the D, *a lot*."

My insides were in turmoil. It felt like I'd drunk sour milk and wasn't sure how things were going to turn out in the near future. The thought of Holden with another woman was crushing, though I knew I had no right to feel like that. I was freaking engaged, after all.

"I'm sorry I wasn't a better friend," Holden eventually whispered.

"What are you talking about? You've been such a good friend. You've driven me all over the place, fixed everything in my apartment, helped me with my car a half-dozen times…"

Holden shook his head. "A better friend would have kept his distance."

"I've been just as culpable. You said you want me more than I could imagine. Well, you're not the only one with desires, Holden."

He smiled sadly. "I know. Desire can be a fucked-up thing. But whatever is going on between us ends tonight." Holden climbed to his feet. "I care about you too much to be your biggest regret. Take care, sweetheart."

CHAPTER 14

Holden

Owen stopped in the following day after he returned from his Boston trip. He was still wearing his work clothes; I swear, that guy lived in suits. He gave me a scrutinizing look as he headed for my couch, and I knew what was coming. But after the way I'd left things with Lala last night, I was in a crap mood and had no tolerance for his usual bullshit.

"How did everything go with bringing Lala back from New Jersey? Once again, you manipulated your way into spending time with her, huh?"

I fisted my hands. "Shut the fuck up, Owen."

"Is that not the truth?"

"You want the truth? The truth is...I'm gonna kick your ass if you don't cut the shit and stop sticking your damn nose where it doesn't belong."

"Jesus. Chill out." His brows furrowed. "Are you okay?"

"You act like this whole Lala thing is a fucking game to me. It's not. It's been eating at me. And walking away is hard."

He blinked. "Wait—walking away?"

"Yes. You don't need to police me anymore."

"What are you talking about?"

"I got a little drunk last night. Told her I was done. Also told her I didn't want to be her biggest regret. Then I stormed off. And I meant it. I'm done."

Owen narrowed his eyes. "You don't look done, my friend." He placed his hand on my shoulder. "You don't look done in the least. You look...like shit."

"Suck a dick." I chuckled.

Owen stared at me for a few seconds. "You know... I think this might be the first time I've realized how tormented you are over this." He sighed. "I know you care about her. That was never in doubt, nor the problem."

"I haven't been with anyone since Lala came to town, Owen." I pointed to my chest. "Me! What does that tell you? It's fucking weird. I've never had this happen. It's like I have tunnel vision. The more I feel like I can't have her, the more I want her."

Owen got up, went for my fridge, and grabbed a beer. He popped off the cap and tossed it aside. "You need to force yourself to move on somehow. Not only because she's engaged, but for your own good."

"I'm gonna try." I let out a breath. "Starting tonight. I really am."

"It'll be easier when she goes back to Pennsylvania," he said.

"Yeah," I muttered, even though the thought of that—or worse, her going to California—gutted me.

"You know I'm just looking out for her like Ryan would've." He took a sip. "But I'm sorry for giving you such a hard time. I can see now that *you've* probably been the hardest on yourself, more than anyone."

"Are you apologizing to me? That's so unlike you."

"Don't get used to it." He grinned. "And for the record, I'm proud of you for not pushing things any further and for trying to do the right thing."

While Owen knew about the hotel night, he *didn't* know about the phone sex. I didn't want to betray Lala's trust by spilling those details, so I kept that to myself. I wasn't sure he'd be so forgiving right now if he knew exactly how far I'd pushed things.

"In a weird way, I envy you," Owen said.

I blinked in confusion. "Which part do you envy—my blue balls or my inability to get it up for anyone else?"

"Neither." He laughed. "I guess I envy the passion you have for her, even though you may not be right for each other. At least you know you have the ability to feel this way about someone."

"Believe me, you don't want this, brother. Wanting someone and not being able to have them is the ultimate torture."

Owen stared down into his bottle. "I would love to feel something for someone…to not feel so damn dead inside. Sometimes, I doubt whether I'm capable of it. It just hasn't happened for me."

It hit me that I'd had my head up my ass with this Lala thing for so long that I might have been missing that my boy Owen was pretty down. He was a workaholic, and I'd always just assumed he was too busy for anything else or that he was too damn picky. Never thought he felt like he was missing out. But maybe there was something more to him not having a love life.

I lifted a brow. "You think you're broken or something?"

"I honestly don't know, man. The last couple of women I slept with, it was like I couldn't get out of their apartments fast enough. I'd have given anything to *want* to stay—to stay up all night and talk, to not be able to get enough of a person. I feel like I might be ready for that with the right person, but I haven't come across anyone who makes me feel that way." He paused. "You know, the way *you* seem to feel about Lala."

I shook my head. "I'd rather be in your predicament than feel this way and not be able to do anything about it. I miss the days where I felt nothing. I truly do." I groaned. "I can't wait to feel nothing again."

"We're on two different ends of the spectrum at the moment." Owen looked at his watch. "Shit. We'd better get to Colby's. We're late."

I'd nearly forgotten about our dinner plans. "Speaking of which, any clue what the hell this is all about?" I asked.

Colby and Billie had invited us over and specifically requested that we try not to bail—because for some unknown reason, it was important that we all be together tonight. That made me wonder if something was up. I had my suspicions.

"No clue," Owen said. "I guess we're about to find out."

When we arrived at our friends' apartment, the smell of garlic bread wafted in the air. There were five large pizza boxes stacked on the dining room table and some wine set out. Colby and Billie's place was definitely lived-in. Between Saylor's toys strewn about and Billie's art everywhere, it was hard to believe Colby had once been the most quintessential bachelor among us.

Little Saylor came running toward me. "Holden! You need to come see Guinevere. She's getting so fat!"

I smiled at the mention of the guinea pig I'd given her.

Colby chided, "Yeah, Holden, why don't you clean up the cage while you're at it? Thanks again for that gift, by the way."

"The gift that keeps on giving." I winked. "Anytime, my dude."

After a quick jaunt to Saylor's room to say hello to Guinevere, I returned to the living room. Owen had taken off his jacket and rolled up the sleeves of his collared shirt as he made himself comfortable, noshing on the chips and salsa laid out on the coffee table.

Brayden made his entrance a few seconds later. "Okay, so what's this all about?" he asked. "Random Friday-night dinners are a rarity. Something you want to tell us, Colby?"

"Wait. Is everyone here?" Colby asked, turning to Billie. "Didn't you say Lala might come?"

The hairs on the back of my neck stood to attention at the mention of her name. For some reason, it hadn't occurred to me that she might show up.

"Actually, Lala can't make it. So we're going to have to go ahead without her. But she already knows."

Knows what?

"Alright, guys." Colby clapped his hands together and took a deep breath. "We told Saylor right before you got here, and we're gonna let *her* do the honors because she's been so excited to share." He turned to his daughter. "Saylor, what do we have to tell your uncles?"

She hopped up and down and squealed. "I'm gonna be a big sister!"

I beamed. That's what I'd suspected. I was relieved that it wasn't some kind of bad news.

Brayden's eyes practically bugged out of his head. "No freaking way!"

Owen grinned. "Congratulations, guys!"

"I knew it." I hugged Billie.

"You did, huh?"

"I suspected, yeah. Congratulations, Mama."

"Thank you, Holden."

I opened my arms to hug Colby next. "And you, sir...well done."

He patted me on the back. "Thanks, man. We're over the moon."

I couldn't have been happier for my friends. Colby and Billie were perfect for each other, despite appearing to be total opposites. When they'd met, even *I* was surprised that my spunky tattoo artist had gone for my straight-laced, single-dad friend as opposed to, well, *me*. I always said they were like yin and yang. And even though Billie had truly become a mother to Saylor, whose birth mom had bailed, it was cool that she and Colby would have a biological child of their own. Speaking of yin and yang, I used to always associate that term with Colby and Billie. But it now also reminded me of Lala and me. She and I were true opposites, and that might have been part of the intense attraction between us. Still didn't mean I was right for her. But there's no doubt that opposites attract. Basically, I wanted to yin her with my yang—and that was precisely the problem.

With the big announcement out of the way, we all sat down to eat. The mood was jovial, with everyone speculating about the gender and tossing around name options. I couldn't help wondering why Lala had chosen not to be here.

After the meal, I found myself alone in the kitchen with Billie as I brought my dirty plate in.

"So...you said Lala already knew about your news?"

Billie cleared her throat. "She and I went to dinner recently, and I told her in secret. I had to tell someone. I couldn't hold it in anymore."

"Well, she didn't let on that she knew."

"Yeah. I told her not to tell you guys because we wanted to tell you all together."

Billie had given me a couple of odd looks tonight that told me she knew something about what was going on between Lala and me. I couldn't help digging for info.

I rubbed my hands together. "Can I ask you something, Billie?"

She tilted her head. "Sure."

"Am *I* the reason Lala decided not to come tonight?"

She bit her bottom lip. "I don't know, Holden. That's the truth. She told me she was working late. Whether that's legit or not, I couldn't say. She didn't say anything about not coming because of you. And I have no reason not to believe the excuse she gave me."

"Okay." I nodded. "Fair enough."

"Is there a reason she would be avoiding you?" She smirked.

"Be straight with me, Billie. How much do you know about what's gone down between Lala and me lately?"

Billie looked out toward the entrance to the kitchen and lowered her voice. "Enough to know you might have a second career as a phone-sex operator."

Well, alright, then. "I guess she didn't hold back."

She sighed. "Lala needed someone to talk to. She trusts that I won't tell anyone, and I haven't told Colby. I don't want him to give you shit. The way I see it, this is between you and Lala. And you can trust me not to say anything. But part of the reason I'm telling you I know is that I want to talk to you. I'm curious about where your head is, Holden. Because this situation can't be easy on you, either."

"Does it matter where my head is?"

"Of course, it does. I care about both of you. And despite your reputation, I believe that deep down, you're as soft as they come. I don't want you to get hurt."

"You mean *really* deep down I'm soft, right? Because there ain't nothing on this surface that's soft. Just to be clear." I chuckled.

"Yes." She laughed. "Of course. On the inside only."

I let out a long, frustrated breath. "It's been rough, honestly. I've crossed the line with her, put her in some tough spots because of my weakness—more than once."

"You don't put anyone anywhere they don't want to be, Holden. She's obviously smitten with you and struggling with her feelings, too."

"My crush for her goes way back, and old habits die hard, I guess." I paused. "But she's engaged. I have to respect that."

"What's with the whispering?" Colby's voice registered from behind me. "You're not trying to hit on my wife like the old days, are ya?"

I crossed my arms. "We were just chatting about…life."

"Life." He glared. "*Lala*, you mean?"

Billie looked at me and mouthed, "I didn't say anything."

"What makes you think we're talking about Lala?" I asked.

"Because I'm not dumb. I saw your face earlier when Billie said she wasn't coming. And you've been avoiding me lately, which, when it comes to you, means there's something you don't wanna tell me. I know you, Holden."

"Nothing is going on with Lala," I insisted. "She's still engaged. I'm still…me. And I'm moving on from any fucked-up feelings I might have for her. End of story."

"Wow. Sounds so simple," he taunted. "Which makes me suspicious. Sort of like the time I snuck over to Ryan's house in the middle of the night to steal his bike as a prank. I happened to notice you and Lala on the roof. You made up some elaborate story when I called you out on it and expected me to believe it. Then you proceeded to avoid me for a week." He laughed. "Just like back then, I think you're full of shit now."

I'd most definitely been avoiding Colby lately. Out of all of the guys, he'd always seemed able to see through me, even if I was putting on a front.

"Anyway…" I attempted to change the subject. "I'm really happy for you guys. I can't wait to be an uncle again."

"No more animal gifts, though, please," Billie said.

"As long as Colby doesn't piss me off, you won't get any more surprises." I winked. "Although, I hear capybaras make great household pets."

"What am I missing in here?" Brayden said as he burst into the kitchen.

"Nothing," I said.

"Damn, I was hoping you were whispering about Holden's thing for Lala."

Colby and Billie laughed, while I remained stone-faced.

178

"We were talking about the baby and future family pets," I said.

"I can't wait to see what he or she looks like. Hopefully the baby gets lucky and looks like Billie." Brayden chuckled. "No offense, Colby."

Owen entered the kitchen. "Why is everyone hiding in here?"

Brayden turned to him. "They're pretending they weren't talking about Lala."

"Ah." Owen turned to me. "You told them about the hotel night?"

Colby's eyes widened as his head whipped toward me. "Hotel what?"

I pulled on my hair. "Nothing happened! It's a long story. Her car broke down and I—"

"Seriously!" Billie intervened. "You don't owe us an explanation, Holden." She turned to her husband. "Even if anything *were* happening with Lala, it's none of our business."

"Lala will *always* be our business," Colby corrected.

Billie placed her hands on her hips. "Lala's a grown-ass woman. She doesn't need any of you big goons looking out for her. And as for Holden, leave him alone, too. He's done nothing wrong. And if there's anyone here who would kick his ass if he did, it would be me. Got it?"

"Ass?" a little voice asked.

Saylor had joined us.

Billie sighed. "Nothing, honey. Forget you heard that."

Saylor giggled. "Are you talking about Lala?"

Not her, too.

"Why would you think that?" I asked.

"I was listening. I heard her name. I like Lala. She has pretty hair."

Fuck yeah, she does. I dream about pulling it while I—

"Uncle Holden! You have to say goodbye to Guinevere before you leave."

Colby's eyes darted to me. "You can take Guinevere back home with you, while you're at it, Holden."

"Saylor…" I flashed a mischievous grin. "Have you ever seen a capybara?"

After saying a proper goodbye to the guinea pig I'd nearly murdered via Hot Cheeto, I went back to my apartment, unable to shake the uneasy feeling I'd had all night. Knowing that Lala couldn't stand to be around me long enough to show up for her friends' big announcement felt like a punch to the gut. It was proof that I'd gone and done what I'd feared: I'd pushed her away and was losing her as a friend. That was unacceptable to me.

Before going into my place, I stopped in the hallway, debating whether to knock on her door. There was always a chance that I'd blown things out of proportion. Maybe she did have to work late. I needed to know whether that was a lie.

I continued to stand in the hallway and debated texting her, but I had to figure out a new normal, and the sooner I faced her again, the sooner I could practice being around her without screwing up.

I finally knocked and stood there waiting as my pulse raced.

When Lala opened, she looked as beautiful and flustered as ever with her wild hair and wide eyes. Then I looked down. Her neck had broken out in a rash, which only happened when something was really bothering her. It took me all of two seconds to figure it out. Because when I looked to my right, I realized she wasn't alone.

Warren was standing there.

CHAPTER 15

Lala

"**U**h, Holden…hey. What are you doing here?"

Holden's eyes moved between me and Warren. His jaw clenched. "I just came to check on how that leak in the kitchen is holding up. I put some putty around the drain earlier while you were at work, to shore up the seal."

I hadn't had any leak in the kitchen, but I appreciated him making up an excuse for stopping by. "Oh, it must have worked. I don't think it's leaking anymore. Thank you for checking."

The three of us stood staring at each other in silence until it got awkward. Eventually, Holden lifted his chin to Warren and forced a smile, but I could see he was anything but happy. "Hey man, what's up?"

Warren placed his hand on my back. "Not much. Just surprised my fiancée for the weekend."

Holden glanced to me. "Cool. Well, I'll let you guys go since the faucet is holding."

"Actually," Warren said. "I'm glad you stopped by. I knocked on your door earlier, on my way in, so I could speak to you about something in private…"

My eyes widened. "You did?"

Warren nodded before looking back to Holden. "Could you possibly recommend a restaurant? Something romantic, perhaps?" Warren leaned in and kissed my temple. "Tomorrow is the anniversary of our first date, and I don't get to see my girl so often these days. I'd like to take her somewhere nice."

Oh God. I wanted to throw up.

Holden glared at Warren. "I don't eat out much."

"Really? I figured you'd have an arsenal of romantic places, with all the dating Laney tells me you do…"

I shut my eyes. When I opened them, Holden's glare had shifted from Warren to me.

"I never said Holden was a serial dater."

Holden's face reddened. "Just a manwhore, right?"

"Holden…"

He held up a hand. "It's fine. I mean, the truth is the truth. Though, I guess one of the reasons I can't think of a romantic restaurant off the top of my head is because some of my most memorable times with women aren't at places like that. The best times I've ever had were just evenings sitting on my fire escape, drinking wine and talking. I don't think you need a fancy, overpriced place when you're with a special woman."

Holden caught my eyes one more time. "But I'll let you know if I think of any restaurants. Have a good night."

Once I closed the door, I told Warren I needed to use the bathroom so I could buy myself a little time to clear my head. But I could probably have stayed in there for days and still felt like a jumbled mess. After I came out, I went straight to the wine, poured a glass to the brim, and drank. I didn't realize how much I'd gulped back until Warren's eyes zoned in on the nearly empty glass.

"I was really thirsty," I said.

"I can see that. Although water quenches thirst better than alcohol. That stuff will only dehydrate you more."

VI KEELAND & PENELOPE WARD

"Right…of course." I refilled my glass. "I'll take this one a little slower. Would you like a refill?"

Warren gestured to the glass I'd poured him a half hour ago. "I've barely had a sip."

I'd been feeling awkward ever since I opened the door to find Warren on the other side a few hours ago, but suddenly I didn't even know how to act.

Did I sit down?

What should I say?

Was he looking at me funny?

Warren rubbed his lip with his thumb. "What does that guy do for a living again?"

I immediately felt defensive. Maybe it was the use of "that guy" when I knew he knew his name. "Holden plays in a band called After Friday. He's also the building super."

"Pushing thirty is a little old to be holding on to the hope of becoming a rock star, isn't it?"

"Holden's a very talented drummer. Just because he hasn't made it big yet doesn't mean he doesn't have what it takes. So much of the creative arts is about right time, right place."

"But when do you call it quits? Thirty? Forty? Sixty? We all have to grow up sometime."

"Are you saying Holden isn't a grown-up because he does something he loves? Not everyone is willing to give up their happiness for a job that pays better or has a more structured schedule. I think you're forgetting that Holden, and all of the guys who own this building, experienced something that taught them a valuable lesson: Life is short. Don't waste it on things that aren't worth your time."

Warren's face fell. "I'm sorry. I didn't think of how Ryan's death might've affected them."

I blew out a breath and shook my head. "It's fine. I'm sorry if I got a little snippy. I'm tired, and you know how I get when I don't get my sleep."

He reached out and stroked my cheek. "Why don't we go to bed? I'm tired too. I went into the lab early this morning so I could get a jump on traffic this afternoon."

Warren and I hadn't seen each other in a few weeks, so I suspected we wouldn't be going to sleep once we went to bed. And I wasn't in the right headspace for fooling around at the moment. So I told a little white lie. Or should I say *another one*…

"I need to get a few things done for work by the morning. I didn't know you were coming, so I left some of my tasks to finish at home. But why don't you go relax and watch some TV in bed, and I'll join you as soon as I'm done?"

Warren frowned. "Okay. Hopefully you won't be too long?"

I attempted a smile. "I'll try to hurry."

Not wanting to get caught in my lie, I did work on an Excel spreadsheet I'd been avoiding. Entering data and creating graphs were my least favorite parts of running research trials, yet I picked them over fooling around with my fiancé. After forty-five minutes or so, the numbers on my laptop started to blur, so I tiptoed to the door of the bedroom to see if I could hear Warren moving around. I exhaled a huge breath when I heard his gentle snore.

It might've been safe to go to bed, yet I still felt wired by the evening's turn of events—first Warren surprising me and then Holden showing up at my door. So I poured myself another glass of wine and tried to unwind, but my mind kept wandering to the man next door. I couldn't stop replaying the hurt on his face when he'd seen Warren. Worse, he thought I'd told Warren all about what a womanizer he was. Unable to shake the thoughts from my head even with the help of more wine, I took out my phone and scrolled through TikTok. Normally when I was stressing about something, I could scroll through one of the gazillion *dogs* hashtags and find some adorable lab who let a pet duck ride on his head to change my mood. But tonight, in between every video, I looked up at the window that led to the fire escape.

I couldn't...

A basset hound running around with sunglasses on.

I shouldn't...

A goldendoodle eating dinner in a highchair like a child.

What if I just went out for five minutes...

A boxer who can play piano.

Warren would never even have to know...

A sheepdog who uses his teeth to pull the covers up for a sleeping child.

I could be quiet...

I picked up the almost empty magnum of wine and guzzled the last of it straight from the bottle. *Fuck it. I'm doing it. I'm going out there.*

Double checking at the bedroom door that Warren was still snoring, I quietly pried open the window and climbed onto the fire escape.

Each and every time I'd come out here, Holden was either already here or had joined me pretty soon after. So I waited.

And waited.

And waited.

And waited.

After about a half hour, my phone buzzed with a text.

Holden: Chez Josephine in Midtown. Enjoy your romantic dinner.

Just when you think it's safe...

I hadn't seen or heard a peep from next door over the last twenty-four hours. But the moment the elevator doors slid open, none other than my neighbor was standing inside. It felt like the wind had been knocked out of me.

Holden's face fell as he took in Warren and me all dressed up. "Oh, hey."

I smiled halfheartedly. "Hi."

Holden had drumsticks in his hand. He tucked them into the waistband of his jeans and lifted two amps from the ground, one in each hand. His eyes did a quick sweep over my little black dress as he stepped out of the elevator.

"Looks like you're all ready for your romantic evening. Hope it's everything you dreamed it would be."

I just wanted to get on the damn elevator and put distance between us, but Warren didn't immediately follow me in when Holden got off. He held one side of the elevator doorframe to keep the doors from sliding shut. "Are you playing tonight?"

Holden turned. "Yep."

"Where? Maybe Laney and I will stop by after dinner."

Holden's eyes flashed to me and back to Warren. "It's okay. You don't have to do that. You should enjoy your romantic evening. Plus, I don't think the place is really your vibe."

"Maybe not, but Laney told me how talented you are, and I think it'll be fun."

Holden's lips pursed, but eventually he nodded. "The Villager. It's downtown."

Warren nodded. "Great. Maybe we'll see you later."

"This place was really nice." I wiped the corners of my mouth with a napkin. "Thank you for finding it and making the plans."

I hadn't told Warren that Holden had texted me with a recommendation for a romantic restaurant last night. The thought that he'd probably been there with someone else was too much for me to handle. But Warren had reached out to one of his colleagues, who had given him the name of this place.

"Everything was delicious, but I think the company is what made it special." Warren tucked his credit card into the leather portfolio and reached across the table for my hand. "I think we needed this, my love. Lately I've felt like we've had a bit of a disconnect. I'm sure it's because of the distance between us, but it's made me realize that I need to come visit more often and put in more effort."

It was screwed up, but my gut reaction to my fiancé saying he wanted to visit more was one of dread. Dinner had been really nice—the food was delicious, our conversation flowed naturally, and a talented piano player played softly from the other side of the room. I should've felt wooed and special—but instead I was... bored. Just thinking that made me feel like a horrible human being. But the thing about feelings is, while they may not be pretty, there's usually a lot of truth in them. And the truth was, I couldn't stop comparing what I felt like with Warren to how I felt when I was around another man. Holden made me feel alive, while I'd felt numb making dinner conversation with my fiancé. There was just no spark, no butterflies, no electricity running through my veins. Sadly, I'd had no idea any of those things were even missing before I came to New York. I'd blindly settled into a routine of *nice*, not really having anything to compare it to. And now I worried that what I'd felt around Holden couldn't be *unfelt*. Could I tuck what I knew a relationship *could* feel like back into the box when I left New York and go back to being happy with *nice*?

That was the big question—one I didn't have the answer to.

I smiled and nodded. "I could come home to visit more, too."

When we were ready to go, Warren stood and held his hand out to help me up.

"Thank you."

He pulled me close for a spontaneous hug. "Did I tell you that you look beautiful tonight?"

"That's sweet of you to say."

Outside the restaurant, Warren stepped to the curb. He raised his hand to hail a cab coming down the block. "You ready to go party now?"

"You mean Holden's show?"

Warren nodded. "I'm looking forward to seeing his band play."

"You are?"

The cab pulled up, and Warren opened the back door. "I feel bad for insulting his career last night. Your brother's friends are important to you, so they're important to me."

"I appreciate that, but…I'm sort of tired. It's fine if we skip it."

"We don't have to go for very long. Let's just stop in for a few songs."

I sighed and ducked into the cab. "Okay…yeah, sure."

The Villager was packed when we walked in. I felt slightly relieved that we were stuck at the back bar, and Holden probably wouldn't even notice we'd come. Warren talked to the bartender while I looked around the club. Most of the women were dressed very differently than I was in my demure little black dress that came to my knee and conservative pumps. They had on cropped tops with abs showing, skimpy strapless dresses, and jeans that looked painted on. It made me feel uncool and super out of place.

Warren slipped some money across the bar and finished talking to the bartender. A minute later, a woman walked over and the bartender pointed to Warren and me.

"What's going on?"

Warren beamed. "I got us a table up front."

"What? How?"

"Gave the bartender a hundred dollars, and one of the two round tables with the little reserved signs suddenly became available. I told him we would only be about an hour, though."

188

The last thing I wanted was to be front and center. I shook my head. "It's fine. I'm good here. We're only going to stay a little while anyway."

But it was too late. The woman motioned for us to follow, and Warren put his hand on my back, guiding me to walk.

Holden spotted us before we even sat down, his eyes tracking my every step as he drummed away.

Warren pulled out my chair, and we sat. He looked pleased with himself as he leaned forward and yelled over the music. "Now isn't this better?"

No, it makes me want to throw up. Yet I had to muster a smile. "Yes, thank you."

The next half hour was brutal. After Friday played seven songs in a row, each one going right into the next, but Holden and I couldn't stop staring at each other. I'd force my eyes away after a few seconds, but somehow they kept finding their way back. And each and every time, I found Holden looking at me. I started to worry that my fiancé was going to notice. But when I glanced over, he seemed completely oblivious and smiled. I smiled back, and the brief interaction caused Warren to reach across the table and lace his fingers with mine. The next time I stole a peek at the drummer, Holden was no longer looking at me; he was staring at our joined hands—actually *glaring* was more like it. His playing also seemed to get louder and louder. We were sitting so close that I'd already been feeling the beat in my chest, but as time went on, my heart pounded so hard I started to sweat. When the band finally stopped playing, the lead singer said they were going to take a short set break, and I told Warren I needed to use the ladies' room.

The hallway had a line of six individual bathrooms, and I was glad to get a few minutes alone in one. Once I caught my breath, I decided as soon as I got back to the table, I'd tell Warren we needed to leave. I couldn't possibly handle another round of what had been going on out there. But when I opened the bathroom door, Holden was waiting right on the other side. He backed me up, locking the door behind him.

"What are you doing?" I said.

Holden looked crazed. He kept walking forward, making me step back, until I hit the sink. Then he put one hand on either side of me, blocking me in.

He leaned down so we were eye to eye. "Tell me, when you hold his hand, do you feel like you do right now?"

My heart raced, and I couldn't speak.

"Answer me!" His eyes were so angry. "How do you feel right now, Lala? Does it feel the same when he touches your hand?"

I shook my head.

"How about when he was in your *fucking bed* last night? Did that feel like this?"

I shook my head again.

"That's fucking sad." Holden trailed one finger along my arm, and goose bumps broke out all over my skin. "Does he make your hair stand up like this? Give you goose bumps?"

I shook my head yet again.

Holden leaned in, bringing his mouth to my ear. "Can he make you *come* just by talking to you? Without ever laying a finger on you?"

This time I didn't answer. I wasn't even capable of moving my head anymore. Holden's hot breath at my ear had my body trembling with need.

But he stepped back. An angry smile spread across his face.

"I didn't think so. Enjoy the rest of your dull evening, *Laney*."

He unlocked the door and walked out without looking back, leaving me standing there like a puddle of mush.

It took people banging on the bathroom door to get me to come out after that. I was an emotional wreck and needed to get the heck out of the club and away from Holden. But when I walked back to the table to tell Warren we needed to leave, I found Holden sitting in my chair. And now he wasn't alone… A scantily clad, beautiful woman was sitting on his lap. It stopped me in my tracks. Out of the corner of his eye, Holden noticed. He flashed an evil smile and nuzzled his face into the woman's neck. Coming out of the bathroom, I'd been a sad, emotional mess. But seeing Holden that way flipped a switch inside me. Sad and emotional became angry and jealous. I marched over to the table and spoke to Warren.

"We need to leave. I have a migraine coming on, and I just got sick in the bathroom." I turned to face Holden and glared at him, ripping my jacket from the back of the chair as they continued to canoodle. "It must've been the loud music. Enjoy the rest of your night, Holden. Though it looks like you already have that covered."

❤CHAPTER 16

Holden

A week later, the fog of jealousy had barely lifted.

Sure, I felt like shit for what I'd pulled at the club last week-end. It was immature and selfish. But every word out of my mouth had been true. And every reaction from her proved how she felt. I still had no right to act like a jealous dick, though. Warren showing up had caught me off guard and brought to the surface just how strong my feelings were.

Once again this week, I'd had to remind myself to take a step back. Luckily, I'd successfully avoided running into Lala since that horrible night, because if I'd done or said anything else stupid and gotten her into some kind of trouble with him, I wouldn't have been able to forgive myself. Even so, at this point, I stood a very good chance of losing Lala as a friend forever.

I desperately needed to get out of my damn apartment before I lost my mind. Thankfully, this afternoon was poker with the guys. It was Brayden's turn to host.

When I showed up to his apartment, I'd apparently done a crappy job of hiding how I was feeling.

"You look down. What's going on?" Brayden said as he stepped aside for me to enter.

"Nothing," I muttered, heading straight for his kitchen to grab a beer.

I then took a seat at the table, where Owen and Colby were already situated. The usual pizza boxes were stacked off to the side. The smell of pepperoni made my stomach growl.

Everyone had been busy lately, so it had been a while since the guys and I had caught up, just the four of us.

Colby dealt the cards. "So what's new with everyone?"

"I'll go first," Owen said, grabbing a cigar and lighting it. "I currently have a client looking for a building to house his, wait for it…" He paused. "Private sex club."

"Well, damn." I laughed.

"I had to sign a non-disclosure agreement in regard to the exact nature of the establishment. So keep this among us. But this is certainly a new one."

"What type of space fits that criteria?" Brayden asked.

"There are apparently certain necessities, like enough private rooms and a certain ceiling height for sex swings in the common area."

Brayden bent his head back. "And I thought I was going to be the one with the most interesting story to tell tonight."

"Why? What's up?" Colby asked.

Brayden spoke as he arranged his cards. "So…I went on a date with this girl last night who I met on Tinder, and apparently she didn't trust me, so she brought her friend as a buffer. The entire time, all I could think of was how beautiful and funny her friend was. I wished I was on a date with her."

"Well, that's awkward." I laughed.

"Yeah, tell me about it. I got a vibe from her friend, too—you know, that the feeling was mutual."

"That's a tough spot to be in," Colby said. "What can you do in that situation?"

"Pretty much nothing." Brayden shrugged.

"Do you know the friend's full name?" I asked.

"Only her first name, Julia. But what would it have mattered if I had her last name?"

"You could look her up online after some time passed. Slide into her DMs," I said.

"Yeah, well, so much for that." Brayden chugged his beer.

I scratched my chin. "What if you reach out to the girl you were on a date with after some time has passed and ask for her friend's name?"

He arched a brow. "You don't think that's tacky?"

I lit one of the cigars I found on the counter behind me and blew smoke out. "Who the fuck cares? It's not like you're dating her."

"Yeah, maybe. I don't know." Brayden sighed. "Anyway, what's new with you, Colby?"

"Well…" Colby flashed a big, goofy grin. "I happen to be holding in my pocket the very first photos of Baby Lennon."

"No way." I reached my hand out. "Hand them over!"

Colby took out a few ultrasound pics. "As you guys know, Billie doesn't want to find out the gender. It was really difficult for me not to ask the ultrasound tech about it. But I promised, so I didn't. Plus, Billie said it's too early to tell." He placed them on the table. "I've been trying to figure it out by looking at the photos. Any guesses?"

Brayden pointed to a certain spot. "That's a total dick! It's huge."

Colby chuckled. "See, that's what I thought at first, but Billie says it could be the umbilical cord. I don't know what these things normally look like. I never saw Saylor's images. But that *does* look like a penis to me."

194

"It's a pretty sizable one." I winked. "Must take after his uncle Holden."

Owen blew out some smoke. "I'm gonna laugh when it turns out to be a girl because that's so obviously *not* a penis. It's an arm."

The guys and I went back and forth, debating the sex of Colby and Billie's baby. I was thrilled that they'd passed right by me in the rotation of updates about what was going on in our lives. Because if I'd told them the truth about what happened at the club with Lala, it wouldn't have gone well.

But I jinxed myself, because as soon as Colby returned the photos to his shirt pocket, he looked over at me.

"Holden, what's going on with you?"

I fidgeted in my seat. There was a lot on my mind that I wanted to unleash, stuff I really did want my friends' take on. I just didn't want to get shit for even asking. But in a split-second decision, I did it anyway. "How the hell do you know if you're in love with someone?"

All three of their heads turned in my direction at the same time, but no one said anything. They looked at each other, then back at me. You could've heard a pin drop.

Colby leaned in. "Why are you asking that?"

I rolled my eyes. "Take a wild guess."

"Well, I know where *my* mind is going," Owen chimed in.

I put my head in my hands. "I don't even know if it's love I'm feeling. All I know is that every single time I'm around her, I make a goddamn fool of myself. I can't seem to make the right decisions… or think about anything else." I lifted my cards and arranged them mindlessly. "I'm all messed up."

"Is this about her fiancé being in town?" Brayden asked. "Is that what pushed you over the edge?"

"Partly." I lifted my chin. "You knew he was here?"

He nodded. "I ran into them in the hallway last weekend. Lala seemed really on edge."

My stomach sank. "That was probably because of me," I con-fessed. "I sort of put her in a weird position last Saturday night."

I gave in and told the guys what had happened at my show at The Villager. Needless to say, they weren't happy with me.

Brayden leaned back in his seat and shook his head. "Dude, that was so wrong."

"I know it was wrong. I should be doing better, but I don't know how to stop. I know I'm wrong for her. But it doesn't change how I feel." I tugged on my hair. "Look, just pretend I didn't say anything…"

Colby held out his palm. "No, no. You asked a question. I think we should all do our best to answer it."

Owen shrugged. "Don't look at me. I've never been in love. I can't even find a woman I can stand spending more than a few hours with."

"Same here, dude." Brayden smirked. "Well, except for freak-ing Julia last night, but that doesn't really count." Brayden turned to Colby. "Looks like you're the one who's going to have to answer the question."

"Okay, don't mind if I do." Colby cleared his throat. "Ob-viously, there are many things you can feel about someone when you're in love. But the thing that sticks out to me is that when you truly love someone, you're willing to give your life for them. That person means more to you than anything—including yourself."

Looking down at the table, I knew I would jump in front of a train for Lala, if that meant saving her. There was no doubt in my mind that I would die for her. I thought that a little bit much to announce at this poker table, though. But I guessed I probably *was* in love with her. Unfortunately, being in love still didn't make me the best choice. You can prove your love by letting someone go just as easily as you would by staying in their life and potentially ruining it.

"Thanks for the input," I muttered.

"That's it?" Colby's eyes widened. "You're not going to say anything else?"

"Nope." I fiddled with my cards. "I need to keep my thoughts to myself. I've had diarrhea of the mouth enough. I don't need you guys busting my balls. I shouldn't have even asked the damn question. But I've felt like I'm going out of my mind since Warren showed up."

"God, this brings new meaning to the phrase lost in La-la Land," Owen chided. "That's exactly where your head has been lately."

"Yeah. No shit." I laughed along with the other guys.

Thankfully, they got off my back for a while as we started our game, and the cards kept us relatively focused until Colby ended up winning.

When we took a break, I went into the kitchen. Colby followed.

He lowered his voice. "Hey, man, I just wanted to talk to you one on one for a bit."

"There's nothing more to say."

"What you said you did last weekend, how you acted out at the club, it reminded me of the time I made a fool of myself when Billie was on that date—before she and I officially got together. Remember that night? You saw her at the restaurant with the guy and texted me photos. I made the biggest idiot of myself by texting her jealous rants. My feelings were splayed out everywhere like a rodent flattened by a truck. There was nothing I could do to stop myself that night. That's what jealousy does when you really care about someone. What you did was no different." He tossed his trash in the garbage. "Here's the thing… I never got anywhere by doing shit like that, dancing around my feelings for her. Ultimately, I had to be straightforward."

I nodded. "Easier said than done."

"I had some of the same issues with Billie that you do with Lala. Not only were we seemingly opposites, but I never felt like I was quite right for her. Of course, there was also the issue of me having a kid." He sighed. "Yet we still couldn't stay away from each other. We just went around in circles until we started to communicate in an honest way. I think you've gone long enough doing the same dance with Lala."

"I always get in trouble when I dance with Lala," I muttered.

"Once she marries him, dude, that's it," Colby said. "There's no going back after that. Lala strikes me as the type of person who's going to do whatever she can to make a marriage work. I don't see her getting divorced, although anything is possible." He exhaled. "I know it's strange for me to be encouraging you to go for it, but I care about both of you. While I'll always want to protect her, I don't know that you're going to shake this. I'm starting to believe you have true feelings for her. And as your friend, I think you need to take your shot."

He's supporting this? A pressure I'd never felt before built within my chest. "Say I take the chance and take my shot. That doesn't change who I am, though. I'm not the type of guy who settles down, who lives in a house in the suburbs with a white picket fence. Everything I've ever worked toward has been about having a music career and being on the road. I don't think it's fair for me to tell her how I feel if I can't be the type of guy she needs."

Colby shrugged. "Well, that's certainly a decision you're going to have to make. I think you have to decide whether you're willing to give up some of those dreams. Or maybe you'll find you don't have to choose. The bottom line is, there won't be a choice soon if you continue to play games." He nodded. "But you're afraid. I get it."

It was more than just fear. I had a moral obligation to protect Lala from me. "I'm not safe, Colby."

He shrugged again. "The safe choice isn't always the right one. That's something I've learned with my own relationship. Billie was not the type of woman I thought would ever want to settle down with a guy like me. She was wild and free-spirited, and I didn't want to hold her back. We were the dangerous choice for each other—but ultimately, our feelings superseded everything. And we learned to make it work."

"Just to confirm… Are you saying you're okay with me expressing these feelings to *Ryan's sister*? Because you always used to be against the idea of me and her."

He smiled. "You can call it *cautious* support. I see things a little differently now, how pervasive your feelings for her have been. That counts for something. From everything you've shown me, you seem to really care about her. Moreover, you told me you haven't been with another woman since she got here? That says a lot."

"Speaking of other women, you should've seen her reaction at the club when I had that girl on my lap."

Colby made a face. "Clearly, she has some strong feelings for you as well. Aside from that, I also worry she's not ready to get married, though at one time she might've thought that was what she wanted. But she strikes me as the type of person who'd sacrifice her own happiness just to avoid hurting someone. She might go through with it if she doesn't have a strong reason to reconsider. That's another reason to open up to her."

"Yeah." I exhaled. "Well, you've certainly given me a lot to think about."

"You just need to lay it all on the line; be brutally honest. You need to tell her exactly how you feel without worrying about the consequences. Because when we keep feelings inside, they eat away at us, and eventually…we die. Well, figuratively, I guess." He shook his head. "I can't picture you at her wedding. Can you? You know we're all going to be invited. How do you stand there and watch her marry him? I can't even imagine that."

"I wouldn't go," I said without hesitation.

"You really wouldn't go?"

"Wouldn't go where?" Brayden asked as he burst into his kitchen.

"Up your ass," I said.

"Are we having more secret Lala conversations?" he teased.

I rolled my eyes.

"You and I need to go out more," he told me. "I can't count on Owen or this old married dude here."

"You're right," I admitted. "I've been stuck in a rut lately, and I've only been going out when I have gigs. I need to force myself."

"Force yourself to stay away from Lala?" Owen said as he entered the room.

"That, too," I agreed.

Brayden smacked Owen's shoulder. "Hey, when your client's sex club opens, can I get first dibs?"

"Again, I'm not even supposed to be talking about it, so keep your trap shut."

Thank God everyone dropped the subject of Lala for the rest of the night after that.

Once I got back to my apartment, I felt like I'd reached my breaking point. I needed to reach out to her—tonight. I grabbed my phone, knowing if I thought about what to text her for too long, nothing would come. After all, it had taken me what felt like years to decide on a message last weekend when I gave her that bullshit restaurant recommendation. But this? Pouring out my feelings? There was no way to plan for this shit.

So I decided to type exactly what was on my mind. Because Colby was right. This situation was driving me mad.

I could always erase it and not press send, I told myself.

Holden: Hey, Lala. I want to apologize for what I pulled last Saturday night. (I feel like I'm always apologizing to you for my behavior.) This text should have come

200

sooner, but I've been so fucked up and didn't know what to say. While I'm sorry for backing you into a corner like that, I'm NOT sorry for what I said. Because it was the truth. I'm not going to claim that what I'm about to say is good for you. But it's also the truth. Here goes: I cannot stop thinking about you. I think about you from the moment I get up in the morning until the moment my head hits the pillow at night. I have never felt this way about anyone. I know I'm wrong for you. That's the thing. That's why this is so unfair, but I've gotten to the point where I just don't give a fuck about that anymore. I haven't been with anyone since you got to New York. I've been incapable of feeling anything for anyone other than you because I'm not interested in anyone else. That girl you saw me with last weekend was no exception. I wanted to make you as jealous as seeing you with Warren made me. It was a game. But I don't want to play games anymore, Lala. I'm done holding back. I want you to leave Warren. If not for me, then for the sheer fact that, even though you might care about him, he doesn't satisfy you like I could. He never will. The problem is, I can't promise anything about what a future with me might look like. That's the shitty part of all this. What I can promise is that I'll give you what I know you want right now: to take your body to places it's never been before. I don't want to die and not know what that feels like, Lala. I want you. All of you. Do with this information what you need to, but if there's any chance you feel the same way, you need to let me know, and you need to handle stuff on your end first. On the other hand, if there is no chance of us ever becoming more than we are now, I'll move on. For good this time. If you love Warren and intend to marry him no matter what, you need to tell me point blank that nothing more will ever happen between us. I promise you, when I hear those words come out of your mouth, I will stop this. It will HAVE to stop. But make no mistake about it, I will continue to crave you.

My heart pounded as my finger hovered over the screen to either erase or send.

Three.

Two.

One…

I paused.

Send.

♡CHAPTER 17

Lala

I pulled into the same parking spot I'd pulled out of yesterday morning. My building was a few doors down and across the street. Looking around, everything appeared exactly the same as when I'd left to drive up to Philadelphia, yet nothing was the same at all for me anymore. I sighed. What a whirlwind two days I'd had.

I'd left New York determined to fix things with my fiancé. Warren had known things between us were off when he left last weekend, and he'd called every night this week to see if we were okay. I hated that I was making him feel uneasy. He didn't deserve that. So I'd driven home to surprise him, like he had me the week before, in order to assure him everything was good between us. I swear I'd had the best of intentions when I'd left just yesterday.

Warren worked at the lab on Saturday afternoons, so I drove up early and visited my parents. After, I went to his favorite bakery and picked up his favorite dessert—gluten-free carrot cake with vegan, dairy-free "cream cheese" frosting—before heading to his place. But just as I pulled up, a text from Holden arrived. And after that, my visit to smooth things over didn't go exactly as planned. In fact, it turned out to be one hell of a bumpy ride. I wound up sitting outside of Warren's house for more than an hour, reading Holden's text over and over. Then my fiancé noticed my car and came out to see if I was alright.

The moment I opened my mouth to tell him everything was great, tears started streaming down my face.

I couldn't do it.

I just couldn't do it anymore.

Now it was late on Sunday, almost eleven o'clock at night, and I still hadn't responded to Holden's text from yesterday. I wasn't sure if he was home, but I was about to find out. Because things between us needed to be settled once and for all.

Adrenaline pumped through my veins as I got out of the car, walked across the street, and rode the elevator up to our floor. I could've used a glass of wine to calm my nerves before going to Holden's apartment, but I was afraid if I went to my place, I'd chicken out and never knock. So I unlocked my door, tossed my bag inside without crossing the threshold, and walked next door.

My hand trembled as I lifted it to knock.

But my heart nearly broke when Holden opened the door, and his face fell finding me on the other side. I never wanted to be the cause of that pain.

He closed his eyes. "I'm so sorry, Lala. I should never have sent that text, and I should never have done what I did last weekend at the bar. I'm a complete asshole."

"Can I come in so we can talk?"

Holden nodded and stepped aside for me to enter.

My insides felt like a shaken bottle of champagne, and I was afraid when I opened my mouth, I'd spew all over the place. I needed something to calm my nerves. "Do you have any wine?"

"In the kitchen." He motioned to the other room, and I followed. An unopened bottle of my favorite pinot grigio was in the door of his fridge. He uncorked it before filling a glass and passing it to me. After, he put it away and leaned against the kitchen counter.

"Aren't you going to join me?" I asked.

"The last thing I need is alcohol when I'm around you. I do a pretty bang-up job fucking everything up when I'm stone-cold sober." He looked down. "I really am sorry, Lala. I had no right to act the way I did last Saturday night. And I should never have sent that text and unloaded on you. Even if everything I said is true, it was selfish to dump it all in your lap. You're engaged to be married to another man, and I haven't shown any respect for that commitment." He lifted his head and our eyes met. "I've done some dumb shit when it comes to you. Can you ever forgive me? Can we pretend I never sent that text and go back to being friends? I know I've said it a dozen times, but I will back off and be on my best behavior if you just give me one more chance. I don't want to lose you completely, Lala."

When I said nothing, Holden looked pained.

"Please, sweetheart," he groaned. "I'm so sorry, so fucking sorry."

My heart pounded as I tried to figure out where to begin telling him everything I'd come to say.

"Tell me I'm an asshole," he pleaded. "Tell me I acted like an immature idiot. Just don't *not* speak to me. I couldn't take that, Lala. Say something. Anything."

I lifted the wine to my lips and gulped back half the glass before taking a deep breath. "I'm not engaged anymore, Holden."

His eyes widened. "What? What did you just say?"

"I'm not engaged anymore."

"Fuck." He shook his head. "Is it my fault? Did Warren break things off because of what I did?"

"No, Warren didn't break things off. I did."

"Why?"

I looked down for a long time before meeting his eyes again. "Because everything you said in that text? I feel the same way, Holden. You're all I think about. You said you think about me from the moment you get up in the morning until the moment your head hits the pillow. Well, I do the same, but I can't even stop thinking about you when I fall asleep. I dream about you." I took another deep breath. "And my dreams…are dirty."

Holden's eyes jumped back and forth between mine. "You're really not engaged anymore?"

I shook my head and held up my ringless hand.

He stared at it for the longest time before taking a step toward me. "You're not engaged anymore."

"Nope," I whispered. "Very single."

He closed the remaining distance between us and put one hand on either side of me on the kitchen counter. Every nerve in my body zapped to life. It felt like I had an electrical current running through me.

"Tell me what this means for us, Lala. Tell me what you want from me."

I swallowed. "You. I want *you*, Holden. And every which way. I want you inside of me more than I've ever wanted anything in my entire life."

"Say that again…the part about wanting me inside of you."

My chest heaved up and down. "I want you inside of me."

His voice turned gritty. "Come closer. Tell me in my ear."

I leaned in and whispered, "I want you inside of me, Holden."

When I pulled back, a wicked smile spread across his face. He lifted his thumb to my mouth and traced the outline of my lips. "Do you want me in here?"

I nodded.

He pushed his thumb inside. "Suck."

I closed my eyes and sucked hard.

When I opened, Holden slipped his finger from my mouth and traced a path down over my chin, along my throat, and kept heading south through the center of my body. When he reached between my legs, he dipped his hand under my skirt and rubbed two fingers over my panties. "Do you want me in here?"

I nodded, breathless.

His eyes gleamed as he bent and trailed his fingers even farther back. When he stopped at my ass, I felt a little panicked. Warren and I had never done that before. But I wanted to experience it *all* with Holden.

His finger pressed into the crack of my ass through my underwear. "How about here? Do you want me in here?"

I swallowed and nodded.

He smiled wickedly. "I'm going to leave marks. *Everywhere.*"

Oh God. I wanted him to do that, too. In the moment, I was pretty sure there wasn't anything he could say that I wouldn't agree to.

Holden lifted his hand to my face and cupped my cheek. "Are you sure about all of this? Because once I touch you, I'm not going to be able to stop, sweetheart. You need to be sure this is what you really want."

My answer was to crush my mouth to his. Holden laughed between our joined lips. "I'll take that as a yes."

"Oh my God. Shut up and kiss me already." I threw my arms around his neck and hoisted myself up, locking my legs around his waist.

"Yes, ma'am." He grabbed my waist and hitched me up higher as he started to walk. In his bedroom, he sat me on the edge of the mattress and dropped to his knees before pulling back to look at me. "I don't remember a time I didn't want you, Laney Ellison."

"I want you, too." But when I reached for him, he caught my hand and kissed the inside of my palm.

"I need to taste you first," he said. "I want you dripping wet when I slide inside of you."

I held my breath as he bunched up my skirt and bent to place a gentle kiss over the front of my panties. If I wasn't out of my mind with need, I might've been self-conscious that they were already soaked.

"You said you want me inside of you. But first you get my tongue." He hooked his thumbs into the sides of my panties. "Lift your ass or they rip."

I lifted, and he slid my underwear down my legs before nudging my knees apart. "Open for me. I want to see all of you."

My knees fell apart shamelessly, but Holden guided them still wider. He licked his lips as he looked between my legs. "Your pussy's even beautiful. Pink and perfect and so fucking wet for me already."

Holden lifted my right ankle and placed it over his shoulder before settling between my legs. His very first touch was a simple flick of his tongue over my clit, and I almost jumped off the bed. It felt like he'd hit a live wire. He smiled up at me before sucking the bud into his mouth, and my hands wound into his messy hair.

"Oh God. Please don't stop."

I felt him smile against me. "A bomb could go off, and you wouldn't be able to stop me. There's no going back now, sweetheart." He licked up and down my opening, his magical tongue pushing inside and exploring, then returning to focus on my throbbing clit. He hollowed his cheeks and sucked as one finger slipped inside and began to pump. When he added a second finger, I felt my body start to tremble. All of the muscles in my legs tightened as my orgasm built.

"Oh God," I gasped. "Holden…"

"Say my name, baby. Say it again."

He sucked harder, and his fingers thrust faster.

"Holden!" I was already about to come, and I tried to pull back. "Slow down."

"No fucking way. Come in my mouth, sweetheart. Come all over my face."

While my head wanted to rein things in and go slow, my body didn't need to be told twice. I flew over the edge, crying out Holden's name as he crooked the fingers inside me and hit a spot that made my entire body shake. I'd never had an orgasm explode like fireworks on the Fourth of July before.

After, I collapsed back on the bed, still panting. "Holy shit..."

Holden climbed to his feet and unbuttoned his jeans. "Jesus Christ. I can't wait to feel that on my cock."

I heard the zipper go down, denim brush over his legs, and the opening and closing of a drawer somewhere. Yet I was still in a fog, unable to really focus. That is...until Holden's boxer briefs came off.

I pushed up to my elbows and blinked a few times, making sure I wasn't seeing things.

"Holy crap, Holden. You're huge."

It might've been the first time this cocky man looked a little embarrassed. No wonder he was always so popular with women. Between what he looked like, that talented tongue, and the thick erection bobbing against his abdomen, it felt like I'd died and gone to sex-god heaven. And if the tatted and muscular package weren't enough, the way his beautiful, blue eyes looked at me so intensely stole the remaining air from my lungs. I'd never felt so wanted or desired.

"God, Holden. You really are perfect."

He shook his head. "I'm far from that, but I am going to make you feel like you've never felt before."

The scary part was, I already did. And it wasn't because he'd given me an earth-shattering orgasm; it was the way he made me feel inside—more alive than I'd ever been.

Holden scooped me from the edge of the bed and set me down in the center before he climbed on himself. He straddled me, one knee on either side of my hips, and used his teeth to tear open the condom wrapper before rolling it on.

I'd thought things were going to continue at the same frenzied pace they had been, but Holden didn't rush this time. He lowered himself onto me, weaved our fingers together, and pulled my hands up and over my head before taking my mouth in a sweet kiss. When his tongue dipped inside, I could taste myself, and it wasn't lost on me that Warren had always gone to the bathroom to brush his teeth after oral sex. This way was so much more erotic and intimate. Of course, Holden also really knew how to kiss; his touch was confident, with just the right amount of aggressiveness.

After a while, Holden pulled back to look into my eyes as he pushed inside me. The veins in his neck bulged as he eased in and out.

"Fuck. You're so wet and tight. If you don't relax a little, this is going to be really embarrassing for me."

Considering I'd been in a state of nirvana since his first touch, I didn't think that was possible, but I tried. It helped when Holden took my mouth again. His kisses were like drugs—they made me forget where I was and everything going on in the world around me. Not to mention, I was reasonably certain they were as addictive as the hardcore stuff.

When Holden pulled back the next time, he smiled. "I didn't think it was possible for me to think you were any more beautiful, but the way you look when I'm inside you is easily the most incredible thing I've ever laid eyes on." His face grew serious. "I want to watch you come."

Holden was hard as a rock and rubbing along a spot that made my eyes roll into the back of my head. So he wasn't going to have to wait very long to get what he wanted. Especially once he started to move faster. His gentle thrusts grew more intense, and he rooted deeper with each plunge down. But he never broke our gaze. The way he stared into my eyes made me question if I knew what the hell I was doing, yet it also made me question how the hell I'd accepted anything less than this feeling before.

Holden reached down and guided one of my knees up. The change in position allowed him to sink deeper, and I moaned as my muscles began to pulsate around him.

"Holden…"

He gritted his teeth. "Right there with you, baby." His pupils dilated as he continued to stare down, watching my face as he drove into me over and over.

Unlike all the other times I'd had sex, my orgasm didn't take its time to bloom. It shot out of a cannon, making my toes curl and my nails sink into the flesh of his back. Holden kept going, pumping into me ferociously until my body finally gave out and went slack. Then he buried himself deep with a groan and let go.

"You know…" I played with the light smattering of hair on Holden's chest. "The first time I ever masturbated was because of you."

"Oh yeah? Tell me about it."

I'd been curled up on top of Holden since we woke up an hour ago. My cheek was pressed to his chest, but I turned now and propped my chin on my fist to look up at him while I spoke. "You were in the pool in our backyard with Nancy McDonald."

"Who?"

"Nancy McDonald."

He shrugged. "I don't think I remember her."

"Seriously? You had your tongue down her throat and you don't remember her?"

"What did she look like?"

"Brunette, long hair, big boobs. She had on an American flag bathing suit. It was a day or two after the Fourth of July."

Holden squinted. "American flag bathing suit sounds familiar."

I shook my head. "I can't believe I remember you kissing her and *you* don't."

"I remember *you* had a blue bathing suit with silver stars on it."

"I did. It was my first string bikini. I'd had two-piece suits before, but never a string bikini. I'd talked my mother into buying it for my thirteenth birthday by reminding her I was now a teenager. She'd made me agree not to wear it anywhere but in our yard." I smiled. "That worked for me, since I only wanted it to get your attention anyway."

"Oh, it got my attention alright. But go back to your masturbation story. I want to hear how you got off the first time to thoughts of me."

"You're lucky you redeemed yourself by remembering my bathing suit because I was considering not sharing my story when you couldn't even remember Nancy McDonald."

Holden kissed my forehead. "I only remember the important things."

"So anyway, while you were busy kissing Nancy in the pool, I was watching from my bedroom window. Getting busy with myself, with my hand down my pants."

"*Whoa!* Lala Ellison, you naughty girl. I didn't know you were a voyeur. My sweet little brainiac is a little bit freaky, getting off on watching others. I like it."

I laughed. "I spent most of the time pretending I was Nancy, so I think it was more about sparking my imagination and less about me getting hot and bothered watching the two of you together. So you might not want to get your hopes up. I'm pretty sure that's the freakiest thing I've done in my life."

"We can fix that, you know."

I bit down on my bottom lip. "I know you're teasing, but I wouldn't mind exploring my sexuality a bit with you."

"That can be arranged. What did you have in mind?"

"I don't know. Nothing specific really. But I'm not too experienced, and obviously you are. I trust you, and I think it could be fun to try something different."

"I'm game. But you should give me an idea about what would be new to you."

"*Everything* would be new to me, Holden. I haven't done anything daring."

"Ever been tied up?"

I shook my head. "Nope."

"Sex in a car?"

"Nope."

"Sex in public?"

"Definitely not."

"Sixty-nine?"

I shook my head.

"Anal?"

"Never."

My cell phone alarm interrupted with a loud buzzing. I reached over to the end table and turned it off, looking at the time. "I can't believe it's six thirty already. I need to get to work." I leaned up and brushed my lips over Holden's. "I gotta go next door and shower."

"You can't leave me now." He took my hand and slid it between his legs. "Look what you did…"

"I didn't even touch you. I think you're just perpetually hard."

"You didn't have to touch me. You just told me I'm going to be the first one to do sixty-nine with you *and* anal. Of course I'm hard."

I laughed. "I never said you were going to be the first to do either of those things. I said I'd never done them."

He pulled me to him and flipped us, so I was suddenly on my back, and he hovered over me. "Oh, I'm going to be your first for lots of things, sweetheart."

"We'll have to discuss this later, because I really need to get to work."

"What about my erection?"

I pressed my lips to his and smiled. "You'll just have to do what I did when you were busy kissing Nancy McDonald."

Holden pouted. "How about I shower with you?"

I wiggled out from beneath him and got out of the bed. "That will definitely make me late."

"Can I see you later then? After work? We can order in and eat naked."

I smiled and leaned down for a kiss. "Okay."

Holden watched as I collected my clothes off the floor and got dressed. When I got to the door, he stopped me. "Lala?"

"Yeah?"

He folded his hands behind his head. "Since you're running out on me before finishing our conversation, you need to bring a sex to-do list when you come tonight."

"A sex to-do list?"

"That's right. I want a list of everything you've ever fantasized about."

I couldn't believe I was doing this. I'd cheated and Googled *sex bucket list* to give me some ideas. Then I'd gone through one by one and written down the things I thought might have potential.

Looking at the last entry on my list, I scribbled out *sex in public* and chewed on the top of my pen. *Could I have sex in public?*

Too many people have cameras.

Is it even safe to do?

I doubt it.

But damn…I had to admit the thought of doing it in public with Holden was pretty enticing. Then again, the thought of doing it *anywhere* with Holden made me feel tingly all over. So I put it back on the list, but added a big question mark after it.

What about a threesome?

With another girl?

Definitely not. I couldn't share Holden.

How about another guy?

What did I need that for? Holden was more than enough.

Sex toys with a partner?

Sure. Why not? I had a few of my own toys, but it wasn't something Warren and I had ever explored together. I bet it would be hot if Holden used one on me.

Mutual masturbation?

That one was definitely going on my list. Just envisioning Holden stroking himself while I watched made it difficult to sit still in my seat.

Being dominated by your partner?

I think I might be able to get into that, too.

I'd already discovered Holden had a naturally commanding way about him when it came to sex, which I loved. And because I already trusted him, the thought of submitting wasn't scary. It turned me on a little. But I did have a lot of work to do today, and making this list had me unable to think straight. So before I forced myself to focus on my job, I texted the man responsible for my distraction.

Lala: This list was a bad idea.

My phone buzzed with a response right away.

Holden: The sex to-do list?

Lala: Yes. I have a ton of work to do, and now I'm completely distracted, thinking about the things I wrote.

Holden: What was the last thing you wrote on your list?

The last thing I'd written was the most dicey, so I debated, but then I said *screw it*. I'd spent twenty-eight years being conservative. It was time I lived on the edge a bit.

Lala: Being dominated by your partner.

The dots started to jump around, then stopped. A minute later, they started again and paused once more before a message finally came in.

Holden: What time do you take lunch?

♥CHAPTER 18

Holden

Where to begin...
Where to begin...

I felt like a starving man at a buffet.

There was so much I wanted to do with Lala, and I couldn't seem to contain myself. We'd just been together this morning, but I needed to see her again already. I couldn't wait until tonight. In my defense, I'd waited a *long* time for this.

She finally responded to my text.

Lala: I take lunch in an hour.

My dick twitched. I'd always had a strong sexual appetite, but now I was Holden on steroids.

Holden: Good. I'm coming to meet you.

Lala: Okay. Anywhere in particular you want to go?

Holden: Down on you.

Lala: Where are we supposed to do that?

Holden: Oh, Lala, you have no idea how resourceful I can be.

Lala: OMG

I made a quick stop at the drug store before driving over to Lala's work.

A couple of minutes after I texted her that I'd arrived, she exited the revolving doors of her building. I reached out and pulled her into a kiss right there on the sidewalk in front of the lunchtime crowd. It didn't matter to me how many spectators we had. I'd waited too damn long for this to care.

When I let her go, I took her hand and led the way.

Her blond curls blew in the wind as excitement filled her eyes. "Where are we going?"

I smirked. "My van, actually."

"You want to have sex in your van? What if someone I work with sees us?"

"Don't worry. That ain't gonna happen."

We arrived at the garage where I'd parked my now completely blacked-out vehicle.

She looked it over. "I'm not even gonna ask why you have these window coverings on hand."

"Probably better if you don't."

"Creepy-van man," she teased.

"Guilty." I held up my hand. "Welcome to the dark side, Lala."

"You're the hottest creepy-van man I've ever seen, though. Pretty sure women would volunteer to be kidnapped by you."

"Flattery will get you everywhere, Miss Ellison." I leaned her against the van, pressed my body into hers, and nuzzled her neck. "I fucking missed you."

"It's only been a few hours, but this morning has been torture, hasn't it?" She bent her head back and closed her eyes, letting out a satisfied breath as I sucked on her skin.

I led her into the back of the van, which I'd cleared out, and Lala removed her jacket. "By the way, I already ate," she said. "Since I suspected no actual eating would be happening during lunch."

"Oh, there will be eating. Trust me. Speaking of which, take off your pants and spread those beautiful legs for me."

She eagerly removed her pants before slipping off her undies so she was naked from the waist down. Then she slipped her shirt over her head, leaving her in nothing but a lace bra.

Lowering my head, I ran my tongue along her clit in slow but intense circular strokes, eventually going lower and lower until my tongue found its way to her asshole, licking around it and then up and down her ass crack. Her breathing intensified.

I wasn't sure if that was a good or bad thing, so I stopped. "I know you've never had anal, but has anyone ever done *this* to you?"

"No."

"You want me to keep going?"

"Yes." She panted. "Please. That felt good."

Practically shaking with need, I began to explore her ass with my tongue, moving it ever so slowly in and out of her perfect, tight little asshole.

Her legs became restless. No longer able to hold back, I lifted myself up and grabbed the condom out of my pocket.

"Tell me what you want," I rasped.

"I think I…" She hesitated.

"What, Lala?"

"I want to try anal."

"Now?"

"Yes. What you just did to me made me want it."

Fuck, yeah. "I'm just warning you, if we jump right into that, I won't last very long."

"It's okay. I feel like I can come at any moment anyway."

Well, alright, then. I took a deep breath to grab my bearings. *She's never done this before, so you can't just go for it.* I needed to take it easy and make sure I didn't hurt her. That *also* reminded me…

"I want you to know, I had a doctor's appointment and got tested for everything two weeks ago. This might feel better for you if I don't use anything. But I don't know how you feel about that. Would you let me?"

After a moment, she said, "Yeah. I trust you."

Yes.

"Thank you."

There were no words to describe how turned on I was by what I was about to do to her. I tossed the condom aside, unable to fathom how freaking lucky I was. I reached into the front seat for a tube of lube I'd bought *just in case.*

"I came prepared. And no, I don't carry lube around in my creepy van." I chuckled. "I took a little trip to the drugstore this morning so I could be prepared for anything."

She looked up at me, lying on her back, and smiled, awaiting my next move. I opened the lube and squirted some out before using my middle finger to explore her hole. I inched it inside her ass until it was all the way in.

"How does that feel?" I whispered.

"Good."

"You want me to add another finger?"

She bit her bottom lip and murmured, "Yes."

As I slowly inserted a second finger inside, I used my other hand to massage her clit. My fingers were all the way in now. She was still so tight, and I wasn't entirely sure my dick was going to fit easily. There was only one way to find out.

"Do you feel ready for me?" I asked.

"I am."

"Spread your legs wider. I want you to touch yourself while I fuck your beautiful ass."

Lala began massaging her clit as I lowered my pants to my ankles. I took my rock-hard dick out and jerked it a few times, ready to come from the mere idea of what I was about to do.

"Tell me if I hurt you, okay? I'll stop."

"Okay," she breathed.

I squirted lube into my palm and rubbed it over my shaft. Placing the head of my cock at her opening, I moved it around in slow, circular motions for a while until I finally made my first attempt to enter her. Inch by inch, I eased in, moving gradually deeper and deeper. It took several minutes before I was able to push halfway inside of her. I moved in slow, controlled movements, not only because I was afraid of hurting her, but because I was in danger of losing it at any moment.

"You're so freaking tight…" I groaned. "Okay if I try to go deeper?"

She nodded through heavy breaths. "Yeah, it feels good."

Lala bent her legs back farther and tilted her ass to allow me better access. Eventually, I was all the way in and moving freely.

"Nothing in my entire life has ever felt like this," I muttered. It was the damn truth.

"You can go faster…" she said.

I was trying to go easy here and she wanted more? I wasn't sure I could handle it.

"When I come inside you, Lala, I want you to think about how you're mine and only mine, sweetheart. You got it?"

"Mmm-hmm." She tightened around me for a moment, nearly causing me to come.

Sliding in and out with ease now, I said, "You tell me when you're ready."

I continued fucking her slowly, my eyes alternating between rolling back in pleasure and watching myself enter and exit her, which was pretty much the hottest thing I'd ever had the pleasure of witnessing.

A few minutes later, she began to massage herself faster. "Come inside my ass, Holden. I'm ready."

Her words totally undid me as I thrust deep inside her once, my balls slapping as I exploded, filling her with my hot cum and pumping in and out until there was nothing left. *Holy shit. What just happened? That was phenomenal.* After we both came down from it, I lowered my head to her chest.

Her body shook with laughter. "I'm almost afraid for you to pull out."

"Don't worry. I'll clean you up nice and good before you have to go back."

"Not sure there's much you can do. I may have to use the work bathroom for like a half hour." She laughed.

"Sorry, yeah." I leaned to kiss her forehead. "I get that."

"Don't apologize. That felt amazing. Especially when you came."

"Amazing doesn't even properly describe what that felt like for me, beautiful." I ran my thumb across her lips. "Thank you for trusting me."

I slowly pulled out before lifting myself off her and reaching over to my bag to take out a towel I'd packed, knowing she might need it. I handed it to her. After she cleaned up—as best as one could in the back of a van—I looked at my phone.

"We still have like fifteen minutes before you have to be back. You said you ate, but do you want to get ice cream or something?"

"Anal and ice cream?" She broke out into hysterical laughter. "Why, you romantic man!"

"What can I say? I'm a romantic kind of guy." I pinned her under me and tickled her. "That's how we do it in the Creepy Lunchtime Van Express, baby."

Lala came over to my place straight after work, and we had sex a few more times that evening.

That might have seemed like a lot, but if you took into account our prolonged weeks of foreplay, we were simply making up for lost time.

It was after 9 PM before we finally rolled out of my bed and went to the kitchen so I could figure out what to make us to eat.

Lala leaned against my counter as I perused the fridge.

"So, you knocked three items off my list today," she said.

"Let me see…analingus, anal, and sex in a car, right?"

"Yup." She giggled.

"Not bad for a day's work, eh?" I winked.

"You're a workhorse, Holden." She sighed. Then her tone changed. "So… there's something I need to say."

I shut the fridge and turned to her, giving her all of my attention. "What's up?"

Lala fiddled with her hands. "Even though I told you I'd be up for *anything*, there is actually one thing that I wouldn't be willing to do with you."

"Okay…" I blinked. "I'm listening."

"I know I might appear eager and curious and all that, but I want to make it clear that I would *never* be okay with sharing. So threesomes are out of the question."

I couldn't help smiling as I walked over and wrapped my hands around her ass. "That's so funny."

"Why?"

"Because I can't even think about anyone else right now, let alone invite them into our bed, Lala. I would never want to share you with anyone—man or woman. The thought of anyone else touching you makes me sick to my stomach. You're the only girl I've ever felt that way about." I kissed her nose. "Anyway, I have a rule as far as threesomes go."

"What is it?"

"I would never expect a woman to share me if I couldn't also share her. It needs to be a two-way street. And under no circumstances would I ever be willing to share you."

"How long have you had that rule?"

"I just made it up." I smirked.

She smacked my chest. Our eyes locked, and then her expression turned serious again.

I pulled her in closer. "What's on your mind, sweetheart?"

She looked up at me. "I don't ever want this carefree feeling to end. Let's just take this day by day, not worrying about where it's going. I'm not ready to think about how to define what we're doing."

"We don't need to define anything right now," I said, though I already worried about what was going to happen when her research project was over. "We'll obviously have to figure things out when your contract ends, but that's not today."

"Yeah." She frowned. "I can't think about that right now."

"Let's not, then."

I ended up running out to the market since my fridge had been pretty depleted. We had rotisserie chicken, instant mashed potatoes, and steamed broccoli for dinner. It wasn't fancy, but it was edible, and Lala demolished what was on her plate.

We were hanging out in my kitchen, having a glass of wine after dinner when she said, "I should probably go back to my apartment so I don't wake you in the morning when I have to get up for work."

I put my glass down. "Stay with me. I promise to let you get some sleep."

"I don't know if I believe that." She poked my chest.

My dick stiffened. Jesus, all she had to do was poke me with her index finger, and I was already ready to poke *her*. She was right. She wouldn't get any sleep if she stayed over. Damn, I was weak.

Still, I persisted. "What do I have to do to convince you to stay?"

Just then there was a knock at the door. Without thinking it through, I opened it without checking who it was first. *Bad idea.* Standing there was a blonde I vaguely recognized. *Shit.*

"Hey, Holden." She smiled. "Please tell me you remember me."

I think her name was Piper? We'd had a one-night stand earlier this year. *This is not good. Why the fuck is she here?*

"Do you? Remember me?" she asked.

I ignored her question. "What are you doing here?"

"I know it's been a while since that time we hung out after your show. I was just in the area, and it reminded me of you. I figured I'd take a chance, come by, and say hello." She looked past me to Lala, who had her hand on her stomach, like she was about to throw up.

The woman's cheeks reddened. "Oh…gosh. I'm sorry. I didn't mean to interrupt."

"Yeah, I don't mean to be rude, but I'm…"

"Well…" She shook her head. "Yeah." She stepped back. "Forget I came by."

Piper (I think?) turned and headed back down the hall.

But the damage had been done. If I didn't feel so badly for Lala, I might've felt bad for how cold I'd just been to someone who really didn't deserve it. But I didn't give a crap about anyone but Lala right now. I looked over at her, feeling like a piece of shit.

I cleared my throat. "That was…someone I hadn't seen in at least six months, Lala—well before you ever moved here. I—"

Her face grew redder by the second. "It's fine. You don't have to explain."

"Really? Because I can see on your face that you're not okay, which tells me I *do* have to explain."

Now her neck was breaking out in a rash. *Great.*

She shrugged. "I mean, no explanation needed, right? I obviously *know* what she came here looking for."

"Maybe," I admitted. "But it doesn't fucking matter what she came here for. She's just a ghost from the past."

As much as I tried to pacify the situation, it still sucked and certainly didn't help my cause. My manwhore past was hard enough to overcome without it literally knocking on my door.

"Tell me how you feel, Lala. Don't hold back. If you don't trust me, tell me."

"It's not that." She let out a long breath. "It just makes me feel ragey when I think about you with other women, even if it's a part of life I can't erase."

I lifted my brow and slowly approached her. "Ragey, huh? Why don't you take your anger out on me, then?"

Lala looked at me a moment, panting, before she lifted my shirt off and dug her nails into my chest. "I feel like this is mine."

My dick rose to full staff. *That's so hot.*

"Then take what's yours," I demanded.

Her eyes filled with desire as she stared at my body. I had no idea where this was going. Then Lala dropped to her knees and unzipped my jeans.

Fuck yes. I was definitely into Angry Lala.

She began stroking my cock before she took me into her mouth as deeply as I could fit down her throat. She nearly gagged before she retreated back, only to swallow me whole again. She was claiming me with her mouth. Needless to say, I came pretty hard and fast, and she swallowed every ounce of my cum.

Lala licked her lips as she stood.

"Wow." I struggled to catch my breath.

"Any more girls show up here, that's what you're gonna get."

"An angry blowjob? I might line them up to come over, then."

She laughed as I wrapped my hands around her face. Our lips smashed together, and I could taste myself on her tongue as we fell into a deep kiss. I lifted her up as she wrapped her legs around me. I groaned into her mouth, pretty sure Laney Ellison was going to be the death of me.

Though delayed a little, Lala still insisted on heading back to her place that night. I longed for her every second she was gone, still feeling like crap that Piper (Petra?) had stopped by. Although Lala had handled it like a champ, I was certain it reminded her of all the reasons she should be wary of me. She'd likely conclude that this whole thing was a bad idea once the sex fog wore off. Who knew when that would happen? Sure, she'd broken off her engagement with Warren, but the whole thing just seemed too good to be true. I got the feeling her ex-fiancé wasn't going to go without a fight, either.

The thought of him coming back to knock some sense into her haunted me.

The next morning, Owen stopped by on his way to work.

"How's the sex-club search?" I asked as I poured some coffee.

"We still haven't found him the right place."

"I think you need to ask your client for a reduced membership fee, once it's all set."

"I won't be joining."

"Come on! It would be good for your sorry ass. When was the last time you had any action?"

"Why do I feel like you're asking me that to avoid having to talk about what you've been getting into lately? You've gone quiet, so I know that spells trouble."

As much as I didn't want to admit anything to Owen, I was glad he'd stopped by, because I needed his advice.

Maybe he could read my face because he immediately asked, "What have you done, Holden?"

I arched a brow. "Sure you want to know?"

He narrowed his eyes. "You had sex with Lala, didn't you?"

"Before you get on my ass, she broke off her engagement."

His jaw dropped. "Really?"

"Yep."

"That's one powerful dick you have, Catalano." He chuckled.

"Just to clarify, she broke off her engagement *before* we had sex."

"Okay…" He shook his head. "I don't need to know the details—please spare me—but why do you look so damn down? Isn't this what you wanted?"

"Let me ask you something," I said. "And be honest with me."

"Okay." He pulled out a chair, took a seat, and crossed his arms.

"Do you think maybe she's just using me for sex and doesn't even realize it?"

He scratched his chin for a moment. "That's an impossible question to answer. But there's no doubt that whatever you're giving her is unlike anything she's had before. I'm sure the newness and excitement of it is part of the intrigue for her. And I can't guarantee that's not going to wear off. Honestly, Holden, I think what happens after, though, is going to depend on *you*, not her."

"What do you mean?"

"We know by now what Lala is looking for. She wants an exciting sex life. She also wants a trustworthy man she can depend on. She basically wants it all, and who can blame her? But is a stable life something *you're* going to be able to give her? I mean, surely the excitement is going to wear off for *you*, too, at some point."

I hoped to God it never did and couldn't imagine that.

"What happens then, Holden? I think that's the biggest question. She's probably only going to walk away if you're not worth sticking around for."

I sighed. "Yeah…"

"Can you be the type of man Lala needs for the long term? That's still the lingering question here." He sighed. "And if the answer is yes, you have a lot of work to do to prove it. I don't think anyone would put their money on you being a reliable life partner. Your track record is the pits. But I hope you'll prove us wrong."

CHAPTER 19

Lala

The smile fell from my face as I read the name flashing on my cell phone.

Warren.

I'd assumed it would be Holden, since we'd been dirty texting back and forth all morning. I debated not answering, but I had so much guilt after breaking things off a week and a half ago and then running straight to another man's bed. It felt like the very least I could do was act like an adult and communicate.

So I swiped. "Hey, Warren."

"Hi, Laney." He was quiet for a few seconds. "Is this okay? I mean, am I allowed to call?"

My heart squeezed. "Of course. Why wouldn't it be?"

He sighed. "I don't know. This is new territory for me, and I'm not sure what to do."

"Well, I'm sorry if I made you feel like it wasn't okay to call. How are you?"

He went silent again. "Maybe we can talk about work or something. I don't want to start out on a negative note."

"Of course. Yeah, sure. How are things at work?"

"Pretty good. I've been working a lot, keeping myself busy, and this week I've made some solid progress on the immune cells I've been engineering, the ones from healthy donors that I'm using to target the blood-cancer cells in stage-two and -three patients."

"Oh, wow. Congratulations. Tell me more about it."

For the next twenty minutes, Warren explained how he was using Gamma T cells to promote cancer progression by inhibiting antitumor responses. Our conversation almost started to feel normal, like maybe we could be friendly without it being weird, until we came to a lull and he cleared his throat.

"How much time, Laney? Is it a week, a month, a year?"

I wasn't sure what we were talking about, considering ten seconds ago we'd been discussing the fact that his latest research might move to a human clinical trial at some point. "How much time for what?"

"You'd said you needed time apart, to live as a single woman. But I don't know what that means. Is it just a few weeks, or do you need longer?"

My gut twisted. "I don't know, Warren. I'm sorry I can't be more definitive, but I'm very confused, and I thought it was unfair of me to keep things moving down the same path when I wasn't ready to go where we were ultimately heading."

"I know I haven't been a great partner. I work too much and haven't been attentive enough. I took what we had for granted."

I shook my head. "No, Warren, it's not your fault at all. I meant it when I said you didn't do anything wrong. This is entirely about me. You were always a very good boyfriend."

His voice strained. "I should've moved to New York with you. I could've taken a leave of absence and showed you that you and your work meant more to me than staying here."

"Warren, no. What happened between us is not your fault. If you would have offered to come to New York, I wouldn't have let you. Your work is very important, and our relationship should have been able to weather a few months apart while I was here. Where we are today doesn't have anything to do with New York, really. I think sometimes we get on a path and keep following it without giving the destination any real thought. We fall into a nice routine and keep going. Being here just made me stop and question a lot about myself."

"I loved our routine, and I know where we were heading is exactly where I want to be, Laney. I'd marry you tomorrow, if that would make you happy."

That was a kick in the gut. But that's what I deserved. I'd committed to him and told him I felt the same, and then pulled the rug out from under him with no warning. "I'm sorry, Warren. I'm sorry you're hurting."

"Don't be sorry. Just take the time you need and come back to me. I'll be waiting. You're not wearing my ring anymore, but that doesn't mean my heart isn't with you. I'll be loyal to you, my love."

Oh God. I put my hand on my stomach, feeling a little queasy. I didn't know how to respond, so I didn't.

Eventually, Warren broke the silence. "I'll let you go," he said.

"Thank you for calling, Warren. I hope things continue to go well at work."

"Bye, Laney."

I lowered my phone and was just about to swipe to end the call when I heard Warren yell. "Wait! Laney!"

I raised the phone back to my ear. "Yes?"

"You'd tell me if there was another man, right? *Is there* someone else?"

Caught completely off guard, I panicked. "No. No, Warren, there isn't anyone else."

"Hey, stranger." Billie smiled.

I'd been staring straight ahead as I walked past the tattoo shop and hadn't noticed her walking out the door, only a few feet away.

I blinked. "Oh. Hey, Billie."

"I wasn't sure if you saw me. You looked lost in thought."

I attempted a smile. "Just tired."

Billie wiggled her eyebrows. "I heard you aren't getting much sleep these days." She laughed. "Sorry, the guys can't keep a secret. But I probably should've waited until you told me about you and Holden getting together before I started cracking jokes."

I shook my head. "It's fine. I've been meaning to come down to tell you."

She squinted at me. "What's the matter?"

"Nothing."

Billie put her hands on her hips. "I will kick that boy's ass if he's upset you already."

I laughed halfheartedly. "Holden hasn't done anything wrong. I swear."

"Then what's going on with you? I can tell something is off by your smile. Your mouth is moving, but the rest of your face isn't getting in on the action. You're usually a full-face smiler."

I took a deep breath and exhaled. "Warren called today."

"Oh boy." She rubbed her pregnant belly. "I can't have anything to drink, but it sounds like this conversation needs wine for at least one of us. There's a new café two blocks over that serves alcohol and dessert. What do you say we go get you a drink and this little guy, or girl, a brownie ice cream sundae?"

"That sounds perfect. Except I think I might need wine *and* dessert."

She hooked her arm with mine. "Now you're speaking my language."

Fifteen minutes later, we had three desserts on the table, and I'd already downed almost a full glass of wine.

"So is your ex giving you a hard time?" She shoveled a heaping spoon of brownie with vanilla ice cream into her mouth.

I shook my head. "Warren's been really amazing about everything. I just have so much guilt over jumping into bed with Holden. I went straight from breaking up with my fiancé to Holden's apartment."

"Can't say I'm surprised, though. You two have been playing the cat-and-mouse game for a long time. There must've been a lot of pent-up frustration."

I nodded. "We've spent *a lot* of time working that out the last few days."

Billie smiled. "I'll bet."

I looked down into my wine. "We've had an amazing time together. And I definitely have feelings for Holden. But I also still have feelings for Warren. I might not be engaged anymore, yet a part of me feels like I'm cheating on him."

"Well, our feelings aren't like light switches. We can't just turn them on and off. Ideally, it would have been nice if you had some time between one relationship and the other. Even when you're the one who ends a relationship, you still need time to heal from it. But you and Holden..." Billie scooped more brownie and ice cream and spoke with her mouth full. "I don't think anything could have stopped you. You've been on a collision course since that dance you shared at my wedding. It was impossible not to notice the way you were looking at each other."

I guzzled the rest of the wine in my glass. "I can't stop thinking about what would've happened if I hadn't come to New York. What if I hadn't realized I needed to see what else is out there until after I said I do? Would I have cheated on my husband?"

Billie shook her head. "Don't play the *what-if* game. No good can come of it. Look forward, not back."

Our waitress stopped at our table. "Another wine?"

"That would be great, thanks."

After she walked away, Billie pointed her spoon at me. "You just said you needed to see *what else* is out there. Is that true? Or is it only Holden you're interested in seeing?"

"You know, for my entire life, I've been the type of person who could tell you where I planned to be in five or ten years. I knew in middle school what I wanted to study in college, and when I finished college, I had my sights set on getting my own research study. A few months ago, I thought I saw my future with Warren. But right now, I can't seem to see farther than today and tomorrow, and those days I want to spend with Holden."

"Sometimes we need to live in the moment."

Billie and I sat at that café talking for more than two hours. During that short time, I knocked back four glasses of wine. They didn't hit me until I stood, but then I wobbled. And my pregnant friend wound up walking me home, when I should've been the one walking her.

I hugged her in front of the building. "Thank you so much for listening to me."

"Anytime, my friend." She smiled. "You look better."

"I actually feel a lot better." I leaned into her but forgot to whisper. "Alcohol makes me horny, so I think I'm going to stop by Holden's."

A man who had to be in his seventies stopped on the street. "I live at 210 West Street, apartment 3B, if Holden isn't available."

Billie and I cracked up. She yelled to me over her shoulder as I walked toward the door to the building. "Go get 'em, tiger."

Upstairs, Holden answered the door wearing a pair of low-hanging sweatpants and no shirt. He had a set of drumsticks in one hand, headphones around his neck, and his skin glistened.

"Oh my God." I hiccupped and covered my mouth. "You look so freaking hot."

He flashed a crooked smile. "Are you drunk?"

"I think I might be." I grinned and leaned forward. "And I'm also really horny."

He grabbed my hand and yanked me into his apartment. I yelped, but loved every moment of it.

"I can't wait to fuck you drunk."

I giggled. "And here I was worried you might refuse me because you were too much of a gentleman to have sex with a drunk girl."

"My dick was in your ass in the back of a van not too long ago, sweetheart. I think gentleman, when it comes to fucking you, is long gone."

"You're a pig." I snort-laughed.

"Damn right. And you're knocking on my door anyway." Holden scooped me off my feet and into his arms.

While he strode toward the bedroom, cradling me, I licked a line up his chest. "Yum. Salty. I wasn't sure if it was sweat or water from a shower."

"I've been playing the drums for an hour. What were *you* doing?"

"Drinking with Billie."

"Seems like you drank hers and yours."

I smiled. "Maybe. But I needed it."

"Bad day?"

"Warren called and told me he was going to be loyal to me. Then he asked me if there was someone else."

Holden froze two steps into the bedroom. "What did you tell him?"

"I told him there wasn't."

He set me down on my feet. Too tipsy to notice that the mood in the room had changed, I kept going in horny Lala land. Dropping to my knees, I reached for the waistband of Holden's sweats. But he caught my hand and moved it away.

"What are you doing?" I said, still oblivious and flirting. "I want you in my mouth."

Holden put his hands under my armpits and hoisted me back up. "You're too drunk."

"But you just said—"

"I'm going to go get you Motrin and water."

Before I could argue, he was halfway down the hall on his way to the kitchen. I was too drunk to fully understand that I'd upset him. After a few minutes, I realized I was also too drunk to remain upright. So I sat down on the edge of the bed and let myself fall back. A few more minutes went by, and he still hadn't come back, so I yawned and shut my eyes. And that was the last thing I remembered happening when I woke up at six thirty the next morning.

Propping myself up on my elbows, I was momentarily confused about where I was. Holden's apartment and mine looked a lot alike. But the big pile of drums in the corner of the bedroom helped me figure it out. Though Holden wasn't in the bed next to me. I rubbed sleep from my eyes and went in search of him.

"Hey."

I found him sitting in the dark at the kitchen table, drinking a cup of coffee. Wrapping my arms around him from behind, I kissed his neck. "What are you doing out here?"

"Thinking."

"About what?"

He turned and caught my eyes. "Why you didn't tell Warren you were with someone else."

Oh shit. A needle on a record scratched to a halt. Last night was a bit fuzzy, but I must've shared the conversation Warren and I had on the phone.

I sighed and sat down in the seat across from Holden. "I didn't tell him because I didn't want to hurt him. I just ended our engagement a few days ago, and everything happened so fast between us."

236

He nodded, staring down at his coffee mug. "So you'd rather hurt me than him…"

"No, no, it's not like that, Holden. Really it's not. It's just… He caught me off guard with that question, and I didn't have time to think things through. He'd sounded upset when he called, and I don't like to hurt people, especially ones who have always been kind to me. I absolutely wasn't thinking that the answer I gave to avoid upsetting him would hurt you. I don't want to hurt either of you."

Holden lifted his eyes to meet mine. "Is that all he wanted? To know if you were seeing anyone else?"

I shook my head. "He wanted to know how long I needed. I guess when I ended things, I told him I needed time for myself."

He frowned. "So things between you two aren't over for good? They're just…what? On hold? You're on a break of some kind? And I'm just the fuckboy you needed to get out of your system before you married the good guy?"

"No, Holden. It's not like that."

"Tell me what it *is* like, then. What am I to you?"

"I care about you. You know that. I've had a crush on you as far back as I can remember."

"Are you still in love with Warren?"

All of these questions made my head feel like it might explode. I'd broken things off with Warren and jumped into bed with Holden and not taken the time to figure out what I was doing. Yet I didn't want to lie. That would only make things more complicated.

"I don't know what my feelings are, Holden. I have a lot to sort out."

He pushed back from the table, the legs of his chair scraping along the tile, and stood. "It seems like the only thing you *do* know is that you want to fuck me." He thumbed toward the hall that led to his bedroom. "Should I go jerk off so I'm ready for you when you're in the mood?"

"Holden…"

He dragged a hand through his hair. "On second thought, I'm going to go shower. The lady in 408 needs her pipes snaked. It seems that's all I'm good for these days."

Later that night, I was still feeling down when I climbed out onto the fire escape with a glass of wine. I hadn't heard from Holden all day, and I couldn't say I blamed him for being upset. No one likes to feel like they aren't important enough to mention. Over the course of the day today, I'd thought a lot about why I'd lied to Warren. And it had nothing to do with Holden. I was embarrassed about my own actions, how I couldn't wait twenty-four hours after breaking off my engagement before jumping into bed with another man. I had no self-control when it came to Holden Catalano. And while I'd been selfishly enjoying the perks of that lack of self-control, I hadn't stopped to think about the consequences giving in came with.

Lost in thought about how I could've handled things better, I was a few sips into my wine when Holden opened his window. He climbed out and took a seat at the edge closest to where I sat.

"Hey," he said.

"Hi."

He looked down, shaking his head. "I'm sorry about how I acted this morning."

"I'm sorry, too. I swear to God, Holden, lying to Warren had nothing to do with you. I wasn't trying to hide you. I just didn't want to hurt him. And if I'm honest, I'm a little ashamed about my lack of self-control. I jumped you the minute I got back to New York after breaking things off with my fiancé. I didn't stop to think that not having my emotions sorted out could hurt other people." I sniffled back tears. "I just acted on impulse."

Holden reached through the bars of our fire escapes and cupped my cheek. "Don't cry, sweetheart." He smiled. "Your lack of self-control is the best thing to happen to me in a very long time."

I covered his hand on my cheek with my own. "I hope you can accept my apology."

"Only if you can accept mine. I get that you need some time, and I shouldn't have tried to force you to put a label on whatever is going on between us. You were upfront about what you wanted from the beginning. Let's just have some fun."

My shoulders relaxed for the first time today. "Really? Do you mean that?"

"I do." He held up a finger. "In fact, I bought you a little apology gift aimed at just that—having fun. I'll be right back."

Holden climbed into his apartment and came out a minute later carrying a red box with a big white bow tied around it. He slipped it through the bars of our adjoining fire escapes with a smile.

"This will make us both forget our little disagreement this morning."

The box was unmarked. I shook it. "Is it liquor? Because I think the glass of wine I'm drinking is more than enough after my evening with Billie last night."

"Open it and find out."

"Okay!" I felt like a kid on Christmas morning as I ripped the bow open and pulled the lid off the box. The inside was lined with velvet and contained two items, one of which I recognized. I smiled and covered my mouth.

"Oh my God. You bought me a vibrator?"

"It's from your list. I believe it was number six: playing with toys together. By the way, I didn't realize all we have to do is write down what we want and our wishes come true. Santa's definitely going to be getting an eyeful from me this year..."

I laughed. "You're so crazy. But what's this other thing?"

"We each got a toy. That one is for me." He dug his cell from his pocket and held it up. "It syncs up with a phone. I've already connected mine. We insert that part inside of you, and I can make it vibrate, pulse, or rumble from anywhere in the world."

My eyes widened. "Rumble?"

He grinned. "You want to go try it, don't you?"

I covered my smile with my hand.

"I'll take that smile as a yes," he said. "Now go get naked. I want you spread-eagled on the bed before I get next door so we can consummate my apology."

❤CHAPTER 20

Lala

It was amazing how much more exciting weekends were now that I knew I'd be spending them with Holden. The end of the work week couldn't come fast enough.

Friday night after I got home, I took a long shower before going over to his apartment. As the water poured down on me, I felt on top of the world, growing more excited by the minute about our weekend plans, even if I had no clue what they were.

All refreshed and ready for whatever the night would bring— hopefully amazing sex—I went next door to Holden's place.

When he opened the door, he looked amazingly hot in his gray beanie and a plain burgundy tee. My nipples hardened at the mere sight of him. But my horny haze was interrupted when I looked into his eyes and sensed that something wasn't right.

"What's going on, Holden? You look kind of down," I said.

He sighed. "Yeah, we need to talk. Something's come up."

Oh no. My stomach sank as a number of worst-case scenarios flooded my mind. *Are we done?* "Okay…" I gulped.

"So…our manager called a little bit ago to let me know she booked us a bunch of new gigs."

I blinked. "That's good, right?"

He frowned. "They're all out on the west coast, Lala."

It took a few seconds to set in. He didn't say west side. He said west *coast*. *He's leaving?* "Oh…" A feeling of dread filled me. "Did you know this was a possibility?"

He nodded. "I knew she was working on getting us booked out there at some point, but she'd made it seem like it wasn't going to happen for a while. Now she's telling us she's lined up several stops from Oregon all the way down through southern California. Apparently, she met a booking manager out there who made it all come together."

I took a deep breath. "When is this all happening?"

Holden's jaw flexed. "We're supposed to fly out there some-time next week."

What? "Wow. Next week." I rubbed my nauseous stomach. "How long will you be gone?"

"At least two weeks. That's what's lined up as of now. But it could be longer."

Two weeks wasn't that long, but somehow I knew it would feel like forever.

Holden must have sensed my inner panic as I stood there speechless.

"You know what? Come here," he said as he brought me into his arms. "I hadn't even hugged you yet before I sprung this on you." He breathed into my neck. "If this amazing thing wasn't hap-pening between us, I would be happy about leaving, but every-thing's different now. I want nothing but to soak up every minute with you while you're in New York."

When Holden let me go, I gazed at the streetlights outside his window for a moment, unable to meet his eyes. "How is it even possible for your manager to spring something like this on you with so little notice?"

Holden scratched his chin. "Well, that's the thing about the music business. You're sort of expected to drop everything and take opportunities when they come. I'm fortunate that the guys and I have an understanding about that in terms of my job around here. They know the music comes first."

Right. The music comes *first. Don't forget that, Lala.* "What about the other band members?" I asked. "They have day jobs they can just drop?"

"They all do jobs similar to mine, and they have deals with their bosses. If an opportunity comes up, the music takes priority. Obviously, with all that I handle around here, we'll have to hire a temporary service to do the maintenance, which we have in our budget. The guys have always known this could happen and I would need to be gone. So we've planned for it."

I was sure I'd be the only one *not* okay with him leaving. But it wasn't because I didn't want him to have the opportunity. I wanted all the success in the world for him. I just didn't want to be apart when things were just starting between us.

I stared back out the window in a daze.

Holden placed his hand gently on my chin and brought my face up to meet his eyes. "Talk to me, Lala."

"Well, obviously I'm completely bummed about this, but I would never in a million years try to stand in your way. It is what it is, and I'm so proud of you, Holden." I reached up and placed a chaste kiss on his lips.

"Thank you, sweetheart. It's a pretty big deal, since there are a lot of music execs out there. The goal is to try to get a few of them to our shows."

"Yeah. That makes sense." My gaze drifted to the ground.

Holden again lifted my chin to meet his eyes. "The last thing I want to do right now is leave. The thought of it is killing me."

I ran my hand along his stubble. "It's only two weeks, right? And I'll still be here when you get back."

"Two weeks will feel like two fucking years. We both know it."

I exhaled. "Any person in your life has to expect this kind of thing. I would never want to hinder your musical aspirations or tie you down."

"Well, you can always tie me down in a literal sense. We haven't tried that one yet," he joked, forcing a smile. "And if this is really upsetting you, I want you to be honest with me, even if I still have to go. I want to know what you're thinking right now."

I sighed. "It's only upsetting because I won't get to be with you. But just because I'm sad doesn't mean I'm not also incredibly happy that you have this opportunity."

He took me in his arms and scooped me up off the ground, spinning me around as he groaned. Wrapping his hands around my ass, he said, "How about this? We have a week together before I have to leave." He put me down. "Let's just vow to make it the best fucking week ever—not let anything stand in the way of fully enjoying each other."

"Okay." I grinned, trying my best to hide my feeling of impending doom.

I had not seen this coming, but I *should have*. That's the thing. This news was a slap in the face from reality about what being a musician's girl was like. Maybe it was better that I experienced this now rather than later. I needed to understand what I was getting my heart into.

That evening, Holden made his best efforts to take my mind off of his leaving. He took me out to a nice Italian restaurant called Vincente's Trattoria that I had been wanting to try. I vowed to relax and enjoy my time with him—especially now that I knew how precious that time was.

Under the dim lights, with distant Italian music playing, I had just about managed to forget the bad stuff when our beautiful waitress appeared.

Rather than greeting us in a normal fashion, the attractive brunette simply looked toward Holden and said, "Oh."

It didn't take me long to figure out what was going on.

"I didn't know you worked here," he finally said.

"Well, I just started a few weeks ago." She turned to me. "Uh, hi, I'm Sasha...a friend of Holden's."

A *friend. Sure.*

Seeming flustered, she shook her head. "Anyway, what can I get you guys to drink?"

The table fell silent for a few seconds before Holden said, "I'll take a glass of cabernet." He turned to me. "Lala?"

I swallowed. "I'll have a glass of chardonnay."

Sasha cleared her throat. "I'll be right back with those."

After she walked away, I placed my cloth napkin on my lap. "Well, I would ask who that was, but I'm fairly certain I can put two and two together."

Holden's eyes seared into mine. "I didn't know she worked here. I wouldn't have taken you here if I did."

"Why?" I shrugged, trying not to lose my cool. "I mean, what's the difference? I've seen girls at your shows who you used to hook up with. It seems we can't go anywhere in this city without running into them." I snorted.

While I know bitterness and jealousy didn't look good on me, my feelings were impossible to hide. I'd already been struggling with the news that he was going on the road for two weeks. This just added fuel to the fire.

Holden reached for my hand. "I'm fucking sorry."

Feeling my emotions spiral, I blurted, "Exactly how many women have you slept with?"

His eyes widened.

I couldn't help it. I'd always been curious.

"I have no problem talking about this, Lala. You know I'm an open person. But the topic upsets you, so I'm curious as to why you'd want to go there right now, when you're already upset enough as it is?"

My heart hammered against my chest. "Well…I might have this ridiculous number in my head, and maybe it's not even as bad as I think it is."

Holden's face turned a little red. I'd officially made him uncomfortable. That wasn't my intention. I knew I'd gone too far, but there seemed to be no turning back now.

"The truth is… I don't know exactly how many women I've slept with," he said after a moment. "I never counted. I was always safe, but there have been…lots. I won't lie to you."

"Hundreds?" I asked, as my curiosity continued to get the best of me.

He didn't say anything.

Oh my God. Thousands?

"Not hundreds plural," he answered. "But…*dozens* maybe, if I had to guess." He exhaled and shook his head. "I never cared about being judged for any of that before. But I do care about *your* opinion of me." His face held a serious expression. "I hate that my past keeps coming back to haunt me. But I was who I was. And I hope you know that despite that, nothing has mattered to me as much as being with you right now."

My chest tightened. I was a horrible human for having shamed him. I suddenly snapped out of my jealous haze enough to see it. "God, I'm sorry, Holden. I'm actually really upset at myself right now for how I've handled this conversation."

"You had every right to ask me that question. I get it, sweetheart. I really do. I couldn't even handle the thought of you with Warren, let alone if the waiter who came to our table was someone you had been with on top of that. I understand how jealousy feels.

I'm just sorry you've had to experience this feeling multiple times because of my history. That's on me."

"You owe me no apologies, Holden."

When Sasha came back with our drinks, I vowed to calm down. I tried to accept the fact that she was beautiful. I tried to accept the fact that she had slept with Holden, and I did my best to move on and treat her like I would treat any waitress—not someone who had fucked my boyfriend.

Is he my boyfriend?

At one point, after she'd dropped off our entrees, Holden said, "I appreciate you trying to pretend you're not upset. But Lala, when your neck turns red, that's always a dead giveaway. That's telling me you're still affected."

Damn. "It's not so much that I'm still upset about her," I admitted. "It's just that my feelings for you are getting stronger, and I'm sensitized right now to every little thing since you're leaving. I know it's not a huge amount of time, but it's a reminder of what life might be like if we were together." I took a long sip of my wine. "Just something I'd have to get used to."

He swallowed uncomfortably, and I knew he understood what I was getting at, even if I hadn't said it: I still doubted whether he could ever be the type of man who settles down.

For the next week, Holden and I made every effort to spend each night together and not focus on the fact that he was leaving. We had dinner together every evening after I came home from work, and lots of sex.

But the night before he had to leave for his trip, reality set in hard. The one thing we hadn't done this week was sleep over at each other's apartments, because I always had to get up early, and I knew if we spent the whole night together, neither of us would get any rest. But tonight was different.

We were just finishing cleaning up after dinner when Holden wrapped his arms around me from behind.

"I know you need to get up early in the morning, but I really need to spend the night in your bed tonight," he said.

I turned to face him. "You read my mind. Of course. I don't need sleep tonight. I just need you."

"You're *all* I need lately…period." Holden lifted me and carried me to my bedroom, kissing me passionately. As he began to undress me, I raked my fingers through his thick hair, eventually lowering my hands to pull off his shirt. It felt like I couldn't have him inside of me fast enough.

Once we were naked, we fell lazily onto the bed. Holden locked my hands over my head before entering me in one swift movement. I let out an unintelligible sound of pleasure.

"I don't want to leave you," he muttered against my mouth as he slowly fucked me.

I relished every powerful thrust, unsure if this would be the last time we'd have sex for two weeks.

Our bodies rocked together in sync as Holden looked deeply into my eyes and never once moved his gaze away from me. That had to be the sexiest thing he'd ever done—so simple yet so intense.

Jesus. It terrified me how hard I was falling for this man.

"You're so fucking beautiful," he whispered as he moved in and out. "I'm gonna miss you…" *Thrust…* "So…" *Thrust…* "Fucking…" *Thrust…* "Much." *Thrust.*

That undid my resolve. "Come inside me, Holden," I panted.

His eyes rolled back as he groaned, and I felt the heat from him seep into me as he covered my neck and chest with kisses.

We'd had sex in many ways over the past several days, but this time was special. It felt different, and I didn't dare mention that to him. Because then I'd have to admit the reason: it felt like he was making love to me, more than just having sex. I didn't want to scare him away.

After Holden got up to get a towel, he returned to bed, wrapped his arms around me, and pulled me close. We never did have sex again that night. And despite the worries still swirling around in my head, I managed to fall asleep peacefully in his arms.

The following morning, I was no longer able to hide my sadness. Holden was set to take a car to the airport about an hour after I left for work. We had to say goodbye now since I was already late.

We stared at each other blankly as we chugged down our coffee.

He shook his head. "I have no desire to leave you. Please tell me we're going to talk every night and you're not going to worry about anything when it comes to me. I give you my word that I won't do anything stupid." He sighed. "Yes, I was who I was back then. But right now? I'm not him, Lala. I don't want you stressing while I'm gone."

My stomach hurt even more knowing he'd felt he had to give me that assurance. That was my fault because of how insecure I'd acted recently. "I trust you, Holden. As much as I sometimes get jealous, please know that it has nothing to do with a lack of trust."

He took my hands in his. "I want you to call me anytime you feel like you need me—doesn't matter if you think I'm in the middle of something." Holden opened his backpack and took out a sheet of paper. "Also, I've printed out a detailed itinerary of every place we'll be and when, along with the contact info in case you can't reach me on my cell for some reason." He handed it to me.

This was adorable. I suspected he'd never printed out an itinerary for anyone else in his entire life.

"The guys all know you're leaving this morning, right?"

He nodded. "They've hired a maintenance service to cover for me." He opened his arms. "Come here. I need to hold you one last time before I leave."

After leaning my head against his chest for several minutes, I looked up at him.

Holden placed one last firm kiss on my lips. "I already miss you so damn much, and I haven't even left yet."

"I feel exactly the same." I looked over at the clock. "Shit, I have to go."

"Okay," he murmured.

I gave my gorgeous maybe-boyfriend one final-final kiss on the lips, took one last look at his beautiful face, and walked out of my apartment, feeling empty and worried for the future, despite all of Holden's assurances.

♥CHAPTER 21

Holden

"**W**hat the fuck, Catalano?" Dylan, our bass player, said. "You got an STD or something?"

I looked up from breaking down my drum set. "What the hell are you talking about?"

He motioned to the woman who'd just stopped over to tell me how much she'd enjoyed the show…and asked if she could buy me a drink.

"Oh, that. Not interested."

"Really?" Monroe chimed in. "She looks right up your alley. Long hair, big tits, nice ass. Not to mention those plump lips look like they would make some really nice dick pillows for your head."

I chuckled but shook my other head. "I only have one type these days, boys—a certain brainiac blonde who's back home waiting for my return."

Dylan raised a brow before glancing around to the other guys. "I got fifty he doesn't make two weeks."

"A hundred says he doesn't make it out of Oregon without at least a blowjob," Kevin added, putting away his guitar.

Monroe pulled a wad of cash from his front pocket and twirled the microphone in his hand. He motioned to two women I hadn't noticed, who were gazing my way and smiling. One sucked on the straw in her drink suggestively. "Oregon? I'm pretty sure those are identical twins. They were sitting in the front row. The one in red has a tongue ring. I got two hundred he doesn't make the *night*."

I shook my head as I dismantled the tension rod from the bass drum. "I'll take every single one of your bets, you fools. Because the only thing I'm looking forward to taking to bed with me tonight, or any other night during this trip, is my iPad, so I can FaceTime with my girl."

Dylan nodded. "It's definitely gonorrhea."

After we finished loading the van, the guys went back into the bar for drinks, but I decided to call it a night. I was all too familiar with the attention we got when we stuck around after playing, and I didn't want to put myself in that situation. Not that there would be any temptation on my part—I was a blissfully satisfied man these days—but even hanging out with women I knew would be into fooling around seemed wrong. The guys could joke all they wanted, but I was living my best life getting to play on stage and then going back to my room to tell my girl all about the day. Which was exactly what I did.

"Oh my gosh. You need to put a shirt on." Lala's face came on the screen, and she smiled. "It's unfair that I should have to look at that and then go to bed alone."

I was sitting with my back against the headboard, wearing only boxer briefs. Locking my hands together behind my head, I made sure to flex my biceps. "Are you saying you like what you see, sweetheart?"

Lala sighed. "I wish I could *lick* what I see right now."

I smiled. "How was your day?"

"Good. Busy. I went to one of the assisted-care centers I'm working with to check in on how everyone is doing."

"Is it going well?"

She nodded. "I really love working with older people. They have so many stories to share. Mr. Wentz, one of the gentlemen in my study, has been married for fifty-seven years. He met his wife at three years old, when her family moved in next door to his in Chicago. They grew up as best friends, but by the time they were teenagers, they were madly in love. When his wife was sixteen, her father got transferred to Switzerland for work. They wanted to get married and stay together, but their parents wouldn't allow it, and eventually they lost touch since she lived so far away. Eight years later, they were both engaged to be married to other people when they wound up on the same subway car in Manhattan. Mr. Wentz was there on a business trip for only that day, and Mrs. Wentz was there to visit her sick grandfather. According to Mr. Wentz, his heart started beating again on that train. That very night, he broke off his engagement and quit his job, since they wouldn't let him extend his trip in New York. He said he wasn't letting her out of his sight a second time."

"Wow. Sounds like it was fate. It's not as impressive as winning the girl from her fiancé by acting like a complete douchebag in a bar, but it's a decent story."

Lala laughed. "How was your show tonight? I didn't expect to hear from you this early. What time did it end?"

I shrugged. "About a half hour ago, maybe. I took a shower before calling you."

"I thought you guys usually had drinks after your shows?"

"We do. The guys stuck around, but I wasn't in the mood for it. I wanted to come back and call you."

She smiled. "I'm glad you did. I thought about you a lot today."

"Yeah?"

"I was thinking maybe we could take a weekend trip after you're home?"

"I'm game. Where to?"

"Up to the Hudson Valley. When we were kids, we went to a wedding at this place called Mohonk Mountain House. I think staying there is really expensive, so we can stay somewhere else nearby, but they have all these beautiful hiking trails and the most amazing views of the mountains. I thought it would be nice to go while the weather is still warm."

"So you've been thinking about getting away just the two of us, huh?"

"Yeah, is that weird?"

The fact that she was thinking about doing things with me—going hiking and taking a road trip together—gave me hope. As much as I loved fucking her, I wanted more with Lala. And this was the first real sign that maybe she did, too. "No, it's not weird at all. I'd love to go. I love the outdoors, and it gives me something to look forward to. I've only been gone four days, and I miss you already."

Her face went soft. "I miss—"

Her cell phone started ringing. It must've been nearby, because for a second I thought it was mine. "Ummm... Hang on a minute. Okay, Holden? It's my parents calling, and it's pretty late here. I want to make sure nothing is wrong."

"Yeah, of course. Go ahead."

I watched as she swiped to answer. "Hello?"

I could only hear one side of the conversation, but I didn't need to hear the other person. From the look on Lala's face, I could tell the call was *not* good news.

"When? Is she okay? Where is she?"

Fuck. It's her mother.

Lala put her hand over her mouth as she listened. "I'll be there as soon as I can. Will you be at the hospital?"

Quiet.

"No, I want to come, Dad. It should be a pretty quick drive at this time. I'll call you when I'm close."

More quiet.

"Okay, bye."

She swiped to hang up, and my heart was already racing.

"What happened?"

"My mom…" Her eyes filled with tears. "She had a heart attack, Holden."

"Fuck. Is she okay?"

Lala got up and started walking with the iPad. She went into her bedroom and began to toss clothes into a bag. "My dad said she's stable now, but they found a blockage. She was taken by ambulance, and they're probably going to do surgery tomorrow." She rubbed her forehead. "Thank God I didn't have that wine I thought about earlier, or I might not be able to drive. I never gave any thought to what I would do in an emergency."

"Don't think about that now. One of the guys could always drive you, if you needed."

"Holden, what happens if my mom…" She got choked up.

Fuck, I wished I was there to hold her, to go with her, to be by her side. "She's going to be okay, sweetheart."

"You can't know that!"

I raked a hand through my hair. "She's okay now, and she's in a hospital where she's going to get the help she needs. What hospital is she in?"

"Jefferson."

"That's a great hospital. It's known for cardiac care. She's in good hands."

"I need to hang up." She looked around the room and zipped up a duffle bag. "I've got to get on the road."

"Maybe we should call one of the guys? I don't want you driving in the dark while you're upset."

"No, I'm fine."

I frowned. "Can you do me one favor before you go, at least?"

"What?"

"Sit down."

"I can't. I need to leave, Holden."

"Just for one minute…I promise."

She sighed, but sat. "What?"

"Take a deep breath."

She took a small one.

I smiled. "A bigger one. Actually, close your eyes and give me three deep breaths."

She didn't look happy about it, but she nonetheless did what I asked. I watched as she closed her eyes and counted three deep breaths. When she opened, I smiled.

"Thank you. She's going to be fine. Drive safe, okay?"

"Yeah." She nodded. "Okay."

"Call me after you get there. Or shoot me a text. Whatever is easier. Just let me know how Mrs. E is doing and that you arrived safely."

She nodded. "I will. Bye."

I didn't sleep at all. Lala hadn't called or texted. The drive from Manhattan to Philly shouldn't have been more than two-and-a-half hours at the time she left, but four hours had gone by without a word. Every bad scenario played out in my head.

She had an accident.

Mrs. E had another heart attack and didn't make it.

She and her father are too much of a mess to call anyone.

Fuck. I hated that I wasn't with her. And as selfish and immature as it was, I also couldn't help but worry about what would happen when she was in Philly again. Would she turn to Warren for comfort? Lala's mother—a woman who'd been like a second mother to me for most of my life—was in the hospital with a serious medical condition, and I was so damn self-absorbed that I couldn't stop thinking about Lala being near her ex. That made me feel like an even bigger piece of shit.

More hours went by. I tried to convince myself that maybe she'd fallen asleep on the chair next to her mom's bed and everything was fine. But by 7 AM Philly time, I was pacing my hotel room and figured it was a somewhat okay time to call.

Her phone rang once and went straight to voicemail. I hated not reaching her, but left a message anyway.

"Hey, sweetheart. It's about seven your time. I just wanted to check in and see how things were going. Just let me know when you get a chance." I paused. "I'm thinking about you and your mom, and I'm sorry I'm not there with you."

A half hour later, I had to start packing for our next stop. The band needed to get on the road this morning, and we were supposed to meet downstairs for the free breakfast before that. Just as I opened my hotel room door, my phone buzzed with an incoming text. I stopped to read it.

Lala: Sorry I haven't called. Mom is stable, though she's still in Afib—atrial fibrillation, where the heart beats irregularly. They don't allow phones to be used in the ICU, so I had mine off. I haven't wanted to leave the unit in case a doctor came by. Rounds finally just started. There's a group of doctors going bed to bed, and they're currently three beds away from us. Hopefully, they'll get to us soon. I'll try to call you after.

Holden: Okay. Good luck.

I didn't hear from her while we had breakfast, loaded the SUV with all of our equipment, or for the first two-and-a-half hours into our drive. I tried my best not to be a pest, but eventually I sent another text.

Holden: Sorry. Just wanted to check in. Did you get to meet with the docs yet?

My phone rang a few minutes later. I was in the backseat with two guitar cases on the seat between me and Dylan, while Kevin was up front with Monroe, who was driving. I had zero privacy.

"Hello?"

"Hey, I'm sorry I didn't call sooner with an update. It's the first time I've left the ICU since I got here. I came outside to take a quick walk and get some fresh air."

"No worries. I just wanted to see how your mom was doing. And how you're holding up?"

She blew out an audible breath. "They took Mom into surgery a few minutes ago. They're doing a bypass. The blockage couldn't be cleared with angioplasty."

"Shit, I'm sorry, babe. She's young and strong, though. I'm sure she'll do okay."

"The doctors are optimistic, but I can't help being terrified. And I could tell Mom was, too, before she went in."

"Yeah, of course. It's got to be scary."

I heard a man's voice in the distance. "Hey. How's Jean doing?"

"Oh…hi, Warren. What are you doing here?"

My teeth gritted as I listened to their conversation.

"My mom heard from your parents' neighbor, Irene Davis, that there was an ambulance at the house. She called me, and I called you, but your phone went to voicemail. I called Bill, and he filled me in."

"My dad filled you in?"

"I spoke to him about a half hour ago."

"Oh. He didn't mention that you'd called."

My jaw clenched so tight, I was surprised I didn't crack a tooth. First of all, he was there, and I wasn't. But also…*Bill?* Not Mr. Ellison, like I'd always called him. And I certainly didn't have her father's phone number. I realized all over again what Warren had been to her, what he'd been to her entire family.

"Are you on the phone?" Warren asked.

"Oh…shoot. Yes, I am. Excuse me a minute."

She came back on the line. "Hey. Umm…Warren just showed up."

"I heard."

"Oh…okay."

So many emotions hit me, and I didn't know what to do with any of them. I guess I was quiet for a while.

"Are you still there?" Lala asked.

"Yeah, I'm here."

She lowered her voice. "I'm sorry."

I frowned, but had to suck it up for Lala's sake. "Nothing to be sorry about, sweetheart. I'm glad someone is there for you. And I'll let you go, so you can go back and be with your dad."

"Are you sure you're okay?"

The last thing she should be worrying about right now was me. "Of course. Call me later and let me know how everything goes. Okay?"

"Alright."

"I hope everything goes smoothly."

"Thanks."

"Bye."

Dylan eyed me when I hung up. I hadn't told them what had gone down yet. "Everything okay?"

"My girlfriend's mom had a heart attack last night. They just took her in for a bypass."

"Shit. Sorry, man." He was quiet for a moment, then cracked a small smile. "Girlfriend, huh? Don't think I've ever heard you use that word."

The funny thing is, I hadn't even realized I'd said it. But deep down, that's what Lala was to me…*my girl.* Unfortunately, I wasn't sure if I was *her guy*…and she was currently with a man who I was certain still wanted her.

❤CHAPTER 22

Holden

"**L**ook what the cat dragged in!" Dylan said.

That night, we were setting up for our second show in Oregon when I turned to find our manager, Daisy, walking toward the stage.

She held her arms in the air. "Surprise!"

Each of the guys walked over and greeted her. Daisy was really cool. She'd been our manager for almost two years now. Right before we'd signed with her, she and I had a little thing together. It only lasted for two months, since she lived out in California and was looking for a husband-type, and I was on the east coast and looking for a good time. But we'd parted as friends, and our past had never been an issue since we'd started working together. She was also engaged now.

"What's up, Daze?" I kissed her cheek. "Looking good, as always."

She smiled. "And you're looking the part of a rock star, as always. Good to see you, Holden."

"What brings you to Portland?" Dylan asked. "I know you don't go this far north for nothing."

"You're right, I don't. It's too freaking cold up here. But I made an exception to watch my favorite clients play and to give you some good news." She clapped her hands. "I have a record label coming to see you when you get down to San Francisco in a few days. And not a small one—a *major* one with a shitload of Grammy-winning artists: Interlude."

"Holy shit," Dylan said. "Interlude is huge!"

"I sent them your newest demo, and one of the scouts really loved a few of your songs, enough to come hear you in person."

Dylan lifted Daisy off the ground and spun her around. The rest of the guys and I settled for high fives.

After we caught up for a little while, it was almost time for us to go on. Daisy took a seat at a table off to the side of the stage, and the guys started warming up. I walked over to her.

"Hey, Daze? Can you do me a favor and keep my phone?"

She smiled. "You want me to field calls from groupies and arrange for them to come by your room at different times?"

"Nah. I'm waiting for a call from someone. If you could just let me know if it rings. You don't have to answer it. But if the call comes in, we'll take a quick set break so I can call back."

"Sure, of course."

I pulled out my phone and handed it to her. "Thanks."

She tilted her head. "You okay, Holden?"

I shrugged. "I've been better."

"You want to talk about it?"

"Maybe later. We gotta get started."

"Okay."

I pointed to my phone. "Lala. That's the name of the person I'm waiting for a call from. If you can just give me a signal if she pops up."

"You got it, Holden."

Over the next ninety minutes of our set, I must've looked over at Daisy a hundred times to see if Lala had called. But she never did. After we were done playing, the guys headed to Daisy's table for drinks. I didn't much feel like partying, but the mood among the rest of the band was celebratory, and I didn't want to be a downer. So I joined in. After two rounds, the guys were all talking to different women at various places around the bar, and it was just me and Daisy. She'd had a few drinks already, which was unlike her.

"How about a shot of tequila?" she asked when the waitress came to check on us.

I'd been nursing my second beer for the better part of an hour. Before I had the opportunity to decline, she turned back to the waitress. "Two shots of Don Julio, please. And I'll take another tequila sour."

I lifted a brow when the waitress left. "You're celebrating pretty hard tonight. Does that mean you're feeling good about the producer who's coming to see us?"

She let out a big sigh. "I broke things off with Rob last night."

"Your fiancé? Why? I thought he was such a great guy."

"He is. He's the *greatest guy*. That's why it sucked to have to dump him."

"What was the problem?"

"We just had no chemistry. I've tried a bunch of things to get some sparks going, but it just wasn't there." She shook her head. "I'm too young to be in a dull marriage. I like sex too much."

I finished off my beer. "That sucks. You can force a lot of things, but chemistry isn't one of them."

The waitress brought over our shots and Daisy's drink. "You want another beer?" she asked.

"No, thank you."

Daisy held up her shot, so I raised mine. "To good sex, like we used to have."

I clinked but didn't add anything, not wanting to give her the wrong impression.

"So who's this Lala you were waiting for a call from?"

263

"A woman I'm seeing."

"And you're waiting on her, not the other way around? That doesn't sound like the Holden Catalano I know."

I smiled. "Yeah, it's definitely new to me. And I can't say that I'm enjoying being on the receiving end of the person not calling when they said they would."

"She must be special."

I nodded. "She is."

"I'm guessing you have chemistry together?"

"We do."

She started to laugh. "I bet no woman has ever complained about not having enough chemistry with you. You're too sexy for your own good." She pointed to my face. "The eyes, the scruff, the whole I-don't-give-two-shits attitude. Hell, even a damn beanie is hot when you wear it." Daisy chugged back half her drink.

"Maybe you should slow down a little?"

"Fuck that. I'm on the road to getting shit faced."

An hour later, she arrived at her destination. Somehow I'd become her babysitter, and now I was stuck helping her into an Uber to get back to our hotel. She was so drunk, I had to keep my arm around her to make sure she stayed upright when we got out. At her room, I opened the door and flipped on the lights. Two steps inside, she dropped her purse. It landed upside down, and the contents spilled all over. I helped her to the bed before gathering all the crap from the floor. Then I put everything, including her leather clutch and phone, on the end table and walked down to the foot of the bed to take off her sandals.

"Alright, Daze. You're in your room. I'm going to head out. You going to be okay?"

She smiled with her eyes shut. "Where are you going? Don't you want to fuck me? I'm single now, you know."

It was probably the alcohol talking. But drunk or sober, I had zero interest in any other woman than Lala. In fact, just being alone in a hotel room with another woman made me feel uneasy. So I leaned down and kissed Daisy's forehead.

"I'll check on you in the morning."

I thought I might've heard snoring as I pulled the door closed behind me.

Back in my room, I was relieved to be alone. I couldn't wait any more to call Lala. Her lack of communication was freaking me out. I needed to get some sleep tonight, so I was going to reach out, even though she was supposed to call me. I kicked off my shoes and chugged half a bottle of the free water the hotel left each day, then sat down on the bed and took out my cell.

Except…my code didn't work.

I tried a second time. Then a third, before turning the phone over.

A purple case? Mine was black. *Fuck,* this wasn't my phone. I'd had my cell in my hand when I picked up Daisy's shit from the floor, including her phone. I must've taken hers by mistake and not mine.

Fuck.

I hated to be a dick and wake her, but I really needed my phone. I didn't even know Lala's number without it. So without bothering to put my shoes on, I went back to Daisy's room and knocked.

No answer.

Great. Just great.

I knocked louder, then put my mouth near the crack of the door.

"Daisy! It's Holden. I think we have each other's cell phones! Can you open the door?"

The third time I knocked, a door opened, but it wasn't the one I was knocking on.

"People are trying to sleep, goddammit!" An older man yelled.

I waved. "Sorry."

He slammed the door, and my shoulders slumped. I put my ear to the door, hoping maybe the commotion had stirred Daisy, but the only thing I heard was a loud-ass snore.

Fuck my life.

The following morning, I waited until seven o'clock before going back to Daisy's room. I hadn't slept yet again, and I was going out of my mind not having my phone and being able to communicate with Lala with everything she was going through.

Daisy had always been a morning person, so I hoped that hadn't changed. I knocked lightly, not wanting to piss off the guy next door again. Thankfully she answered this time. She was still wearing the clothes from the night before and looked like crap.

"I'm sorry to bug you so early." I held out her phone. "But I think we have each other's phones. I must've taken the wrong one when I left your room last night."

She nodded. "Yeah, we do. I was going to go down to the lobby and see if I could schmooze your room number from the front-desk guy once the Tylenol I just swallowed kicked in and took the edge off the pounding in my head."

She walked inside and grabbed my cell, while I held the door to her room open and waited. "I didn't realize it wasn't mine when I answered it a few minutes ago. That's what woke me up."

"My phone rang? Who was it?"

"Lala."

I closed my eyes and dropped my head. "Shit."

"Yeah, I'm sorry. I told her you weren't here, and you must've left your phone here when you helped me to my room last night, but she didn't sound like she believed me."

Awesome. Just freaking awesome. "Alright. Thanks, Daisy. I'll see you later at checkout?"

She nodded. "I'm sorry for being such a lightweight last night. I hope I wasn't inappropriate or obnoxious. Some of the evening is a little fuzzy."

I forced a smile. "Nah. You were all good."

Rather than go back to my room, I went downstairs and got some coffee and fresh air. I was going to need to be more alert than I felt right now for my conversation with Lala. Searching my missed calls, I found that she'd called twice last night and then again this morning when Daisy had picked up. Given my history with women, I knew it wasn't going to look good. But I hung onto the hope that she and I had built some trust over the last two months. Though that hope went in the toilet when she picked up and I heard her curt tone.

"Yes?"

"Hey, babe."

"Seriously, Holden? You're going to *hey, babe* me like nothing happened? Or did your groupie forget to tell you I called?"

I shut my eyes. "It wasn't a groupie. It was Daisy, our manager."

"Who was in your bed…"

"No, she wasn't in my bed. She was in hers. And I was in mine—not sleeping because I couldn't contact you. I accidentally took Daisy's phone and left mine with her last night. She'd had too much to drink, and I walked her to her room, where she proceeded to drop her purse and spill everything inside all over the floor. I picked her stuff up, and I grabbed the wrong phone."

"Oh? I see. So you're a gentleman, then?"

I didn't have to ask if she was being sarcastic. "I'm telling you the truth, Lala."

"Whatever."

"No, not whatever. I'm telling you the honest-to-God truth that nothing happened. And I think you should believe me. I've not done anything to make you doubt my loyalty to you."

"You don't have to. Your history tells the story, Holden."

I didn't have any right to get angry. I knew exactly how it looked. But for some reason, her blaming my history for her lack of trust in me pissed me off. "How about giving me some credit, Lala? I know you think I'm a big manwhore because I have more experience than you. But not once have I cheated on a girl I was in a committed relationship with. I slept around when I was single. I know you don't like to hear that, but I can't go back and change it."

"No, you can't," she said.

"As long as we're on the topic of sleeping around, where did *you* sleep last night? Last we talked, you were with Warren and were going to call me back. My phone didn't ring all day. Have you gone back to him? Are you done with me already? Did you get what you needed and I'm dismissed?"

"I can't do this right now." Lala sniffled. "My mom is in the ICU, and I can't take any more stress."

Oh fuck. I made her cry. "I'm sorry, sweetheart. I didn't mean to upset you. I just…I feel so frustrated that you don't believe me. Trust me, if you understood how much I think about you, you would not have any questions about whether I could be with another woman. I'm freaking crazy about you, Lala."

"I'm sorry, too."

"Can we start this conversation over?"

"I can't right now. I need to go back inside for rounds in a minute. They just started when my phone rang, so I stepped out."

"Alright. But tell me how your mom is doing first."

"They were able to clear the blockage, and she tolerated the surgery well. But it's open heart, so they had to cut through her breastbone to get in. She's in a lot of pain and groggy still. But her doctors think she'll make a full recovery."

"Oh, thank God."

"Yeah."

268

"I hate to let you go, but I know you need to get back in there. Are we good? I swear nothing happened, Lala. I would never do that to you."

"Yeah, we're good." She didn't sound too convincing.

"Will you call me later?" I asked.

"I will."

"Alright. Bye, sweetheart."

"Hey. Sorry to bother you all so early."

Two days later, I'd texted the guys in the band at nine o'clock in the morning, asking if everyone could meet me in the lobby. We weren't supposed to get on the road to San Francisco until check-out time, which was eleven. Today would be a lot of driving, and tomorrow night was the gig the record producer was scheduled to come to. I rubbed the back of my neck as I spoke to the group. "I need to leave for the day today. But I'd like you to all be okay with it."

Everyone started to freak out.

"What do you mean leave?" Kevin said. "We have the producer coming tomorrow night. We can't play without a drummer."

"I know. And I promise I'll be back in time. I booked a noon flight out today, and tomorrow I'll be on a noon flight from the east coast, which gets in at three because of the time change. We don't go on until ten, so I have a good cushion."

"What if they cancel your flight back?"

"I'll get on another one. I'll take three planes if I have to. Or if there's high winds or some reason why I can't fly into San Francisco to meet you, I'll fly as close as I can get and drive the rest. I won't let you guys down."

Dylan shook his head. "Don't fuck us over, dude."

"I won't."

"You've never once flaked on us, so if you say you'll be there."
Monroe shook his head. "You'll be there."

I nodded and looked to Dylan. He looked less confident, but
nodded.

Kevin frowned. "Can you at least tell us what's so important?"

"Lala's mom is sick." I paused and was going to leave it at
that, but then decided better of it. "And Daisy answered my phone
when she called the other morning. I wasn't even with her. We'd
inadvertently switched phones the night before. But it didn't look
good, especially with my history and all. We've been talking, but
things are off, and I don't want to leave it any longer. I need to see
her in person."

Dylan nodded. "You want a ride to the airport?"

"Yeah, if you don't mind. That would be great."

Nine hours later, I pulled up at Jefferson Hospital. I went to
the waiting room closest to the ICU and texted Lala. She had no
idea I was coming, and I had no idea if she was even here...or if
Warren was still hanging around.

Holden: Are you still at the hospital?

She texted back a few minutes later.

**Lala: Yes. I'll probably leave in an hour or two. Dad's
going to stay overnight tonight.**

**Holden: Can you go to the waiting room for a minute? I
have a surprise there for you.**

**Lala: A surprise in the waiting room? Which one? And
how?**

Holden: The one closest to the ICU entrance.

Lala: Okay.

I leaned against the doorway. It was directly at the end of the
hallway that led to the ICU ward, so I figured I'd see her when the

double doors opened. Thirty seconds later, they did, and Lala's eyes went wide.

"Oh my God." She ran to me.

I engulfed her in a bear hug, lifting her off her feet.

"What are you doing here?"

"I wanted to make sure you were okay."

"But you have your big show tomorrow night. The one with the record producer."

I nodded. "I know. I'll be back in time. I'm on the noon flight out tomorrow."

She looked into my eyes. "I can't believe you're here."

"I'm sorry I couldn't come sooner." I pulled her against me and took her mouth in a kiss. "I'm sorry for upsetting you, Lala."

She softened. "Thank you for coming. It means a lot."

The double doors leading to the ICU opened again. Lala's back was facing them, but I saw the man coming out before he saw me...before he saw us.

"Your father..." I whispered.

Lala stepped back and smoothed her top. Mr. Ellison noticed his daughter at the end of the hall and smiled. Then his eyes lifted to my face and his smile wilted.

Bill is definitely not giving me his cell phone number anytime soon. "Hey, Mr. Ellison."

"Holden. What are you doing here?"

I looked at Lala, and she gave me a face that confirmed what I'd suspected—her parents had no idea about us. Extending my hand, I smiled as best I could. "I'm in town for a gig, and I heard about Mrs. E. I figured I'd come see how she was and check on Lala."

He smiled. "That was very nice of you. Jean is doing much better. Thank you."

"I'm glad to hear it."

"I was just heading to the men's room, if you'd like to go in and visit. They only allow two people at a time. Lala can take you in."

I nodded. "Thank you."

I followed Lala down the hall to her mother's room. Mrs. Ellison was sleeping, but she looked better than I would have thought. "She looks really good."

"I put a little makeup on her and did her hair. My mom is old school and would hate for anyone to see her without her face on." Lala made air quotes.

"Whatever makes her happy."

We visited for a little while, and then Mr. Ellison returned. The three of us made small talk. Lala had been here since last night, and Mr. Ellison was taking the overnight shift this evening.

"Dad, I'm going to get going," Lala told him. "I don't want us to get in trouble for having three people in here. And I'm really tired. All the bells and whistles kept me up last night again."

Mr. Ellison nodded. "Go get some sleep."

"I'll be back in the morning before rounds."

"Alright, honey."

I extended my hand to Lala's dad. "I'm going to head out, too. It was good seeing you, Mr. Ellison. I hope Mrs. Ellison makes a speedy recovery."

He smiled warmly. "You're going to be thirty soon. I think you can call me Bill now, son."

Well, well, well…maybe there's hope after all.

❤CHAPTER 23

Lala

The following morning, Holden and I were lying in bed, neither of us ready to get up and face the world.

I still couldn't believe he'd come all the way here.

After we got back to my house last night, we'd almost started fighting again until he'd grabbed my face and kissed me, hard. Then he carried me to my room and made love to me like he had the night before he left New York—slowly, sensually, and in a way that made me certain my heart was all-in to the point of no return.

The morning sun streamed through the window. As we lay side by side in my old bed, I grew anxious, knowing I was about to bring up the subject of the woman who'd answered his phone. I trusted his explanation, yet I still felt unsettled about it—both the situation itself and my reaction to it.

"You should get to the airport early to make sure you don't miss your flight," I said.

"I want to go to the hospital with you first."

"You don't have to, Holden."

"Yes, I do. I want to be here for you every second I can until I absolutely have to leave." He searched my eyes. "You're hesitant

273

about me going? Don't worry. I'll make up a story again for your dad."

"You shouldn't have to do that."

"Yeah, but come on. We have no choice right now since they don't know about us." He shrugged. "It's not a big deal."

There was another reason why Holden's being there might cause a scene today.

"Warren said he might be stopping by this morning."

Holden took a deep breath in and let it out slowly. "Okay. Whatever. I'll feed him the same story." He rolled his eyes. "I fucking hate that you care what he thinks. But I get it. You don't need the drama right now. I can put my ego aside for a day."

"Thank you for understanding." I ran my fingers along his chest and added, "Speaking of which, I owe you an apology for the way I reacted to that woman answering your phone."

"No, you don't. You reacted the way I sure as fuck would've if the situation were reversed. The whole thing was just bad luck. I don't blame you for freaking out."

"If she's your manager, why didn't she just explain who she was? She could've easily done that. But she sounded shady, to be honest."

Holden sat up straighter in bed and turned his whole body toward me. He hesitated. "Daisy is my manager, but...she and I had a quick fling once."

My stomach turned as I moved back and muttered, "Of course."

"Fuck." He shut his eyes briefly. "Would you rather I lie to you, Lala?"

"No, I wouldn't."

"We'd both moved on. She got engaged earlier this year. I was really happy for her, because the dude seemed like a nice guy. But then she told me she broke it off with him recently. I think she might've been hoping something would happen between us during this tour. But when she insinuated that, I told her about you." He sighed. "Anyway, she might not have properly explained herself out of spite since I'd turned her down."

I nodded. "Thank you for explaining. I'm sorry I'm so on edge. You've had to put up with a lot, too, when it comes to Warren being around. We have to trust each other."

"Tell me you really mean that, Lala. Look into my eyes and tell me you trust me. I need to hear it before I go back on tour."

I got up and straddled him, wrapping my hands around his stubbly cheeks. "I trust you, Holden. I do."

He placed his hands over mine. "I came to make you feel better, not to cause you any more stress."

"You leaving the tour and coming here means so much to me."

After we dragged ourselves out of bed, Holden whipped us up some eggs and coffee before we headed out.

The hospital visit went more smoothly than I'd anticipated, since Warren never did show. That was a huge relief.

Holden fed my dad a story that I'd offered to drive him to the airport today. I couldn't imagine what my father would've had to say if he knew Holden had spent the entire night with me.

But despite that little awkward lie, we got the best news ever: my mother was out of the ICU, and her condition was stable. I felt confident enough to leave the hospital when it came time to take Holden to the airport without feeling like I'd be missing anything important.

When we got to the drop-off area at Philly International, Holden towered over me as he enveloped my body in his. The hair not covered by his beanie was blowing in the wind.

"Your visit went by way too fast." I spoke into his chest. "I wish so badly that you didn't have to leave."

"I can't even begin to express how much I wish the same, sweetheart. This fucking sucks."

THE RULES OF DATING MY BEST FRIEND'S SISTER

I looked up at him. "If my mother continues to get better, I'm gonna go back to New York in a few days."

"Okay." He squeezed me tighter. "Call me day or night. Seriously, Lala. You're my priority. None of the other shit matters right now."

"Knock 'em dead tonight at the show. I'll be thinking of you."

"I'll be thinking of *you* every fucking second." Holden lifted me up in grand fashion.

I giggled at the gesture.

He looked into my eyes and said, "I…" He hesitated as he put me down.

My heartbeat sped up…

"I'm gonna miss you so fucking much," he finally said.

And just like that, my heart deflated.

A few days later, I was at my parents' house packing my things. Since my mother was set to be discharged soon, I was clear to return to New York.

It was a huge relief that Mom was going to be okay, and I was so grateful that I'd been able to be here, even if I was now super behind with my research project. Ultimately, that didn't matter. Nothing mattered more than family.

My father appeared at the doorway to my bedroom. "Can I come in?"

"Sure." I put down the shirt I'd folded. "I didn't know you were here."

"Just came home to grab a few things and stock the fridge." He went silent for a bit as he watched me pack. "How long have you been messing around with Holden Catalano?"

I froze. "Why are you asking me that?"

"I saw him with his arms around you that first day he showed up at the hospital, Lala. But more than that, I'm not stupid. You don't think I'm able to put two and two together? You end your engagement to a great guy. You live next door to Holden. He randomly shows up at the hospital and just so happens to be in town. Do you think your dad is blind?"

I exhaled. "Okay. Yes, Holden and I have been seeing each other." Admitting that felt like a huge weight had been lifted.

He raised a brow. "Are you telling me you left Warren for him?"

"No. I mean, Holden might have been a mitigating factor, but I ended my engagement because I wasn't ready to be tied down, Dad. Plain and simple. Holden and I are just…having fun right now. Seeing where things go."

"Jesus, Laney. I don't have to tell you why this sounds like a really bad idea."

"I know you have preconceived notions about him, Dad. But Holden and I care about each other. I can't say with a hundred-percent certainty that I know where it's going, but I trust him. He's not gonna hurt me."

"I know he was a damn good friend to your brother. But his reputation certainly precedes him. I just hope you know what you're doing."

"I *don't* know what I'm doing exactly." I laughed. "But right now, I'm happy. In a different way than I've ever been happy before. I feel…" I paused. "Alive."

He nodded. "Well, then I have to accept that."

The doorbell rang, interrupting our conversation.

"Are you expecting someone?" I asked.

"No."

Dad and I walked together to the front door.

When he opened it, I saw Warren standing there, wearing a short-sleeve collared shirt and a bow tie.

"Hi, Bill. Just came to say goodbye to Laney before I have to head to work."

My father stepped aside. "Come on in, son."

"Hey." I waved.

"Hi." A look of sadness crossed Warren's face.

My father grabbed his keys. "I'll, uh, give you guys some privacy. I need to get to the market and pick up some things before Mom comes home anyway. I'll be back in time to see you off, honey."

"Okay, Dad."

After my father left, I looked up at Warren, who was twiddling his thumbs nervously.

"You seem preoccupied. Is everything okay?" I asked.

"No," he said. "Things really aren't okay, Laney."

"Come sit."

He took a seat across from me on the couch in the living room.

"Talk to me, Warren."

"Well…" He sighed. "I got it—the job in California."

"You did?" I smiled. "That's amazing!"

There wasn't a shred of joy on his face. "Is it?"

"Yes."

"This might be the opportunity of a lifetime. But if it meant us getting back together, I would turn it down in a heartbeat. I know you never wanted to move out there. And you mean more to me than a job."

My chest constricted. "You need to take it."

He hung his head. "I guess I know what that means."

My voice shook. "I'm so sorry, Warren."

He lifted his gaze to meet mine. "I can only hope to God that when you come to your senses, you'll want to join me out there. I'm not giving up hope on us, even knowing you haven't been hon-

278

est with me. Even knowing you broke my heart, I still can't give up on us."

His words took a moment to register. "You said I haven't been honest with you. What are you referring to?"

His stare was penetrating. "Was *he* the reason you left me?"

I gulped. "Who?"

"Holden."

My mouth opened and closed a few times. "How…"

He stared at the lamp vacantly. "I came to the hospital a few days ago. He was there with you, holding you—when it should've been me. You were tucked away in a corner by a vending machine, probably hiding. You likely didn't know I'd be coming from that direction, but I'd stopped to use the bathroom. You were too wrapped up to notice me." Warren rubbed his temples. "I left because I wasn't in the mood to make a fool of myself."

That tore my heart into a million pieces. "I'm so sorry, Warren. I should've told you I'd started seeing him. He's not the main reason I ended things. It was more about a need to experience life before settling down. But—"

"It just so happens *he* was right there when you made that decision, I suppose?" Warren stood. "I need to go. I'm late for a meeting." He walked toward the door but turned around before leaving. "I'm not going to judge you for your choices. He would not be the type of man I'd choose for you. He's a phase, Laney. And you *will* come to your senses. I am confident of that. I plan to wait for you to do that, but I don't know that I can wait forever."

Mentally spent, I arrived back in New York that night feeling terrible about myself. At the same time, I was happy that Warren had gotten the job in California. He deserved a change of pace, in a new environment where every corner wouldn't remind him of me.

That said, his words about Holden being a phase had gotten into my head a little, especially since I'd had ample time alone in my car to let everything fester.

After taking a shower and getting into comfortable clothes, I curled into my sofa and decided to check out After Friday's Instagram page. There were photos posted of the last couple of gigs, including the one the night Holden returned from Pennsylvania. He'd told me that one went particularly well and that the music exec had told their manager he'd be in touch.

They must have put someone in charge of taking these supposedly candid shots, because they looked fantastic—Monroe making love to the mic, Dylan playing bass with his eyes closed. I particularly loved the shots of Holden swinging his drumsticks under the neon lights. His eyes held so much passion. It made me miss the heck out of him. I would've given anything for him to be next door right now.

Almost as soon as I had that thought, my phone began to ring. It was a FaceTime call from Holden. As fast as humanly possible, I answered, "Hey! How did you know I was thinking about you?"

"Are you back in New York?"

"Yes. I got stuck in killer traffic, so I just got back a little while ago."

"Damn. It's almost eleven there. That sucks. But I'm so glad you got back safely."

Holden had mentioned the band would have a tour bus for the last leg of their trip, and I could see he was lying down in a cramped space. His hair was going in all directions. How I wished I could've run my hands through it.

"What are you up to tonight?" I asked.

"We have the night off. A couple of the guys are heading out clubbing, but I'm just gonna order a pizza and hang out on the bus and watch movies."

"Why aren't you going out with them?"

"Just no interest. I'm wiped, and all I want to do is talk to you."

"Syphilis!"

I cocked my head. "Did someone just say syphilis?"

"That was Monroe. Ignore him."

"Chlamydia!"

"Who was that?"

"Dylan."

"Why did he say that?"

"The guys have a running joke that the reason I'm not into partying is because I have an STD. I've told them why I have no interest in hooking up with random women out here, but they're having too much fun ragging on me. They're acting up worse right now because they see me on the phone with you. Ignore them, please."

I laughed. "That's crazy."

He suddenly got up and began walking to the back of the bus. "Hang on. I'm going to the bedroom for some privacy."

Holden lay back on a bed. "Ah. That's better." He reached to his side and lifted up a lace thong. "Monroe had a little too much fun in here earlier today."

"Ew." I laughed.

I remember him telling me they'd take turns using the main bedroom as opposed to sleeping in the bunks.

"I wish I were there lying in that bed with you."

"Why don't we pretend, beautiful?" He slipped his shirt over his head, showcasing his gorgeous chest and tats. The man was a work of art.

Every nerve ending in my body rose to attention. I'd planned to spend this phone call filling him in on what happened with Warren, but forgetting about everything sounded like a much better idea.

"Can anyone barge in on you right now?" I asked.

"Nope. I locked the door."

With that, I slipped my own shirt over my head.

Holden's mouth dropped. I guess he hadn't been expecting me to do that. "Are you trying to kill me?"

"I just thought since I get to look at your beautiful chest, you might want to look at mine."

"You know I love those tits, but it's like torture since I can't suck on them. If we're doing this, though, I'm down, Lala."

I began to circle the tips of my fingers around my nipples.

"Oh…it's on, then?" Holden's eyes filled with mischief as he moved to adjust something. He lowered the phone momentarily. "See what you did?"

He was completely hard, his marvelous cock sticking straight up in the air.

Feeling hornier by the second, I murmured, "I want to watch you stroke it."

"Oh, you dirty girl. I fucking love it when you talk like that." He grinned. "And of course, I'll touch myself for you, but only if you do the same for me."

I raised the phone to an aerial position so that he got a full view of me as I slipped my shorts down and began massaging my clit.

Holden's head bent back as he jerked his cock up and down and groaned. "Keep the phone like that so I can watch you. That is so freaking hot, Lala."

Closing my eyes, I got lost in our mutual masturbation.

"I'm gonna lose it," he finally groaned.

I looked over at the screen to see the explosion of cum spurting from the tip of his cock.

I let go, too, feeling the muscles between my legs contract as I surrendered to this much-needed ecstasy after a long few days. I let out a long sigh. "That was so good."

He panted. "We need to do that more often while I'm out here."

"Now that I'm home, we can."

"Yeah. Probably wouldn't have been wise to get off to me on FaceTime while your dad could've popped in at any time back in Pennsylvania."

That reminded me. I could at least tell him this part of the story right now. "Speaking of my dad…"

Holden pulled his pants up and sat straighter. "What's up?"

"Well, he saw us hugging at the hospital, and he put two and two together."

He shut his eyes. "Shit."

"It's okay. I admitted we've been seeing each other. He accepted it."

"Was it really that easy, or are you holding back?"

I didn't want to lie… "He's concerned about your reputation, but I think that's understandable considering you were pretty wild and always had a different girl around the last time he spent any amount of time with you."

Holden pulled on his hair and seemed to be contemplating something.

"What are you thinking?"

"I'm thinking I'd want to kill me if I were him."

I ended up telling him about Warren getting the job in California and the fact that I'd admitted to my ex what had been going on between Holden and me.

We stayed on the phone a while longer, until I could no longer stay awake. While the future still remained uncertain, I closed my eyes to the sound of Holden's voice, knowing that for now, moments like tonight with him were all I needed.

♥CHAPTER 24

Lala

I felt like I might jump out of my skin.

Lord knows nothing was holding me back, since most of my flesh was already on display. I took one last look in the mirror and drew in a deep breath. *I look good… No, I don't look good. I look hot, if I do say so myself.* After thirteen days of not seeing Holden, he was finally coming home today. To celebrate the occasion, I'd stopped at a lingerie store and picked up something spicy. I'd initially tried on a pretty white baby-doll nightgown, which had probably fit my personality better. But then I'd decided to go outside my comfort zone and try on something I thought Holden might like. In the end I bought a red, one-piece teddy with a tie-neck halter, side cutouts, a thong back, easy-access crotchless panties, and a quarter-cup bra top that my breasts literally spilled out of. The get-up was completed with a garter belt, fishnet stockings, and a pair of matching satin high-heel mules with whimsical faux-fur pom-poms. I couldn't wait to see Holden's face when he walked into his apartment and found me waiting for him like this.

Luckily, I didn't have to wait long. Less than half an hour later, I heard a key in the lock at the front door of his place. Feeling bold in my outfit, I positioned myself leaning against the kitchen counter in the sexiest way I knew how and waited for him. My heart thumped in my chest as the door opened and Holden stepped inside. But it stopped beating when I realized *he wasn't alone...*

"Oh shit," Holden said. He spun around and smacked his hand over his bass player's eyes.

I immediately bolted to his bedroom, though I was grateful he'd done that since I was just as naked from the back as I was the front. Mortified, I grabbed my clothes from the top of the dresser, yanked the shirt I'd worn earlier over my head, and started to tug on my jeans. They were halfway up my legs when Holden opened the bedroom door.

I closed my eyes. "Please tell me a giant hole has opened up in the center of your living room that I can go jump in."

"Take those pants back off," he said. "Shirt too."

I shook my head with my eyes still squeezed shut. "I think the moment has passed. I'm so sorry. I had no idea you were bringing someone home with you."

"He's gone. Now take those clothes back off and let me look at you in that outfit."

"I'm too embarrassed, Holden."

"You have *zero* to be embarrassed about, sweetheart. But you do have less than five seconds to get undressed, or I'm going to do it for you."

I finally opened my eyes. The way Holden was ogling me went a long way toward restoring my self-esteem. His eyes were dark, and there was an undercurrent of something dangerous as he bit down on his bottom lip.

I shook my head again. "I cannot believe that just happened."

"Forget anything but right now. You have no idea how much I fucking missed you." Holden paused and cocked his head. "Do you know how magnificent you are, waiting for me to come home dressed like that? How insanely sexy you looked?"

I have no idea how the man managed it, but I started to put what had just happened in the kitchen out of my mind and began to believe I was everything he said. The heat in his eyes made me feel so wanted. So I did as he asked and slipped out of the clothes I'd thrown on to cover up.

Holden ran a hand through his hair as he dragged his eyes up and down my body. "Jesus Christ. I'm the luckiest son of a bitch on this planet." He shook his head. "I definitely don't deserve you, but I'm way too selfish to give a fuck anymore."

The air in the room crackled as Holden approached. If I'd had any doubt about whether he was only trying to make me feel better, that went out the door when I saw the bulge in his pants. It looked like his arousal was trying to escape by forcing the zipper teeth on his jeans apart.

Holden reached around to my ass with one hand and hitched me up and off my feet. My legs wrapped around his body as he took my mouth in a kiss that quickly grew out of control.

"Holy shit," he groaned. "I can feel how wet you are through the crotch of your outfit and all of my clothes."

"No, you can't." I bit down on his bottom lip and tugged. "Because this outfit *has no crotch.*"

"I want to tie you up. Every night for the last week, I've had a recurring dream of binding your hands together. But tying you up in this outfit? I couldn't possibly have dreamed of something this good." He pulled his head back and caught my gaze. "Are you good with that, sweetheart?"

I swallowed. "Yes."

A wicked smile curved his lips. "Then let's get you on that bed."

Holden set me down on the mattress. He walked over to one of his drawers and pulled out a belt. Folding it in half, he snapped the leather together, making a loud whip-smack sound that was the most erotic thing I'd ever heard.

"Arms over your head. Clasp your hands together."

He shook his head, staring down at me as I did what he asked. "I could look at you like this all day, sweetheart."

Holden stripped out of his clothes, never taking his eyes from me. I grew hotter at the sight of his beautiful, tanned skin, decorated with all of his sexy tattoos. His six pack was sculpted, and his muscular arms each had a thick vein that ran the entire length of them. But when he slipped off his pants and underwear, my mouth went dry watching his thick erection bob against his stomach. He lifted a knee onto the bed and crawled up, straddling my waist as he leaned and fastened the leather belt around my wrists.

"Try to get out," he said when he was done.

I attempted to unclasp my hands, but couldn't.

Holden smiled. "Don't pull too hard. The leather might chafe your skin and leave marks. I need to get something softer for next time."

"Okay."

He propped a pillow under my head and then looked around the room before climbing off the bed. "Give me a minute." Inside his closet, he unhooked a full-length mirror hanging on the door, then positioned it on top of the dresser at the foot of the bed, laying it sideways.

"Can you see yourself with this angle?" he asked.

I nodded. "Part of me."

"Which part?"

"The top half."

He fiddled with the angle of the mirror again. "Now what do you see?"

"From my waist to my feet."

He smiled. "Perfect. Spread your legs. I want you to watch while I eat you."

"Uh, okay." I was barely coherent as he climbed back onto the bed and positioned himself between my legs. Holden gently blew against my wetness, and a shiver ran from the top of my head down to my toes. His eyes blazed as he looked up at me and licked me from one end to the other.

"Oh God," I whimpered. His tongue moved to my clit, and he sucked hard. Without thinking, I went to reach for him, forgetting that my hands were bound together, and the leather strap bit into my skin. The ache shot directly down between my legs.

Oh wow. I had no idea I liked a little pain. Holden speared his tongue inside me, and I pulled at my wrists again, this time a little harder.

I moaned. "Holden…" My orgasm was going to happen embarrassingly fast. I already felt it brewing. "Slow down…please…"

But my plea only made him go faster. Holden sucked and licked, adding two fingers as I headed over the edge. When it hit, I cried out so loud, I was pretty sure the people on the street three floors below me heard.

After, I panted as Holden climbed up my body.

His eyes sparkled. "My girl likes to be tied up."

"I think it's just you," I breathed.

He brushed a hair from my face. "That's good. Because I think it's just you for me, too."

"How's your mom doing?" An hour later, Holden and I were lying on our sides. It was the first time we'd had any real conversation since he'd walked in the door.

I tucked my hands under my cheek. "She's doing really well. She had a doctor's appointment yesterday, and they said her incision is healing nicely and all her vitals are stable. She doesn't need another check for three months now. But they're keeping her on blood thinners, so she has to be really careful not to fall or anything because it would be hard to stop any bleeding."

"Wow. Is the bubblewrap next door in your apartment?"

My brows dipped.

Holden smiled. "I figured you'd have ordered a shitload to wrap her up in case she bumps into anything."

I laughed. "Trust me, I would if I could. Getting that call was one of the scariest moments of my life. I think I'm going to drive down to Philly to see her again in two weeks."

"I'll go with you. While you spend time with your mom, I can work on getting to know your dad as an adult. Now that you've told him we're together, I think it's important that I show him I'm not the same teenager he knew back in the day."

It was a sweet impulse, but… "I'm not sure that's such a great idea. I don't think my dad is ready for that."

Holden frowned. "Why not?"

"I don't know. It just feels like it's too soon."

"Too soon after your breakup with Warren? Or too soon because you haven't figured out if I'm really a changed person yet?"

I hated to hurt his feelings, but I needed to be honest. I bit my lip. "Maybe a little of both?"

Holden mulled that around for a minute. "Can you see a future with me, Lala?" he finally asked. "I get that it's too soon for you to jump into anything serious, but can you see something more than just fooling around happening between us down the road?"

I placed my hands on his chest. "Holden…"

"You look like you're afraid to answer because you don't want to upset me. But I'd always rather have the truth from you."

I nodded. "It's not that I don't want to see a future with you, but I guess I have trouble imagining what that might look like. Your lifestyle is so different from mine, and I've only ever seen you in that light. It's difficult to imagine you being happy in a long-term, monogamous relationship."

Holden looked down and nodded. "I hate that you feel that way, but I guess that's fair. You only know the person I've shown you. And if I'm being honest, I'm not sure *I* knew there was another side of me until recently." He lifted his eyes to meet mine. "I need to prove to you that I'm not the same guy I was. I know that won't happen overnight, but will you give me the chance to do that? Keep an open mind?"

I'd known Holden practically all of my life, so I was pretty good at reading him. I could see his heart was in the right place. I just wasn't so confident that he wouldn't change his mind once the fun was over. Relationships weren't easy, especially not ones where one of the people traveled as often as he did. Not to mention, he was a drummer, gorgeous, and women had always thrown themselves at him. I wanted more than anything to not have that doubt, but my inner self-protection mechanism was afraid. Holden Catalano was the one man who could swallow me whole and annihilate me if he spit me back out. I knew that in my bones.

But Holden was watching me and waiting for an actual answer. So I offered my best positive smile, even though my insides were laced with hesitancy. "Sure."

"Oh my gosh," I said, setting my keys on the kitchen counter the next evening when I arrived home. "I got nervous when I opened the door. I didn't even realize it was you and thought maybe I'd walked into the wrong apartment."

Holden was in the kitchen with three burners going on the stove. He had on a button-up cardigan sweater and slacks, and his always-wild hair was slicked back and neat. He also wore horn-rimmed glasses, though I didn't think he had a vision deficiency. Basically, he was dressed like Warren.

He walked over and placed my slippers at my feet. "Good evening, darling."

Darling? I squinted. "What are you up to, Catalano? Did you accidentally break something or buy some new sex toys you want to try out?"

He gave me a quick peck on the lips. "I'm not up to anything. Just wanted my lady to come home to a nice dinner after a long day of work."

"*Mmm-hmmm.*"

Holden placed his hand at the small of my back and ushered me into the living room. "Dinner will be ready in about twenty minutes. Would you like a glass of sauvignon blanc?"

"Sure."

He disappeared and came back a minute later with wine. Handing it to me, he guided me to sit on the couch, then lifted my feet up onto the coffee table and slipped a pillow underneath. "Give me two minutes and I'll join you. I just need to check on the chicken cordon bleu and saffron rice."

I raised my brows. "Are you sure you don't mean chicken nuggets and tater tots?"

Holden went into the kitchen and fiddled with the knobs on the stove before returning again. He took the seat at the other end of the couch, leaving a large gap between us. I might've been able to believe his wardrobe change was a new style, and that he was secretly a good cook, but Holden Catalano did *not* leave three feet of distance between us when we hadn't seen each other all day.

"So, what do you think of the political turmoil going on in Bosnia?"

I laughed. "What?"

"You know, the threats of secession that are causing instability for the Balkan nation."

I sipped my wine. "No, I don't know. I guess I'm not up on my Balkan news."

"That's okay. What about the financial crisis? A pretty big hedge fund just warned that hyperinflation might lead to a major collapse of our economy."

"Did you hit your head, Holden?"

"No, but I read *The New York Times* from cover to cover today."

My brows raised. "From cover to cover? How long does that take?"

"About six hours."

"Why on Earth did you spend six hours reading the *Times*?"

Holden shrugged. "You're smart. I want to be able to discuss things with you."

"You don't need to do that. I like you the way you are, Holden."

He shook his finger at me. "Ah… But that's not true. You need more from me to see that I can be a good partner, and I want to show you I can give you what you need."

Grinning, I set my wine down and crawled over to his side of the couch, lifting one knee over his legs to straddle him. Then I shimmied my hips up to sit on his crotch. "You already give me *exactly* what I need."

Oddly, Holden didn't take the bait. His face grew solemn. "I'm serious, Lala. I want to make you dinner, take you out, have meaningful conversations with you… I want to show you I can be more than just a good fuck."

I shook my head. "That's not all I think of you."

He looked down at his lap where I was perched. "Sometimes it feels that way."

I started to climb off, but Holden stopped me. "No, don't go anywhere. Let's talk."

I shook my head again. "I'm sorry, Holden. I didn't realize I was making you feel like a piece of meat. I feel bad."

"Don't feel bad. I understand why our relationship would be about sex. Hell, that's the only man you've ever known me to be. But I meant it last night when I said I wanted more than that. I want a lot more, Lala."

"Why?"

"Because I…" He stopped and cleared his throat. "Because I like you a lot."

Adrenaline sparked through me. Was Holden about to say he *loved me*?

He pushed a lock of hair behind my ear. "Listen, sweetheart. Maybe I went too far trying to change things up this fast. But I really would like to try to shift the focus of our relationship, to show you I can be more to you than you think."

"You *are* more to me than just sex."

"Can you let me prove it to you? Do something for me?"

"Of course. What?"

"Let's not have sex for the next two weeks."

My eyes widened. I wasn't sure if it was because I was astounded Holden would ever want to abstain that long, or because I wasn't sure I could go that long myself. The man was more addicting than drugs.

"Really?" I said. "You mean no intercourse or no…everything?"

"How about we stick to kissing?"

I'd already made him feel like all he was good for was sex, so I couldn't let on how disappointing the thought of two weeks without it sounded. So I forced a smile. "Sure. Of course. Whatever you want."

Holden looked relieved. He leaned forward and gave me a tender, closed-mouth kiss. "Thank you."

A minute later, he got up to serve dinner. The food he'd made was delicious, and after we ate, we snuggled together on the couch and watched an incredible movie he'd picked out. When I yawned, Holden kissed my shoulder.

"I'm gonna go. You should get some sleep."

"You're not going to stay?"

He sat up. "I think it's better if I don't."

I pouted. "Okay."

Holden rubbed his nose with mine. "You're cute when you're celibate."

"I might turn hangry. Except the h is for horny instead of hungry."

He laughed and stood, offering me his hand. "Come on. Walk me to the door so you can put the safety lock on."

At the door, Holden gave me a peck on the lips.

"You said we could kiss. Can I at least get a real one?"

His lip twitched, but he hooked a hand around my neck and pulled me to him. Then hit me with a kiss so passionate, I blinked a few times when he let go.

"Goodnight, sweetheart." He smiled.

"Uhh… Yeah. Goodnight."

After he was gone, I leaned my head against the closed door, still reeling from that kiss. *It's going to be a long-ass two weeks.*

♥CHAPTER 25

Holden

"**D**amn, to go without sex—by choice?" Owen took a bite of the apple he'd stolen from my fridge after stopping by on his way home from work the next evening.

Lala hadn't gotten home yet, so I was killing time and entertaining my friend's curiosity about my probably asinine decision.

"Can't believe it was *my* idea." I shook my head.

"Talk about shooting yourself in the foot." He laughed. "I know one person who'd be happy about this, though."

"Who?"

"Ryan. He'd be thrilled you're keeping your hands off her."

"You're probably right." I sighed. Owen had touched my sore spot. I swear, I had dreams about Ryan coming back to this life just to strangle me.

A knock at the door interrupted my thoughts.

When I opened, Brayden stood there with a goofy smile on his face.

"What's up, man?" I waved him in.

"This is just a welfare check. Owen texted me to get down here. He said he thought you might've lost your mind."

"I haven't lost it—yet." I rolled my eyes. "*Yet* being the operative word."

Brayden leaned against the counter. "What's going on?"

Owen took it upon himself to answer. "He wants to prove that what he and Lala have isn't driven solely by sex, so your boy here made a decision. He's denying her the D for two fucking weeks."

Brayden's eyes widened. "Since when did Catalano grow up? I guess we've all been too busy to notice." He chuckled. "But seriously… Withholding sex? Isn't that going to be a little…challenging for you?"

"Believe me, even one day has been hard—on both of us. I think Lala's taking it worse than I am."

"It must be tough being wanted so badly for your body, huh?" Owen chided.

"I used to be just fine with that, dickhead. But not with this girl. It sounds sappy, but…" I cringed at the words about to exit my mouth. "I want her to like me for me."

"Who are you, and what have you done with Holden?" Brayden joked.

"Lala certainly never had a lack of brainiac shit to talk about with her last boyfriend," I said. "I want to stimulate her mind as much as I stimulate other parts."

"What if *you* unexpectedly start to feel differently now that sex is removed from the equation?" Brayden asked.

I shook my head. "No way. Even when Lala and I weren't having sex, I wanted to be around her twenty-four-seven. I love just talking to her, spending time with her. That's what we do best—before we got sidetracked by the mind-blowing sex."

"Is this the part where I'm supposed to feel sorry for you?" Brayden taunted.

Then came another knock on the door. I hoped to God it wasn't Lala walking in on this conversation. I was sure the guys' faces would be a dead giveaway as to what we'd been talking about.

Thankfully, it was just Colby. "What's up?"

"Hey, man," I said.

"Brayden just texted me to come down here. Said something funny is going on with you."

I turned to Brayden. "Are you kidding?"

Brayden shrugged. "I'm sorry. But it *is* funny."

After they filled him in, Colby reached his hand to my forehead. "You sure you're okay, dude?"

"I might've lost my mind," I conceded.

"Nah." Brayden smacked my shoulder. "I think our boy is growing up."

Colby chuckled. "This is like if Owen woke up one day and decided there were more important things than work. I wouldn't recognize him."

Owen took a bite of his apple and spoke while chewing, "Hey, don't knock me when I don't currently have anyone worth neglecting work for—unlike you two whipped pricks. Plus, I've decided I'm not getting married. Most women want kids, and those two fuckwad teenage brats in 410 have made me decide I'm never having any."

"What did they do now?" I asked.

"I saw them in the elevator this morning. They asked me if I had change for a twenty. I did, so I gave it to them. When I got to the train station, I realized my wallet was gone. And my damn watch. They laughed when I went up to their apartment pissed off. They claim they were just screwing around, but I didn't find it too amusing."

I chuckled. "At least we won't be putting kids out on the street when we evict them for not paying the rent someday. They'll get two hots and a cot in prison."

"Getting back to our celibate boy here," Brayden said. "What happens after this two-week period? Say you prove that you can have a great relationship without sex. Then what? Does that solve all your problems?"

I took a moment to ponder that. "I don't know. The biggest challenge for me is what things will look like if shit starts taking off with the band."

"Speaking of that…" Colby popped the cap off a beer he'd taken out of my fridge. "You never really told us how everything went out west. Any prospects?"

"More than one, actually. The trip was as successful as it could have been."

"You seriously didn't *mess around* with anyone out there?" Brayden asked.

"Of course not," I said, a little insulted. "I wouldn't do that to her."

"Good for you," he said.

"It wasn't effort. I didn't *want* to. It's as simple as that."

Colby interrupted, "So what's the next step? Is someone getting back to you guys?"

"There were at least two interested execs. We're waiting to hear more. That's putting me on edge somewhat."

"Well, I, for one, am proud of you for never giving up," Owen said. "It seems like it might finally be paying off."

"Be careful what you wish for…" Brayden laughed. "You might just get it all at once."

I nodded. "That's exactly what this feels like. Everything is going great with my personal life and my career, but the two are trying to cancel each other out."

The guys hung around and busted my balls for about an hour before leaving me alone. Venting to them had done me good.

After they left, I took a shower and jerked off before heading over to Lala's. The latter would be a must over these next several days, although it didn't help the need much when she was right in front of me.

As I walked next door, I had to stop myself from getting too excited. I'd almost forgotten for a split-second that we weren't going to be having sex. Instead, I'd be offering her another evening of "platonic fun."

When she opened the door, my eyes immediately fell to her chest. Lala's nipples were piercing through the thin fabric of her white T-shirt.

"Hey, handsome. I missed you today."

I gritted my teeth as I entered. "Lala, what are you doing?"

"What do you mean?"

"Your nipples are staring at me like you have a second set of eyes. I want to fucking suck on them right now, and that's not good."

"Oh." She looked down. "I must've forgotten to put on a bra."

Her face turned red as I glared at her.

"Is that it, or are you just trying to torture me?"

She flashed an impish grin.

"That's what I thought."

Her blond curls were especially unruly tonight—just the way I loved them. I envisioned bunching all of her hair into a ponytail and pulling on it while I fucked her from behind. And God… I'd been so fixated on her chest, I nearly missed the fact that she'd put on that cute leather skirt that she'd worn out to a couple of my gigs.

I was practically salivating as I pulled her toward me. "Fuck. Come here."

I threaded my fingers through her hair as our lips smashed together. When Lala moaned into my mouth, my dick stiffened. It took everything in me not to carry her over to the kitchen counter and break my "fast." I was going to be in trouble if I didn't put a stop to this—so I pulled away.

"What's wrong?" she asked. "I thought kissing was okay."

"It's never *just* kissing with you." I panted. "I know I said we could kiss…but it's making it harder for me right now."

She looked down at my crotch. "I can see that." Lala sighed. "This is more difficult than I thought it would be. Everything is turning me on more than usual. This afternoon, you texted me, and even your name on my phone made my body react. Who the hell gets aroused by a text they didn't even read yet?"

"Well, that's all the more reason to condition your brain not to associate me with sex."

Lala's expression turned serious. "What is this really about? Are you seriously concerned that I'm only interested in one thing from you? Because if that's the case, I find it a little insulting after we've had years of history together that didn't involve a single *second* of sex."

Fuck. "Of course, I know you care about me for reasons besides sex. But I do think the sex part of our relationship could be masking some things you might be inadvertently turning a blind eye to."

"Like what?"

Shit. What am I doing?

"Are you trying to warn me or something? I'm confused, Holden."

Am I?

"Look… The no-sex thing is about us connecting more on another level, but it's *also* about you figuring out what you're getting into with me. When we're constantly fucking our brains out, it's hard for you to see everything clearly."

Why was I trying to sabotage things? I couldn't seem to stop myself. I tugged on my hair. "I feel like things are starting to happen with After Friday. I know my being away wasn't easy. But that could be just the beginning, Lala. It's gonna be tough for you with me away. What if you can't handle it?"

"You're putting words in my mouth, Holden. Obviously, I've thought about that. But all I know is, if my head starts going there—into tomorrow or some imagined future scenario—I'm losing these moments with you right now. So maybe my blocking out reality is intentional because I don't want to lose this time with you."

I shook my head, looking down at my shoes. "I'm sorry for ruining the mood."

"Don't apologize for being honest. You're admitting what you're worried about. And I was honest in admitting that I wasn't ready to deal with it. Even if we don't always love the other person's answers, we should *always* talk about what's bothering us." She tugged on my shirt. "And by the way, opening up to each other like this is a better use of the no-sex period than you dressing up like Mr. Rogers and pretending to be someone you're not."

Breaking my vow to not kiss her, I leaned in and took her mouth in mine. Speaking over her lips, I muttered, "I just don't want to lose you. *That's* what all of this is about."

"I know," she whispered.

My damn emotions were all over the place. Lowering my mouth to her neck, I sucked on her tender skin, needing to be inside of her like I needed my next damn breath. "I want to fuck you so badly right now."

She laughed. "Did someone flip a switch inside you, Catalano?"

"That's how it is when you…" *Love someone.* Fuck. Every time I'd nearly said it, things didn't feel right. Now wasn't the time—I'd already fucked tonight up.

I repeated, "That's how it is when you want someone as badly as I want you right now, sweetheart." I forced myself back. "But I'm gonna stick to the plan."

She spoke against my chest. "Not gonna pretend to be happy about that."

I switched the subject before I gave in. "Here's something that might take our minds off sex…"

"What?"

"I want to talk about your dad."

"Yeah, okay. That might work." She chuckled as she moved away from me. "What about him?"

"I'm not gonna pressure you about me spending time with him, but I'm secretly hoping you change your mind about that."

"Why does it matter so much to you?"

"I think it's two-fold." I paused. "Part of it is that Ryan can't be here to give me the official seal of approval. I still can't figure out if he'd be happy about us or want to kill me, and most days I feel like it's the latter." I sighed. "So getting on your dad's good side would be like the next-best thing."

"What's the other component?"

"I'm not gonna lie…knowing how well your father got along with Warren irks me. It's because your dad trusts him. And he sure as fuck doesn't trust me yet."

"He also had a really long time to build that trust with Warren. I don't want you to feel like you need to rush. That happens with time. There's nothing you can say or do that's going to make him trust you right now."

"Gee, thanks."

"What I mean is that if you stick around and he gets to know you naturally, that's how he'll end up trusting you. You can't make that happen overnight."

"I get it." I exhaled. "Okay, here's what I propose. It's been too damn long since I've spent some quality time with my parents. You said you were going back home in a couple of weeks. Why don't I drive us out there, but I'll stay with my folks. My mother has been bugging me to come home for a long time. Then I can drive you back and maybe sneak in some time with you there, too."

"You don't have any gigs scheduled that weekend?"

"I'll let the band and our manager know that those days are blocked off for me. It's non-negotiable." Showing her I meant business, I took my phone out. "Matter of fact, I'm gonna text them right now to let them know that time is off limits."

After Lala took out her calendar and confirmed the three days she'd planned to go home, I sent a group text to my bandmates and manager, specifying the dates I'd be home in Pennsylvania.

Within a minute, I got a text back from my manager.

Daisy: I'm sorry. You can't take those dates off. We just received word that Seal Records wants you guys to go back out to L.A. and record a demo. Those days overlap with the dates they booked the studio. Sorry!

A rush of adrenaline hit me as I typed a response.

Holden: There's no flexibility on the dates?

Daisy: Nope. Studio is booked solid otherwise. We don't want to fuck around with these guys by acting like a bunch of divas off the bat. Non-negotiable.

I stood there frozen, looking down at my phone incredulously.

"Holden, what's wrong?"

"Sweetheart…I'm so sorry. I can't believe I'm saying this, but I can't go to Pennsylvania." My stomach ached.

"What happened?" She blinked.

"Daisy just told me one of the record companies wants us to go out to California again to record a demo. They booked the studio during the time you're going to Pennsylvania."

She leapt toward me and wrapped her arms around my neck. "Oh my God. That's amazing!"

Sure, that was great news, but it wasn't even fazing me. Grasping at straws, I asked, "I assume you can't go any other time?"

"No. We have that Monday off—some sort of government

holiday I've never heard of, which is the only reason I can take that long weekend. Since I'm already behind, I really can't take any other time off."

I gritted my teeth. "I'm so fucking pissed right now."

"It's okay." She rubbed my arm. "Please don't stress."

I wanted so freaking badly to prove to Lala that I could be there for her. But how could I let my band down after we'd worked for years to get to this place? It was literally the opportunity of a lifetime.

My gut told me if I thought I could seriously pursue this music career *and* be the kind of man who's good for Lala, I was probably kidding myself.

❤CHAPTER 26

Lala

"**A**nd our next subject evaluation will occur in sixty days. If you look at the last page of your presentation, you'll find a schedule of all of the various checkpoints, including hormone-level testing, cognitive assessment, and overall health evaluations." I paused and looked at the five members of the National Institute of Health grant-compliance team. All of the faces were new except for Dr. Reston, who had been part of the team that had approved the funding for my research grant. "Does anyone have any questions?"

They all shook their heads and looked at each other. Dr. Reston smiled. "Not surprising. Normally when I listen to a proposal, I have a laundry list of questions when the presenter is done. I didn't have a single one when Laney pitched her study to us. She's incredibly thorough." Dr. Reston closed the binder on the table in front of her. "I'm going to make it a challenge to myself to think of a few questions you haven't already answered next time we meet."

I smiled. "I'm always available by email or phone if you think of any after the fact."

Everyone got up. It was already after four o'clock, so one by one, each of the members of the team said their goodbyes, except for Dr. Reston. She helped me clean up the coffee cups and papers scattered around the conference room. After, she extended a hand back toward the chairs where we'd been sitting. "Do you have a minute, Laney?"

"Sure, of course."

We took seats across from each other.

"Is everything okay?" she asked.

And here I'd thought things had gone well. "Yes. I'm sorry. Was my presentation not good?" I shook my head. "I knew I should've included a better introduction and spoken about the norepinephrine research that recently concluded in Germany."

Dr. Reston raised her hands. "Your presentation was more than sufficient. In fact, I wish every grantee put as much effort into their summaries as you do. Many researchers get the science, but PowerPoint is scarier to them than quantum physics."

My shoulders relaxed a little. "Oh, okay."

She tilted her head. "Perhaps I should've clarified that I wasn't referring to your work. I was asking more on a personal level. You seem… I'm not sure what it is exactly, but you seem different than the last few times we've met. I thought maybe there was something going on, perhaps here at the facility or something personal bothering you? You're a little less peppy than usual, and it looks like you might be getting less sleep. I'm not asking in an official capacity; I just wanted to check in woman to woman. We STEM ladies need to be there for each other as more than just coworkers, and I know you took some personal days a few weeks ago."

"Oh." I shook my head. "That's very kind of you, Dr. Reston."

"It's Barbara, please."

I nodded. "That's very kind of you, Barbara. I didn't realize I was so easy to read. But you're right, I haven't been sleeping that great. I took some time off because my mom had some health issues. She had a heart blockage and needed to have open-heart surgery, which was pretty scary. My mom and I are particularly close.

We lost my only brother eight years ago, and we were each other's support system."

"I'm very sorry to hear that. I would imagine that left you two with a special bond. Does she live here in the City?"

"No, she's back in Philly with my dad. That's why I took some days off, to be at the hospital."

Barbara nodded. "That's hard. My parents lived on the west coast when my dad got sick. We lost him to cancer a few years back. It was difficult not to be there all the time while he was going through his treatments. But I hope I didn't insult you by saying I could tell you weren't sleeping. You look just as beautiful as ever; your eyes just don't have the sparkle they normally do."

She didn't know the half of it, since I hadn't mentioned to anyone here that I'd broken off my engagement and started sleeping with a guy I'd had a crush on for twenty years, who was probably all wrong for me. Not to mention, who could *sleep* when Holden left me hot and bothered every night because of his current no-sex policy.

"I really appreciate you taking the time to check on me," I said. "But I promise, nothing that's going on with me personally will distract me from getting my research done."

Barbara smiled. "I really have no worries about that, Laney. But you have my number. Call me anytime if you need to talk, about work or personal stuff. We scientists look at things differently than a lot of people, so it's nice to have a friend who doesn't think you've lost it when you break out a Venn diagram to overanalyze every little thing."

I laughed. "I appreciate that. It's very kind of you."

"You know, you could probably finish the remainder of your initial research back in Philadelphia. At least all of the data-gathering and analysis is able to be done offsite. Perhaps you could just come back for the next round of interviews and medical assessments with the participants. If you want, I'll ask the grant committee to approve a change in your primary site location so you don't need to come to this building every day and can go back home early. You're supposed to be here for another few months, right?"

Oh. Wow. I wasn't sure what to say. Of course, I would love to be closer to my mother and be able to help out with her recovery. It would take some of the pressure off my dad, who still worked full time and had taken weeks off already. But that would also mean leaving Holden. Even thinking of that made my heart squeeze inside my chest. "Can I think about it and get back to you?"

"Of course. You figure out what will make things easier for you."

Later that night, Holden and I were out to dinner at a fancy restaurant. He looked so damn sexy in a shirt and tie. But something else about his outfit was distracting the heck out of me. I held up the menu, but didn't really read any of the words.

"What are you going to get?" I asked.

Holden looked up at me. "Whatever you get. To be honest, I can't think straight sitting across from you wearing that dress."

I'd worn the sexiest thing I owned, hoping we'd have a few drinks with dinner and maybe Holden would let his guard down a little. We were twelve days into our fourteen-day sex sabbatical, and I was ready to explode. I set my menu on the table.

"*You* can't think straight? You know what you're wearing, right?"

Holden looked down. "A clown outfit?"

I laughed. "No. And I do love you in that shirt and tie. But that's not what I was referring to." I leaned in and lowered my voice. "That belt you're wearing is the belt you used to bind my hands a few weeks ago."

Holden groaned. "*Fuck*, don't even mention that. My dick hasn't gotten over your dress yet."

I bit my bottom lip. "Don't mention how you tied me up and made me watch as you licked me?"

His eyes darkened. I was definitely poking the bear. "Laney…"

"Laney? Oh boy. You sound pretty serious. You know what *I'm* serious about? Taking that tie from around your neck and begging you to tie me up with it. Would you like that, Holden? If I begged. I can do it from my knees, if you want…"

There was so much heat in his eyes, it looked like my taunting might actually pay off this time. So I leaned in closer to try to close the deal, intent on describing what I could do to him on my knees inside the ladies' room at this fancy restaurant, but my cell buzzing on the table stopped me. Ever since Mom's health scare, I couldn't ignore my phone.

My eyes shifted to read the name flashing. It wasn't a name I expected. *Dr. Reston.* Barbara.

Holden noticed the change in my face, and his eyes dropped to my cell, too. "Shit. Is it your mom?"

I shook my head. "No. Dr. Reston is one of the members of the grant-oversight committee for my research, one of the people I presented to today."

"Do you need to get it?"

I nodded and lifted my cell. "I probably should. It's not like her to call me after hours."

"Go ahead."

I swiped to answer. "Hello?"

"Hi, Laney. It's Barbara Reston."

"Hi, Barbara. Is everything okay?"

"Yes, I'm sorry to call you so late. But I was just going through my emails and wanted to give you the good news."

"Good news?"

"I know you said you wanted to think about relocating and finishing your initial research back home, but I shot off a note to the committee anyway. I didn't expect to get a response so quickly, but the team was unanimous in their decision. Everyone agrees you're doing a great job, and a change in your official site would be fine."

"Oh…wow."

"It's still up to you, of course. But I thought it might make your decision easier if you knew it was possible to go back. Anyway, I don't want to bother you after hours. Just wanted to let you know we're good with whatever you decide."

"That's really generous of you."

"Like I said, we STEM ladies need to stick together. If there's anything else I can do to make things easier for you, just let me know."

"Thank you very much, Barbara."

When I hung up, Holden was waiting with a smile. "From where I'm sitting, that sounded awesome."

"Uh. Yeah. It was good news. The committee was really happy with my presentation today," I said. It wasn't a lie, though it also wasn't the reason for the call. But I wasn't ready to discuss what had just been offered to me with Holden. I first needed to figure out what I wanted. "Dr. Reston just wanted to let me know that. She knows I get worried about having to make presentations."

"Of course you killed it. My girl is like Lois Lane and Superman balled into one. Smart, strong, and *hot*."

I smiled, though inside I felt terrible for not sharing the truth. The news from Barbara also left me a bit distracted during dinner. My brain wanted to start analyzing the pros and cons of what had just been offered. I might've even needed to work up a Venn diagram. But by the end of the night, after a few glasses of wine, I'd managed to put it out of my head and focus on my handsome date.

It was a beautiful, clear evening, so Holden and I walked from the restaurant back to our building. We took the elevator up to the third floor, and I opened my apartment door. But Holden didn't follow me inside.

He stayed in the doorway and motioned toward his place. "I'm going to go next door…call it a night."

"What? Why?"

His eyes raked down my body and did a slow sweep on their way back up. "Because I'm struggling with you in that dress…those heels."

I put my purse down and returned to the door, bunching his shirt into my fists. "It's been twelve days. Don't you think that's close enough to two weeks?" Pushing up on my tippy toes, I pressed my lips to his and whispered, "I don't have any underwear on."

Holden groaned. "Fuck, Lala. I want more than anything to end it. But we're doing so good, and the last thing I want is to show you I can't even commit to something for two weeks and stick to it."

"I know you could make two more days. You don't need to prove it."

"Yes, I do. I think I need to prove it to both of us."

I pouted. "But we're leaving soon. Will I even get to see you before I leave for Philadelphia to visit my parents and you go back to California to record? Your flight is early on Friday, and you don't even know how long you're going to be gone."

Holden ran his thumb over my bottom lip. "Trust me, sweetheart. You're going to see me *and* you're going to feel me. I plan to send you home sore so you have no choice but to think about me every time you sit down."

I sighed. "Okay."

"Now give me that mouth and then help me out a little by locking the door and holding on to my master key for the evening."

Holden: Take a nap. I'll be over at midnight, and you won't be getting much sleep.

It was the third time I'd read the text since it had come in this afternoon. Each time, it made me giddy. Since we were both leaving tomorrow morning, I spent the evening at home packing, running errands, and finishing some last-minute work things that needed to be done. I didn't want to waste a second of the time Holden and I had together before we left by doing anything but ravaging him.

It was now 11:55 PM, and I only had one thing left to do— reply to Barbara's email. This morning she'd sent a follow-up message, telling me she'd reached out to a contact at UPenn in Philly, and I could use their administrative offices for whatever I needed, if I decided to go home early—printing, copying, even office space. That really gave me no reason to turn her down. Well, no work-related reason anyway. Yet I still wasn't ready to make a decision. So I responded to her email, letting her know I'd get back to her by Monday, hoping that maybe my trip home would help me figure out what I should do. Immediately after I pressed send, I looked up at the time on my laptop, and the clock changed from 11:59 to 12:00. Seconds later, there was a knock at my front door. Holden must've been waiting out there. I smiled and tossed my laptop on the couch, running to answer and practically ripping the door off the hinges as I swung it open.

Holden leaned casually against the doorframe. He looked *insanely* hot in that beanie I loved so much. He held a set of fur-lined handcuffs in one hand and some bunched-up rope in the other.

"Time to play…" he crooned.

I leapt into his arms, causing him to stumble back a few steps with a laugh. "Hello to you, too, beautiful."

My arms wrapped around his neck and my lips glued to his as he carried me inside my apartment. I vaguely registered him kicking the door shut behind us.

Holden took me straight to the bedroom. Neither one of us seemed to be able to get our clothes off fast enough, though things slowed as I positioned myself in the middle of the bed and Holden climbed over me. He laced our fingers together, kissed the top of both my hands, and brought them up over my head. Then he stared into my eyes for the longest time.

"I missed you so much," he whispered.

"I missed you, too."

"I don't know what the last two weeks proved to you, but it proved to me that I don't want to be away from you that long ever again."

I forced away the thought that crept into my head about Barbara's offer and cupped his cheek. "As much as I missed the sex, I still enjoyed every minute of our time together over the last two weeks, Holden."

He closed his eyes for a moment. When he opened them again, they were watery and filled with emotion. He nodded and swallowed before taking my mouth in a kiss and easing inside of me. "Fuck." Holden moved in and out of me slowly. "This is... everything. You feel so fucking good."

He kissed me until I was breathless and then pulled back to look at me. His pupils were dark and huge, filled with so much emotion. Everything else in the world faded away as we moved in unison.

I never wanted the moment to end, but before long I was already heading over the edge, and Holden's jaw went rigid as he tried to hold back. His thrusts became faster and harder, and our bodies grew slick with sweat.

"Holden..."

"That's it. Come with me. At the same time..."

His command was all it took for my muscles to start to pulsate. Holden felt it.

"Fuck. Take all my cum. Feel it deep inside you…"

I moaned through the best orgasm of my life. Holden kept pumping and grinding until every last tremor worked its way through my body.

After, we were both spent. It felt like I'd turned to jelly.

"Wow. That was…"

Holden's lip twitched. "Very long overdue."

A few minutes went by, and Holden moved to get up. I grabbed his arm. "Where are you going?"

"To get you a towel."

I shook my head. "Not yet. I want to keep you inside of me."

He smiled and kissed my lips. "That's good. Because you're already deep inside of me."

I woke in a panic, pushing up onto my elbows in the dark. "Oh my God. We fell asleep. Holden, wake up. What time is it? Your flight…"

But Holden was already awake next to me. He was fully dressed, staring up at the ceiling. "It's five thirty. I have a few minutes still."

I covered my heart with my hand. "Oh, thank God. We didn't set the alarm last night. I thought we'd overslept."

"I set the alarm. I got up to go to the bathroom a few hours ago, and I realized I left my phone next door. I couldn't find yours, so I grabbed your laptop from the living room and set the alarm on that. It went off a little while ago, but I hadn't ever fallen back asleep."

I settled back into the bed and turned to face him. "Oh. Good thinking. But I'm sorry you didn't fall back asleep."

"It's fine." Holden's voice was somber.

"You must be tired?"

"Not really."

"Is something bothering you?"

He shrugged, but then shook his head. "Just a lot on my mind."

"You want to talk about it?"

"No, I'm going to go next door to make a cup of coffee and grab my phone and suitcase."

"Okay."

While Holden was gone, I slipped into the T-shirt he'd had on last night. Lifting it to my nose, I took a big inhale. I really hoped he didn't need to take it with him because it smelled so good, and I planned to keep it for a while. He came back a few minutes later with his luggage and two mugs. His was half empty already.

"Uber will be here in a minute," he said.

"Oh. Okay. I was hoping to get a few minutes to kiss you."

Holden guzzled back the rest of the coffee, set his mug in the sink, and walked over to me. He cupped my cheek and pressed his lips to mine. "I'll see you soon."

Something seemed off. "Are you sure everything is okay? Did I say or do something to upset you?"

"I'm fine. I'll call you when I can, okay?"

Talk about depressing goodbyes. I nodded and tried to force a smile, but I failed miserably. "Okay. Have a good flight."

Shutting the door, my shoulders slumped. I don't know what I'd been expecting, but after the intensity we'd shared last night, I thought we'd have some sort of a big farewell moment filled with emotions. Instead, that was more like the way Warren and I would've said goodbye. Anticlimactic. Which was fine. It really was. It just seemed very anti-Holden.

But whatever. He was probably just feeling as down as I was about going our separate ways. I briefly considered going back to bed, but since I was up early, I thought I might as well hit the road for Philly and get a jump on traffic. So I took a quick shower, dried my hair, and finished putting my toiletries into my weekend bag. I grabbed my laptop from the bedroom nightstand and started to pack it into its case, but when I remembered I needed to send an email to my admin, I pulled it back out.

The power saver screen was on when I opened. But after it woke up, I went to type and froze.

Oh no.

Holden said he'd set the alarm on my laptop, so he must've opened to the same screen I just did—front and center with the email from Barbara Reston, the email with a first line that read:

Great news! Not only can we get you back to Philly as soon as next week, but we can get you a place to work in a local government building.

Holden's mood when he left made a lot more sense now…

♥CHAPTER 27

Holden

The ride to the airport was a blur. My thoughts raced so fast that it felt like it took two minutes to get here.

We were waiting at the gate to board our plane when Monroe plopped into the seat next to me. "Hey, man. You alright?"

"Yeah," I muttered, staring out at what looked like our plane.

He handed me a donut hole out of the greasy bag he was holding. "This trip is supposed to be a good thing, you know. Why the fuck do you look so down right now?"

I popped it into my mouth. "No offense, but you wouldn't understand."

In all the years I'd known Monroe, he hadn't been in a single relationship. I doubted he would do anything except chastise my ass if he knew the truth about what was bothering me.

"This business is a lot easier without girlfriends. You know that, right?"

I guess he wasn't *that* clueless as to what was on my mind. My eyes darted over to him. "Thanks for the insight. I do know that, yes."

"Out of all of us, I thought you'd be the last one to fall into that trap."

"It's not a trap if you want to be in it." I sank into my chair and crossed my arms.

"This is the worst timing for you, Catalano. Everything is finally starting to happen for us. It would be one thing if you could have your cake and eat it, too—if you know what I'm saying. But what you're doing—trying to be true to this chick when we very well could be hitting the road again very soon—is not gonna be sustainable. You'll end up slipping with some groupie, and then you'll feel like shit. It's better to just end things before that has a chance to happen."

I wanted to cuss him out for his assumption, but settled on a simple truth. "I would never cheat on her."

He chewed. "Look, I've met her, obviously. She's a good girl—smart. Not someone who's gonna put up with our lifestyle anyway. So just put her out of her misery."

His trite opinion of Lala irked me. She was a hell of a lot more than just "smart" and a "good girl."

"What happened with her anyway?" he asked as if he truly cared, when I knew damn well he didn't.

I wasn't going to waste my energy venting to someone who would never understand. Monroe was a friend, but he was the wrong person for this conversation.

Our talk was interrupted when my phone rang.

Lala. I stood up, walking a few feet away, and answered. "Hey."

"Hi. Are you all checked in yet?" she asked.

"Yup. Just waiting at the gate until we have to board. What's up? You on the road?"

"No, I was just about to leave, but then I noticed something and had to call you first." She paused. "Did you happen to read an email on my laptop that referred to a relocation to Philly?"

I cleared my throat. "I did."

"I was afraid of that. You were acting strange this morning, and then I saw it opened on my computer after you left." She sighed. "Holden, that wasn't my idea. Dr. Reston noticed that I'd seemed off lately. When she found out about my mother's health, she took it upon herself to look into a relocation option for me. It wasn't something I asked for."

Dragging a hand through my hair, I said, "Why didn't you mention this to me?"

"It was barely an afterthought. I had no idea her offer was going to come to fruition."

"I'm not gonna be the asshole who tries to convince you to stay in New York if what you need is to be closer to your mother right now, Laney."

I'd called her Laney again. I'd done that at the restaurant the other night, too. It hadn't been intentional. Apparently, it just came out when I was pissed.

"I feel like you still think this is something I instigated," she said.

"I didn't say that. But think about it. You leaving New York is inevitable anyway, right? I mean, if you haven't been acting like yourself at work and people are noticing... Maybe you need a change."

Maybe she *did* need to go back to Philly now in order for us to know whether this would work. "The sooner we get to what the true normal will be for us, the better, I think."

Her voice cracked. "You mean me back in Philly all alone and you on the road?"

I looked around at the people passing me by. "Look where I am, sweetheart—at an airport instead of accompanying you home. Prioritizing the band and my music career. It's unfair of me to try to get you to stay in New York when, for all I know, I could get called away again like this."

She went silent.

"I'm sorry I didn't admit I saw the email before I left," I finally said. "I *did* jump to conclusions. But ultimately, I wanted you to be the one to tell me about it. It's all good now."

"All good?" she laughed angrily. "Why doesn't it *feel* good?"

I closed my eyes and blew out a breath of frustration. All I wanted was to get the hell out of this airport and go back home to her.

"I could've handled it if you'd just told me, Lala. You didn't need to hide it."

"I *wasn't* intentionally hiding it…"

"Whatever you decide to do," I told her, "staying in New York or going back to Philly early, the choice won't change what's meant to happen with us, sweetheart."

"It sounds like you're encouraging me to leave, though."

Maybe subconsciously I *was* pushing her to go, not because I wanted to lose her, but because the sooner she left, the sooner I could know whether we stood a chance in the long term. With Lala in New York, it felt like we were in a temporary fantasy. It wasn't our eventual reality.

I could hear her breathing heavily. I didn't want to upset her when she was about to get on the road. What if she got into an accident? I'd never be able to forgive myself.

"Look, Lala… Don't stress, okay? The answer of whether or not to move back early will come to you, maybe based on how your mom's doing when you see her. But don't base it on me… It won't impact our…"

I hesitated. *Relationship?* I wanted to believe that was what we had versus a temporary thing, but time would tell.

I continued, "Be careful driving. Enjoy the visit with your parents, and try not to worry about anything else." I exhaled. "Promise me you won't get on the road if you're upset."

"Do you believe that I wasn't intentionally hiding this from you?"

"I do, Lala. Okay?"

Her voice was barely a whisper. "Okay."

VI KEELAND & PENELOPE WARD

♥

I could finally breathe.

From the moment we'd landed in L.A., we'd been locked away in that dark studio, working on the demo through the entire freaking night. I hadn't had a moment to think straight.

Being busy had been a good thing, though, because it kept me from ruminating about Lala. I felt bad for the attitude I'd given her during our phone call at the airport yesterday. In fact, I'd pretty much thought of nothing else for the first half of the flight over here before I started writing some lyrics to stop myself from totally drowning in my thoughts.

There was no part of me that wanted us to be apart sooner than we had to. Rather than opening up about that like I should've, though, I'd acted like her leaving didn't matter to me. Like maybe *she* didn't matter to me. I wasn't sure whether I was trying to protect her from me or myself from her at this point.

But I'd gone long enough—more than twenty-four hours—without hearing her voice. That needed to end now.

Palm trees blew in the breeze as I stepped outside the building, feeling like I'd just emerged from a black hole into daylight. Leaning against the wall of the recording studio, I could see the Hollywood sign in the distance as I took out my phone to dial her.

"Hey…" she said when she picked up. "How did everything go?"

"We just wrapped up. I'm wiped, but we got some good stuff down."

"I'm so glad, Holden."

I could hear silverware clanking in the background. I knew it was close to dinner time on the east coast.

I sat down on the ground. "Are you in the middle of eating?"

"Yeah, no biggie, though. I'm so happy everything went well."

"If I had to miss being with you this weekend, it better damn well have been productive and not a waste. I worked my ass off to make sure of that." Looking up at the sun, I sighed, "I fucking miss you. I'm sorry I was a dick the last time we spoke."

"It's okay. You were upset. I'm sorry to have caused it."

"Lala, listen. I'm…" I was about to explain why I *didn't* want her to move back to Philly early when I heard a certain voice in the background. A *male* voice. And it wasn't her dad, either.

I narrowed my eyes as my heart pumped faster. "Who's there right now?"

"Hang on," she said. There was some rustling, and then she came back on the line. "I needed to step away from the table."

I tugged on my hair and snapped, "Why?"

"That was Warren you heard," Lala whispered. "I didn't want to talk about him in front of his face."

Sucking in a breath, I seethed. "What is he doing there?"

"He stopped by the house to say goodbye before he has to leave for California this week. It turned out they needed him there sooner than originally planned. I didn't want him to stay for dinner, but my parents insisted." When I stayed silent, she asked, "Are you mad?"

"Why would I be mad? You wouldn't care if I was having dinner tonight with one of my exes while I was out here, right?"

That was a cheap shot, but I couldn't help myself.

"Point taken. I'm sorry if I upset you. I seem to be doing that a lot as of late."

Listening for a moment to the sounds of traffic coming from Mulholland Drive, I took a long, slow breath to calm myself. "No, sweetheart." I rubbed my tired eyes. "I'm the sorry one. It was bad enough that I was incapable of being there for you this weekend, but *him* being there in my place is a bitter pill to swallow. You can't help it if he stopped by unannounced, though."

"I didn't have the heart to tell him to leave. This is probably the last time I'll see him—possibly forever, for all I know."

I doubt that. "Don't think he's not hoping you'll try to change his mind about leaving. That's why he's there, Lala."

I stopped myself from saying anything else about that. I was making this about Warren, when deep down, he wasn't the problem. The problem was *me*. It would've been impossible to feel insecure about Warren, if *I* were secure in my ability to be the right man for Lala. He was with her and her family right now, and I was sitting outside a recording studio in L.A. while one of my bandmates got blown by some random girl in a car parked diagonally across from me.

The sooner we knew whether this could work between Lala and me, the better.

"I think you should take them up on the offer to work from Philly," I blurted.

"You're just saying that right now because you're pissed Warren is here. I get it. But don't give me advice when you're angry."

"While I'm not happy he's there, that's not why I said it. If things are meant to work out between us, the distance between Philly and New York shouldn't matter."

I could hear her mother's voice in the background. "Why are you in here, Laney? Is everything okay? I just put out dessert."

"Yeah. I'll be right there, Mom. Everything's fine."

Just dandy.

"I have to go," she said.

I chewed on the inside of my cheek. "Alright."

"Will you call me later?" she asked.

"I'll try."

Lala hung up without saying anything else. I couldn't blame her. *I'll try?* I'd acted like a prick again—and I immediately hated myself for it.

After at least five minutes of staring into space, I finally stood up.

"Hey, Holden," I heard someone call.

I turned around to find a curvy blonde in six-inch heels walking toward me. She was one of a few women who'd hung around for much of our session. I didn't exactly know who was who, since several random people kept popping up behind the glass while we were recording. She could've been with the label, or just someone connected to the studio we were renting.

"Hi," I said.

She gave me a once-over. "Man, do you know how to work a pair of sticks. You were amazing in there."

"Thank you. I appreciate that."

"You guys play off of each other so damn well. Great work ethic, too. No one complained when you had to do several takes. Even when it was the tech's fault. That's a rarity."

"Well, we don't have a lot of time out here. So we want to make sure the demo is as good as it can be."

"Hopefully it's only the beginning. Something tells me this won't be your last visit."

I wanted to ask her who the hell she was, but didn't want to insult her in case she was someone important.

"I'd love to get to know you guys better while you're in L.A. Does the band have plans tonight?"

I was just about to tell her I wasn't sure when Dylan appeared out of nowhere.

He practically flew over and skidded into place in front of me. "We don't, actually. We're all yours."

"Awesome." She chuckled. "Carrie and I will send a car to your hotel to pick you guys up." She raised a brow. "Say eight?"

"Perfect." Dylan beamed.

She turned to me and smiled. "Catch you later, Holden."

I waited for her to disappear from sight before turning to Dylan. "What the fuck was that all about? Who is she?"

His eyes gaped. "You don't know?"

"I know she was hanging out watching us for a while, but no, I have no clue who she is." I shrugged.

"She didn't introduce herself to you by name because you're supposed to *already* know who she is, fuckface." He smacked me lightly on the head. "That's Alana Styles. She's the head of A and R at Seal Records. She could single-handedly decide if we get this deal."

My jaw dropped. "Oh shit. Okay. I had no idea."

"You'd better do whatever the fuck she wants tonight, and I mean it."

My body went rigid. "Are you suggesting that I'm supposed to fuck her?"

"Whatever you need to do to *seal* the deal—no pun intended."

I pushed him. "Get the fuck out of here."

He stumbled a little, and his expression turned dead serious. "Holden, listen. I overheard her gushing about you to the other woman, Carrie, who works in PR. Alana kept saying how talented you are. We need you to do whatever she wants."

"Who's getting whatever they want?" Monroe asked. He'd finally emerged from the car he'd been sitting in with some chick.

"Alana Styles," Dylan said. "And Holden here is going to be the one to give it to her."

"Niiice." Monroe laughed. "I saw her walk over. What did she say?"

Apparently, I was the only one who had no damn clue who Alana was.

"She's sending a car to pick us up at the hotel at eight," Dylan announced.

Monroe's mouth spread into a huge smile as he high-fived Dylan. "Fuck, yeah."

"What are the chances I can play sick and skip out?" I asked.

Both their heads turned toward me at the same time.

325

"Well, you could," Monroe said. "But then I'd have to staple your balls to the bed while you sleep tonight."

I hung my head. "Dude, I really don't think this woman wants me. She's a big deal and was nothing but professional in there. Besides, even if it came to that, I wouldn't be sleeping with her. But to be safe, maybe I shouldn't go."

Dylan glared at me. "The old Holden would have come through for us tonight."

"Well, you have me freaked now. I get this is important, but I'm not about to prostitute myself for you, dickhead," I spat.

The sad thing was, he was right. If this had been before Lala? I wouldn't have had to think twice about sleeping with someone to further my career, if that's what it took. *Seal* the deal. I was a little ashamed to admit that to myself.

"Look, you guys figure out what to tell her about me. But as of now, I'm officially sick." I walked away before they could say anything else.

Realizing I'd left my jacket in the studio, I headed back inside. One of the techs was still lingering.

"Are you closing up shop?" I asked.

He swiveled in his chair. "Nah. I have someone else booked in about an hour. Just chilling until then."

An idea came to me. "You mind if I tool around in there? I've got a song I wanted to try out a cappella."

He grinned. "You sing?"

Fair question, since he'd only seen me on the drums.

"Occasionally, I dabble. Wrote some lyrics on the plane out here, and I've got this melody in my head to go with them. Curious as to how it sounds."

He hit some buttons and pointed to the booth. "Head on in."

I situated myself in front of the mic and pulled up the lyrics I'd written on my phone.

Can you meet me tonight?
On the rooftop under the moonlight.
I have a secret and can only pray,
When I say it, you don't run away.

I've tried so hard not to cross the line.
Tried not to wish you were mine.
But I'm telling you as a friend,
Loving me is a dead end.

La…La…La…La
This is my warning.
Will you look at me the same in the morning?

La…La…La…La
Tell me you'll stay.
Even if I warn you to walk away.

Now I'm going out on a limb,
Admitting you'd be safer with him.
But even if that's true,
He won't love you like I do.

I won't take offense.
I know we don't make sense.
The truth cuts like a knife.
But you'll still be the love of my life.

La…La…La…La
This is my warning.
Will you look at me the same in the morning?

La…La…La…La

Tell me you'll stay.
Even if I warn you to walk away.

La…La…La…La
I love you. I love you. I love you.

♥CHAPTER 28

Lala

Almost a week later, I stood in my bedroom and looked around for the tape to make another box. The mess reminded me of the day I'd moved in, when the bottoms of all my boxes had busted because I'd used nearly decade-old tape. Holden had made me laugh about it, not gotten annoyed like Warren or my dad would have. That was one of the things I loved about Holden—he didn't sweat the small stuff. Car broke down in the middle of nowhere? It's an adventure, not a reason to complain. Forget the music in the middle of a song? Turn the moment into a drum solo and flash an irresistible smile to the crowd. He had an uncanny ability to go with the flow and believed that when we did, we all ended up where we were supposed to be.

That thought made me sad. Because he seemed to be applying the same easy-come, easy-go logic to us. But was that the way relationships were supposed to be? Weren't we supposed to fight for the things that mattered most to us? That's how I'd always believed things were supposed to work. Though if I was right, what did that say about how much I meant to Holden? I didn't matter enough.

A tear trickled down my face as I grabbed another sweater and folded it before placing it into a cardboard box. I hated that I was doing this. I wasn't ready to leave New York yet. But Holden had been so distant since our call last week when he'd told me I should go back to Philly, and I wasn't about to stay where I wasn't wanted.

After I packed the last of my clothes from the closet, I decided to take a break and treat myself to a glass of wine. Mid-pour, there was a knock at my door. I figured it was one of the guys coming to check on me, since I'd mentioned to Owen earlier that I was leaving Sunday. But when I opened the door, my heart stopped at the sight of the beautiful man standing on the other side.

"Holden? What are you doing here? I thought you weren't back until tomorrow night?"

"We finished a little sooner than expected, so I was able to jump on a flight after we wrapped last night."

He glanced over my shoulder, and the smile on his face wilted. "What are you doing?"

I turned and looked at all the boxes. "I started to pack."

Holden seemed surprised, though I wasn't sure why since he'd been the one to tell me to go back home.

I opened the door wider and stepped to the side. "Come on in."

He shoved his hands into his pockets and looked down. "I need to shower and unpack. I just wanted to let you know I was back."

"Oh…okay."

He lifted his eyes, but they didn't meet mine. "I'll see you around later?"

It felt like I'd been run over by a bulldozer. "Yeah, sure."

No kiss. No hug. Nothing.

A few weeks ago, we would've both been naked within ten seconds of him knocking.

Tears stung my eyes as I shut the door. I'd been secretly hoping Holden would see me packing up to leave and it would scare him into fight-or-flight mode. Sadly, it had, only he didn't choose the option I'd hoped. Holden had run away as fast as he could.

Somehow I managed to not burst into full-blown tears. Over the next two hours, I didn't hear a peep from Holden. I went back and forth about how to handle things, debating whether I should just pack up my car and go now, without any goodbye or warning, or if I should march next door and tell him my feelings had grown and I needed him to fight for me to stay. In the end, I wound up doing something I wasn't proud of, something that would probably make me feel even more like shit if it didn't work. I resorted to sex.

Knock. Knock. Knock.

Holden opened his door, and his eyes dropped right to my cleavage. He certainly couldn't have missed it with the push-up bra and low-cut cropped top I'd changed into.

Desperate times. Desperate measures.

I twirled a piece of my hair as I spoke. "Hey. Do you think you can help me with a few of my boxes? I packed a couple of them a little too heavy, and I want to stack them up at the door. I'm afraid the bottoms will fall out if they're not carried right."

"Sure." His eyes stole another peek at my cleavage before he pulled his door closed and followed me into my apartment. In the living room, he looked around with his hands on his hips. "Which ones do you want stacked?"

"The ones in the bedroom."

He swallowed and frowned. "Oh."

The lackluster response hurt my heart, but I did my best to pretend it didn't harm my self-esteem. Walking to the bedroom, I exaggerated the sway of my hips knowing Holden had a weak spot for my tight yoga pants. Inside, I even pretended to rummage through a box on the floor without bending at the knees. My ass was impossible to miss. I caught Holden looking a few times, but he just seemed sad rather than turned on. When there was nothing left for me to pretend I needed help with, I still refused to give up.

"Thank you for the help," I said. "How about a glass of wine?" Holden looked reluctant, so I pulled out the big guns to make sure he wouldn't say no. "I can fill you in on my mom's health, and I want to hear about how your recording went out in California."

He nodded, but didn't look happy. "Sure."

Over the next hour, we had a nice conversation and caught up, but it felt like I was talking to Owen or Colby. Holden sat on the chair diagonal to the couch and made no attempt to touch me. This was the least physical connection I'd ever felt while near him. We'd had more of a spark when I was fifteen and sitting on the roof of my parents' house with my brother sleeping ten feet away. And I got the feeling he couldn't wait to get the hell out of my apartment. So I made one last-ditch attempt at kindling something by reaching over my head and doing a big, fake stretch. Holden's eyes zoned in on my exposed midriff, but then he frowned and rubbed his hands on his jeans.

"It's late. I should get going."

Well, that move backfired.

After he was gone, it felt like I had a lump stuck in my throat. I guess the positive side was that it clogged up all the tears that were threatening. The way I'd acted had left me desperate and sad, and at two o'clock in the morning, I was still staring up at the ceiling in the dark, searching for answers I didn't have. So I ripped the covers off and sat up, reaching for my phone. There was only one way to get answers, and that was by going straight to the source. Without giving myself a chance to change my mind, I shot off a text to Holden, even though it was the middle of the night.

Lala: Hey. Are you up?

He answered quickly.

Holden: Yeah. I think the time change and sleeping on the redeye screwed me up. What's your excuse?

Lala: Will you meet me on the fire escape in a few minutes?

The dots started moving around, then stopped, and then finally began again.

Holden: Sure.

I grabbed a bottle of wine and two glasses before opening the window and climbing out. Holden was already seated on the adjoining fire escape.

"Hey," I whispered.

"You should be sleeping," he said.

"There's too much on my mind, and I need to talk, Holden."

Our eyes caught, and he nodded.

There was so much I wanted to say, but my thoughts were all jumbled. So I took a few minutes to compose myself as I poured us each a glass of wine and passed one through the bars to Holden.

"Thanks," he said.

I nodded and took a deep breath. "Why didn't you kiss me tonight, Holden? We haven't seen each other in a week."

He looked down. "I didn't want to crowd you. You have so much on your plate right now."

"But I *wanted* to be crowded by you. I think I made that pretty obvious."

Our eyes met and for a second or two, I saw the familiar spark in his gaze. But then he turned away. "Sex will just make it harder. I don't want you to be sad or feel bad when you leave New York. Your happiness means more to me than my own." He paused for a second. "Over the last week, I've been thinking a lot about Ryan. I promised him I'd always look out for you, and that's what I'm trying to do. I don't want to say or do anything that makes things more difficult for you. That's one of the reasons talking was so hard when we were inside your apartment before. I don't want to screw up."

"Just be yourself, Holden. You can't screw up when your intentions are good."

He scoffed. "Didn't you ever hear that saying, *the road to hell is paved with good intentions*? That's me, Lala. I *am* the road to hell."

We were both quiet again. Eventually, he chugged his entire glass of wine.

"How did seeing Warren make you feel when you were back home?"

I frowned. "It was sad. He cried and told me he still loved me. And before he left, he gave me an open-ended plane ticket to go out to California, so I can visit him if I ever want to. It's hard to see someone you care about hurting."

Holden nodded. "Do you think it was a mistake that we got together? I basically wormed my way between you two and broke you up."

I shook my head. "You didn't worm your way into anything. I wanted what happened between us as much as you did, maybe more. I'll always love Warren in some way. He was very good to me and a big part of my life for a long time, but being with you made me realize something important was missing." The moment had become really sad and heavy, so I tried to lighten the mood. "You know, like good sex, for one."

Holden nodded. "At least I'm good for something."

"I'm teasing, Holden. Yes, sex with you has been great, but it was more than that."

"Yeah…"

This time it was me who chugged my wine. I'd been meandering around with small questions because I was afraid to ask the big one. But I needed to know.

"What will happen between us once I'm back in Philly?"

Holden shook his head. "I don't know. Why don't we just play it by ear?"

It felt like my insides were being torn up, yet I forced a smile. "Okay. That sounds good."

A minute later, Holden thumbed toward his apartment. "I'm wiped from traveling. I should probably get some sleep."

"Oh. Yeah. Of course."

I hated to end this conversation, yet I climbed to my feet when Holden did and opened my window. "Goodnight. I hope you get some sleep."

"You, too. Goodnight, sweetheart."

Halfway through the window, I panicked and froze. "Wait! Holden?"

He paused with one leg already inside. "Yeah?"

"I'm going to leave on Sunday. Do you think we can spend tomorrow night together, since it will be my last night here?"

"I'd like that."

"Me, too."

Miraculously, I managed to keep it together as I climbed back inside and brushed my teeth. But as I crawled into bed and pulled up the covers, all of my emotions hit me at once. And I started to cry.

And cry.

And cry.

CHAPTER 29

Holden

"Hey, stranger." Billie smiled.

"What's up, Mrs. Lennon?" I looked over at Deek, the tattoo artist whose chair was across from hers, and lifted my chin. "What's up, man?"

He was currently working on a skull tattoo for a guy who would've been scary *without* a head full of tats.

Deek lifted his chin. "'Sup, rock star?"

"Where've you been?" Billie asked. "Oh wait. I know *exactly* where you've been. Doing the dirty with lovely little Lala." She took one look at my face and turned off her machine. She set the needle in her hand down in its holder. "Oh, no. What happened?"

I shrugged. "Nothing. I just came down to ask you for a recommendation for a special restaurant."

She squinted. "What's the occasion?"

"Lala's last night in town. She decided to go back up to Philly early, to be near her mom. She leaves tomorrow."

"Shit." Billie took a rag and wiped the excess ink from the arm of the guy she was working on. "I'll be done in five minutes. You want to go get some ice cream? I've been craving peanut butter chunk since I woke up."

It wasn't like I had anything better to do. "Sure."

Fifteen minutes later, we were down the block at an old-fashioned ice cream parlor. Billie licked her lips as the kid behind the counter scooped two heaping mounds of the flavor she'd ordered onto a cone. She rubbed her pregnant belly as she waited.

"How you feeling?" I asked.

"Pretty good, considering I haven't slept through the night in a month." She patted her stomach. "This little guy has taken up residence on my bladder. I don't drink or eat three hours before bed, yet I *still* get up at least twice to pee. Last night, Colby was snoring, and it pissed me off, so I kicked him and *accidentally* woke him up."

I raised a brow. "Accidentally?"

"Well, yeah. I only meant to bruise him a little. Not wake him."

I chuckled. "I gotta tell you, I love that a five-foot-nothing little lady is getting even for the shit he did to me when we were kids. He's a year older, so he used to kick my ass back when we were six and seven, just for fun."

Billie motioned to one of the tables inside the ice cream store. "Why don't we sit? I don't have another client for a half hour."

"Okay." I took my strawberry shake and sat across from her as she went to town on her cone.

"So talk to me," she said between licks. "What's going on with you and Lala? I thought you were having a great time."

"We were. But that's all it was for her—a good time." I shook my head. "I guess I'm finally getting a taste of my own medicine, after being a love-'em-and-leave-'em guy for the last decade."

"You have real feelings for her though, right?"

I raked a hand through my hair. "I'm in love with her. I think I have been for most of my life."

Billie put her hand over her heart. "Oh my God. Don't say things like that. Because aside from being a pee machine, I'm also super emotional. I think I might cry."

337

"Well, then it might turn into two of us bawling." I sighed. "Man, it really sucks to be used for sex."

"I don't think Lala used you for sex. You two had a lot of fun together, didn't you? I mean, outside the bedroom, too?"

I shrugged. "Yeah, but it's not enough."

"Did you tell her how you feel?"

I shook my head. "I don't want to make it harder on her."

"Then how do you know Lala doesn't feel the same way you do?"

"She pretty much told me on more than one occasion. Last night, I asked her if she regretted dumping Warren, and she said no, because being with me made her realize something was missing from her relationship—*like good sex*."

"That sounds more like an example of things that were missing than the full list."

I shrugged again. "It's not the first time she's made it clear what we are. Plus, her mom is sick, and she just got out of a long-term relationship. I basically pushed her to jump into bed with me. I'm just her rebound guy."

"You're assuming an awful lot, Holden."

"I'm not assuming anything. I'm hearing how she feels loud and clear through her actions. Lala wasn't even supposed to leave New York for a couple of months. She got an opportunity to go back home early and jumped at it. I don't know a lot about relationships, but I'm pretty sure when you're in love with someone, you run *to* them and not *away* from them."

Billie licked her ice cream and shook her head. "I think you're making a mistake to leave so much unsaid."

"If it's meant to be, she'll find her way back to me."

Billie pursed her lips. "You know that old saying about loving someone and letting them go to see if they come back is horseshit, right? If you love someone, you fight for them. You tie them up to keep them, if that's what you need to do."

I wished that were true, but the only kind of tying up Lala wanted from me was to the headboard when we fucked.

That evening, Lala and I were on our way to One if by Land, Two if by Sea to have dinner and celebrate her last night in New York. Was it really a celebration, though? It felt more like the end of something.

I'd called a car to come get us.

The mood was somber as Lala leaned her head on my shoulder. We both gazed out at the city lights from the backseat. My nose was buried in her soft curls. It still hadn't fully hit me that tomorrow she'd be gone. I felt numb.

Then my phone vibrated. When I looked down, I saw it was a group text from my manager to the band, and the first word was: URGENT!

I clicked on it.

Daisy: URGENT! You guys, I need you to get down to The Palace stat. The band that was supposed to be playing there tonight had to bail. They called to see if you were available. Of course, I told them yes. Show starts in an hour. If you don't have time to grab your stuff, they have a house set of instruments.

"Shit," I muttered.

Lala lifted her head off me. "Who's that?"

I didn't want to explain because I planned to refuse to go. But I had to tell her.

"My manager. She wants us to get down to The Palace to play tonight."

"The Palace?" Lala's eyes widened. "Even *I've* heard of The Palace. That's huge. You need to go."

Despite the fact that my phone was now blowing up with messages from my stoked bandmates, I still insisted that I couldn't abandon her again, like I had when I'd chosen California over accompanying her home for the weekend.

"No. Fuck that. It's your last night here. I'm telling her I can't."

My fingers were on the keypad when Lala reached her hand over mine to stop me. "You can't. If you don't play, no one plays."

"No," I insisted. "They can find another drummer to replace me for the night. There are plenty of guys in our circles champing at the bit for that opportunity."

She shook her head. "No, Holden. It *needs* to be you." Lala sighed. "You haven't come this far to refuse big opportunities like playing at The Palace. Besides, what makes you think I'd rather go out to eat than see you play one more time before I leave the City? We'll still be together. And I truly love watching you perform. It brings me so much joy."

My chest tightened. There were two things in this world that brought *me* joy. Music and her.

Before I could refute it anymore, Lala turned to the driver. "Can you please take us to The Palace instead? I realize that it's in the opposite direction. I apologize. We've had a change in plans."

The man nodded and turned around at the next intersection.

By the time we arrived at the club, there was barely any time to think. Monroe arrived shortly after we did, followed by Dylan and our guitarist, Kevin. Lala watched as we set up, and within thirty minutes, we were on stage performing.

This show felt especially powerful, not only because of my emotional state tonight, but because I could see Lala clearly in the audience. I particularly loved watching her reaction to my solo. I wondered if this was the last time I'd get to experience having her with me while I played, but I tried to shake that thought from my mind.

Song after song, I beat the shit out of those drums, needing to take out my frustration on something. We definitely rocked it out there, though. The crowd went wild after each and every song, and I suspected we'd be invited back here, on our own merit next time.

When our set ended, I couldn't fly off that stage fast enough. I abandoned my sticks and ran down to meet Lala in the crowd.

She wrapped her hands around my face. "You're so amazing, Holden. Do you have any idea how beautiful you are to watch?"

I lifted her up, spinning her around, and kissed her long and hard. "Everything I did up there tonight was for you. All I cared about was whether you were watching me."

"Are you kidding?" She ran her fingers through my hair. "I couldn't take my eyes off you."

Putting her down, I said, "Let's get the hell out of here."

I wrapped my arm around her as we headed out of the club, not even bothering to say goodbye to the guys.

"I'm not that hungry," she said. "I just want to go home with you—because it's the last night I can say that."

She'd read my mind. All I wanted was to take her home and make love to her all night long—send her off to Philly in the best way I knew how.

So that's what I did.

The next morning, I got up first to make coffee for Lala since she'd be hitting the road early. While it was brewing, I also decided to... move some things around in her apartment.

Her eyes widened after she wandered out of the bedroom and noticed what I'd done.

"Why are all of the kitchen chairs up against the door?"

Shrugging, I flashed a crooked grin. "I figured if you can't get outta here, you won't be able to leave."

She shook her head and laughed as she walked over to wrap her arms around me.

I lifted her up. "I'm so fucked up right now, Lala. I must've been crazy for ever encouraging you to leave early."

As we fell into a kiss, I decided I needed to have her one more time before she left. I lowered my pants a few inches before sliding her underwear to the side. After leaning her ass against the counter, I slowly spread her legs and pushed inside of her.

"You want me to stop?" I rasped.

"No…" She panted, raking her hands through my hair. "Please… Don't you dare stop."

Lala lifted her hips to meet my thrusts, each pounding more intense than the last.

"That's right. Give me that beautiful pussy," I groaned.

This was something we were absolutely exceptional at: dodging reality with sex.

"I don't want you to fucking go," I muttered into her neck as I sank deeper into her.

When I felt the muscles of her pussy clamp down around me, I let out a guttural sound as Lala's orgasm echoed through the kitchen. I came so hard that I nearly saw stars.

As we started to come down from it, I said, "I should just stay inside you. That's another way to keep you from leaving."

She reached for my face and cupped her hands around my cheeks. "What's all this getting-me-to-stay stuff all of a sudden? I thought you felt my going back now was the right thing?"

I couldn't blame her for being confused. "I know I encouraged you to leave so we could figure out if this really could work. But now that the day's come, I just want to turn back time."

"This has been the best time of my life, Holden. But I get it. This was always a temporary situation."

"It's not the end, Lala. We just have to figure out a new normal." I kissed her nose and finally forced myself to pull out of her.

Lala returned to her room to get dressed while I prepared bagels for us.

We had a quiet breakfast. Outside the window, I could see it was starting to drizzle. That definitely fit the crappy mood.

After we ate, I carried all of her things out to the car. We lingered on the sidewalk, neither of us wanting to be the first to say goodbye.

I scratched my chin. "I should've disconnected your car battery. Then you wouldn't have been able to leave." I tugged on her jacket, pulling her to me and placing one last kiss on her lips. "Call me the second you get there. Be careful driving."

"I will."

The sun suddenly came out, even though it was still drizzling—perfect symbolism for the indecisive mess I'd become as of late.

I hugged her tightly, then finally let her go.

♥CHAPTER 30

Lala

Why am I back here again?

So much had changed since I'd last lived here. My fridge was empty. The apartment was freezing. I missed the warmth of my New York City place. But most of all, there was no Holden next door here. That was most definitely the worst part.

Being back in Pennsylvania was just as bittersweet as I'd thought it would be. Well, more bitter than sweet, if I was being honest. Pretty much the only good thing since arriving was getting to see my mother last night. She'd seemed to have more energy than the last time I was here, and I felt very fortunate that things were looking up with her health.

I'd spent much of today unpacking and getting my apartment back to a livable state. But no matter what I did, it still felt cold and barren. I also spent some time taking down photos of Warren and me. I hoped Holden would be coming to visit soon, and I sure as hell didn't want him seeing those. My chest felt tight, thinking of Warren and how badly I'd hurt him. Perhaps I deserved the crappy way I felt right now.

Before leaving New York, I'd packed a shopping bag with some of the snacks from my cupboard there. I'd just gotten around to emptying it out when I found a little surprise inside. Holden had stuffed one of his black hoodies in the bag with a note pinned to it.

In case you're missing me, wrap this around you tonight. (Only fair since I stole a pair of your underwear.)

Smiling, I took the sweatshirt to my face and breathed in the painfully awesome scent. I then wrapped it around myself and zipped it all the way up. It was like a warm hug from Holden. This hoodie wasn't coming off of me tonight.

Reaching for my phone, I almost texted him but remembered he had a gig this evening. I didn't want to disturb him.

Instead, I read over the text Holden had sent me earlier today.

Holden: I just listed your apartment for rent, and now I want to vomit. I miss you a fuck ton already. How have you been gone less than twenty-four hours?

I'd been asking myself that question all day.

Needing to get out of this funk, I decided to drive over to my parents' house. It was after dinner, so we'd probably just sit around in front of the TV or talk.

Mom and Dad were lounging in the living room together when I entered using my key.

My mother straightened. "Laney! I didn't know you were coming by. I would've left some food out. I've already put it all away."

"I'm not hungry, Mom. I'm actually feeling a little sick to my stomach tonight. I just came by for some company."

Her eyes narrowed. "You're sick?"

"I think it's just…depression, honestly. I have no appetite and feel a little queasy."

"That's nerves." My dad nodded.

"I don't need to tell you we're happy to have you back early, but what good is it if *you're* not happy?" My mother frowned.

My father lowered the volume on the television. "I've sensed that something was off with you from the moment you arrived last night, Laney. I'm guessing this is about Holden?"

I sat down on the couch and kicked my feet up. "He and I are sort of in a weird place right now. His career is taking off, and I just moved away, so we're figuring out where things go from here."

My mother flashed a sympathetic smile. "You've really grown to care about him, huh?"

Caring about Holden wasn't a strong-enough sentiment. "I love him," I blurted without thinking it through—because it was the truth.

"Wow." My mother's jaw dropped.

Dad sighed. "Okay."

"Does he know how you feel?" Mom asked.

"I haven't told him I love him, mainly because I need to hear him say it first. I also don't want to freak him out or make him feel obligated. If he feels the same, I want it to come from him, without any added pressure from me."

"You're not sure he feels the same?" my father asked.

"I know he cares about me, but he's always stopped short of saying those words. There were times I could've sworn he was about to say them, though. He might be scared. Or…he might not feel the same." I sighed. "But I'm not sure it could ever work between us logistically, regardless of how strongly we feel about each other."

My mother squinted. "What does that even mean…*logistically*? Is there some formula that determines whether something fits perfectly into a neat, organized box? Who's making these rules?"

Her comment gave me pause. Who *was* making the rules?

"Never mind what you think life should look like." Mom looked into my eyes. "What do you want, Laney?"

I blinked, pondering her question for a moment. "There's really nothing else I want right now than to be with him. But this isn't just *my* decision. He would have to decide whether he wants

346

the pressure of a relationship in the midst of his music career taking off."

My mother adjusted her throw blanket and posed another question. "In your mind, what would a future with Holden look like?"

Crazy.

Sexy.

Amazing.

Unpredictable.

"He'd be constantly on the road. I'd be left alone a lot." I looked away. "Not sure how you have a family with someone who's gone half the time."

"Military families do it," she pointed out.

"Does Holden want kids?" Dad asked.

"I don't think it's something he ever really saw in his future."

She shrugged. "People's wants and needs change as they mature."

"That's true," I agreed. "Though, I'm in no rush to get married or start a family, either."

"Sounds to me like fear is the biggest thing keeping you guys apart, then," she said. "Can I give you some advice?"

"Of course, Mom."

"I've learned a lot about myself and about life since this recent health scare. It's changed my outlook on certain things."

I nodded.

"I think sometimes we overthink things to death when we should just be following our hearts and enjoying each moment."

"You think I've been overthinking this?"

She grinned. "Lala, I have never seen you so engrossed in anyone, not even Warren at the height of your relationship, and not even after he asked you to marry him. That says something. Say what you want about Holden, but he's making you feel things, and that's not something anyone in this family has had an easy time of since Ryan's death." Her smile faded. "We've all been pretty much numb for years. Even if it doesn't work out with Holden, I think you should enjoy this experience for what it is: an important chapter in your life. Chapters don't last forever. But sometimes they lead to other chapters that lead to happily ever afters."

"My life is a book? Is that what you're saying, Mom?" I chuckled.

She laughed. "Every person in our lives comes into it for a reason. We just haven't figured out if Holden is a supporting character or a leading man for the long haul."

My father interrupted. "I'll tell you one thing. If you'd told me years ago that you'd end up with Holden Catalano, I wouldn't have believed it. I still don't quite believe we're having this conversation." He sighed. "But as I've told you before, I trust your judgment, Laney."

"If she loves him…" Mom said. "She's just going to have to adjust her expectations about what the future looks like." She turned to me. "When you were with Warren, you imagined a life where you were at home some of the time and perhaps working part time, with your husband returning from work on the dot every night. But maybe a future with Holden looks different. Maybe it's not as predictable, but maybe it's equally as fulfilling. Maybe you would need to take on a little bit more responsibility at home. In the end, if he's who you were meant to be with, that might be something you'd be willing to do."

She was right. And I'd been thinking a lot about what a future with Holden might look like, what sacrifices I might be willing to make in order for him to fulfill his dreams. But of course, none of that would matter if he didn't feel the same way, if he didn't *want* me to make those sacrifices. Holden had always seemed to think he might not be right for me. But didn't *I* have a say in that?

"I appreciate your perspective, Mom. I always assumed you'd be against the idea of me and Holden, but it's good to know you'd support me if I decided to do some things differently in order to be with him."

She smirked. "I should also point out that I ran into his mother the other day at the supermarket."

"Oh really?"

"Yeah, it was very interesting. We both sort of looked at each other a certain way at first. Like we both knew what the other was thinking, but neither of us was sure what we were allowed to say."

I laughed. "Awkward, huh?"

Mom nodded. "Finally, she came out with it. She said to me, 'Have you talked to Laney lately?' I asked her why she was asking. She said she was wondering if you'd happened to mention anything about Holden. I admitted that I knew there was something going on between the two of you, but I wasn't entirely sure of the status with you moving back and all. She said she'd pretty much written off any hope of Holden ending up with a nice girl, and she was hesitant to get too excited about the prospect of him dating you. But she wanted me to know that Holden would be incredibly lucky to end up with my daughter, and she hoped he would change his ways and settle down someday."

Of course, that made me miss Holden even more. It meant he'd spoken about me to his mom, which I knew had to be a big deal.

I left my parents in the living room and went to the place I often did when I needed to think—Ryan's old room. I looked over at his bulletin board with all the photos of him and his friends.

"Oh, Ry. I would give anything to know what you're thinking of all this. I often wonder if Holden and I would've had the balls to go for it if you'd been here. We might have been too scared to hurt you. But I'd like to think you're not upset at us." Tears formed in my eyes. "I really wish we could talk right now. I wish a lot when it comes to you, big brother."

I looked over at a photo of Ryan with his arm around Holden. Their eyes looked hazy, as if they'd been drinking.

I took out my phone and texted Holden, unsure whether his gig was over.

Lala: You never mentioned that you told your mother about us.

He responded right away.

Holden: Why? Did she say something?

Lala: She ran into my mom at the supermarket, and they sort of talked in code until they both acknowledged that they knew we were dating.

Holden: I don't open up to my mom much. Only about the most important stuff.

My heart fluttered. I beamed and typed.

Lala: Got it.

The little dots moved around for a while before he sent another message.

Holden: Lala...I don't know if I can do this.

My heart sank to my stomach, and a rush of heat shot straight to my head. *Do what? Is he breaking up with me?*

Holden: I can't go too long without seeing you.

I took a deep breath. If my near heart attack wasn't an indication of my true feelings, I didn't know what was.

CHAPTER 31

Holden

Owen looked me up and down when he opened the door. "Rough night?"

"Rough *sixteen* nights." I couldn't believe it had been that long, and I still hadn't seen Lala.

The card table was set up in the middle of the living room for our monthly poker game. Colby took a beer out of the cardboard box he was unloading into the mini fridge and chucked it to me. "You look like balls, dude."

I frowned. "Thanks."

He shrugged. "Actually you look worse than balls. My sack is looking pretty spiffy these days. Billie told me I needed to do a tidy-up down there. When I didn't get around to it fast enough for her, she told me she wanted ice cream and then shoved me into the waxing place next door to the ice cream parlor for grooming while she ate her cone. She'd booked me an appointment for a bro-zillian."

"A bro-zillian?" Owen covered his junk over his pants. "Like, someone poured hot wax on your balls and ripped it off?"

"It actually wasn't as bad as I thought it would be. I kinda liked the hot wax part. It was warm and nice, like having your balls cupped in two soft hands. The skin-ripping part, I could've done without."

I shook my head. "How did this conversation take a turn so fast?"

Colby stood and cracked a beer with a loud *tssSSS kr-POP*. He pointed at me as he lowered the can. "Your face looks worse than my pretty balls."

Brayden strolled in from the kitchen. He looked between me and Colby and held his hands up. "I'll take your word for it."

I chuckled. It might've been the first time that had happened in more than two weeks. I think I needed this. The guys took their usual seats around the table, and Brayden doled out the chips in exchange for cash.

When he got to me, he lifted his chin. "So why do Colby's balls look better than your face? Or do I want to know?"

I sighed. "I don't want to talk about it."

He shrugged. "Fine with me. Now give me your fifty for the chips so I can start dealing."

I pulled my wallet from my back pocket and tossed the cash on the table. Brayden added it to the empty coffee can that we kept the chips in and dealt the first hand. I went through the motions, tossing a chip into the center of the table and picking up my cards. But I couldn't have told you what suits or numbers I had in my hand to save my life. I guess I also got lost in thought while the guys were making bets and taking cards because suddenly, a chip hit me in the face.

I rubbed my nose. "What the fuck?"

"You want any cards or not, pretty boy?" Brayden asked.

"Yeah." I looked down at my hand, but I couldn't concentrate enough to make a decision. "Actually, no. I'm good."

Owen was seated to my left. He tipped his chair back on its hind legs and snuck a peek at my cards.

"You got nothing, shit for brains," he said. "Take some damn cards."

I studied my hand once again and nodded. But still couldn't make a decision.

So I gave in and shook my head. "I'm in love with Lala. I think I fucked up."

Brayden tossed his cards into the air and groaned. "Oh fuck me."

Owen frowned. "What the hell did you do?"

Colby blew out a jagged breath. "I'm really going to hate fucking up your pretty face. Did you cheat on her?"

I held up two hands. "No, nothing like that. I meant I fucked up by encouraging her to leave. I should've never pushed her to go."

"Wait. Let me get this straight," Brayden said. "It wasn't Lala's decision to go back to Philly? You *made her* leave early?"

"Maybe *made her* leave is too strong. But I told her I thought she should go back. I sure as hell didn't do anything to stop her."

"Why the fuck would you do that if you're in love with her?"

I rubbed the back of my neck. "Because I'm an idiot?"

"Well, we knew that," Owen said. "But seriously, man, why would you tell her to go if you wanted her to stay?"

I heaved a loud sigh and shook my head. "I thought it was the right thing to do. At least that's what I told myself at the time. But maybe I was just too much of a chicken shit to tell her how I really felt and ask her to stay and be with me. Deep down, I don't feel like I deserve her. She's so smart and beautiful and...unspoiled. Part of me feels like she should be with Warren."

"Jesus Christ." Colby shook his head. "I never thought I'd see the day."

"That I fell in love?"

"No. The day that your egotistical ass had your confidence rocked. When you were eighteen, you thought you could score our super-hot, thirty-year-old English teacher."

I smiled halfheartedly. "Ms. Renzo put her hand on my thigh. She wanted me."

Colby pointed. "You see? Never once have you doubted yourself with a woman. Do you think I feel good enough for Billie? Of course not. But you gotta get over that shit. When you're in love with someone, you don't push them away because you're not worthy. You spend the rest of your life trying to become the man who's good enough to be by her side."

I wanted to believe I could be a man worthy of Lala. But I wasn't sure it was true. "What if I fuck up?"

Brayden motioned to the three of them. "Then we're going to kick your ass. We owe that to Ryan."

Owen caught my eye. "If you hurt Lala, you're definitely getting a beating. But I'm going to go out on a limb and say something I never thought I'd say… I think if Ryan were here listening to how you feel about his little sister, he'd give you his blessing. So you have mine."

Colby nodded. "Mine, too."

Brayden shrugged. "Same. So stop being a pussy and tell the woman how you feel. And maybe we can also quit talking about feelings and manscaping now and play some cards?"

I smiled. "Yeah, let's do it."

I wasn't sure I'd actually solved anything, but it was good to know the guys thought maybe things could work out with Lala. Now I only had to convince myself…

The following morning, I was lying in bed, kicking around the idea of driving up to Philly this weekend to lay my heart on the line with Lala, when my phone buzzed from the end table. It was our manager, Daisy. I read the message in preview and frowned.

Daisy: Hope no one has any plans for the weekend...

Lately, her timing had really sucked.

Though if that wasn't fate telling me not to profess my love to Lala, I wasn't sure what was. I sighed and went to type back. But when I unlocked my phone and it opened to the full text, I realized there was more to the message.

Daisy: Hope no one has any plans for the weekend. There's a new club owned by a group of celebrities that's impossible to get booked at. One of the owner's daughters saw you play recently and told her father he needs to get you guys on stage.

Before I could respond, my bandmates typed back.

Dylan: I'm in. Where we heading?

Monroe: Could be Pluto for all I care. I'm in.

Our manager responded.

Daisy: It's a little more convenient than Pluto. It's in Philadelphia.

I sat up, feeling adrenaline pump through my veins. Maybe fate had other plans after all...

Holden: Definitely in.

Once we'd all responded, Daisy sent through the details for the Saturday-night gig. Still feeling the high of the coincidence, I couldn't wait to text Lala.

Holden: Hey. We just booked a show for Saturday night in Philly. I'm stoked to play back home, but even more stoked to see you. We're the first act, so we should be on by nine and done by ten or ten thirty. Come to the show, and we can skirt out.

I didn't even put down my phone as I waited for her to respond.

Lala: Oh that's great. I'll try to make it.

Try?

It felt like I'd been listening to the theme song from *Rocky*, ready to run up the stairs to grab my girl at the top, when suddenly the needle screeched to a sudden halt.

I typed back.

Holden: Do you already have plans?

I watched the dots jump around, then stop for a minute or two, before finally starting again.

Lala: Just some work I need to catch up on.

At nine o'clock on Saturday night, which was four days away? She couldn't even figure out a way to free up a few hours with that much notice? Whatever optimism I'd felt sank like lead to the bottom of my stomach.

This is it. The beginning of the end.

She might as well have told me she had to wash her hair. Though something inside of me was afraid to call her out on it, for fear she'd just end things now. I needed to at least see her one last time if this was where it was heading. So I sucked it up.

Holden: Okay. Have a good day.

Her response was a smiley face, *a damn emoji.*

Over the next few days, I spent a ridiculous number of hours contemplating how I should handle things. I bounced back and forth between professing my undying love and making her life easier by being the one to formally break things off so she could have her freedom. My head was a fucking wreck. The only thing I knew for sure was that I wanted to do the right thing by Lala, not make things harder on her.

In the end, I decided I needed to see her in person to figure out what that right thing was. So I drove up a day early without telling her, hoping that catching her off guard would help me make the decision. I wanted to see how she reacted when she opened the door after not seeing each other for three full weeks.

My heart started to pound when I pulled up in front of her apartment Friday evening. Beads of sweat formed on my forehead and upper lip as I walked up the path, though it wasn't the slightest bit warm out. Standing at her door, I wiped my hands on my pants and took a deep breath.

Knock. Knock. Knock.

But it wasn't Lala who opened.

It was…*her mother.*

I tried to hide my disappointment and act polite. "Oh. Hey, Mrs. E."

"Holden? Laney didn't mention you were coming."

I shoved my hands into my jeans pockets. "That's probably because she doesn't know. I thought I'd surprise her."

"Oh. Well, she's not home right now. I'm waiting for a delivery that was supposed to come earlier this afternoon, but the shipping company got a flat tire and said they were going to be a few hours late."

"Is Lala still at work?"

Mrs. E shook her head. "She had a doctor's appointment and then some errands to run."

"Oh. Okay." I forced a smile. "So much for surprises. But I'm glad I got to see you, Mrs. E. You look great."

"Would you…want to come in for a cup of tea, maybe? It'll probably be a few hours before Laney is back, but perhaps we could catch up for a few minutes?"

"Sure. Of course."

I'd practically lived at the Ellison's house when I was a kid. Yet I suddenly felt awkward. That might've had something to do with being certain she'd invited me in to tell me to keep the hell away from her daughter.

We made small talk as she filled the teapot and got everything ready, and I did my best not to sweat rings under the armpits of my shirt.

"Here we go…" Mrs. E set two mugs down on the kitchen table and took the seat across from me. She smiled warmly. "My husband said he might stop by to keep me company. So we might not have too long with just the two of us. I hope you won't mind if I speak candidly and don't beat around the bush."

Fuck. Here it comes. I swallowed and nodded. "Of course. We go way back, Mrs. E. Say whatever is on your mind."

"Thank you, Holden." She cleared her throat. "I'm not usually one to meddle. But I know you have feelings for my daughter. And I also know how close you and my son were."

I looked down, ashamed. "I'm really sorry, Mrs. E. I know Ryan would want to kill me if he was here. And I also know I'm not a parent's ideal pick as boyfriend material." I shook my head. "I didn't mean for it to happen. I swear, I didn't."

Mrs. E reached across the table and patted my hand. "I want to tell you a story. I'm not sure if you'll remember this or not, but about a week before Ryan died, he started sleeping on the couch downstairs. He was too weak to go up to his room."

My heart felt heavy as I nodded. "I remember."

"Well, this one day in particular, you were over, and Ryan had fallen asleep on the couch. Laney was outside raking the leaves on the front lawn, and you went out to help her. At least that's what you said you were going to do." Mrs. E smiled fondly. "But when you got out there, you scooped up a big bunch of leaves and threw them at Laney. The two of you had a leaf fight on the lawn. You chased each other around for the better part of an hour, laughing nonstop like two schoolkids."

I smiled. "I remember that day."

"What I don't think you know is that Ryan woke up in the middle of the leaf fight. He was thirsty and went into the kitchen.

358

I'd been folding laundry in the other room, and I came in to find him watching you and Laney through the window." She turned to stare out Laney's kitchen window and covered her heart with her hand. "The smile on his face as he watched was as big as the ones you two wore. And you know what he said?"

"What?"

She turned back to look at me. "He said you two had had it bad for each other for years."

My jaw dropped. "He knew?"

She nodded. "He told me you weren't right for his sister."

I frowned.

"But then he said he hoped one day you'd find the girl who'd change you, and he hoped that girl was Laney."

Tears filled my eyes. "Really?"

"Really." She held up a finger and laughed. "Well, full disclosure, after he said that, he also told me that if you *didn't* change and went after his little sister, I was supposed to have my husband kick your ass."

I smiled. "That sounds more like Ryan."

Mrs. E squeezed my hand. "Only you know if you've changed to become the man we both know Laney needs. But I thought it was important that you know Ryan believed you had it in you." She paused. "And so do I, Holden."

My eyes met hers. "Really?"

She nodded. "Really."

Whatever hope I'd left with after talking with Mrs. Ellison had long faded by the next day. Lala had texted when she'd gotten home last night. Her mom had told her I was in town and had stopped over, but she said she was too tired for me to come back by. And this morning, she'd told me she had to go into work. She was supposed to have texted me when she was done, but checking my phone a hundred times did nothing to make her message arrive. Still, I clung to the hope that she'd just been really busy and would show up for our gig. But she never did.

By the end of our show, I was miserable and wanted nothing more than to go home. So when Monroe announced that we had a new song to play for everyone—the song I'd written about Lala—I was in no mood and shook my head.

"Not tonight, buddy."

He waved me toward the front of the stage anyway, as he spoke into the microphone. "I think our drummer is being uncharacteristically shy and needs some encouragement. What do you say, everyone? Can you make some noise if you want to hear a *brand new song* that has never been played to a crowd before? If you'd like our resident stud-muffin drummer to come up and sing for you all?"

The crowd clapped and yelled. Meanwhile, I wanted to punch Monroe in the face. But there was a reason he was the front man for After Friday. He was a relentless showboat and kept egging people on to get me up there. When he had them all chanting *Hold-en, Hold-en*, I knew I had no choice but to get up from my seat. I'd wanted Lala to be the first person to hear me sing the song besides the band, but it kind of felt like that was never going to happen anyway. So when the music started, I closed my eyes and poured my heart into singing every word I'd written. I didn't even realize tears were streaming down my face until I was done and opened my eyes—and saw *Lala* standing near the back door with matching tears on her cheeks. I blinked a few times, making sure I wasn't seeing things. But sure enough, she was there.

I shoved the mic at my bass player, oblivious to the crowd giving me a standing ovation, and took off from the stage. "Take a set break. I'll be back."

I couldn't get to her fast enough. Pushing through the crowd, I ignored people congratulating me and gushing with compliments. Nothing mattered except for Lala.

When I finally reached her, I cupped her cheeks in my hands. "I didn't think you were here."

She sniffled. "I wasn't going to come. I'm sorry, Holden. I'm so sorry."

I swallowed. It hurt like hell, but it was more important to me that she wasn't upset. So I wiped her cheeks with my thumbs. "It's fine. I understand. We can be friends, sweetheart. We can keep in touch. Don't cry. Don't be upset."

"I don't want to keep in touch, Holden."

My jaw flexed. I knew I needed to walk away at this point. I was emotional after pouring my heart out on the stage. I didn't want to say something I'd regret. "Fine. Whatever you want. Take care, Lala."

I turned abruptly and took two steps, but Lala grabbed my arm. "Holden, wait!"

"Why? What the hell else is left to say? That I'm so in love with you that it hurts? That I can't fucking eat? I can't fucking think? I don't even want to get out of bed without you near me?" My voice grew louder. "Tell me, Lala. Is that what you wanted to hear me say?"

She shook her head. "No."

"Then what the hell else is there?"

Lala took a deep breath. "I'm pregnant, Holden. With your baby."

CHAPTER 32

Holden

I felt the world around me spinning. Every single sound and light in the club faded into the distance as I tried to comprehend the words she'd just uttered.

Did Lala really just say what I thought she'd said?

She's pregnant?

My heart raced as I took her hand and led her out of the venue. I needed to hear it again with no distractions.

We walked around the corner of the brick building until we were alone, aside from some passing cars.

My hands shook as I wrapped them around her face. "Lala… say it again. What you just said in there, so I know I'm not hallucinating."

"I'm pregnant, Holden."

"Are you sure?"

"I've taken multiple tests. And it was confirmed by the doctor. That's where I was when you stopped by and spoke to my mother."

This news shouldn't have come as a surprise. We hadn't been careful a hundred percent of the time, a risk I'd never taken with anyone else. I'd gotten carried away.

Dazed, I asked, "How long have you known?"

"A couple of weeks ago, I realized the nausea I'd had ever since I left New York wasn't going away. I thought it was nerves at first, but then started to suspect it could be more."

I nodded as everything finally started to make sense.

"That's why you went silent on me."

"Yeah."

"Why didn't you tell me what was going on, Lala? I could've been there for you."

She shook her head. "I needed to be absolutely sure before I sprung this on you."

I closed my eyes, letting it all sink in.

Lala…was carrying my baby.

Our baby.

I'm going to be a dad.

What?

Holy shit.

Holy shit.

Holy shit.

She interrupted my thoughts. "I need to let you know, Holden, that I've decided to keep it. I know it's the worst possible timing, and you're nowhere near ready for—"

"Whoa. Whoa. Whoa." I pulled back suddenly. "Did you think I would *ever* consider not keeping our baby?" My heart pounded. "I might not be *ready* to be a father, but Lala…" I lifted her chin. "Look at me. Look into my eyes. I need you to understand something."

She nodded, her tears starting again as she stared up at me.

"This news? It's the best thing that's *ever* happened to me. The fact that my baby is now growing inside you is more important than music. More important than *anything*. It's…" I paused to reflect on what this meant. "It's everything I never knew I wanted."

Her eyes widened. "You're happy about it?"

I placed my trembling hand over her stomach. "I'm so fucking happy, sweetheart. So happy."

"I'm so relieved." She placed her hand over mine. "I was worried this was going to blindside you. I was prepared to raise it alone, if I had to."

"If for some reason you didn't want to go through with this, that would be your choice. But that would've killed me, Lala. Because after only a few minutes of knowing about its existence, I love this baby." I paused to look into her eyes. "And I love *you* so much. I haven't known how to express it. I tried through that song obviously, but saying it to your face has been long overdue." I finally removed my hand from her belly and placed it around her face. "I love you, Lala. And I promise you, I will do whatever it takes to make this work, to give you the kind of life you've always dreamed of."

Her eyes glistened. "Any life I dreamed of before you doesn't exist anymore, Holden. You're my dream." She wiped her eyes. "When I heard that song you performed tonight, it gave me the confidence to finally tell you what was going on. I would never want you to say you loved me for the wrong reasons. Knowing you loved me before you found out I'm pregnant… That was perfect."

I caressed her cheek with my thumb. "I've loved you for a long time, sweetheart. Just didn't want to scare you away."

She stepped back a bit. "I have to say something…"

"Okay…"

"I don't want you to change anything because of this news. I would never be able to live with myself if you gave up a career you've worked so hard for because you felt obligated to stay in one place. I want you with us, of course, but even before I found out I was pregnant, I'd been thinking a lot about adjusting my expectations so we can make this work. If I want you in my life, I need to accept that you might not always be physically around."

I blinked. "I can't even think about music right now. That all seems so…unimportant compared to this." I shook my head. "I can tell you one thing—I'm not going to wanna be away from our kid, or you, for any length of time. So while I do need to figure out what that means in terms of the band, it's not gonna be tonight. Right now, I just want to bask in this—because, Lala…we're having a baby." My mouth curved into a smile. "There's nothing bigger than that. I'm scared as fuck…but so happy."

She beamed. "I'm happy and scared, too. But I know you're gonna be the best dad to our child. Even if neither one of us knows what the hell we're doing."

Our child.

It felt surreal in the best possible way.

A disheveled man approached us. "Spare some change?"

"Dude, I just found out I'm gonna be a father." I lifted my arms up and repeated, "I'm gonna be a dad!"

The man flashed a toothless grin. "Well, that's great, man."

I reached into my pocket and handed him a wad of cash. "Tonight's the best night of my life, and hopefully this makes *your* night."

The man looked down at the money in his palm and started to cry. "You don't know how much this means."

I patted him on the shoulder. "Take care of yourself."

"You, too. And congratulations!" he said before limping away.

After he left, the shock started to wear off, replaced by nothing but pure excitement.

I yelled out into the street. "I'm gonna be a father!"

"Fuck you!" someone from one of the apartments across the road yelled back.

Lala wiped tears of laughter from her eyes.

I wrapped my arms around her and kissed her forehead. "Let's go home."

That night, in Lala's bed, I lay my head gently against her stomach. I'd been in such a stupor earlier that I'd forgotten to ask how long she'd been pregnant. She told me she was about six weeks along. The idea that her belly would be growing larger by the week brought me more joy than you could imagine. The crazy thing was, in my wildest fantasies, I'd imagined Lala pregnant with my baby inside of her. But I'd never dared to think it might actually happen.

"Who else knows?" I whispered against her belly button. "I mean, besides half of Philadelphia after I yelled it out tonight."

Her belly shook as she chuckled. "My parents. That's it."

A rush of adrenaline hit at the thought of her dad wanting to kill me.

I cringed. "How did your father take it?"

"He was shocked, like I was. But I think when he finds out how you reacted, he's gonna be just fine. He knows I love you."

I turned to look at her. "He does?"

"Yeah. I told him. We've talked a lot about you these past several weeks, even before I knew I was pregnant." She massaged her fingers through my hair. "He knew how down I was being away from you. I couldn't hide it from anyone."

Knowing she'd told her dad she loved me gave me a sense of pride. No one could argue with that.

"We should probably wait until at least twelve weeks to tell everyone else," she said.

I nodded. "Okay…so you think it's too soon to tell even the guys and Billie?"

Keeping this inside for another six weeks would kill me. I wasn't known for holding secrets very well—just the opposite.

She sighed, looking conflicted. "Well, they say to wait twelve weeks or so, because anything can happen before then." Lala must have noticed me pouting. "Okay…just the guys and Billie. And your parents. But no one else."

I smiled. "Cool."

She rubbed her stomach. "It's only the size of a bean right now."

My heart sank as fear filled me. *That's freaking small.* So incredibly fragile. The thought of anything bad happening to our baby scared the crap out of me. I vowed not to focus on that and to try to believe everything was going to be okay.

"You're making me want to bubblewrap you, Lala."

"But then you couldn't get at me yourself." She winked.

"Yeah. What was I thinking? Forget that." I squeezed her side. "I want you to know something…"

"Okay…"

"Even if you hadn't told me you're pregnant… I was going to come see you before I left Philly and suggest that we do whatever it takes. Because the past few weeks have been unbearable. We might have no solid logistical plan, but we're a team. And now… We're a *family.* There is absolutely nothing I won't do to make this work."

Lala smiled down at me. "Thank you."

"Thank *you.*" I returned my attention to her stomach and spoke softly into her skin. "Hey, little bean. It's your daddy. I don't think you can hear me yet, but I want you to know I'm rooting for you. I'm gonna start praying really hard that you continue to grow healthy. I don't want to disrupt the peace in there so early, but I also want you to get ready for some music in the coming months. Because I'm gonna sing to you, whether you like it or not. You're gonna come out drumming your little fists, too."

Lala laughed.

"And I want to apologize in advance for my lack of preparation for you," I added. "I'm probably the last guy you would choose to be your dad. I almost killed a guinea pig with a Hot Cheeto once. But I promise to love you enough to make up for the fact that I'm not perfect."

The following day, I had a few hours to go before I'd reluctantly return to New York. Since Lala had agreed that I could tell my parents, I'd visited them this morning and explained that not only was I in love with Lala Ellison, but we were having a baby. My mother had nearly fainted, while my dad just kept laughing in disbelief. Despite having funny ways of showing it, both of my folks were overjoyed—especially since I was an only child.

I'd already planned to drive back to Philly the following weekend to see Lala again. But I needed to make one important stop during this trip before I left Pennsylvania. It simply couldn't wait. And I needed to go alone.

It was cloudy when I showed up to the cemetery. Whenever I was home for any length of time, I stopped to visit Ryan's grave. But this time was perhaps the most important visit of all.

Kneeling down, I laid an ice cream cone in front of his gravestone. Most people brought flowers when they came to a cemetery, but I always brought Ryan his favorite cookies and cream from Mickey's.

Taking a deep breath in, I looked up at the sky. "I'm just gonna come out with it." I returned my gaze to the headstone and exhaled. "I knocked up your baby sister, Ry."

I paused for the harsh reaction I imagined he was exhibiting up in heaven—some expletives thrown my way and perhaps a *"How the fuck could you do that to me?"*

"Did you ever dream you'd hear me say that?" I continued. "Or maybe you did dream it, and it was your biggest nightmare." I shook my head. "Either way, I never imagined I'd have to admit this to you."

Then I remembered my conversation with Lala's mom. Maybe I was blowing Ryan's imagined reaction out of proportion.

"I want to believe what your mother told me you said to her, that you would've approved of this on the condition that I'd changed. But it's hard to know whether you'd think I've changed *enough*."

I picked at some grass. "I'm here to tell you I believe I have. I'm not sure anyone but Lala could've made me *want* to change, Ryan. But love does that, I guess. The time was never right all those years ago when you noticed how I used to look at her. I wasn't the right man for her then."

A plane flew overhead.

"The thing is…I don't know that I'll ever be the man she deserves. But I do know I'll love her and our baby more than I've ever loved anything. I need *you* to know that. And I need you to trust me. I've got her, brother. I do. I won't let you down." I chuckled. "Oh! And if for some reason you had anything to do with that nerd Warren getting that job out in California, thank you."

I'd promised myself I wouldn't cry, but my eyes watered when I thought about how unfair life was. "It should've been you, Ryan. You're the one out of all of us who always knew you wanted a family someday. It kills me every day to think about you not getting to experience that. I owe it to you to not fuck this up because you never got the chance to be a dad. My kid is your niece or nephew, which is pretty damn cool, if you ask me. And if it looks like Lala, that means it will have your face, too." I shook my head. "Okay, that's fucking weird that I only now realized I'm in love with someone who looks like *you*. Don't overanalyze that one, okay?"

I wiped my eyes. "Anyway, I hope you don't hate me. I mean, let's face it, if you're able to see *everything* that happens down here, I've been on the chopping block for a while now."

Patting the gravestone, I said, "I love you, man. I always will. And my kid will always know what an amazing guy their uncle is. I can't wait to tell them all of the stories of our childhood. I promise not to make it all about what we lost—but about what we had when you were here. Because, Ryan, you were so much more than your sickness. And I will make damn sure that's not what you're remembered for. You were the tie that bound all of us guys. And any one of us would've traded places with you, if it meant keeping you here. We love you so much."

Now my tears were falling again. *Damn, it was good I came alone.* I stood. "Anyway, take care, my guy. I'll be back soon. I promise."

As I walked to my car, a burst of wind knocked the Eagles cap I'd been wearing right off my head. It blew so far away that I would've had to sprint to catch it. Instead, I smiled and chose to let it go. That had been Ryan's favorite cap. He'd always tried to steal it from me.

It seems he finally did.

❤CHAPTER 33

Lala

I licked my lips.

Seriously. Freaking. Hot.

Holden finished wiping the sweat from his forehead and let the hem of his T-shirt fall back in place. He glanced over to where I sat as he picked up the sledgehammer again. But when he saw my face, he set it down.

"Again?"

I bit my lip and shrugged. "I can't help it. It's the pregnancy hormones. And your muscles are bulging, your abs are glistening with sweat, and you're mesting. It's ridiculously sexy."

His brows quirked. "Mesting?"

"Male nesting. There's something so seductive about a man doing physical labor to get ready for the arrival of his child. Would it be weird if I asked you to take off your shirt, bang on your chest, and say, '*Me, Tarzan. You, Jane*?'"

Holden peeled the work gloves from his hands. "How about I bang something else instead?"

I giggled. I was insatiable lately. I couldn't get enough of this man, especially since he'd started breaking down the wall between his apartment and my old one last week, after I finally moved back to New York for good. It was such a turn-on to watch him swing a sledgehammer and saw through wall framing to make room for our growing family. Who knew?

Holden stalked over to me and wrapped his arms around my waist. "You do realize, I'm going to have to keep you knocked up since you're a little nympho when you're pregnant."

"It's okay. I want to have lots of your babies."

"We're going to have to be quick this time. I need to take a shower to clean off before I touch you, and then we have your twelve-week OB appointment in an hour, too."

"Take a shower before you touch me? No way. I want you sweaty."

Holden chuckled. He leaned down and scooped me off my feet and into his arms. "Your wish is my command, sweetheart."

In the bedroom, we stripped out of our clothes and fell to the bed, tangled in a kiss. We'd started our day with slow and sweet early this morning, and I wanted it hard and fast now. So I wiggled out from beneath him and climbed up on all fours. Holden didn't need any prompting. He knelt behind me and reached down between my legs to test the waters. Finding me ready, he groaned. "I love how wet you are before I even touch you."

"No time for foreplay," I breathed. "I need you inside of me now."

No matter how wet and ready I was, Holden was always a tight squeeze. He nudged the head of his cock inside, and my inner muscles clamped around every glorious inch of him as he eased in. When his hips were flush against my ass, his body started to shake. He pulled halfway out with another groan.

"I love to watch your face when I'm inside you. But this view is pretty damn spectacular, too." He eased a few more inches out and pushed back in, painstakingly slowly. "Jesus Christ, I could watch this forever."

Holden found his rhythm, gliding in and out at first, then speeding up and powering deep and hard. He folded his body over my back and reached around to massage my clit.

"Come for me, sweetheart, so I can fill this sweet pussy up."

The mix of dirty and sweet detonated the climax that had been building, and my orgasm rushed over me. I moaned through every second of it. After, I felt like a puddle of mush, and it was difficult to hold my weight up as Holden finally took his turn. His fingers dug into my shoulders, and his hips powered against me in a long release. I felt aftershocks pulse through our joined bodies for a long time when he was done. Both drained, he turned us so we collapsed on our sides rather than our stomachs. I smiled to myself, knowing that was Holden being protective of the baby.

He kissed my shoulder from behind. "I have a dumb question, one I should probably know the answer to."

"What?"

"How long can my swimmers live inside you?"

I turned over to face him. "Sperm can survive in the female reproductive tract for up to five days. Why do you ask?"

He grinned. "You know how many times I've filled you up over the last five days? I'm wondering if the sonogram tech is going to think she's looking into a packed fishbowl when she does your ultrasound."

I laughed. "Your swimmers have proven to be powerful, but I'm pretty sure they're still microscopic. But speaking of the ultrasound, you better jump in the shower so we're not late. I'll go in after you."

"Why don't we save time, take one together?"

"Because we'll never get out of here."

"I can be good. I mean, we've had sex three times already today. I can probably keep my hands to myself for an hour or two."

I shoved Holden off the bed. "I wasn't worried about *you*."

Forty minutes later, we were at the obstetrician's office. Dr. Resnick did a quick exam and then a technician came in, rolling a machine with her. I was suddenly as nervous as I was excited. She set everything up, then pulled a condom over the wand and squirted lube on my belly.

Holden stood beside me, holding my hand so tightly. He looked as nervous as I felt.

The technician rolled the wand around, and a loud heartbeat echoed through the room. She fiddled with some knobs. "Strong heartbeat. Running a hundred and forty-eight beats per minute."

Holden squeezed my hand. "Does everything look good?"

"I'm just going to take some measurements, and then I'll give you an anatomy tour. But so far everything looks perfect."

"Thank you for saying that," I said. "Because I think I might be losing the circulation in my fingers." I looked over at Holden, who took a minute to realize what I'd meant. When it clicked, he loosened his grip.

"Shit. Sorry."

The ultrasound tech and I shared a smile.

She spent a few minutes scanning my belly and then pressed a little harder while pointing to the screen with her other hand.

"Eyes, nose, mouth. Little chin."

I leaned forward, amazed at how clear it was. "Wow, it looks like a real person."

She moved the wand again and a hand with five fingers came on the screen, clear as day. "I think he's waving."

"He?" Holden said. "It's a boy?"

"No, sorry." The tech shook her head. "That just came out. I actually don't know to tell you if it's a he or a she. We can't usually see sex at the twelve-week exam." She showed us the spine, knees, and feet. It was the coolest. I'd known I was pregnant, of course, but seeing a real human inside of me on the screen was mesmerizing.

Suddenly, the tech gasped and lifted the wand off my belly.

"What's the matter?" I said.

She shook her head. "Oh my gosh. Nothing. I'm sorry again. I didn't mean to scare you. I was scanning the reproductive organs. Like I said, normally I can't tell the sex at twelve weeks. But I definitely can with this baby."

My eyes bulged. "Really?"

The tech laughed. "I think this little peanut might go down in the books as the biggest gender-reveal show off I've ever seen. The legs are wide open, flaunting its sex organs."

Holden and I looked at each other.

"This is *definitely* your child," I said.

"Sex organ? Does that mean it's a boy?"

"I said sex *organs*, not organ." She looked between us. "But do you want to know?"

I said *no* at the exact same moment Holden said *yes.*

The woman smiled. "I can tell just one of you, if you'd like."

I shook my head. "No way. Telling him would be like telling me. This baby's father is the worst secret keeper in the world. Six weeks ago, we agreed we would tell a small, select group of a few friends and wait until the second trimester to tell anyone else. Every day I have strangers in the building we live in coming up and congratulating me."

Holden shrugged. "What can I say? I'm happy. I want to tell the whole world you're having my baby."

I knew he meant that, which was why it was impossible to get mad at him for blabbing. The sonogram tech finished up her exam. She set the wand back in the holder and gave me a wad of paper towels to clean the lube off my belly. A row of pictures printed out from the machine, and the tech handed them to me.

"None of these show the sex. I'll let you two talk for a few minutes. If you decide to find out, just tell the front desk to grab me."

"Thank you."

I looked down at the images as she finished packing up her

machine. Glancing over each, I smiled. It was surreal to hold the first photos of our child. Each picture was a black square with a thin white border around it. On the bottom, there were tiny little letters and numbers typed within the white edges. I thought I could make out what they were, but I had to be wrong, had to be imagining what was there. So I pulled the strip of pictures to my nose for a closer inspection.

It can't be.

The technician was halfway out the door already. "Wait!" I yelled.

She stopped.

I turned the sonogram images to face her and pointed to the bottom. "What are these letters down here? Is this your name?"

She leaned and squinted. "Oh, no. That's the practice name. It's abbreviated."

I blinked a few times. "Really?"

"Yes, why?"

"I guess I just never saw it abbreviated like that. Thank you."

"No problem."

Once she shut the door, I turned to Holden.

"You're never going to believe this…"

"What?"

I held the photos out to him. "Look for yourself."

Holden's eyes bulged when he saw what I saw.

"What's the practice name again?"

"Resnick, Yanez, and Nussbaum."

RYAN was printed on the bottom of every page.

"Holy shit," Holden said. "I guess he's okay with it after all."

My eyes filled with tears. "And I guess we have our baby's name, if it's a boy."

❤EPILOGUE

Holden

Six months later

The sterile smell of the hospital waiting area hit me. I'd just walked out of Lala's room when I spotted Colby approaching. He was wearing an infant carrier. And following him was his entire family.

I held my hand up. "Hey, Lennons. What's up?"

I'd known Colby and the guys planned to visit tonight but was surprised to see Billie, Saylor, and the baby, too.

Billie reached out to hug me. "We didn't have a sitter, but I had to come anyway."

"I'm glad you did." I kissed her on the cheek.

"How is Lala?" Colby asked.

"She's good." I looked behind me at the door to her room. "But they're both sleeping."

"Oh no." Billie's smile faded. "So this is a bad time?"

"Pretty sure they'll wake up soon if you don't mind hanging out for a little bit."

"We can wait!" Saylor said as she hopped excitedly. "I want to see the baby!"

"Cool." I ruffled her hair. "It seems like just yesterday *you* were the baby."

We all moved to the seating area, and I filled them in on Lala's long labor, which had lasted over twenty-four hours until she gave birth this morning.

Brayden showed up a few moments later.

I turned to him. "Hey."

We clasped hands.

"How is everyone?" he asked.

"Great. They're sleeping, though."

I hadn't gotten much sleep myself over the past couple of days. But it didn't matter. I was on cloud nine and didn't want to miss a moment of my life right now.

"Why don't I grab coffee?" Brayden patted me on the shoulder. "You look like you could use it."

"Thanks, man. I could definitely go for some."

After Brayden left, Owen emerged from the elevator and headed toward me.

"Congratulations, Daddy!" He smiled. "Why is everyone sitting out here?"

"Lala and the baby are sleeping. I'll check on them in a minute and see if they're awake."

Owen nodded and exhaled. His tie was undone, and his hair was unruly. He looked a bit frazzled. I wondered if it had anything to do with things back at the building. When Lala went into labor, I'd had no choice but to put him in charge of things.

"Thanks for covering for me, by the way," I said.

"You neglected to tell me about the smokeshow in 410."

"Smokeshow?" I laughed. "The middle-aged lady with the crazy kids who drive you nuts?"

"No." He shook his head. "The woman who answered the door was in her twenties."

I scratched my chin in confusion. We'd had a number of run-ins with the teenagers we'd dubbed Frick and Frack. I'd been meaning to go over there and issue a warning to them after yet another series of disturbances and another missing rent payment right before Lala started having contractions. Owen had offered to handle it for me when she and I headed to the hospital.

"No one in their twenties lives there, Owen. It's just that lady, Maureen, and her kids. You sure you didn't go to the wrong apartment?"

"No, because Frick and Frack were there." He sighed. "She's gorgeous and has quite the mouth on her, too—a bit of a firecracker. I haven't been able to stop thinking about her." He chuckled. "Especially after she slammed the door in my face."

"Wow." I laughed. "So she left an impression. I haven't seen you react to a woman since... I can't even remember."

He shook his head. "You don't understand. I didn't think I'd ever see her again."

I squinted. "Again?"

Owen looked behind his shoulder then lowered his voice. "A few nights ago, I'd had a hard day at work. I couldn't relax, so I went to that bar down the street. I met her there. We both had too much to drink. I hadn't wanted anyone like that in a long time. She wouldn't tell me her name, which I thought was a little weird, but I went with it. We ended up at the hotel next door to the place and..." He sighed. "Best freaking sex of my life. But she snuck out before I could convince her to give me her name and number."

My mouth fell open. "No shit?"

"So you can imagine my shock when she opened the door at 410 today." He exhaled. "Anyway, she kicked me out before I had a chance to find out who she is or why she's apparently living there."

"What are you guys whispering about?" Brayden appeared, holding two coffees.

Owen glared at me. I assumed that meant Brayden didn't know the story, and he was in no mood for our friend to bust his balls right now.

"The mystery woman in 410," I simply answered.

He handed me a cup. "Oh…the hot chick?"

Owen's eyes widened. "You know her?"

"No, but I've seen her."

Owen leaned in with great interest. "Who is she?"

Brayden peeled back the corner of his plastic coffee lid. "I don't know if she's visiting or what. Or maybe she's their babysitter. But I've seen her coming in and out of the building a few times."

"Aren't those kids too old for a babysitter?" I asked.

"Believe me, they need *more* than a babysitter. They're tyrants," Owen said.

"I'm sure they're no worse than us when we were their age." I chuckled.

"Anyway, I saw her carrying a bunch of groceries in the other day," Brayden explained. "I offered to help her, but she wouldn't let me."

Owen arched a brow. "I *bet* you offered to help her."

Brayden shrugged. "Can you freaking blame me?"

I looked between them. "I'm not gonna have to break up a fight between you two over this new girl in town, am I?"

"Mr. Catalano?" A nurse turned my attention away from the conversation.

I turned. "Yep?"

"I just went in to check your wife's vitals. She's awake and looking for you."

My wife. Except she wasn't my wife—yet.

"Thank you." I nodded. "I'll be right back," I told the crew before walking away.

Lala's voice was groggy when I entered the room. "Hey."

She held the baby to her breast. Her curly hair was disheveled, but she'd never looked more beautiful than she did lying there breastfeeding our child.

"Everyone's here to see you guys," I said, putting my coffee down on the table.

"Really?" She scooched up. "Tell them to come in."

"Well, you just woke up. I figured I'd give you a few."

My beautiful daughter was perfectly latched onto Lala's breast, sucking away. She'd gotten the hang of it so quickly. I ran my thumb along the peach fuzz on the side of her soft little cheek.

"She's such a good girl," I whispered.

"She loves to eat. I was so worried I'd have trouble."

Her tiny hand curled into a fist on Lala's chest. I gently slid my fingers along her hospital bracelet and smiled at the name written on it: *Hope Ryann Catalano*. We'd decided to keep Ryan as a first-name option if we ended up having a boy someday.

"The nurse called you my wife, by the way. We need to make that happen for real," I told Lala.

She smiled. "I know. I feel left out. My two favorite people in the world are Catalanos. I want to be one, too."

Lala and I had decided to have a massive wedding in the near future and would start planning it once everything calmed down and we became acclimated to our new life as parents. Everything was up in the air in the best way. Lala would be taking some time off in between research projects to stay home with Hope and wasn't entirely sure what she'd be doing in a few months. As for me? My music career was still up in the air, too.

The band hadn't gotten any offers out of California, which gave me a bit of a reprieve from having to worry about letting the guys down. But from the moment my daughter was born, I knew I wouldn't be able to handle missing a single second of her growing up. That meant if the band ended up going on the road, they'd have to find another drummer, because I was more than likely going to quit. Personally, I didn't look at that as a failure. It would be my choice. I knew Lala would never ask me to step away from the band, but it didn't matter. There was only one place I *wanted* to be, and that was with my family. Music would always be a part of my life. It just would no longer *be* my life.

"Let me know if you're ready for the storm of our friends to blow in," I said.

She covered her breast a little. "I'm ready."

A minute later, I went out to the hall and gave them the all clear.

Colby had taken his son out of the carrier. Little Maverick had a massive amount of black hair for a baby who was only a few months old. He looked like he was wearing a toupee.

"Look at the hair on Mav's head!" I laughed.

Billie fluffed it. "I know, right? Where did it come from?"

The crew bustled into the room and spent the next several minutes oohing and ahhing over baby Hope. It was crazy to realize that there were now three children in the mix among us.

I looked down at my daughter and pointed to Colby's son. "You know, these two are gonna grow up together. He'd better not get any ideas."

"I think Ryan might find that pretty funny, actually." Brayden laughed.

Owen nodded. "Yeah. He'd get a kick out of Holden having to protect his daughter from Colby's son—since he couldn't protect Lala from you. Sweet revenge, you know?"

Lala looked up. "Well, thankfully we have some time before we have to worry about that love story."

"But you know what you don't have all that much time for?" Colby asked.

I raised a brow. "What?"

"The minute baby Hope here can identify rodents, you'd better believe her uncle Colby is going to gift her with one. Maybe two or three."

Billie chimed in. "Oh, you know it."

"Fair enough," I conceded.

Our friends didn't stay long. I think they could tell how tired Lala and I were. I was looking forward to heading home to the

382

apartment tomorrow. My mother and Lala's mom were both staying in a spare apartment in the building and would be sticking around to help for a while. We certainly had no lack of love and support around us.

Lala turned on *Jeopardy!* as Hope lay sleeping in her arms. I sat at the bedside and alternated between looking at the TV and admiring my daughter's little face. She looked so much like Lala. I wondered if she'd have the same crazy curls. I'd thought I loved Lala more than I could possibly love anyone. But then I met Hope. If I could cover her in bubblewrap forever to protect her, I would. I planned to drive ten miles per hour on the way out of here.

"Today was the best day of my life," I said.

"Me, too," Lala said as she turned to me. "Can you guess what the second-best day was?"

"Well, you once told me the best day of your life was when I proposed to you atop your parents' roof."

"Bingo." She winked.

We'd been visiting our parents in Pennsylvania one weekend. Lala had gone to the grocery store, and I climbed up on the Ellisons' roof so that when she pulled back into the driveway, she'd see me standing up there holding a gigantic Will You Marry Me? sign.

"You know…" I said. "I'd wanted you up there with me when I proposed, but I was too scared you'd slip and fall or something and hurt the baby."

"If you had asked me to go up there, I would've suspected something. So it was perfect the way it was. I never saw it coming."

"Some of the best things in life are those we don't see coming, huh?" "I smiled down at Hope. "Yeah. I'm talking about you, little girl. The surprise of my life."

Our daughter cooed and looked up at me.

"She has Ryan's eyes," I said.

"I know. Genetics is amazing, isn't it?"

I frowned. "I really felt his absence when everyone was here today."

"Me, too," Lala murmured.

We turned our attention back to *Jeopardy!*. A few minutes in, one of the categories was Daytime TV.

The question was: *ABC soap set in Washington Heights.*

One of the contestants pressed the buzzer and answered, "What is Ryan's Hope?"

Lala and I looked at each other.

He always made sure to let us know he was here.

GUESS WHAT'S COMING IN 2023!
OWEN'S BOOK

Dear Readers,

While we were writing *The Rules of Dating My Best Friend's Sister*, we decided we adored this world so much that we needed to continue telling the guys' stories. And you don't have to wait long to find out what fate has in store for Owen!

The Rules of Dating My One-Night Stand
is coming in November, 2023
and is available for pre-order now
(https://bit.ly/3ZhLTIB)!

ACKNOWLEDGEMENTS

Thank you to all of the amazing bloggers, bookstagrammers and BookTokers who helped spread the news about *The Rules of Dating My Best Friend's Sister*. Your excitement keeps us going, and we are forever grateful for all of your support.

To our rocks: Julie, Luna and Cheri – Thank you for your friendship and always being there day in and day out.

To Jessica –Thank you for making sure Lala and Holden were ready for the world. We are fortunate to have you as our editor.

To Elaine – An amazing editor, proofer, formatter, and friend. We so appreciate all you do.

To Julia – Thank you for being our eagle eye and making sure our manuscripts are squeaky clean.

To our wonderful agent, Kimberly Brower – Thank you for helping to get our books into the hands of readers internationally. We look forward to seeing where Holden and Lala land.

To Kylie and Jo at Give Me Books Promotions – Our releases would simply be impossible without your hard work and dedication to helping us promote them.

To Sommer – Thank you for bringing Holden to life on the cover. We say this often, but this cover might be our favorite yet.

To Brooke – Thank you for organizing this release and for taking some of the load off of our endless to-do lists each day.

Last but not least, to our readers – We keep writing because of your hunger for our stories. We are so very excited for our next adventure with Holden and Lala! Thank you as always for your enthusiasm, love and loyalty. We love and appreciate you!

Much love,
Vi and Penelope

OTHER BOOKS BY
Vi Keeland & Penelope Ward

The Rules of Dating
Well Played
Not Pretending Anymore
Happily Letter After
My Favorite Souvenir
Dirty Letters
Hate Notes
Rebel Heir
Rebel Heart
Cocky Bastard
Stuck-Up Suit
Playboy Pilot
Mister Moneybags
British Bedmate
Park Avenue Player

OTHER BOOKS FROM VI KEELAND

The Game
The Boss Project
The Summer Proposal
The Spark
The Invitation
The Rivals

Inappropriate

All Grown Up

We Shouldn't

The Naked Truth

Sex, Not Love

Beautiful Mistake

Egomaniac

Bossman

The Baller

Left Behind

Beat

Throb

Worth the Fight

Worth the Chance

Worth Forgiving

Belong to You

Made for You

First Thing I See

OTHER BOOKS FROM PENELOPE WARD

Toe the Line

Moody

The Assignment

The Aristocrat

The Crush

The Anti-Boyfriend

Just One Year

The Day He Came Back

When August Ends

Love Online

Gentleman Nine

Drunk Dial

Mack Daddy

Stepbrother Dearest

Neighbor Dearest

RoomHate

Sins of Sevin

Jake Undone (Jake #1)

My Skylar (Jake #2)

Jake Understood (Jake #3)

Gemini

CONNECT
with the Authors

Enjoy *The Rules of Dating My Best Friend's Sister?*
Then connect with the authors!

Join Vi Keeland's reading group
https://www.facebook.com/groups/ViKeelandFanGroup/)
Join Penelope Ward's reading group
https://www.facebook.com/groups/PenelopesPeeps/

Follow Vi Keeland on Instagram
https://www.instagram.com/vi_keeland/
Follow Penelope Ward on Instagram
https://www.instagram.com/PenelopeWardAuthor/

Check out Vi Keeland's website
https://www.vikeeland.com
Check out Penelope Ward's website
http://www.penelopewardauthor.com

Check out Vi Keeland on TikTok
https://www.tiktok.com/@vikeeland
Check out Penelope Ward on TikTok
https://www.tiktok.com/@penelopewardofficial

Vi Keeland is a #1 *New York Times*, #1 *Wall Street Journal*, and *USA Today* Bestselling author. With millions of books sold, her titles are currently translated in twenty-seven languages and have appeared on bestseller lists in the US, Germany, Brazil, Bulgaria, and Hungary. Three of her short stories have been turned into films by Passionflix, and two of her books are currently optioned for movies. She resides in New York with her husband and their three children where she is living out her own happily ever after with the boy she met at age six.

Connect with Vi Keeland

Facebook Fan Group:
https://www.facebook.com/groups/ViKeelandFanGroup/)
Facebook: https://www.facebook.com/pages/Author-Vi-Keeland/435952616513958
TikTok: https://www.tiktok.com/@vikeeland
Website: http://www.vikeeland.com
Twitter: https://twitter.com/ViKeeland
Instagram: http://instagram.com/Vi_Keeland/

Penelope Ward is a *New York Times, USA Today,* and #1 *Wall Street Journal* Bestselling author. With over two-million books sold, she's a 21-time New York Times bestseller. Her novels are published in over a dozen languages and can be found in bookstores around the world. Having grown up in Boston with five older brothers, she spent most of her twenties as a television news anchor, before switching to a more family-friendly career. She is the proud mother of a beautiful 17-year-old girl with autism and a 16-year-old boy. Penelope and her family reside in Rhode Island.

Connect with Penelope Ward

Facebook Private Fan Group:
https://www.facebook.com/groups/PenelopesPeeps/
Facebook: https://www.facebook.com/penelopewardauthor
TikTok: https://www.tiktok.com/@penelopewardofficial
Website: http://www.penelopewardauthor.com
Twitter: https://twitter.com/PenelopeAuthor
Instagram: http://instagram.com/PenelopeWardAuthor/

Made in the USA
Monee, IL
19 June 2023

36240125R00236